D1498005

Orland Park Public Library
14921 Ravinia Avenue
Orland Park, Illinois 60462
708-428-5100

– MAR 2022

stains /liquid damage 2-15-23 BK

ORLAND PARK PUBLIC LIBRARY

BY CLAUDIA GRAY

STAR WARS

Lost Stars

Bloodline

Leia, Princess of Alderaan

Master & Apprentice

The High Republic: Into the Dark

The High Republic: The Fallen Star

EVERNIGHT

Evernight

Stargazer

Hourglass

Afterlife

Balthazar

SPELLCASTER

Spellcaster

The First Midnight Spell

Steadfast

Sorceress

FIREBIRD

A Thousand Pieces of You

Ten Thousand Skies Above You

A Million Worlds with You

CONSTELLATION

Defy the Stars

Defy the Worlds

Defy the Fates

STANDALONE

Fateful

THE FALLEN STAR

THE FALLEN STAR

Claudia Gray

NEW YORK

ORLAND PARK PUBLIC LIBRARY

Gray,
Claudia

Star Wars: The High Republic: The Fallen Star is a work of fiction.
Names, places, and incidents either are products of the author's
imagination or are used fictitiously. Any resemblance to actual events,
locales, or persons, living or dead, is entirely coincidental.

Copyright © 2022 by Lucasfilm Ltd. & ® or ™ where indicated. All rights reserved.

Published in the United States by Del Rey, an imprint of
Random House, a division of Penguin Random House LLC, New York.

DEL REY is a registered trademark and the CIRCLE colophon
is a trademark of Penguin Random House LLC.

Hardback ISBN 978-0-593-35539-8
International edition ISBN 978-0-593-49912-2
Ebook ISBN 978-0-593-35540-4

Printed in the United States of America on acid-free paper

randomhousebooks.com

2 4 6 8 9 7 5 3 1

First Edition

Dedicated to Sarah Simpson Weiss,
who saves me from myself, sometimes daily

THE STAR WARS NOVELS TIMELINE

THE HIGH REPUBLIC

Light of the Jedi
The Rising Storm
Tempest Runner
The Fallen Star

Dooku: Jedi Lost
Master and Apprentice

I THE PHANTOM MENACE

II ATTACK OF THE CLONES

Thrawn Ascendancy: Chaos Rising
Thrawn Ascendancy: Greater Good
Thrawn Ascendancy: Lesser Evil
Dark Disciple: A Clone Wars Novel

III REVENGE OF THE SITH

Catalyst: A Rogue One Novel
Lords of the Sith
Tarkin

SOLO

Thrawn
A New Dawn: A Rebels Novel
Thrawn: Alliances
Thrawn: Treason

ROGUE ONE

IV A NEW HOPE

Battlefront II: Inferno Squad
Heir to the Jedi
Doctor Aphra
Battlefront: Twilight Company

V THE EMPIRE STRIKES BACK

VI RETURN OF THE JEDI

The Alphabet Squadron Trilogy
The Aftermath Trilogy
Last Shot

Bloodline
Phasma
Canto Bight

VII THE FORCE AWAKENS

VIII THE LAST JEDI

Resistance Reborn
Galaxy's Edge: Black Spire

IX THE RISE OF SKYWALKER

A long time ago in a galaxy far, far away. . . .

THE FALLEN STAR

The tragic events of the Republic Fair have galvanized the galaxy. The Jedi and the Republic have gone on the offensive to stop the marauding NIHIL. With these vicious raiders all but defeated, Jedi Master AVAR KRISS has set her sights on LOURNA DEE, the supposed Eye of the Nihil, and has undertaken a mission to capture her once and for all.

But unbeknownst to the Jedi, the true leader of the Nihil, the insidious MARCHION RO, is about to launch an attack on the Jedi and the Republic, on a scale not seen in centuries. If he succeeds, the Nihil will be triumphant, and the light of the Jedi will go dark.

Only the brave Jedi Knights of STARLIGHT BEACON stand in his way, but even they may not be enough against Ro and the ancient enemy that's about to be unleashed. . . .

Prologue

The Longbeam cruiser slipped into the Nefitifi system as smoothly and silently as a sharp needle piercing black cloth. Only a few million years before, a star in this previously binary system had exploded, leaving behind a nebula of extraordinary scale. Trails of deep-purple and dark-blue gases laced between the planets, radioactive and opaque, hiding the entire system within swirls of mist.

Many smugglers had, in the past, taken advantage of that mist.

The Jedi now believed the Nihil were using it, too. It was their last place to hide.

"Any signals?" Master Indeera Stokes asked her Padawan.

Bell Zettifar, next to her, shook his head. "Nothing on any frequencies. It's completely quiet out there."

"It shouldn't be." Master Nib Assek shook her head, her gray hair painted silver by the shadows in which they stood. (When a Longbeam ran on half power to avoid attention—as this one now did—lighting dimmed accordingly.) "Gunrunners have used this part of space for a long time. You'd expect beacons, tagged cargo in asteroids, something of that sort. Instead . . . nothing."

Bell glanced over at a fellow Padawan, the Wookiee Burryaga, who stood by Master Assek's side. Their shared look confirmed that they understood what was implied: The Nefitifi system was *too* quiet. Finding no activity here was like landing on Coruscant and finding it deserted: proof positive that something was very wrong.

Here it could only mean that the Nihil were near.

"They must be using silencers," Bell said to Master Indeera. "Satellites or shipboard?"

"Shipboard, I suspect. We'll soon find out." His Master squared her shoulders; her Tholothian tendrils rippled down her back. Bell felt the shiver of anticipation that went through the Jedi cohort aboard; the Force was warning them of what was about to come. Master Indeera put her hand on her lightsaber hilt. "The other Longbeams report similar readings—or lack thereof. The Nihil must be very near."

Finally, action. A chance to move on the Nihil. Bell had wanted this—*needed* it—ever since the loss of his former Master, Loden Greatstorm. Not for vengeance. Greatstorm would never have wanted that. For the knowledge that Bell had done something, *anything,* to counteract the evil that had robbed his Master of his life. The Nihil were already beaten, it seemed—Master Avar Kriss seemed on the verge of capturing their leader, the Eye, at any moment—but neither Bell nor the rest of the galaxy would be at peace until the threat had been laid to rest forever.

The debacle at the Republic Fair months ago could've damaged confidence in the Republic—and in the Jedi—past repair. Instead the Nihil were now on the run. The corner had been turned. This entire part of the galaxy would soon be wholly safe once more.

Once everyone else had regained their confidence and security, maybe Bell would, too.

As the Longbeam passed through another thick golden cloud of gases, Master Indeera was the first to say, "They're above us. Almost directly overhead." Burryaga growled in assent.

Ship sensors almost immediately began to flash, but the true warning came to them through the Force. Bell's senses heightened; his muscles tensed. Readiness galvanized him on every level.

Here it comes, he thought as he looked out the cockpit. The dark, swirling nebula gases became translucent as the Longbeam rose, revealing the underbelly of the Nihil ship. Bell imagined the warning alarms on that ship's bridge, the frantic rush of activity as they prepared to fight—for by this point, surely, the Nihil had realized that the Jedi had come to fight.

But the Jedi had been ready from the instant they left Starlight Beacon, and their moment had finally come.

For Master Loden, Bell thought, *and that no one else may ever suffer at the Nihil's hands as he suffered.*

The initial boarding attack had been designed for precisely this moment: The mother ship of the Jedi group seized the Nihil craft in its tractor beam, holding it fast, as the Longbeam on which Bell and his compatriots stood angled itself to attach to one air lock and block several others. Docking—rough, uneven, forced—shook the entire vessel, but the team remained steady and alert, recognizing as one the moment when the vibration signaled their penetration of the hull.

"For light and life!" Master Assek cried as they dashed into the Nihil ship.

Bell had rarely felt the Force with him so powerfully as he did at the moment he rushed forward into a blazing array of blasterfire, slashing through the air that surrounded him so closely he could feel the heat. The scent of ozone filled Bell's breath. Yet his lightsaber blade deflected every blaster bolt so smoothly that it seemed to be moving itself, aiming without any conscious work from Bell other than fierce concentration. All around him, he saw a sea of faceless, soulless masks—Nihil shooting, scattering, scrambling—and, advancing upon them, the Jedi swift and sure.

"Now!" Master Indeera called over the fray, acknowledgment of the warning from the Force they all felt. Bell ducked behind a metal girder to shield him for the seconds it took to strap on his breather. No sooner had he done so than the telltale hiss from the air vents revealed that the Nihil's poison gases had been deployed.

Too late, Bell thought with satisfaction. *It's your turn to be too late.*

Master Indeera led the charge toward engineering, or what passed for it on the cobbled-together, jury-rigged Nihil vessel. Bell and Burryaga fell in directly behind. It would be up to Master Assek to hold off the Nihil near the air lock; Bell's job was to paralyze this ship.

Even running at top speed, Bell could tell that this ship was ramshackle to the point of hazardousness; the interior was dismal, dull, and strictly utilitarian. What made someone want to live like this? To join the Nihil, visit infinite pain and destruction upon innocents throughout several systems, and for what? Life on a dark, dank ship creeping along the edges of space, with only the dim spark of potential future riches to provide any light—something that was no life at all.

Bell's wonderings only took up one small part of his consciousness, musings he'd examine later. The present moment was for completing his mission.

Green gas filled the corridors with toxic haze, to which the Jedi remained impervious thanks to their breathers. However, the gases meant that Bell *felt* the door ahead of them before he saw it. Master Indeera and Burryaga must have as well, because they all skidded to a halt at the same moment.

"Should we knock?" Bell asked. Burryaga groaned at the terrible joke.

Master Indeera simply plunged her lightsaber into the door's locking mechanism. The heated glow of melting metal illuminated all their faces in pale-orange light for the instants it took for the door to give way. It stuttered open to reveal only a skeleton crew, most of them young and unarmed, and all too willing to surrender.

It helped Bell, knowing that he wouldn't have to take additional lives. What had to be done, had to be done—but the pain he felt over the tragedy of Loden Greatstorm remained sharp. It could've pushed him in dangerous directions. Instead he was satisfied with their capture, no more.

You taught me well, Master, Bell thought to the memory of the man that he carried within his mind.

Once they'd finished rounding up the prisoners, Burryaga whined curiously.

"Yeah, seems like a low crew contingent to me, too," Bell said. "Do you think Marshal Kriss's pursuit of the Eye of the Nihil has shaken them up? They might have deserters by the hundreds, even thousands." He didn't like the idea of Nihil escaping any justice for the atrocities they had already committed, but the most important thing was making those atrocities stop. If the price of saving so many lives was a few Nihil deserters getting off scot-free, so be it.

We've gone on the offensive, Bell told himself. *We've outplayed the Nihil at their own game. We did it for you, Master Loden, and for every other person who suffered as you—*

Bell couldn't even think about it.

Burryaga didn't seem to notice Bell's distraction, for which Bell was grateful. Instead the great Wookiee shook his head and growled.

"Sure, it was easy," Bell agreed. "I don't know if it was *too* easy, though. No point in worrying about it if the Nihil are finally collapsing."

In that, at least, Burryaga completely concurred.

Regald Coll had more of a sense of humor than most Jedi. At least, that was what non-Jedi told him. Most of the other members of the Order didn't agree.

Or, as Regald would argue, they just didn't have enough of a sense of humor to appreciate his own.

"So what is it with the storm terminology?" he asked his newest prisoners, a fierce-eyed adult named Chancey Yarrow and a young woman who had identified herself only as Nan. "You're all supposed to be one big storm, but each group breaks down into Tempests and Strikes and Clouds. How far does it go? Is one Nihil on their own, I don't know, Slightly Overcast?"

The prisoners had been caught near a Nihil fleet in the Ocktai system, just one of the many raids on the Nihil occurring simultaneously. However, their ship wasn't definitively a part of that group, and at first he'd thought they'd probably just question the women before letting them go. But Nan had pulled a blaster on the first Jedi she saw, which prompted an identity check, which then revealed her true affiliation.

Nan looked furious at having been caught. On the other hand, Chancey Yarrow's face remained utterly unmoved as she said, "You're not as funny as you think you are."

"Probably not," Regald agreed. "Because I think I'm hilarious, and really, nobody's that funny." Enjoying his own jokes was enough for him.

"I'm not Nihil any longer," Nan said. The words sounded strange—as though she had to force herself to say them. "We work for—" She cut off as she caught sight of her companion. Chancey Yarrow's icy glare could've frozen lava. Regald thought about making a "blizzard" joke to go with the whole storm theme, decided against it. Nan finally finished, "We work for ourselves. I haven't been with the Nihil for months now."

"Convenient timing," Regald said. "And who knows? Maybe you're telling the truth. But you'll have to prove it before we can let you go."

Meanwhile, the *Gaze Electric* rested in quiet space between systems far away from the Jedi battle. No one on board even bothered monitoring the current Jedi activity, much less worrying about coming to the defense of their comrades. Instead it seemed as though nothing much was happening other than some random, ordinary housekeeping. Certainly nobody paid any attention as Thaya Ferr—a mere assistant, not a fighter—made her way through the long corridors.

Thaya was a human woman of middle years and nondescript appearance: flat brown hair pulled back into a practical tail, basic standard coverall, no telltale streaks, no mask, no weapon. She held nothing more interesting than a simple datapad.

This 'pad led her to the first door, the crew quarters for an Ithorian woman. Thaya sounded the chime and arranged a blank, uninterested smile on her face before the door slid open.

"Good morning," Thaya said with all the meaningless cheer of a droid. "You'll be happy to know that the Eye of the Nihil has found a new place for you, one ideally suited to your talents. Details are here." She handed over a small datacard never pausing, lest the Ithorian say something. "Please report to the main docking bay for a transport at thirteen hundred hours today. Thank you!"

At that Thaya walked away, still smiling, leaving no opportunity for argument, gratitude, or any response at all. The Ithorian's reaction was irrelevant. She would obey, which meant she would depart the ship days before the Ithorian male she was partnered with. That Ithorian's departure needed to go unnoticed—and getting rid of the main person who would notice helped with that.

It served other purposes, too. But Thaya would turn to those when she'd finished delivering this first set of transfer orders.

As soon as she was done, she hurried back to the bridge of the *Gaze Electric*. To the Eye. To Marchion Ro himself.

He sat in the captain's chair, studying reports. Thaya could tell they had details about attacks on other Nihil ships—ships loyal to Lourna Dee, and therefore hardly Nihil at all anymore, in her opinion—and she gave them all the attention she knew Ro would wish her to give them, which was none. Instead she stood nearby, patiently waiting to be noticed.

Some on the bridge smirked at Thaya Ferr, and she knew why. She wasn't a power player; she was only someone who ran errands for Marchion Ro.

Many people underestimated how much could be learned from such errands, or how much a leader might come to rely on someone who took care of such mundane, trivial concerns.

Thaya Ferr saw things more clearly.

Finally, Ro spoke to her. "You've put through the transfers?"

"Yes, my lord. I'll prepare the next orders for delivery later in the day."

A few ears had pricked up at the mention of "transfers"—evidence, perhaps, that some had lost the confidence and favor of Marchion Ro? There would be an appetite for names, details, the better to sneer over the fallen. As of yet, none of those on the bridge suspected that a transfer order might be coming to *them*—which was precisely how Ro wanted it, and precisely how Thaya intended to deliver.

Marchion Ro moved on to a different subject—one, Thaya noted, guaranteed to draw attention away from any talk of transfers. "It appears Lourna Dee's capture is imminent."

"Do the Jedi still believe she is the Eye of the Nihil?" She said this in precisely the tone of disbelief she calculated would be most flattering to Ro.

He smiled just as she had foreseen. "They'll know the truth very soon, Ferr. For the moment, let them have their fun. Let them enjoy believing they have defeated the Nihil.

"They will never have the luxury of that belief again."

Chapter 1

Stellan Gios was among those Jedi who perceived the Force as the entire firmament of stars in the sky. Points of brilliant heat and energy, seemingly distanced from one another by infinite absence and cold—but actually profoundly connected. Families, friends, tribes, organizations: Each formed a different constellation, carving shape and meaning from the sky. (Were not he, Avar Kriss, and Elzar Mann such a constellation? Stellan had always thought so, even in childhood.) The Force shone forth from them all, illuminating the vast dark; if Stellan but had the ability to perceive every living being, it would have the same effect as being able to see every star in the universe at once: total, pure, all-encompassing light.

Rarely had he felt so close to that ideal moment as he did on this day.

Colorful banners streamed in the sunshine, fluttering over a throng of thousands who were laughing, eating food from tents and carts, and enjoying the beautiful day and—at last—a sense of true safety and belonging. Or so Stellan liked to think.

Finally, he thought, *we've regained the joy the Nihil stole from us for so long.*

At last we can celebrate our unity the way we should've been able to from the beginning.

Stellan stood at the head of the Starlight delegation upon a dais that overlooked the celebration. In the eyes of most of the galaxy, Eiram was an insignificant place, a tiny dot on a star chart too obscure to bother with. But this had been one of the worlds that had led the campaign for this part of space to finally join the Republic, which made their recent mission here all the more symbolic.

Eiram had recently suffered a storm—the kind of vicious cyclone only a handful of planets could muster, one that had at its apex covered almost an entire hemisphere. Terrible winds had badly damaged the desalination structures that supplied the planet's only fresh water. This was a crisis that would devastate an independent planet, leading to a mass exodus or even starvation.

But planets in the Republic had a reason to hope.

"And so, instead of returning to its place in the heavens, Starlight Beacon was transported here, to Eiram!" The storyteller gestured at the holo that showed Starlight being towed through outer space, for only the second time ever, following a lifesaving mission to the planet Dalna. Ringed around the storyteller, dozens of children oohed and aahed in wonder. The shimmer of the holo was reflected in their bright eyes. "The Republic and the Jedi came to save us all, by bringing us water, supplies, and most of all . . . hope."

Stellan felt a faint twinge of regret that he hadn't been here to personally oversee the station's moving and the beginning of the repairs. He'd still been on Coruscant then, so he'd tasked Master Estala Maru with supervising every step—not because he doubted the specialists, but because it was so important for this to be absolutely right. Nobody in the galaxy paid more attention to detail than Maru.

Upon Stellan's return two days prior, the repairs for the desalination plant weren't entirely complete. All they had to do now, however, was attach the sluice gates—something that would be accomplished as soon as the tow craft were available, a week or two at most. The people of Eiram might still have water rationing in place, but the rations were generous, and after several weeks of hardship the planet was ready to celebrate.

Stellan said as much to Maru, who replied, "Right. It's the perfect time for everybody. But it doesn't hurt that this is when the chancellor happened to be free."

"Such is the state of politics," Stellan said.

In truth, it was good of Chancellor Soh to have made the time to attend, even holographically. The flickering images next to him on the dais saw her sitting comfortably in an informal chair, her enormous targons lying on either side of her, dozing in the contentment of beasts. Stellan's eyes met Lina Soh's, briefly—each sharply conscious of the memories of the Republic Fair. The image of Stellan lifting her unconscious body from the rubble had already become iconic: both of the evil of the Nihil, and of the resilience of the Republic. Thus the two of them were in a strange way bound together in the public eye; in the same way, Stellan had become *the* Jedi, the symbol of the Order.

"*If we're a constellation,*" Elzar Mann had said, before leaving for his retreat, "*the Council has made you the polestar.*" Stellan would've liked to disagree, but he couldn't.

Stellan wasn't sure how he felt about that. So he was guiltily relieved that the chancellor hadn't attended in person. Otherwise there would've been pressure to come up with some new iconic image, somehow.

From the Jedi Council, his fellow members Masters Adampo and Poof watched via their own holograms as well. Cam droids hovered amid the streamers and balloons, capturing the event for people from Kennerla to Coruscant. No matter how distant this part of the frontier might be from the Galactic Core, the people of Eiram could know themselves to be truly as much a part of the Republic as any other world.

"They've needed this," Stellan murmured as he looked out at the revelry of the crowd.

Maru surprised him by answering, "*We've* needed this."

And that was the truth of it. Stellan's keen gaze picked out white-and-gold-clad figures among the festival-goers: Bell Zettifar and Indeera Stokes, sipping bright-orange ram'bucha from their cups; Nib Assek helping OrbaLin to make his way toward the dancers, the better to watch their performance; and Burryaga, playing with some of the tinier children. Being a Jedi was a sacred duty—but the light demanded more than obedience and sacrifice. Sometimes a Jedi had to be open to the simple, pure experience of joy. Today they all had that chance.

"A fine thing to see, isn't it?" Regasa Elarec Yovet of the Togruta was there in person, standing near the flickering image of Chancellor Soh.

It was the chancellor who answered, though Stellan entirely agreed: "It is, Your Majesty. And it's about time."

"It is almost time, my lord," said Thaya Ferr.

Marchion Ro gave his underling the slightest nod as he stared into the depths of the holographic star chart. His preselected targets glowed red among the whiter stars, and he studied each one in turn.

These were ordinary worlds. Large and prosperous enough to be of note at least to neighboring systems, not so large as to have strong planetary defenses or to draw undue attention. He walked through the holographic chart, imagining the suns and planets pushing apart to let him pass.

The worlds he had chosen had two things in common: First, they all had good communications systems that would allow them to reach officials on Coruscant within minutes.

Second, they were all very, very far from Starlight Beacon.

He smiled his bloodless smile. "Begin."

Aleen: a planet neither particularly obscure nor noteworthy. Although Aleen had been racked by wars in its distant past, it was now a place where nothing of significance had happened in a very long time— even by its own inhabitants' reckoning—and nothing of significance was anticipated for perhaps an even longer time to come. The legends of the wars were enough to make every soul on Aleen satisfied with an uneventful life.

Yeksom: one of the longest-standing Republic member worlds on the Outer Rim, one that had suffered terrible groundquakes in recent years. The Republic was helping the planet rebuild, but it was a protracted, painstaking process. Its people remained guarded, uncertain, sad-eyed; everyone had lost someone in the quakes, and grief veiled the world's gray sky.

Japeal: a planet on the frontier, newly bustling, with no fewer than three small space stations in various stages of construction. Its temperate climate and plentiful water practically invited settlers to find a place they might call their own. Dozens of species set up storefronts and eateries; engineers mapped bridges and roads; families put finishing touches on brand-new, prefab homes.

Tais Brabbo: Anyone on Tais Brabbo who wasn't up to no good had taken a wrong turn somewhere. Rumor had it the Hutts had considered moving some operations onto Tais Brabbo but decided against it—the place was too corrupt even for them. It was a good place to get lost, and on any given day it housed millions of souls who wanted nothing more than to remain out of sight of any authorities more powerful than the ineffectual local marshals.

On each of these very different planets, under four different shades of sky, millions of very different individuals were going about tasks as divergent as spinning muunyak wool or taking bounty pucks when they each heard the exact same sound: the thudding hum of spacecraft engines descending.

All those millions of people looked up. They all saw Nihil ships streaking down out of the sky—numerous as raindrops—the beginning of the Storm.

Explosives dropped. Plasma weapons fired. The assault slammed into homes, factories, bridges, cantinas, medcenters, hangars. There was no specific target, because everything was a target. It seemed the

Nihil wanted to cause mayhem for mayhem's sake, which nobody who had heard of them found difficult to believe.

One passenger ship leaving Japeal at that very moment got lucky. It took damage—a devastating hit to its port side—but was able to limp out of orbit and even get into hyperspace. Its crew and surviving passengers thought it was a miracle they were still alive and might even remain so, if they could get to help in time.

The so-called "miracle" was, in fact, no more than a standing order Marchion Ro had given before the Nihil attack began. Some people *needed* to escape—because the Nihil needed them to run straight to Starlight Beacon, where they would be given comfort, medical treatment, and the full attention of the Jedi.

No sooner had Stellan Gios returned to Starlight Beacon from Eiram than the news of the Nihil attacks arrived. Estala Maru, normally not given to bad language, used phrases considered obscene on most planets when word came in of the Aleen assault. "Still more Nihil, still attacking, and for what? Nothing, so far as I can tell. They're not even bothering to plunder ships or planets any longer." He shook his head grimly. "The Nihil mean to cause us more trouble so long as there's even one Cloud remaining."

"This isn't close to the scale of destruction we saw from the Nihil at first," Stellan said, reminding himself as much as Maru. "We've made real progress. We ought to have expected to see the Nihil thrash around in the group's death throes. For now, our attention should remain on helping those affected. It looks like some damaged ships are heading our way, no doubt with some injuries aboard—"

"Already on it," Maru said. The man's fanatical attention to detail only sharpened in times of crisis, and Stellan had rarely been gladder of this. "I've sent a couple of the Padawans to ready the medical tower for a few extra patients."

"Excellent." Stellan put one hand on Maru's shoulder, a gesture of gratitude. "Maru, sometimes I think you're the one holding this place together."

"And don't forget it," Maru sniffed. His grumpy demeanor was only a thin shield, however; Stellan saw the glimmer of satisfaction in Maru's gray eyes.

Stellan hurried away, leaving the situation that was being taken care of to deal with the many that had yet to be resolved. A few damaged ships had already signaled their need of a place to land, and more would be coming.

In truth, he was somewhat more disquieted by the Nihil assaults than he'd let on to Maru. Stellan had had misgivings about Avar Kriss's search for the Eye of the Nihil from the very beginning; it felt too much like a personal vendetta. Avar had walked away from Starlight Beacon—her assignment from the Council, the very symbol of the Republic in this part of space—all in the hope of making a capture others could have made equally well. Was it possible that her search had antagonized the Nihil, driven them to lash out instead of skulking off into oblivion?

Or maybe these scattered attacks are a sign that Avar's plan is working, Stellan allowed. *The Eye is fleeing from her, possibly losing contact with the Nihil at large. Perhaps what we're seeing is the Nihil newly decentralized, lashing out wildly before falling apart.*

If so, Stellan would be the first to apologize to Avar for doubting her. Until they knew more, however . . . he would keep his own counsel.

An electronic voice chirped: "Master Stellan Gios?"

Stellan half turned to see a logistics droid rolling toward him, coppery and bright, with a vaguely humanoid body above a rolling base. "Yes—are you delivering a message?"

"The message is that you are my new master. I am Jayjay-Five One Four Five and I stand ready to label, prioritize, sort, file, collate, and otherwise organize every aspect of your existence." The droid practically vibrated with readiness to begin.

"There must be a mistake, Forfive," Stellan said. "I haven't ordered any droid, and the Council would've mentioned—"

"I am a gift," JJ-5145 declared with apparent pride. "I come compliments of Elzar Mann, who sends word that as he can no longer be your right hand, he wished for me to serve in that capacity."

There was almost nothing Stellan would've wanted less than a droid following him around to organize everything.

Which, of course, Elzar knew perfectly well.

Stellan had previously been concerned about sending Elzar off to work through his current crisis without accompanying him—as he had first planned, and in fact promised. In the end, Stellan's many tasks had not allowed him any opportunity to step away, and he'd found an excellent replacement to guide Elzar through this difficult passage. But he'd worried that Elzar might on some level resent it . . . and in Elzar's current state of mind, that resentment could too easily have turned to darkness.

It now appeared that Elzar wasn't resentful in the slightest—and only irked enough to play a practical joke.

JJ-5145 said, "You have remained silent for three point one seconds. Do you lack clarity on how to prioritize your thoughts? Voice them and I can help you order them most efficiently."

"That's quite all right, Forfive," Stellan hurriedly replied. "How about you help the Padawans get the medical tower organized? That would be of great assistance." He guided the droid on its way, relieved to have something else for it to do. Later he would ask it to schedule some other tasks for a few days in the future.

One of those tasks would be, "Think up the ideal revenge for a practical joke."

The first ship to arrive at Starlight Beacon after the Nihil attacks was neither damaged nor carrying the injured; it was the Longbeam tasked with bringing some of the Jedi back from their raids on the Ocktai system, with a handful of prisoners in tow.

Bell Zettifar, fresh from checking supply stores in the medical tower, prepared to assist in the prisoner unloading—but his Master, Indeera Stokes, waved him off. "There are only a handful of captives, and if help is needed, I can supply it," she said. "Take some time to yourself."

No doubt she'd noticed how dark his mood remained, months after Loden Greatstorm's death. Bell didn't want his new Master to think he didn't appreciate her—to let his admiration and grief for his old Master cloud his new apprenticeship. (And it was clear he needed more time as an apprentice. Bell's conviction that he was ready to become a Knight had turned to dust with Master Loden.)

That was something he should consider later. For now, there was little to do besides say, "Thanks, Master Indeera."

She nodded as she began to walk away. "We'll all have plenty to do soon enough. Best to take free time where it can be had."

Burryaga, who was also at liberty, asked with an inquisitive growl whether Bell might want to meditate together. Dual meditation techniques sometimes succeeded where solo efforts failed; it was often easier to calm another person, or to be calmed by them. It wasn't a bad idea, but a shadowy form at the far end of the corridor reminded Bell that there was something much more important to do first—someone he hadn't been able to visit since returning to Starlight from Eiram that morning.

"Hang on just a second," he said to Burryaga before dropping to his knees and opening his arms wide for the shape hurtling toward him. "C'mon, Ember!"

The charhound bounded from the shadows and leapt onto Bell, welcoming him back with all the enthusiasm she could muster, which was a lot. Bell allowed a couple seconds of frantic licking before he put his hand out to calm his pet. Her fur blazed warm against his palm. "Steady, Ember, steady. I'm back now."

Ember wriggled with delight, and Bell couldn't help grinning. There was nothing like a pet to remind you to release your worries and live in the moment.

Burryaga made a low, huffing sound. Bell glanced up to see his Wookiee friend watching Jedi Knight Regald Coll lead the two Nihil prisoners away. One was a tall, fierce woman with long braids and cheekbones sharp enough to cut. The other was a girl not even his own age, her hair pulled back in a tail, her garments slightly too large for her body—creating the illusion she was even younger than her true years.

Bell knew the young woman's face, not from personal experience, but from security briefings.

"*I thought of Nan as almost still a kid*," Reath had warned them, soon after word had come of her capture. "*She's not. She's as capable as any Padawan—arguably more than me, because she fooled me completely. Don't take Nan for granted.*"

Bell figured that speech was mostly about making Reath Silas feel a little better for having been so skillfully deceived. But as he watched Nan walk away, head unbowed despite her cuffed wrists, Bell found himself hoping Regald Coll had heard that warning, too.

"I suggest waiting before you question them," Regald told Stellan Gios. "Our transport was small. The Nihil prisoners might've heard about their comrades' successful attacks, and if so, that'll make them—"

"Overconfident," Stellan finished for him. "Exultant, even. Convinced help will come quickly. When it doesn't, then, perhaps, they'll be ready to talk."

"They claim they're not Nihil any longer," Regald said, "but the girl called Nan was absolutely with the organization just a few months ago, and it's a really convenient time for her to have left it, don't you think?"

"But not impossible." Stellan looked thoughtful. "If she did leave the Nihil, and we can figure out why—it could provide some valuable information about how to psychologically disarm the group."

"It would save a lot of time. Still? I kinda doubt it." Regald missed the old days when he had worked in the Jedi crèche, where when you saw a problem (three-year-old fascinated by fire), the solution was obvious (remove three-year-old from vicinity of fire). "Will you handle the interrogation yourself, or will Elzar Mann take point? I'm happy to assist, but I've got to warn you, my jokes make me a little less than intimidating. Though there's always the chance the captives will reveal all, just to get me to shut up."

Amusement played on Stellan's features. "I'll call on you if I become truly desperate. Elzar, I fear, is unavailable. He's off doing something even more important."

"And what in the worlds would that be?"

"Elzar is taking some time to strengthen his ties to the Force," Stellan said. "Connecting with the greater Jedi he may yet become."

Chapter 2

The oceanic planet Ledalau possessed only a few thousand square meters of land, all within one tiny archipelago. Long ago, this world had possessed mighty continents, but it had been more than a millennium since the waters had swallowed them whole. Few relics of the ancient civilizations remained; the planet currently possessed few resources and less infrastructure. Thus Ledalau was left almost entirely alone. That was what made it the perfect meditative retreat.

It also turned out to be the perfect place to get your pride handed to you on a platter.

Elzar had been skeptical upon his arrival several weeks before. The islands were at an upper latitude, which made the weather disappointingly cool and foggy. He was of the opinion that it was easier to concentrate when you weren't cold. It had then been pointed out to him that nobody needed to practice what came easy, and if he only wanted to do what he could already do, he might as well have stayed on Starlight.

So he'd abandoned his early, halcyon notions of a tropical retreat and set himself to his task. His temporary home was a small stone structure, no more than a room and a privy. Elzar had no comm devices, no forms of entertainment, no droids—only the few items he would need to be totally self-sufficient, and a guide who cut him no slack whatsoever.

Once the mental noise of upheaval had died down, he began grappling with the truths that had brought him here:

I have begun drawing upon the dark side for my strength in the Force.

Elzar had not turned; nor did he feel he was close to turning. This was not a way of life for him—he still believed all the good and true lessons he had learned from Yoda as a youngling, then as a Padawan from his wise Master Roland Quarry. But anger was unavoidable. Fear was unavoidable. Extreme circumstances created extreme emotions. Denying them served no purpose. Why not use them?

Many weeks of meditation later, Elzar still felt those questions were valid. However, he'd also come to realize that every Sith Lord in history had probably asked the exact same questions until the darkness held them completely in its grip.

Where do you draw the line? Elzar asked himself. *You don't know. You can't know. And that's why you can't travel down that path at all.*

It had also become clear to him that part of the reason he was so deeply opposed to denying emotion was because negative feelings weren't the only ones he was trying to deny.

Even here, it had been hard for him to face that truth. But the truth within him demanded to be known. At night, when he looked up at Ledalau's three broad, shining moons, he imagined them as pinpoints of light in Avar Kriss's sky.

They'd never meant to become attached. Padawans often fooled around together on the sly; adolescence, a phase in virtually every sentient species, demanded its due. Instructors and Masters pretended not to notice as long as nobody went too far. When relationships formed, reprimands were rare. Instead a Master would promptly take her apprentice away on a long-term mission far from any Jedi temple. By the time a reunion could take place, both younger people had generally grown up, gained perspective, and moved on.

Elzar and Avar hadn't had to be torn apart. They'd been reasonable. Responsible. They'd known what they were doing and what the limitations had to be.

So Elzar had believed. But even though he had grown up and gained perspective, it appeared he couldn't move on.

How much of my confusion and anger is rooted in my feelings for Avar? So he had asked himself as he meditated on his knees, sometimes for hours at a stretch. *How much energy do I waste, trying to reconcile that which can never be reconciled?*

There, at least, the barriers stood strong. While Elzar felt—no, *knew*—that Avar still had feelings for him as well, he also knew that she would never break her vow. So why did this trouble him so?

Finally, he realized: It wasn't the lack of answers that weighed on him. It was the refusal to even ask the questions.

Once he knew that, the rest began to fall into place. Elzar fell into a rhythm: morning meditation and exercise, a light meal, deeper meditative practices, more exercise, a dinner substantive enough to allow for a good night's sleep. He allowed himself to feel moments of anger and frustration without drawing upon them as fuel. He gave himself permission to think of Avar when he gazed up at the night sky.

And he submitted to the tasks given to him—even his current very wet, cold, and irritating one—out of respect for his guide, a Jedi Knight only a few years his senior, one who made her path as a Wayseeker.

"*Concentrate.*" Orla Jareni always sounded faintly amused, even at moments like this. "Be in this moment. In this very breath."

Elzar inhaled deeply and resumed his handstand in the instant before the next wave crashed.

When Orla had first suggested that he work on meditating in the water, Elzar had been only too happy (even, truth be told, a little bit smug) to reply that he often did precisely this. As he described his meditation method, he'd expected her to be impressed.

But Orla Jareni didn't impress that easily.

"Right," she said. "You go with the flow. You move where the water takes you. Then you're surprised when you wind up someplace you never meant to be. I want you to practice standing firm against the water. Not to reject its power—to coexist with it. To accept it, and yet hold fast."

"Which means . . . ?"

She'd gestured at the rocky shoreline. "Walk out about four or five meters, give me a handstand, and hold it despite the tide." And that was what Elzar had been practicing every day since.

The water—only wrist-deep between waves—went up almost to his waist when the waves rolled in, heavy and shockingly cold. Elzar dug his fingers into the sand and called upon the Force to steady him. Within a few seconds, the wave rolled out again, leaving him wet and gasping, but still in place.

"Excellent," said Orla, safe and dry on the shore.

"I'm not a great meditator," Elzar called back. "But I really enjoy not drowning."

"Luckily you're good at *that*."

Another wave roared toward him, and Elzar closed his eyes. This time it was easier to forget that Orla was there and to accept the gift the ocean had to give him.

He let his awareness flow from his body through the water, until he could sense all the other life-forms teeming around him: fishes, shell-dwellers, plants that sprouted from the depths to sway in the tides. It was a communion he'd relished in the past, but that connection was different now, somehow stronger for his refusal to completely surren-der to it. His body remained still, a cliff against the waves: vulnerable to time, but strong in this moment. It took Elzar a while to realize that each individual wave hardly registered with him now; his breathing had naturally taken on the water's rhythm, and his sense of oneness with the life around him felt more vital, more real, than even the sand beneath his palms.

Equilibrium, he thought, and he remained in that place, mentally and physically, for the hour it took for the tide to start going out.

Elzar flipped back onto his feet and landed ankle-deep in seaweed and silt, an interesting sensation. On the shore, Orla Jareni was drawing her snow-white cloak around her. "You've come a long way. The first time you tried this, I couldn't decide whether you swallowed more seawater or sand."

He grinned. "Praise? From you? I must be doing something right."

"My praise is difficult to earn," she agreed. "That's why it's worth something to you, I hope."

"It is. You can hardly imagine how much." Elzar paused. "I'm going to refrain from 'tinkering' with the Force for a while after this. A long while, I expect."

Orla cocked her head. The cool sunlight made her skin almost glitter, like fresh snow. "When I advised you to stop doing that, I never meant for you to refrain forever. You're an intuitive Force-user, Elzar. It's a strength, not a weakness, once you've figured out your boundaries."

"I haven't yet, though. And I feel strong enough now to keep going as I am."

"You do realize you're still limiting yourself?" Orla raised one sharply angled eyebrow. "Not just in how you use the Force, but in using the Force itself?"

"I know," Elzar admitted. "It feels like . . . like an injured leg. I know I'll be able to put weight on it again, but not yet. Or am I getting that wrong, too?"

"Nope. Sounds reasonable to me. We Jedi spend so much time honing our Force abilities that sometimes other abilities get pushed aside. Maybe it's good for you to spend a while discovering your strengths beyond the Force, too."

Elzar toweled his damp hair, which had grown a bit long and shaggy during his time on Ledalau. "Tell me, though—how will I know when it's time to . . . open back up again?"

When she wished, Orla Jareni had a wicked smile. "Trust yourself, stupid. Now finish drying yourself off and pack up."

"Today?" He knew she had planned for them to depart soon, but she had withheld the specific date, so he would experience time more fluidly.

"Within the hour, if you can hustle."

Elzar hustled. This was the benefit of bringing so little; he was both dry and ready to go within the hour.

Working with Orla Jareni had surprised Elzar from first to last. His friend Stellan Gios had connected the two of them, which—given Stellan's general doubt of Wayseekers—had been odd enough to start with. Then Orla herself turned out to be flinty, funny, and even more of an iconoclast than Elzar himself. Her unflinching tutelage had focused him more profoundly, more swiftly, than he would've thought possible.

(Elzar had been inwardly embarrassed when he realized that, subconsciously, he'd been assuming he'd be able to bring Orla around to doing things his way. He hadn't understood how much he'd been flirting with women lately until he'd met one who had no use for that whatsoever.)

If Orla thinks I'm ready, I must be, he reminded himself as he finished packing up. *Because there's no way she'd ever cut me any slack.*

Elzar was grateful she'd been his teacher, so much so that he almost felt guilty about sending Stellan that logistics droid.

But not quite. He grinned as he fastened his bag, ready to go.

He stepped out of his small stone structure to see that the fog had rolled in, thick and wet. Gathering his cloak around him, he called out, "Orla? Where are you?"

"This way!" Her voice came from the distance, and he set out to follow.

They'd spent nearly all their time on the shore, meaning that the interior of this small island remained almost unknown to him. Once sand no longer mingled with soil, the ground grew foggier, bumpier, almost rolling. Elzar hurried on, aware of Orla some measure ahead of him, and only vaguely curious as to how they planned to leave.

Then, amid the mists, he caught sight of the plinth.

It was not especially tall—perhaps the same height as Elzar himself—nor did it retain any of the ceremonial carvings or paint it must have worn in millennia past. Time had worn away everything but the smooth, brownish surface of the stone. Had this once stood over a sacrificial altar? In this moment, surrounded by silence and the swirling fog, Elzar could not help feeling the sacredness of this place, this moment.

Was it his imagination, or was the Force stronger here? Elzar was pretty sure he hadn't dreamed it up.

I bet our ride isn't even here yet, he mused as he studied the plinth. *Orla wanted me to find this ancient relic, to understand it the best I can. If I can.* Should he kneel? Close his eyes? How best could he pay respect to a culture he neither knew nor could scarcely guess at?

"Elzar?" Orla's voice was closer, and he glimpsed her outline taking shape amid the fog as she strode toward him.

"I'm right here," Elzar confirmed, waiting for her next instructions. The plinth loomed before his eyes, its sense of presence intensely real, almost as though it were looking back at him.

"Oh, good," said Orla, grinning as she finally came within clear view. "You've met our navigator."

Elzar stared at her, nonplussed. Then he turned his head back toward the plinth. It wasn't his imagination; it *was* looking back at him.

"This rock—" he began.

"Is not a rock," Orla finished. She gave the plinth a friendly sort of nudge. It didn't move. "This is our Vintian navigator for the trip back to Starlight. He's known by his nickname, which happens to be Geode. Geode, this is Elzar Mann, Jedi Knight."

"Um," Elzar said. "Pleased to meet you." Geode said nothing, what with *being a rock* and all, and was Orla testing him, maybe?

Orla didn't seem overly concerned with his reaction, though. Instead she continued on toward their ship. Elzar followed, glancing over his shoulder every few seconds. Geode didn't move to follow them. Yes, Elzar decided, definitely just a test.

Their destination proved to be a small cargo ship, blue-tiled with a bulbous cockpit that almost looked comical. On the ramp, a young human girl with tan skin and long, dark hair checked pressure gauges at the air lock. Without turning around, she called out, "Welcome back, Orla!"

"Thanks, Affie." Orla gestured toward the girl, "Elzar Mann, Affie Hollow—and vice versa." Affie acknowledged him with only a nod. "And let me introduce you to the captain of the *Vessel*, Leox Gyasi."

"Greetings, fellow traveler of the void," said a tall, rangy man who'd appeared at the top of the ramp. He had dark-gold hair, richly wavy; a loose shirt that hung open to the middle of his chest; and around his neck, a collection of strands of beads in many colors from many worlds. "A pleasure to make your acquaintance."

"The *Vessel*," Elzar said, comprehending now. "Of course. I heard about your trip to the Amaxine station."

"That was a hell of a thing." Leox's stare was distant, as though he were more focused on that past adventure than on the here and now. If in fact he was focused on anything. Given the distinct whiff of spice in the air, Elzar suspected that was a big *if.* "Geode, buddy, looks like it's time to fly. Let's get prepped."

Elzar startled to realize that the plinth now stood only about a meter from his shoulder. *So it wasn't a test,* he realized. *Our navigator really is a . . . a rock.*

Okay, a Vintian. But Vintians look a whole lot *like rocks.*

The young woman, Affie, cocked her head as her expression darkened; Elzar realized she wore a small comm piece in one ear and was now alarmed by something she was hearing. "What's wrong?" he asked.

"The Nihil," Affie said. Elzar swore to himself; Orla swore out loud. Affie continued, "We have a few reports of attacks from—from all over, basically. Just a handful of worlds, but they're scattered. They don't have anything in common. And the Nihil aren't even taking anything. Just causing damage and running off."

"No good can come of that." Captain Gyasi either had sobered up in a hurry or wasn't as spice-soaked as Elzar had first guessed, because he was already checking data on a small terminal panel within the boarding bay, his long fingers swiftly bringing up page after page of new data. "They haven't hit anyplace especially close to here, though."

"At least we have a safe path back," Orla said, somewhat relieved.

Elzar couldn't take the same comfort. After the Republic Fair, and given the seemingly imminent capture of the Eye, he'd hoped they wouldn't have to deal with the Nihil again for a long, long time. Instead they were back—just for some low-level harassment, it appeared, but any Nihil activity was enough to set him on edge.

Still, this wasn't anywhere near the scale of the earlier Nihil attacks. *It might mean Avar's given them enough hell that they've learned some respect,* Elzar thought. She seemed capable of that.

Surely Avar Kriss was capable of anything.

Far away, aboard the *Gaze Electric,* Marchion Ro stood before his chosen few.

Werrera was an Ithorian, silent and wary; Leyel was a human, stout and short, with thick graying hair tied in a braid almost to her waist; Cale was a Pau'an with even longer fangs than most but no other distinguishing features. The three of them were all highly competent technicians, but they had not distinguished themselves within the Nihil in any of the usual ways: neither especially ruthless nor merciful, neither brilliant nor weak-minded.

But they *believed.*

The promise of the Nihil—the golden future Ro had spoken of to them all—for most, it was a hope, a dream. Within these three, it *lived.*

They had such faith in that future that, in a sense, they had reached it already. This was their gift to their families and friends, a promised land to which they already held title, one they were helping to give to countless others throughout this part of the galaxy.

Only that level of belief could fuel the task Marchion Ro needed them to accomplish.

As for these individuals' family members and friends—or what, within the Nihil, passed for friends—every single one of them had been reassigned to other ships, far from the *Gaze Electric,* and had departed Ro's ship at thirteen hundred hours. They would have no chance to protest. To change their loved ones' minds about taking on this vital assignment. They'd never even realize these people were missing, not until it was far too late.

"You should wipe all data banks clean upon disembarking, and leave only the false logs and permissions," Ro said to the three loyalists who stood before him. Those false logs identified their ship as a run-of-the-mill independent hauler, notable only for its license to transport wildlife, in this case supposedly a shipment of rathtars. (Nobody would be in a hurry to confirm that information by personally inspecting the cargo.) "Let the Jedi believe in those. You will reveal the truth soon enough."

"Yes, our Eye." Cale—who tended to speak for the group—gazed at Ro with such reverence that it was almost more unnerving than gratifying. But Marchion Ro was not easily unnerved. "We are ready."

"I know that you are. I believe in you all." Ro put hands on both Werrera's and Leyel's shoulders. Cale didn't need it. "You will not disappoint me. You will deliver unto us the greatest victory the Nihil have ever known."

The thrill that swept through them was palpable. Ro knew they would do his bidding. They would never turn back.

Chapter 3

The astromech in charge of the docking bay beeped in dismay upon reading the cargo ship's manifest. Even droids didn't want anything to do with rathtars. But it wasn't the droid's job to assess the wisdom of letting this ship dock on Starlight; its job was to see that the cargo hauler had the necessary permit to transport wildlife. Sensors claimed it did, so the astromech obediently opened the bay doors and allowed the ship to land.

While Starlight's main docking bay was a lively, busy place, the bay designated cargo-storage-only remained quiet most of the time. Werrera, Leyel, and Cale stepped into a vast, ill-lit space large enough for their footsteps to echo. It unsettled them—after all, they didn't want to be overheard—but they soon realized that nobody was there to hear them in the first place. Only two droids witnessed their arrival, neither of which was programmed to confirm that a ship's cargo matched its manifest.

So had Marchion Ro said it would be. The Eye never failed them. They had been right to trust him, to volunteer for this mission, to take on this great work.

"Where do we begin?" Leyel asked. Like the others, she had on a generic dark coverall, the sort of thing worn by engineers, mechanics, and maintenance workers on ships and stations throughout the galaxy. "Straight into engineering?"

Cale shook his head at the human woman. "First we start with their communications. Then the escape pods. This must be done step by step, just as Ro has ordered."

Loyal to Ro and the Nihil as she was, Leyel couldn't help her impatience to strike a real blow. "And if they catch us before we do anything worth the doing?"

"That is not ours to ask," Cale insisted. "Believe in the Eye's plan. It will be many hours before they learn of our presence. By the time they know, it will be far too late for the Jedi to stop us."

Something nagged at Bell Zettifar's attention, but he couldn't put his finger on precisely what it was.

Normally he would have meditated and attempted to identify whatever strange vibration within the Force was signaling him. At that moment, he had other things to do.

He knelt by a wounded Twi'lek who lay on a low cot near the door in the medical tower's admissions facility. Soot darkened her blue skin and her singed clothing, and her eyes were reddened from either smoke or tears. "Has the pill droid seen to you?" he asked. "Is there anything else I can do to help? Somebody I could contact?"

"The droid's been here," she whispered. "I'll be all right. And there's . . . there's no one for you to contact. But thank you." Her eyes never focused on Bell. He sensed that she was imagining someone else, someone who had been lost in the Nihil attack. Even these smaller raids caused real damage, Bell reminded himself. To the galaxy at large, this might have seemed no more than a skirmish. But this Twi'lek had lost somebody so precious to her that the galaxy would never seem the same.

A nasty gash marred one of her lekku—cleaned, treated, but still mending. Another few centimeters, and the tip of the head-tail would have been completely severed.

Like Master Loden's had been . . .

"I'll check in on you soon," Bell said, quickly getting to his feet. He needed to keep his attention on the present moment. Were his late Master able to speak to Bell from beyond the grave, no doubt he would say something like, *Pay attention to those who need you. I am beyond any help now. Let me go.*

But Bell couldn't do it. Helping the wounded who'd made their way to Starlight meant seeing reminders of the countless terrible ways Master Loden had been tortured and maimed during his captivity with the Nihil. Every bruise, every cut, every groan of pain: Bell's mind assigned them all to his late Master, and the worst of it was knowing that the reality as Loden Greatstorm had lived it was probably even worse than Bell's most heinous imaginings.

Nearby, Burryaga set down a large tray of medical supplies for the droids and medics to swarm over. To judge by the look he gave Bell, the distress Bell felt was obvious. Burryaga stepped away from his Master, Nib Assek (currently assisting another wounded traveler), and came to Bell's side.

The Wookiee's inquisitive whine made Bell sigh. "I'm okay. Really."

The answering growl made it clear Burryaga doubted that.

"Maybe I—it doesn't matter," Bell said. "There's no time to worry about it. We've got too much to do."

They stood in the middle of the receiving room, which was filled with roughly a dozen patients in varying degrees of distress. The air smelled of smoke and coolant spray from the clothes and bodies of those who lay groaning around them. According to the latest reports, even more waves of Nihil attack survivors would be arriving shortly. The medics and healer droids were capable of handling this, but the medical tower was crowded enough that a little extra help was more than welcome. Given all this, Bell figured Burryaga would soon leave him alone in favor of any of the myriad tasks before them.

Instead Burryaga pointed out that providing help meant making sure the helpers were able to do their best. If Bell was having trouble, better to work through it, so that he could serve to his utmost.

"I guess," Bell admitted. "Still, there are things that need to be taken care of—"

Burryaga interrupted to point out that they could have even more to do in the hours and days to follow, so if Bell needed a break, he should take it immediately. Later, they might have no chance.

"You win." Something like a smile crossed Bell's face. "Taking a break."

To Bell's surprise, Burryaga left the medical tower by his side—not pushing, not asking questions, just providing silent companionship as they walked through the quieter inner corridors of Starlight Beacon. Although a handful of individuals hurried past them, for the most part they were left alone as they made their way onto the observation deck.

The observation deck was deserted. Alone, they looked out at the broad expanse of space and on Eiram just below them, its seas shining sapphire. It looked so peaceful. Was that a lie?

"I know Master Avar says she's on the trail of the Eye of the Nihil," he began, "but maybe the Eye is someone else entirely. Surely somebody on the run wouldn't be ordering more attacks."

Burryaga growled that he trusted Avar's judgment. In his opinion, these scattered hostilities were probably just the Nihil striking back in desperation now that their leader was on the run. Terrible, yes, but a sign of how badly they'd been hit.

"That makes sense," Bell agreed. "But somehow it seems like we never hit the Nihil hard enough. Like it's impossible."

After a moment's pause, Burryaga asked why Bell felt that way.

If a full Jedi Knight had been asking questions like this, Bell might've been too intimidated to speak openly. Grief wasn't an emotion the Jedi were meant to dwell upon. But Burryaga was a fellow apprentice. Sure, he was significantly older, but still, in Wookiee terms, just past adolescence. They were peers. It was possible to admit things to a peer that could never be comfortably said to a Master.

"From the moment I became Loden Greatstorm's Padawan, he was more than just my teacher." Bell paced slowly along the observation deck walkway, staring at the stars and the half circle of Eiram's surface below. "He was the ultimate ideal of a Jedi. At least, he was to me."

Burryaga agreed. Loden Greatstorm had been among the noblest, most outstanding Jedi Masters of his generation. (Burryaga, aging as a Wookiee did, could assess several human generations with ease.) His death was a loss to the entire Order—but, he gently added, to Bell most of all.

"I thought he was dead, but he wasn't. Master Loden was alive, in Nihil captivity, suffering—so terribly—" Bell's voice caught. He swallowed hard. "And it wasn't like I didn't sense him! But I told myself it was grief. *They* told me it was just grief, or a sense of him through his new communion with the Force. Instead it was him calling for help that never came. I could have saved him. I didn't."

Burryaga stopped him there with a low growl. There was no way to know what Bell might or might not have been able to do, or even what the Order as a whole could have done to rescue him.

"That's the whole point," Bell said. "If I'd failed in an attempt to help—okay, that would be hard, but I could look at what I'd done wrong. I could learn from it. And maybe Master Loden would've known that at least we tried. Instead there's nothing. *I did nothing.*"

Bell braced himself for Burryaga's next consoling words, but they never came. Instead Burryaga whined thoughtfully and continued pacing slowly by Bell's side, simply remaining with him in his distress. That was more comforting than any words could ever have been.

Yes, Bell told himself. *Everything you've said is true. It's hard, and it's awful, and it's how things happened. The past is no longer in motion. There's nothing for you to do but accept it.*

Only now did Bell realize that, to him, *acceptance* had meant something too close to "surrender." That wasn't it at all. Acceptance was strength. It was being able to carry the weight of what had been, and what had not, through all the many days, months, years, and decades to follow. Bell would bear this burden as long as he cherished the memory of Loden Greatstorm.

That meant he would bear it always.

Central communications for Starlight Beacon were maintained through Ops, a heavily staffed, permanently busy area of the station. Therefore, as Ro had said, the trunk of the tree had to remain standing. Werrera, Leyel, and Cale's job was to cut each and every one of the branches.

Werrera, the comms expert, had crammed himself into an ill-lit service corridor built with smaller species in mind; his Ithorian head could easily have become wedged in that narrow space. Despite the darkness and discomfort, Werrera's fingers deftly inserted the timer lock and set it to the precise hour. As soon as he'd clamped it around the correct cables, he gave a grunt of satisfaction.

Cale gave a fanged grin of appreciation. "There's no chance of them even noticing it before the time comes—"

"Celebrate then," Leyel insisted, shouldering a bag of their equipment. Nobody ever questioned people dressed for repairs and carrying tools, no matter where those people might go. "Work now."

On the *Gaze Electric*, Thaya Ferr had just delivered another batch of transfer orders.

"I've sent Roborhyan to the *Spectre*—he's had bad blood with that captain in the past. The infighting should begin shortly." She tapped on her datapad, bringing up images to remind Marchion Ro of whom she spoke. (He remembered everyone—she knew this and was too smart to forget it—but it gave some vitality to an otherwise flat presentation. She wished to serve the Eye, not to bore him.) "As for the

Janikki clan, they've been ordered to coordinate efforts in the Ishbix system . . . where several of them are wanted for crimes that significantly predate their time with the Nihil. They'll be nervous."

"And nervous people make mistakes," Ro said. The Janikki clan remained formidably loyal to one another, so much so that they had been on the verge of claiming the right to run a Tempest together. To allow such a group to share power would be tantamount to splitting the Nihil in two and handing half of it away. But once they'd screwed up a few times, they'd lose whatever alliances they had outside the clan and—if Thaya's plan came to fruition—would soon be divided against themselves. "Well done, Thaya. You've chosen these assignments wisely."

As much as Thaya wished to bask in the praise, she would not waste the Eye's time. "Tonight we'll ship out the rest of the strategic transfers. Tomorrow we can begin the mass reassignments. They'll talk, of course—"

"By that point there's no way around it." Ro understood, of course. "It doesn't matter. They won't have time to spread any sedition before the *Gaze Electric* is once again fully staffed . . . and more formidable than ever. As for their replacements—"

"The receiving orders will arrive within twenty hours." Then Thaya tensed. She had interrupted the Eye. Would he be angry?

Luckily for her, he seemed to be in an excellent mood—so much so he didn't even notice her tactlessness. And his mood would only improve once the new crew arrived.

Affie Hollow strapped herself into the copilot's seat as Leox and Geode checked their readings. From the passenger area nearby came the sounds of Orla Jareni and Elzar Mann preparing themselves for takeoff. Usually, the *Vessel* hauled cargo rather than people; so far, every exception they'd made had been for the Jedi.

"We're developing a specialty in Jedi transport," she said to Leox, who was chewing on a mint stick. "Maybe we should own it. Even advertise. 'For the monk-wizard on the go.'"

"Up to you, boss lady," Leox said.

Affie felt like that ought to make her grin; it was rare to be a ship-owner at her age, and both Leox and Geode had made the switch from her teachers to her employees with good-humored grace. But reminders that she owned the *Vessel* still made her remember that she'd only gotten it by turning her adoptive mother in to the authorities, which had led to the collapse of the Byne Guild.

Scover Byne had, of course, been guilty of the crimes charged, which involved endangering the lives of indentured workers and costing the lives of others . . . including Affie's birth parents. Very, very, *very* guilty. Affie's actions had been wholly motivated by the chance to save people working under terrible conditions. Inheriting a ship had been an unexpected benefit, the only thing that allowed her to escape the mess with anything to her name. She knew she ought to have been satisfied.

Sometimes she was. Other times, she remembered what it had been like to know Scover would always be there for her. Affie suspected her mom would never speak to her again.

Leox and Geode were her only family now. At least they were a good one.

"Attention, all and sundry." Leox spoke into the intercom, even though their only passengers sat less than two meters away. "We'll be taking a hyperspace lane to the Echerta system, dropping out for a swift switchover to a jump point that our navigator says will get us to Starlight in half the time of a direct trip." Affie threw Geode an appreciative glance, which made him look adorably smug. "Shouldn't be out there too long, so relax, appreciate the unique circumstances that have brought you into being at this moment in history, and enjoy the ride."

As Leox reached for the hyperdrive, Affie murmured, "I love this part."

Leox grinned. "So does any pilot worth a damn." With that, he pulled downward, and black space turned electric blue.

The first leg of the jump lasted only a few minutes, barely time enough for Affie to do more than double-check comms. As she did so, however, she saw an alert pop up. That one line of red told her everything she needed to know: "The Nihil are up to something again."

Leox never looked away from the brilliant-blue light beyond the cockpit. "I wish they were easier to discourage."

"So does half the galaxy, by now," Affie replied.

"The most pertinent fact here," Leox said, "is whether these Nihil shenanigans are taking place at Starlight Beacon, or the Echerta system."

Affie searched through the warnings—difficult, as they were updating constantly, but not impossible. "Looks like Starlight Beacon checks out so far."

"That's a relief," called Orla Jareni from the back. "And Echerta—"

"We're about to find that out for ourselves." Leox squared his shoulders in his seat. "Dropping out of hyperspace in three—two—one—*now*."

He pushed the craft back to realspace. Electric blue faded into the blackness of space—

—Or should have. Instead space beyond the cockpit was lit up with weapons fire and flame. Nihil ships were tormenting a nearby hauler, and already, some of them had changed course to target the *Vessel*.

Fear froze Affie's veins as she said, "They're here."

Chapter 4

Elzar Mann had just enough time to clutch the harness before the *Vessel* jarred violently.

"Hang on to your hindquarters!" Leox called as the ship went into a sharp dive. Almost immediately, another jolt—weapons fire—struck the *Vessel*. Elzar exhaled sharply, half expecting to be ejected into space, but the tiny ship was holding together.

For the moment.

Orla Jareni called out, "What kind of weaponry does the *Vessel* have?"

"Not much!" Affie replied. "One gun back behind cargo. It wouldn't open a durasteel crate."

Elzar and Orla shared a worried glance. Elzar said, "Why do you even have it, then?"

It was Leox who shouted back, "It's more there to *look* scary than to *be* scary, psychology being a critical element of most standoffs. Little late for that now."

"Take the gun," Elzar suggested to Orla. "Some defensive fire has to be better than none."

"We're about to find out." Orla unhitched her harness and ran toward the back of the ship. For his part, Elzar made his way to the cockpit, the better to see exactly how much trouble they were in.

As soon as he'd seen it, he wished he hadn't. The Echerta system was swarming with Nihil ships—literally—swooping in every direction, like clouds of Corellian sting-gnats. Were there ten? Twelve? They moved too swiftly to be easily counted. Since Echerta served as a hub among multiple hyperspace lanes, dozens of ships had emerged here—either hoping to stop in at the system's space station or simply to change course, as the *Vessel* had—only to be waylaid. For their part, the Nihil were attacking everyone and everything, with no clear battle lines or directions of assault. What was their goal? What was its purpose? Elzar couldn't fathom it.

Had they fractured the Nihil from one cohesive group into many smaller ones, all with different aims and purposes? Elzar hoped not. But the death throes of the Nihil would apparently remain dramatic for a while to come.

At the sight of this mayhem, Leox Gyasi bit down grimly on his lower lip; Geode remained stoic. But the copilot, Affie Hollow, was too young to look entirely unshaken. "So," she said, almost evenly, "I'm guessing we haven't already jumped back into hyperspace for a reason?"

"That reason," Leox said, "would be that we are currently busy—as in, *very* busy—dodging Nihil fire." As though to illustrate, Leox took them hard to port, just evading a Nihil barrage. "Without a steady location or a predictable vector, even a navigator as good as Geode has a hell of a time getting a ship safely into hyperspace—particularly around here, which is kind of tricky as hyperspace junctions go. A couple of weapons hits, we'll survive. But a hyperspace splice? That's nothing but an invitation to die."

"All the same," Elzar interjected, "I'd rather we didn't take any more weapons hits. These Nihil seem well armed—better than we're shielded, I think."

"You think correctly," Leox said. "However, you will note that the Nihil have not consulted our preferences about how often we'd like to get shot, since our answer would have been a flat zero."

Affie sucked in a sharp breath as Leox steered them down just in time to miss yet another Nihil barrage. Elzar forced himself not to get caught up in the crew's reactions and closed his eyes.

He wasn't yet sure whether he trusted himself to use the Force fully, freely, without falling back on bad habits. But that didn't mean he couldn't call on it at all.

Reach out. Elzar's awareness through the Force emanated beyond this one small ship, expanding like a bubble throughout the system, until it seemed to him that he could sense the life within each Nihil ship like a pinprick of heat within the vast, cold emptiness of space. His breathing slowed along with his perception of time. Elzar traced the path of each Nihil vessel until he could almost see them moving in his mind, their courses like red trails—stretching into both past and future.

Elzar's eyes opened. "Geode, take us to point seven mark three nine by two seven seven."

He sensed Affie and Leox giving each other a look, but Leox said only, "Give it a shot." Although Geode remained motionless, the *Vessel* immediately pivoted toward the coordinates Elzar had named.

"We're clear there," Elzar said. "Clear long enough to launch to hyperspace, anyway."

Affie stared at him over her shoulder. "Wait. Aren't we going to—you know—go to the rescue? Isn't that what you Jedi do?"

"Do you think we can?" Elzar asked. He knew as well as she did that they couldn't. Although it tore at his soul to see lives endangered—and lost—their ship's limitations were clear. Lingering in this system would save no one else; it would only risk those aboard the *Vessel.* At the moment, these were the only lives Elzar could save.

Still, it took Affie a few long seconds to reply. "I guess we can't," she said. "Maybe we should arm this thing someday, Leox."

"Not a bad idea, boss lady," Leox said. "However, barring a highly unlikely retail opportunity occurring in the next few minutes, it does not serve us at this time."

"Wait a second." Orla Jareni appeared behind Elzar, her white robes stark compared with the darkness that surrounded them. "We're just going to cut and run?"

This, in Elzar's opinion, was a very undignified way to refer to a strategic retreat. "We can't beat them. You must see that."

"We don't have to beat the Nihil to help save lives," she insisted. "We just have to *hurt* them, and we can."

Leox's long face split in a grin. "Now, that's the kind of rascality I like to hear. Whatcha thinking, Orla?"

"The Nihil are devastating because they act in concert." Orla elbowed Elzar aside in a way that would've been rude if the situation weren't so dire. "They can't manage coordinated attacks if they can't coordinate. To coordinate they need communication—"

"Which means you want to screw with their communications systems," Affie finished for her. "Sounds great. But how?"

"If any of us knew how to disrupt their systems, we wouldn't have a Nihil problem to begin with," Orla said, kneeling by Geode's side. "There's one thing we could do, though—flood the frequencies."

Elzar frowned. "They'll have us screened out. That's basic defense."

But Orla shook her head, a wide, wicked smile spreading across her face. "They'll have warships screened out. Larger freighters. Even single-pilot fighters. What they won't have screened is a little bitty hauler like the *Vessel.*"

"So few people realize what a gift it is to be underestimated." Leox's smile was nearly as broad as Orla's. "You do comprehend we'll only be able to stall the Nihil a couple minutes before they catch on?"

Orla nodded. "But that's a couple minutes the ships in this area can use to get away."

Elzar finally saw it, too. By refusing to match an opponent—by not only acknowledging their ship's smallness but by embracing it—Orla

Jareni had found a way to claim a kind of victory and to save hundreds of lives. That kind of thinking should be instinctive, to a Jedi; Elzar wondered if it would ever become so for him.

Already Leox and Affie were working swiftly at their controls, setting up a multi-frequency broadcast at top volume. Affie asked, "So what should we play for our Nihil friends?"

"Who doesn't love the margengai glide?" Leox punched a button with decisive glee. "I know I do."

The song—a popular dance tune for at least the last several decades—filled the cockpit of the *Vessel,* jaunty and fast. It was possibly the least appropriate music Elzar could imagine for a space battle, which made it all the more satisfying to imagine it blaring from the comm systems of all these Nihil ships at once.

"Unfortunately, the other ships have to hear it, too," Orla conceded, "but I doubt they'll mind for long."

Indeed, already the Nihil ships were showing signs of disarray. It wouldn't take them long to compensate—individual ships would have battle plans they could follow in the absence of orders being given, and soon surely they would begin blocking frequencies—but their prey required only a few instants. Civilian ships began to vanish into hyperspace, one after the other, tiny bright sparks of white disappearing into the stars. A bubble around the nearest space station shimmered into being as they managed to get their shielding back online.

Sensors began to beep ominously. Affie winced. "The Nihil are scanning for the source of the signal."

"Looks like they found it," Leox drawled, even as Nihil ships began changing course to head their way. "Which means it's time we were going. Ready, Geode?"

Before Geode could answer, the first spray of weapons fire lit up the space around them, and one bolt found its target. The *Vessel* lurched sideways as damage sensors squealed. Elzar stared at the ship schematics, which revealed a direct hit on their starboard engine. "Can we still fly?"

"About to find out," Leox said, still as casual as though he had not a care in the world. He grabbed the lever on the controls, and—

Elzar breathed out in relief. The dazzling blue of hyperspace had never looked so good. Geode must have input new coordinates in the nick of time.

Meanwhile, the margengai glide continued playing. Apparently Leox hadn't been lying when he said he loved the song.

When Orla turned to go, Elzar left the cockpit with her, both because the space was too small for guests to remain comfortable for long and because he wanted a word with her. "What made you think of it?" Elzar asked. "What reminded you that we didn't have to be aggressive? That we could be . . . small, even playful, and in being so, achieve a victory?"

Orla gave him an odd look. "I've never had to be reminded of that," she said gently. "Stay on your current path, Elzar, and you'll see it, too."

Could it be that easy?

Although the initial wave of wounded had resulted in a great deal of work, the atmosphere aboard Starlight Beacon was regaining its equilibrium. Stellan Gios had seen to it that the medical tower was operating smoothly, that resources had been diverted accordingly, and that space traffic to Starlight in the next several days would be limited: only necessary arrivals, only scheduled departures. Even though the current attacks appeared to be small and scattered, they were still doing real damage. Therefore, until the Nihil had been quieted again, Stellan preferred to know the identity and vector of any ship in the system.

This had met with the approval of most aboard the station and all Jedi (and, particularly, Estala Maru). However, not everyone saw the wisdom of this move.

"*I move where my business takes me, and when it takes me.*" This came from Koley Linn, owner and pilot of the cargo ship *Ace of Staves.* He was a thirty-something human with curly brilliant-red hair and a perpetual smirk, which at the moment had twisted into a sneer. "*Not when some* artificial schedule *tells me to.*"

Stellan was grateful they were speaking via holo—Ops to the main cargo bay—and not in person, as that reduced the chances that Koley Linn could hear his pained sigh. "We're not assigning departure times. You can almost certainly choose your own time to leave. You simply have to register the leaving time for *Ace of Staves* at least two hours in advance—"

"*What if I take on a job that requires me to leave immediately?*" Linn demanded.

Even a Jedi's patience had limits. Stellan was nearing his. "First of all, given the recent Nihil activity, I doubt anyone's going to be in a hurry to move cargo until the situation has quieted further. Secondly, if someone *is* fool enough to offer you a job in these circumstances, I strongly suggest you turn it down, because your ship will not be allowed to leave without a scheduled departure time. If you dislike these terms, refusing to schedule your earliest possible departure seems a rather perverse course of action."

Koley Linn looked like he'd rather punch Stellan in the face than simply schedule a departure. This was not a man who wanted to be told what to do—no matter how reasonable the suggestion might be. He simply snapped off his hololink, cutting Stellan off. Stellan considered the rudeness a small price to pay to be done with the man for a while.

"Charming fellow," said Regald Coll, who'd joined Stellan in Ops just before the call. "Makes you wonder who would be in a big hurry to enjoy his company."

"Makes you wonder what rules he's willing to break, if people hire him despite that attitude." Stellan rubbed his temples.

Forfive rolled up beside Stellan, brimming with energy. "I greatly anticipate the chance to organize the ship departure schedules for you, Master Stellan!"

"Just call me Stellan, please. You sound like a Padawan." Stellan brightened, however, at the realization that from now on he could make Koley Linn deal with JJ-5145 instead. Maybe Elzar's gift would prove to be far more than a practical joke. "In fact, let's get you set up to—"

"Excuse me," said the operator droid on the comm, "but there's an incoming message from Queen Thandeka of Eiram."

Stellan and Regald exchanged glances. Although Thandeka was only the queen consort—her wife, Queen Dima, was queen regnant and the true ruler—she had a history with the Jedi. That history made her not only one of the biggest supporters of both the Jedi Order and the Republic in this area of space, but also her world's designated spokesperson on such matters. Although Stellan would have preferred to go back to checking station preparations before the next wave of wounded arrived, Queen Thandeka was at least a far more enjoyable conversationalist than Koley Linn. Taking his seat, Stellan said, "Put her through."

The holo shimmered into life again, this time revealing Thandeka, a human woman around fifty years of age with tawny skin and wide streaks of silver in her thick dark hair. Her face lit up as she recognized him. "Master Gios. You honor me with your attention."

"Always a pleasure, Your Majesty," Stellan said with a smile. "How may I help you?"

Worry etched a small line between Thandeka's eyebrows. "The people of Eiram have of course heard of the scattered Nihil attacks. We are grateful that Starlight Beacon orbits our world at present, to keep us safe."

Stellan nodded pleasantly, though inside he was thinking that this seemed an odd use of a diplomatic call.

But then Thandeka continued, "You no doubt recall that we were due to use Starlight's tractor beam capacity to help finalize the desalination plant repairs during the next two days—to shift the final layer of the aqueduct into place."

8લે8૨59

"Of course," Stellan said. "I'm afraid other priorities must take precedence now, but we should be able to turn to the work very shortly."

"We understand the delay," she said, "but do any of your scientists or analysts have time to make sure that the desalination plant is stable enough to last for another several days or so, long enough to resolve these few troubles? We used only temporary joisting in its place, since those supports weren't meant to be needed very long—"

"I'll task someone to look into it immediately," Stellan promised. He might not have anyone to spare besides a droid, but an astromech would have more than enough capacity to run those numbers. "Don't be afraid, Queen Thandeka. We will not forget Eiram or its people. We will strive to do our best for all those in need at this time." He smiled at her, genuinely glad to be reminded, for a moment, that his task was greater than running after the latest crisis. This was about unifying space under the peaceful banner of the Republic, and about bringing justice and safety to millions who had never truly known it before. He added, "We are all the Republic."

He was rewarded with Thandeka's own warm smile as she repeated, "We are all the Republic."

ORLAND PARK PUBLIC LIBRARY

Chapter 5

It felt as though Starlight Beacon were a living thing, holding its breath. Bell Zettifar acutely sensed the alertness in most of the beings aboard, from Master Gios himself down to Ember, who paced the perimeter of the training area as though in search of prey. Of course a charhound couldn't know that the Nihil had attacked a few systems, or that some more wounded would soon arrive—but Ember could sense the slight tension in the people around her, and that was enough to put her on edge.

(Or maybe Ember *did* know. Bell tried not to anthropomorphize his charhound, but it was impossible to look into her eyes without sensing the intelligent soul within.)

For the moment, Bell was doing everything in his power *not* to be on edge. He needed to remain calm, steady, and focused for the work to come.

So obviously the best thing to do was to swing a lightsaber around.

"Ungh!" He stumbled backward from the might of Burryaga's blow. Sparring with a Wookiee took full concentration and considerable

YRARBIJ

strength. Bell had the first in hand, but he was increasingly unsure of the second.

Burryaga whined inquisitively, cocking his head. Did Bell need to take a break?

"You wish." Bell grinned, and leapt into the air.

His velocity took him sharply upward, heels over head, pinwheeling above Burryaga—only for an instant, but enough for him to possess, for one second, the advantage of height. Their blades clashed in a burst of light . . .

. . . which was when Burryaga twisted to the side, angling himself perfectly to throw Bell off and send him crashing down. Bell managed not to belly flop—he got his feet under him in the nick of time—but it was hardly a dignified landing.

Burryaga's chuckle made Bell shake his head and deactivate his lightsaber. "Master Loden always said it was a fool who either fought angry or fought a Wookiee."

Self-effacing Burryaga claimed he'd hit a lucky strike, but they both knew better. Bell appreciated it anyway.

Ember trotted over toward them, her tail wagging. Bell knelt down to stroke her head. "It's okay, girl," he said. "Don't worry. Everything's all right."

But it wasn't really Ember who was uneasy, Bell realized. It was him.

Not just him, either, because Burryaga then growled a low, plaintive sound. "Yeah, I sense it, too," Bell admitted. "This nagging sense that something's . . . *off.*"

Burryaga said that normally he would be able to meditate and close in on the source of this disquiet, but it was impossible to separate that from the uncertainty inspired by the recent Nihil activity.

"Maybe it's just that same uncertainty magnified? Like we're all feeding into one another's worry?" Even as Bell asked, though, he knew that wasn't right.

Something else was wrong aboard Starlight. Something profoundly unfamiliar.

Burryaga said as much, his furry brow creasing with consternation. The Force normally allowed them to understand so much—if not the entirety of something, at least its basic outlines or fundamental purpose. At the moment, however, the Force remained silent.

"I wish Master Loden were here," Bell said quietly. "He'd been all across the galaxy. Sometimes it seemed like there wasn't anything he hadn't encountered. If he were with us, I bet he'd be able to tell us everything."

After a moment, Burryaga lay one shaggy paw on Bell's shoulder.

"Thanks." Bell's eyes were hot, but he blinked back the tears. A Jedi shouldn't feel too much grief, for too long. Master Loden had become one with the Force. To grieve too long was to deny that transcendent truth.

But to not grieve at all—that was impossible. Bell didn't think Loden Greatstorm would have asked that of him. He would've understood.

I'm not letting him down by missing him, Bell thought, and then the tears were even closer than before.

At the moment he might've become overwhelmed, Burryaga distracted him by whining and tilting his head. Bell frowned. "I'm not hearing it—human ears can't pick that up from here." All the same, he put away his lightsaber and headed for the hook where he'd hung his jacket. If Burryaga said the docking bay doors were opening, no doubt he was correct.

(The doors were to be used only in times of conflict or when near interstellar anomalies, but the recent burst of Nihil hostility counted as the former.)

Which meant some more wounded might be arriving, and if so, Bell's duty was to rush to their side.

———

The cargo-only bay of Starlight Beacon—which, as it happened, was two levels above and directly over the sparring area—remained quiet. Nobody was allowed to haul goods in during an emergency, unless and until more medical supplies were required.

Werrera, Leyel, and Cale's ship, carrying "rathtars," remained in place, undisturbed, near the station's very heart.

The other cargo bays, however, were filled with light, activity, and noise.

"This way—no—no—does no one look at a flight plan anymore?" Estala Maru huffed before taking the illuminated traffic wands from a signal droid and beginning to direct the offending ship himself. Stellan privately thought the offending ship was no more likely to follow instructions from Maru than from anybody else, but at least it would give Maru the illusion that he had some measure of control.

No one else had that luxury. While most of the small ships coming in to dock were following their flight plans closely enough, there were a few too many craft coming in at once for the effect to be anything other than a mess. There weren't many injured among the arrivals, but they were just numerous enough to pull attention, and thus increase the level of disarray.

"I will attempt to impose order," announced JJ-5145 before rolling out, with the apparent goal of taking the traffic wands from Maru. As amusing as this promised to be, Stellan had no time to watch.

One small ship settled immediately in front of him. The hull showed signs of carbon scoring, but as Stellan hurried over to it, he saw that otherwise it appeared intact.

When the ship's ramp opened, a human woman of roughly forty years helped a human man of similar age from the ship. A blood-stained cloth was tied around his forehead. Stellan took the man's other arm to assist them. "Should you be walking? We can summon a hover-stretcher—"

"I'm fine," the man insisted, then gave the lie to his words with a wince.

"He's *not* fine," the woman said, "but it's not as bad as it looks. I'm Pikka Adren, and this is my husband, Joss, whose forehead had a close encounter with our hyperdrive. Both are the worse for wear."

"I hope the hyperdrive's in better shape," Stellan said as he helped them down. Joss Adren seemed steady enough on his feet, but best to make sure.

"That's just it," Joss groaned. "I managed to knock out the engine display. So there's no telling how bad it is or isn't."

Pikka nodded. "All I can tell you is, when we went into hyperspace to get here, the engine started making brand-new sounds. Previously unknown sounds. I prefer it when everything about my ship's engine is one hundred percent previously known."

"Very wise," Stellan agreed. Now that they were on the hangar deck, he could let go of Joss's arm. "A droid will guide you to our medical tower. Once you're all patched up, Mr. Adren, the two of you can return to work on your ship. I have to warn you, however—we don't have a large reserve of parts, so we can't allow you to leave without a scheduled, preapproved departure."

"Like we're in a hurry to get back out there with the Nihil on the loose." Pikka shook her head in disbelief. "Trust me, Master Jedi—"

"Gios. Stellan Gios."

"Master Gios, now that we're safe aboard Starlight Beacon, we intend to stay put until the Nihil have settled down—whenever that might be." With that, she continued guiding her husband toward a medical droid, which was already blinking to show them the way.

Stellan realized that his altercation with Koley Linn (currently glowering from the far edge of the docking bay) had blinded him to the reality that most of those currently arriving on Starlight wouldn't be in a hurry to leave. In fact, it would probably be difficult to convince them to go unless and until the Nihil threat had finally been, not just diminished or contained as the Jedi had managed before, but truly, completely eliminated.

Who could say when that might be? A day?

A month?

Avar Kriss's mad hunt for the Eye of the Nihil had always seemed dangerous, to Stellan. It seemed far too close to a desire for vengeance, too focused on the enemy at the expenses of their allies. And to abandon Starlight Beacon at its time of greatest need—?

But Starlight Beacon still had a leader. It had Stellan himself.

And if Avar was able to capture the Eye, then there truly was a chance to put an end to Nihil attacks forever. That might be the only way Stellan would ever get Starlight Beacon back. The only way this station could resume its proper mission.

Although he'd never admit it to her, Avar might have had the right idea all along.

Indeera Stokes saw that her Padawan had hurried to help the incoming wounded swiftly—before she could even let him know of the need to do so. *He will become a fine Jedi Knight,* she thought, *if he still believes that he can.*

Bell's grief for his former Master, Loden Greatstorm, colored every interaction Indeera shared with him. She had to walk a very fine line: challenging Bell while respecting the severe shock of Greatstorm's death, forming a bond between Master and apprentice without seeking to replace, or erase, the bond that had gone before. Sometimes she wondered whether she went too far—or not far enough—or if she was getting it wrong by doing both at once.

So thinks every Master with their first Padawan, Master Yoda had told her, back when she'd initially announced her intention to teach. *Certainty, we have not. An individual, each apprentice is. Learn, you must, how to train each one in turn. No two will ever be alike.*

Across the docking bay, Indeera saw Bell directing pill droids toward a more seriously injured individual among this group. Nib Assek moved among the various pilots and crew, assessing ship damage and capabilities, making recommendations. Starlight's resources were somewhat strained by the number of unexpected guests, but not inadequate to the needs of those who had come here seeking refuge.

"Excuse me?" called a muffled voice. Indeera turned to see a Cerean woman of middle age, still sitting in the pilot's seat of her two-engine hopper. She was shouting through the cockpit display. "Could you help me?"

Indeera beckoned. "Of course. We have medical supplies, repair parts—just come out and—"

"But that's the problem," the Cerean said. "I can't leave my ship. Nihil weapons fire seems to have sealed the ramp."

When Indeera paced to the side of the ship, she saw blackened, seared metal almost the length of the ship. The door and ramp had indeed been melted out of shape, fusing with the hull. "Don't worry," Indeera called as she took her lightsaber in hand. "I can cut you out. Stay away from the door."

"No! Don't do that!" The Cerean waved her long arms frantically, visible as a panicking dervish at the edge of Indeera's vision. "How am I supposed to fly a ship with a hole cut in it?"

"Your ship can be fixed, even after I cut through the hull. But we cannot adequately assess the full damage to your craft without getting inside. Nor can we feed you." Hunger sometimes motivated people when nothing else did.

The Cerean slumped over her controls as if in defeat. "All right, all right. Just—make it quick."

Pilots could be so protective of their ships that they saw their vessels as extensions of themselves. Indeera, an enthusiastic pilot herself, found this endearing. Swiftly she ignited her blade and sliced—sliced—sliced—until the ramp fell open with a loud clunk, bringing some of the ship's side along with it.

"There you go," Indeera called. "All over . . ."

What if she had done the wrong thing?

Fear paralyzed her. Indeera was not one to second-guess herself, but at the moment she couldn't stop staring at the jagged hole she'd cut in the Cerean's hopper. It was repairable—so why was she suddenly pierced through with the thought of this poor woman attempting to fly away in a ship halfway peeled open?

Regain control of yourself, Indeera told herself sternly. But the thought would not be so easily banished.

Perhaps the Force was trying to tell her something. Warning her, perhaps, of a risk to come, one in which this woman would badly need her ship.

But Indeera was no stranger to the ways of the Force. She knew what it was like to sense danger coming ahead. This was different. This was . . . slow, creeping dread, coming from a direction Indeera could not identify, somehow outside of the Force itself . . .

There is no such place, she told herself. *The Force is everywhere.*

Yet at the moment, Indeera did not entirely believe it.

Chapter 6

Questioning prisoners was not a duty that Stellan enjoyed. While some Jedi—such as the famed investigator Emerick Caphtor—had particularly strong gifts that allowed them to sense subtle layers of deception, Stellan possessed no exceptional instincts in that area.

(*And do you only enjoy doing that which you do exceptionally well?* he could imagine Elzar saying to him teasingly, lopsided smile broadening as he spoke.)

At least, in this case, Stellan didn't have to pry for time-sensitive information. He hoped only to determine whether or not these two women were currently affiliated with the Nihil. If so, they could provide valuable information on the group's disintegration—in particular, what these scattered raids and attacks might indicate about the state of the Nihil. If not—their information wouldn't be as current, but they'd be a lot quicker to speak up.

Stellan paused in front of the holding cell door, straightened his robes, and nodded. The sentry droid obediently opened the doors, revealing the prisoners inside.

Chancey Yarrow lounged on her bunk as though it were a sofa in a luxury hotel. (Which wasn't that far off the mark—the cells aboard Starlight were meant as temporary custodial facilities, not for imprisoning hardened criminals, and as such were comfortably outfitted.) She was a tall woman with dark skin and a regal crown of braids, and her gaze took him in as though he were a temporary amusement, nothing more.

This one, Stellan thought, *won't reveal a single thing until she's certain it's in her best interest to do so.*

The other woman, however—the young one, known only as Nan—was more difficult to read. She looked younger than her years thanks to her diminutive stature and soft features; Stellan might even have thought her an innocent, had he not read Reath Silas's reports on their confrontation with the Nihil at the abandoned Amaxine space station many months prior. Her dark eyes revealed tension and uncertainty. She was already near a breaking point, but what that break might look like—what direction Nan might turn—was a mystery to Stellan. He suspected it was a mystery to Nan herself.

"Ms. Yarrow," he began. "And Ms. . . ."

"I'm Nan." She folded her arms across her chest.

"Yes, I'd heard that," he said pleasantly. "But I was wondering if you had a surname, any kind of second name."

"I share it with those who mean something to me," Nan said. "Which isn't you."

Fair enough, Stellan supposed. "Ms. Nan. I am Master Stellan Gios, the Jedi in charge here at Starlight."

Nan cocked her head. "The marshal of Starlight is Avar Kriss."

"Was," Stellan said. "You have solid intel—but apparently it's a little out of date."

When Nan's cheeks flushed, he silently noted, *She takes pride in having good information. This one likes to know things others don't.* That could prove useful.

"You're right," said Chancey Yarrow, slowly stretching into an upright position. "Our intel's old. Because neither of us has had anything to do with the Nihil for some months now. Which means you can't prove we've done a thing wrong, and you won't get anything out of us you can use. Might as well let us go, right?"

"I'd rather be the judge of what information I can and can't use," Stellan said. Though he faced Chancey, he paid attention to Nan at the periphery of his vision. Would she begin wondering what she did and didn't have to trade? If he got anything out of either of them, it would be Nan who broke. Chancey Yarrow's polished exterior might as well have been an impenetrable shell. This woman knew who and what she was, and she trusted fate to deliver her where she needed to be. Nan didn't have that kind of confidence. He added, "And if you're no longer affiliated with the Nihil, I'd be very interested to learn who you *are* working for."

"Working *with*," Chancey clarified. Her smile, thin as a blade, indicated that this was as far as she was willing to go.

"Why should we trust you?" Nan retorted. "You arrested us."

"That seems more like a reason for me not to trust you," Stellan said. "As former members of the Nihil, you are responsible for crimes against persons, animals, and property—so many that they're almost without number."

Chancey's lazy smile spread wide across her face. "And you're trying to recruit us? Sounds like a bad plan to me."

"I'm not recruiting anyone. Just—hoping to talk." Stellan judged that he'd pushed as far as he needed to for now. Best to give Nan a while to consider the possibilities before he spoke to her again.

Should he separate Chancey and Nan, put them in different cells? Normally that was a wise move, as prisoners tended to lose their loyalties to their comrades once there was some space between them. However, Stellan sensed that the bonds that tied Chancey and Nan together might be tested more by proximity than by distance. Nan might be quicker to realize that her priorities weren't the same as her mentor's if she was forced to face that difference head-on.

The young girl seemed more tense than before, which Stellan didn't understand until she said, "I know what that means, 'hoping to talk.' What are you going to do to us? Drowning tubes? Electro-stim? Mind probes? If you think we'll crack that easily—"

"Nothing like that is going to happen to you here," Stellan said, rising to his feet. "I don't know how the Nihil handle such things, but that is *not* the Jedi way."

"You sound so sincere," Nan replied. "I almost believe you." She didn't, yet. But she might in time.

He said only, "Take some time. Think things through. Ask yourself what you'd need to start over, to build anew."

"Much appreciated," Chancey answered as though this were a casual chat between friends wondering where to go to lunch. "We'll be thinking."

Stellan studied Nan for a moment longer, nodded at them both, and left the cell—trusting time, and their own differences, to do the rest of the work for him.

Regald Coll had thought nothing could be more exhausting than teaching younglings, no matter how dangerous a mission on the frontier might prove. After a few hours of working with stranded pilots and damaged ships, providing aid and assistance, with new arrivals showing up without warning . . .

Well, he still thought nothing was more exhausting than teaching younglings. The Nihil were bad, sure, but try managing a roomful of toddlers who've missed their nap and *just* figured out they can basically do magic. It was not a task for the weak.

Cleaning up after scattered Nihil raids came close on the exhaustion scale, though. Regald was glad to take a few moments in the mess to sit down, stretch, and summon the strength to decide what to eat.

"Bilbringi?" Indeera Stokes suggested as she took the place opposite his, carrying a tray of spicy food that looked delicious and smelled even better.

Regald found himself sitting upright. "Only Bilbringi food could wake me up like this. Nothing else could even make me move, except maybe a rancor prod."

Indeera gave him a crooked smile. She seemed wearied, too, but her tone was cheerful as she took the place opposite him. "You'll note I brought enough for two."

"That's the kind of sterling character you are." Regald took a meat pie and grinned. "Remind me to nominate you for Jedi Council someday."

"Please, no!" Indeera held up her hands. "A fate worse than death—at least, to me. I don't see how Stellan and the others do it."

"Me either." Regald had never been ambitious in that way. The crèche had been enough for him, until he decided that he should expand his boundaries, take on new responsibilities. But that was only a quest to learn and experience more, not to climb any sort of ladder.

They ate together in companionable silence—or what Regald took to be companionable silence, until he glanced up from his meal to see that Indeera hadn't even touched hers. He ventured, "Are you feeling all right?"

"No. I mean, yes." She winced and rubbed at her temples. "Nothing is physically wrong with me. Tired, but that is of no consequence." Indeera was stoic about such things. Yet even her impassive countenance couldn't fully hide her disquiet.

Regald said, "Nothing's physically wrong, you said. So what's going on is—mental? Emotional? Spiritual?"

"Perhaps all of those, and yet . . ." Indeera shook her head. "It is difficult to speak of such things. But do you not feel it, Regald? At the very edges of your consciousness?"

He nearly asked her, *What do you mean?* Before he could pose the question, however, he understood the answer.

The weariness he was experiencing went deeper than aching muscles or a throbbing head. Bone-deep . . . no. *Soul*-deep. As though the vibrant colors of the Force had all faded to gray. Regald shivered, a fear response he thought he'd left behind as a youngling.

Still, there had to be a sensible explanation. "We're all going through this together," he suggested. "Every Jedi on this station is helping those who've come here for help, dealing with the last remnants of the Nihil. We're each witnessing a lot of anger and fear. Of course that would be a psychic drain on us all."

"Of course," Indeera repeated, yet her eyes narrowed with suspicion. "But we have all been in situations like that before, and in none of those situations did I feel this terrible emptiness."

Truth be told, Regald hadn't ever felt anything like this, either. It wasn't so much the presence of something awful as it was the absence of something else that should've been there. Something so basic and fundamental to the proper workings of the universe that he'd never recognized it and couldn't even get a grasp on it while he was sitting here attempting to come up with a picture . . .

"Is that Bilbringi?" Nib Assek's wrinkled face lit up with a tired smile as she came nearer. "Don't mind if I do."

Regald handed her one of the meat pies as she took a seat between him and Indeera. "Nib, how are you feeling right now?"

"Tired as all get-out," she said, and though Nib still had a smile on her face, he could hear the weariness concealed within her good cheer. "Like my brain's already taking a nap and my body's eager to join it."

"Are you sensing this strangeness?" Indeera said. "The . . . opacity of the Force?"

Nib's valiant smile finally faded. "You, too?"

"We're talking ourselves into it," Regald said. His tone was firm; he'd let himself get sidetracked too easily. "We're worn out, we're emotionally compromised, and now we're convincing ourselves to believe in ghosts."

"Do you really think so?" Indeera kept staring into the middle distance, focusing on nothing.

"Yeah, I do. We like to think we're wiser, we're the Jedi, we're in control of our minds and bodies—but in the end, we can be just as superstitious and suggestible as most people, if we let down our guard." He punctuated this with an emphatic gesture with his meat pie. "Once we eat and give ourselves a breather for a few minutes, the feeling will vanish and we'll hardly even notice."

"You're right," Nib said, with determination. "Of course. Should've thought of it myself." Indeera didn't seem equally ready to believe him, but she started eating her meal, so Regald counted it as a win.

He ate. He tried to relax. And he succeeded.

Mostly.

In the depths of Starlight Beacon, Werrera and Leyel continued their work on the station's communications relays. The central system remained oblivious to their attack—taking each node out, one by one, gave Cale time to provide compensating input for the system, blank energy that would create the illusion of all being well.

This particular relay, however, was of particular importance. When the time came, it would need to be fully functional—the better to send the Nihil's message to the Galactic Core.

Carefully, slowly, Werrera wove his long fingers through the intricate wiring, closing off link after link. Cale routed the signals into the slim silvery box that had previously been programmed by Marchion Ro himself.

It appeared the Jedi remained oblivious to their actions. The only other person aboard Starlight who knew what they were doing was Ghirra Starros—their monitor, the one who would report their deeds to the Eye—and she had already signaled her last. After this, everything they did, they did alone. None would know the individual acts of cunning or courage that lay ahead, not until their work bore its true fruit.

Each of them, at different moments, thought back to the people they'd left behind on the *Gaze Electric*. Not one of them suspected that none of those people remained on Ro's flagship anymore, that instead they had been transferred to Nihil ships that were likely to be used as cannon fodder relatively soon. They might've realized it had they doubted Marchion Ro at all—they knew he erased every trace of his actions—but they were without doubt. Their eyes were blinded by their shining faith.

"I've been thinking," Leyel said. Cale nearly startled; she hadn't spoken loudly, but they'd been tense and silent for so long that any noise jolted his entire nervous system. "Those things back on the ship—don't they have to be fed?"

"None of them will live much longer," Cale reminded her. "But it doesn't matter." A smile spread across his face as he thought of Ro's explanation of what the beasts were, what they were capable of. "I imagine they're feeding already."

Unbeknownst to the Nihil team, one of their "passengers" had already gone in search of heartier fare.

A small astromech droid, whirring about while checking sensors in the cargo bay, heard a loud metal bang—as though plating had fallen off a hull, or a hatch had been forced open. It wheeled toward the sound to find a cargo ship, small and nondescript, with its hatch open. Within, the astromech could see shadowy movement.

Swiftly it checked the cargo manifest, then whistled with alarm. Rathtars? Those were life-forms that required immediate containment.

The astromech rolled forward, connected with the ship's hatch controls, and was rewarded with the almost instant closing of the door. It then turned and scanned its immediate vicinity for rathtars, found none, and went contentedly on its way after a job well done.

Any sentient would've known that rathtars didn't hesitate to burst out of any containment, would've searched for anyone or anything else that might have escaped that cargo ship instead.

But cargo bays were run by droids, and droids were more easily satisfied.

The first scheduled departure from Starlight fell to a small passenger craft that had originally been meant to leave almost a day prior. Most of its few passengers were impatient to go.

One of them had known from the beginning that they would be delayed.

Ghirra Starros checked the full schematic of Starlight. She'd been monitoring it all day—more closely than the Jedi did themselves, since she had the necessary filters to screen the false, planted readouts and retrieve the true data—which was why she'd seen comm relay after comm relay fall under Nihil control. On her screen, what ought to have been an array of bright lights instead lay gray and almost dull, like a night sky shrouded by clouds.

Her personal alarm beeped. Time to go. This was one transport she didn't want to miss.

Ghirra slung a heavy bag over one shoulder; it was stuffed to its fullest capacity, and her shoulder strained beneath the weight. Running to the transport might arouse unwelcome interest, so she walked quickly. If it didn't look particularly senatorial, well, at the moment, Ghirra didn't care. It turned out to be better that way; she didn't have to look too long at the people in the corridors who weren't about to leave. The ones who would be here when—

"Senator Starros?" She turned to see Bell Zettifar, the Jedi Padawan, who'd fallen in beside her. "If you're in a hurry, I can help you—we've got a few minutes—"

"No, no, I'm fine." Ghirra smiled and hoped her expression was convincing. They said the Jedi could read minds. That was the last thing she needed.

But this one was only an apprentice, young enough to make her think of her daughter, Avon. Rarely had she been gladder that she was away at boarding school—safe, and far from all of this.

Bell hadn't picked up on her uneasiness, it seemed. He simply nodded as he headed toward a side corridor. "See you again soon," he called.

"Of course," Ghirra said, and that was the only part that stung. The thought of that young man unknowingly walking away would stay with her far longer than she realized, longer even than the memory of Marchion Ro's joy when she had come to his side.

Something's up with her, Bell thought as he continued on his way. The energy coming off Ghirra Starros had been unsettled in the extreme— and besides, that was one of the fakest smiles he'd ever seen.

But maybe he was reading too much into it. The weird energy that had been clawing at the edges of his consciousness made everything feel strange and wrong. Bell kept telling himself that it was only his doubt, his guilt, the uncertainty that had tugged at him for months. If he kept his mind on where he was, what he was doing, the sensation would stop any time now.

And yet it was always still there . . .

Chapter 7

In his small, makeshift chamber aboard the *Vessel*, Elzar Mann sought peace.

A few moments of silence and stillness would do. To judge from the reports they continued to receive about scattered Nihil activity, he'd be busy on Starlight soon after their arrival, and for a long time to come. If he wanted to center himself—to still the whispers of doubt that haunted his thoughts—this was the time.

Granted, it would've been easier if Leox Gyasi hadn't decided this was an excellent time to play all his favorite music over the ship's intercom. At least this time he'd chosen Chandrilan opera—the sweeping, dramatic melodies washed over Elzar like the waves on Ledalau, reminding him of the stability he had found there.

Darkness will ever be a part of me, he reminded himself. *It will ever be a part of every Jedi, of every living thing. To acknowledge the darkness is to know the darkness. To know the darkness is to begin to control it.*

Elzar's mind—as it often did—flashed to Avar Kriss. He imagined her as she had been on a long-ago mission to Riosa: her long golden hair back in a braid, the jeweled headband she wore sparkling in the pinkish sunlight.

Perhaps one reason he found it so difficult to accept his own darkness as a part of life, no more and no less, came from his inability to believe that any darkness had ever found its way into Avar's soul.

"So," Nan finally said, "what's the catch?"

"Is it not obvious?" Chancey was frankly disappointed. She'd hoped her young protégée would show a little more insight. Sylvestri would've caught on right away . . . But Chancey couldn't think about her estranged daughter, not at the moment. Focus was necessary, as was setting Nan straight.

"I thought you left the Nihil because you wanted to chart your own path," Chancey began. "Not to switch one set of masters for another."

Nan didn't look nearly as crestfallen as Chancey had anticipated. "How are the Grafs not our masters?"

"They're our employers. Big difference."

"I'm not so sure," Nan insisted.

In truth, Chancey had some doubts about this, too; working for one of the wealthiest families in the galaxy came with considerable perks . . . but it had also turned out to come with very short reins.

But still. "Look at it this way, Nan. At the moment, we can't make new friends without making new enemies. Angering the Grafs? That's a seriously bad idea. The Jedi have considerable reach, as do the Nihil, but trust me, money can find you *anywhere*."

"But we won't betray the Grafs, and we don't have to betray the Nihil, either," Nan insisted. "The last we heard, the Jedi were still chasing Lourna Dee because they thought she was the Eye. In other words, they don't know a damn thing. We can feed them old intel, even false intel, and the Jedi will never know the difference! We get free, we go back to work, and—"

"Then the first whispers start to circulate," Chancey said. "That we got out of jail by turning on the Nihil. If even a hint of that reaches Marchion Ro, do you think he's going to wait to determine whether the intel you gave the Jedi was good or not? All he's going to know is, you turned. The minute he knows that, he marks you for death. And if they send someone to kill you, I might wind up as collateral damage. So for both our sakes, I suggest you shut your mouth and keep it shut."

Nan didn't look one bit pleased about being talked down to, even if (in Chancey's opinion) she currently deserved it. But she remained quiet. Hopefully that silence would last a long, long time.

Once again, Chancey's traitor mind whispered, *Sylvestri would've known better, if she were with you.*

Within Starlight Beacon's Hub, Estala Maru walked along the stretch of scanner displays that provided a constant "health" status for the station. They were, as usual, running smoothly, with every single readout within optimal range.

He allowed himself a brief moment of pride—beneath a Jedi, really, but when a mechanism this important and complex ran this perfectly for so long? Well. A little recognition of one's own accomplishments seemed in order, just as long as he didn't get carried away with it.

(And Estala Maru never let himself get carried away, ever.)

Perfection, he thought. *Perfection is satisfying. Perfection is . . .*

. . . impossible.

Eyes narrowing, he began studying some of the readouts more carefully. Yes, each one looked good. Even that comm array that had been giving them trouble lately. Maru didn't recall sending anyone to repair the comms; between the work on the desalination facility on Eiram and the efforts to help the Nihil attack survivors, he hadn't had the personnel to spare.

It runs well most of the time, Maru reminded himself. So why should this set him on edge?

Come to think of it, he'd been oddly on edge all day—

"Master Maru," said one of the techs. "We've got a power surge in the medical tower."

Maru swore under his breath. "No wonder—every pill droid we have must be recharging. We'll reroute." He hurried over to supervise this critical task.

Meanwhile, the unnaturally perfect readouts on the comm array glowed on, unnoticed.

Aboard the *Gaze Electric*, Thaya Ferr watched Marchion Ro from the corner of her eye.

Thaya, a human woman still in her twenties, didn't draw a great deal of attention, generally. Her looks were average, her voice soft, her behavior wholly unremarkable. Her history wasn't a particularly compelling tale, which was just as well, since nobody had ever asked for it. Nor were her ambitions towering. Never once in her whole life had Thaya Ferr dreamed of being the person in charge of anything.

No, she knew her destiny. Thaya Ferr was never meant to lead, but she could be one hell of a second-in-command.

Everyone obsessed over how difficult it was to lead. They didn't recognize that *following* was also a skill, one most people didn't pay enough attention to. They believed that either you were in charge, or you were adrift. Thaya knew better. Being a clever follower meant anticipating needs. Removing obstructions. Ensuring that everything flowed as smoothly for the leader as water in a mountain stream.

Meanwhile, effective leaders noticed those who executed their instructions well while asking for little in return; smart ones knew that those individuals were the ones they could truly lean on.

Marchion Ro was both effective and smart. Thus, over the past few months, he had increasingly turned to Thaya Ferr. At first she had been a flunky, a mere minion, but of late, more complex tasks—more important ones—had been entrusted to her. And Thaya had delivered.

At last, she was proving her value. She didn't hold Ro in the same kind of reverence many of the Nihil did, but she knew she'd attached herself to a leader worth the following. Thaya would never betray him; to do so would only betray her own interests. No, she'd be his right hand—trustworthy enough to remain at the center of things, but quiet enough that the braggarts and bullies who became Tempest Runners would never consider her a danger. That was precisely where she intended to remain.

And this plan currently unfolding . . . this was one of the most important moments of all.

Thaya had finally found her way to the center.

Meanwhile, on the *Ataraxia,* Avar Kriss's hunt had brought her to her quarry at last.

Avar could *feel* the distance narrowing between her and her target. Lourna Dee had run and fought so well—but soon, neither would avail her.

Reason told her that she had every chance of apprehending the Eye in the immediate future. Beyond that, however—the Force told her that it would happen. Every note in its great song was leading to this chorus, one Avar could imagine she knew by heart.

Then, for no reason she could easily name, she found herself wishing that Elzar Mann stood beside her.

He should be a part of this, she reasoned. *We always worked well together.*

But that was the whole problem, wasn't it?

Avar sighed and let the thought go. Time to capture her target.

Starlight Beacon—just like any other station or starcraft that dwelled almost entirely beyond planetary environments—had no natural "day" or "night." Yet most beings functioned better with some kind of diurnal cycle, and so at an appointed hour most lights dimmed and nonessential work shifts were cut to minimum staff. Stellan had never ceased to wonder at how effective these simple changes were. Within only minutes, the pace of living aboard the station had altered. People walked slower. Body language relaxed. Even those remaining with their ships in the principal docking bay, stranded by Nihil activity, slowed down a little. They weren't truly calm—they were away from home, perhaps repairing their ships, annoyed or unnerved by this final burst of Nihil hostility. But the greater ease they felt came close enough to resonate throughout the station.

Stellan was even more conscious of this alteration than most aboard were, and yet it worked on him, too.

A reminder, he told himself, *that our animal selves—our most base natures—live forever within us.*

"Greetings, Master Stellan!" JJ-5145 rolled up beside him, as chipper as ever. "You have a communication coming through!"

Why did a call always arrive just when Stellan thought he might have a chance to sleep? Shaking his head ruefully, he said, "Put it through to the quartermaster's office, Forfive. At least it's close."

"It's very close!" JJ-5145 said as though it were the most important, wonderful news that had ever been delivered. This was pretty much how he said everything. "Very conveniently located, for a number of station systems and locations. Have you considered making the quartermaster's office a secondary control center for Starlight Beacon? It would allow you to have access more easily when in the bottom half of the station."

Stellan opened his mouth to protest, then thought better of it. "That's not a bad idea, really. Is that something you can handle on your own?"

JJ-5145 practically vibrated with delight. "I'll begin immediately, sir!"

"Begin after my communication," Stellan said. "In fact, let me sleep on it—I'll probably tell you to get to work tomorrow morning."

The delay dimmed JJ-5145's glee not one bit. "In the morning, bright and early, as you wish, Master Stellan!"

Happily, the quartermaster's office was already a fairly comfortable, convenient place, wedged in part of the space between the main docking bay and the principal cargo bay. Stellan took a seat at the desk and punched in the code for the incoming communication. The image of Elzar Mann shimmered into being in front of him—lined with static from a weak connection, but nonetheless whole.

Stellan breathed out in relief. "Thank the Force. With the remnants of the Nihil running around like this—well, there were concerns."

Elzar raised an eyebrow. "Did you just admit you were worried about me?"

"If asked, I will deny it," Stellan said. Their friendship was of long standing, but involved a healthy dose of rivalry, and a great deal of banter.

"I'm touched," Elzar replied drily.

"Thanks for the droid, by the way."

Elzar's laugh remained joyful, even through static. "Has he driven you up the wall yet?"

"Actually, Forfive's coming in quite handy," Stellan admitted. "Which doesn't get you off the hook."

"Really? It should." In the background of whatever ship Elzar was on, opera music played, barely audible. "Truth be told, we ran into some of that Nihil action, but we escaped intact and managed to help some others get away as well."

"So you're on your way back to Starlight?" When Elzar nodded, Stellan didn't bother disguising his relief. "You're . . . doing better, then."

"Very much so." Elzar's expression became thoughtful, and more difficult to read. "I have a long way to go, I think—this is a fundamental shift in how I perceive and use the Force. But I've made progress, and the rest of the road, I can only make by walking. Orla's guided me well. Am I ever going to learn how the two of you got acquainted?"

Apparently Orla had done Stellan the courtesy of not revealing the full story. "Someday. But not yet."

Elzar's eyes lit up. "So it's a good story, then."

"Let's just say it's a long one."

"A *very* good one, I think," Elzar said with a grin. "It must be to explain why you'd turn to a Wayseeker. I know you don't care for them."

Stellan interjected, "That's an oversimplification."

"Of *the truth*," Elzar emphasized. "But your opinions of Wayseeking aren't the point. The point at the moment is, I'm on my way back and ready to help in any way I can—as is Orla Jareni, I'm sure."

"Very well. Signal ahead of leaving hyperspace, and we'll have a docking berth ready for the *Vessel* as quickly as possible."

Elzar remained silent a beat too long before asking, "Have you heard from Avar and her team?"

"No. I trust we would have heard were there any troubles." *Or if she had actually succeeded in her quest to capture the Eye.* "No news is good news."

"Of course. I have every confidence in her, and in you. Mann out."

After the holo faded, Stellan stood there for a few long seconds. Was he actually . . . *hoping* that Avar failed? On some level, it seemed so.

This was unworthy of him, Stellan knew. It did no credit to Avar's considerable skills, the very real danger the Nihil had presented until recently, or the ego that Stellan had apparently brought to this disagreement over priorities. He must meditate and purge this needless pride.

But first—sleep.

(Those who did not meditate were sometimes surprised by the idea that it was harder to do when tired, that it involved any energy at all. In fact, it could be profoundly dynamic. Stellan wanted his strength for this and the many other tasks that lay ahead.)

He was tired enough that even his chamber seemed too far away. Instead he went to the one couch in the quartermaster's office, which sat against the wall closest to the cargo bay. It would do. Stellan scarcely had energy to do more than shuck his robe and kick off his boots before he fell back upon the couch and closed his eyes. Surely there were few pleasures more just than resting after a long day of good work.

Stellan would be unable to rest for long.

"Help me—" Elzar Mann called out, looking back powerlessly toward Stellan through thick, billowing smoke.

"Help me!" Avar Kriss dashed forward into Nihil fire, her lightsaber blazing as she charged into the fray alone.

"Why haven't you helped us?" Queen Thandeka of Eiram stood in her ceremonial robe, surrounded by masses of dusty, weary people who had had no water for days.

"You can help us," Pikka Adren pleaded as she stood among the battered survivors of the Nihil attacks in Starlight's crowded medbay. "We're thirsty. We're hungry. We're starving."

"Help us" came whispers from a darkness that surrounded Stellan on all sides. "We're starving. So hungry. So hungry. Feed us.

"Feed us.

"FEED US—"

Waking with a start, Stellan stared up at the ceiling, breathing hard. The desperate hunger he had felt in his dream gnawed at his belly as though he hadn't eaten ample dinner. He tried to banish the illusion, but in the end rose from the couch and made his way to the desk. He rummaged through the drawers and found a small tin of ration powder. A little water and a swirl with his finger produced a sweet bun, which he ate as slowly as he could manage. It took all Stellan's willpower not to devour the thing like a ravenous gundark.

Although the bun sated his hunger, the disquiet from his dream lingered. As always, after a particularly vivid dream, Stellan asked himself if this might be a sending from the Force, a message to which he should pay attention. Could it be a warning about the Drengir? Such hunger called them to mind immediately. Were they not truly defeated, and perhaps returning to threaten the Jedi again? But no sooner had he posed himself these questions than he became certain the answer was no.

It feels like the opposite of that, he thought, then wondered exactly what that meant.

He couldn't articulate the reason, but knew that he was right. The dread that had seeped into his unconscious mind came not from the Force but from something else altogether.

Something that stood *between* him and the Force. Obscuring it, like clouds in front of a moon.

Chapter 8

Some said that consciousness was the galaxy's way of beholding itself. Through Leox Gyasi's eyes, the galaxy looked upon itself with great satisfaction.

Not that he didn't see the galaxy also had a hell of a lot of things wrong with it. But Leox recognized the gift he had been given in being alive, so he didn't waste time on worry or despair. If something was wrong and he could help, he would. If a crisis came, he'd deal with it then. Otherwise each day was one to be savored.

Geode understood this. Leox figured that was one of the reasons they got on so well. Affie Hollow . . . well, she was still learning.

"I don't like this," she said as they cruised through their final seconds of hyperspace flight. "The Nihil make me want to stay safe here forever."

"Traveling without a destination is among the world's most perfect pastimes," Leox said. "But at the moment, we have a passenger run to finish."

Affie frowned as she tugged her long brown-black hair into a tail—a sign that her inner self was readier to complete the voyage than her consciousness was. (Leox was a big believer in the inner self.) She said, "Doesn't it seem like Starlight is the last place we ought to go? It's the symbol of the Republic in this area, the center of the Jedi presence— that makes it the place the Nihil hate most of all."

"First of all, according to the Jedi, what we're seeing is the Nihil's last gasp. So they won't be trouble for much longer. Second, Starlight's the center of Republic attention in that part of the galaxy," Leox replied. "If whatever's left of the Nihil try to raid that place, the Republic's gonna give them a kick in the teeth. Or fangs, or gills, whatever the Nihil in question's got going on. No, they're not coming to Starlight unless they've got something a hell of a lot craftier in mind."

"Sometimes you do this thing where you think you're helping, but you're definitely not," Affie pointed out.

"Either way, Little Bit, it's time to drop out of here. Ready, Geode?"

Geode's answer came in the form of the slight shudder of the *Vessel* leaving hyperspace. The electric blue surrounding them instantly shifted to black. In the distance shone Starlight Beacon—

—and in the nearer distance they saw a ship, a tiny Japealean one-pilot cutter struggling to move forward. Even from here, Leox could tell one of its engines had blown, and the other one wasn't in great shape.

Affie flicked on the comms before Leox's hand could move. "This is the *Vessel*. Are you in need of assistance?"

"*Yes, please—*" The woman from the Japealean cutter coughed. She sounded exhausted. "*—Took fire from the Nihil—just when you think the kriffers are gone for good—*"

At the same instant, Leox and Affie looked down at the readouts. Geode already had the analysis on-screen for them: The ship truly was what it appeared to be, genuinely quite damaged, and the pilot on board was indeed alone. "On our way," Leox said as he angled the ship toward the injured Japealean craft.

Each of the three crewmembers knew what to do without any discussion among them. This was a standard tow job, the same as it would be for cargo containers in space. (Orbital containers were often used by those who didn't want to go through standard spaceport checks. Leox had handled a lot of that kind of cargo back in the bad old days.) Geode brought up precision coordinates, Leox readied the tow cable, and Affie took the controls in hand and fired.

The cable magnetically locked to the Japealean cutter with a satisfying thunk. Leox and Affie shared a quick smile before beginning to slowly move forward, passing over the cutter and preparing to lead.

At the very moment the cutter was directly below them, an explosion rocked the *Vessel*. Red lights bloomed across the ship's controls in one awful wave.

"What the—" Leox hit the comm. "You still alive down there?"

After a few seconds of static, the Japealean pilot whispered, "*other . . . other engine blew . . .* "

So it had. Unfortunately, in doing so, it seemed to have flung metal debris into the body of the *Vessel* itself. Their ship remained airtight, which Leox knew on account of their not being in the process of dying horribly that exact second. But it looked like nearly everything else about the ship had taken damage, to varying degrees. Worst of all: "Hyperdrive is offline."

Affie bit her lower lip, then swiftly regained her cool. "Okay. At least this happened within easy distance of a repair port."

Orla Jareni and Elzar Mann appeared at the cockpit doorway, calm in that preternatural way the Jedi had, but definitely alert. "What happened?" Orla said.

"We paid a little rent on our time in the universe." Leox gestured toward the Japealean craft, still visible at the corner of the cockpit. "Did a good deed, took some shrapnel for it. Hopefully nothing we can't fix at Starlight."

"Anything you need," Elzar promised.

Leox remembered what Affie had said about Starlight Beacon being a target for the Nihil. If he were the worrying kind, he would've seen this as a bad omen.

As it was—well, bad omen or not, they had only one path they could take. Leox intended to take it with a smile.

Knowing that several dozen people had sought help at Starlight after the recent Nihil activity, Elzar Mann had readied himself for a little more bustle than Starlight Beacon generally saw. Yet the sight of the station's docking bay—normally ordered and tidy, to Estala Maru's most exacting specifications—surprised him with its disarray. Several ships of all kinds filled the majority of the available space. Once the *Vessel* settled in, very little space remained in the bay.

As Elzar and Orla led the group off the ship, his attentions shifted from the other spacecraft to the many people gathered in and around them. Most of them were hard at work on repairs—enough of them that Elzar suddenly wondered whether many, or any, spare parts remained.

"I promised you help," Elzar said to Affie Hollow. "I only hope we still have it to give."

"We'll manage." Affie might have been only a seventeen-year-old girl, but she had the knowing smile of a traveler who's spent her life among the stars. "There's not much we can't fix, and we have a few supplies of our own."

"I've got an old-fashioned tool kit in here somewhere," Leox verified. "We can even refit our own couplings, if it comes to it."

Orla raised an eyebrow. "I didn't know anyone made their own couplings any longer."

"What can I say?" Leox's grin widened. "I'm an old-fashioned kinda guy."

Affie added, "We have plenty of parts, Geode's staying on board to test every system, and Leox—Leox? You okay?"

Leox Gyasi was no longer smiling. Instead he had become one of the many staring into the middle distance, but Elzar was pretty sure Leox was staring at something—or someone—in particular. The only reply Leox gave was, "Okay."

Affie frowned in his direction. Elzar wondered whether he should ask more questions, but at that moment two familiar figures bounded up. Burryaga yowled in welcome as Bell Zettifar raised a hand in greeting. "Master Elzar, it's good to see you."

"Good to see you too, you two." Elzar grinned and stooped to pet the charhound that had just bounded to his side. "Excuse me, Ember. You *three*."

Orla greeted them, but absentmindedly; already she was moving on to the next task. Her white robes seemed almost to glow as she strode confidently forward. "I'm not a bad hand with ship repairs, if help is needed there."

Burryaga growled that Master Gios would no doubt want to see them first. "That makes sense," Elzar said. "Let's go."

"Ms. Hollow, Mr. Gyasi." Orla turned to them with a smile. "Please let us know if we can assist you in any way."

Affie nodded. Leox kept staring.

Something's wrong there, Elzar thought. But there was no time to worry about what, and after all, it was probably Leox Gyasi's own business.

As soon as the Jedi had cleared out, Affie turned back toward Leox. "What's gotten into you?"

"Bad news," he said, gesturing toward one corner of the docking bay.

Affie's gaze followed, and she laid eyes on it. "Oh no. Oh, no."

"I'd know that ship anywhere." For once, the ease had left Leox entirely; his wiry body was as tense as a bow pulled taut with an arrow. "That's the *Ace of Staves*."

"Obviously I realize that," Affie said. "As indicated by my repeating 'oh no' a lot of times."

"Sorry. Just making myself face it."

The *Ace of Staves* meant pilot Koley Linn. And Koley Linn meant trouble.

Affie had met Linn on only half a dozen occasions, each of them unpleasant in the extreme. He'd preemptively bought up the spaceport's spare fuel on the tiny world of Todouhar, stranding the *Vessel* for three extra days; then he'd tried to steal their cargo on Kennerla, very nearly making it so they had to pay to even be there. Both she and Leox were pretty sure he'd fouled the waters for them in other spaceports, too.

And those were only the issues Affie personally knew about. The bad blood between Leox and Koley Linn predated her time aboard the *Vessel*. Leox had never shared the details, and Affie had never pried for more information—though, she realized, that might be about to change.

Bad had gone to worse after the collapse of the Byne Guild. Although Koley Linn had not truly been a member, he *had* worked with the guild regularly. When Affie had turned in her mother, and the guild crumbled, it had disrupted Linn's credit flow enough to royally tick him off. As such, Affie had taken her place alongside Leox on Koley Linn's hit list.

Affie lay one hand on Leox's arm as she said, in a low voice, "I know you won't start anything, but—"

"—But I can damn sure finish it," he replied, never taking his eyes off the *Ace of Staves*.

"*But* if we have to interact with him at all, can you leave that to Geode? I know he doesn't like Linn any more than we do, but Linn never can get a rise out of him." Not that the man hadn't tried. It took more than one red-haired jerk to scrape their navigator's flinty surface.

"I will if we get the choice." Leox finally turned to Affie then, and he smiled—but it was a rueful, wary expression. "Though Koley Linn doesn't always leave us with a choice."

Bell smiled as Ember made her way along with the party of Jedi, as if she were one of them, at least in her own mind. Once in a while Stellan Gios gently reprimanded him when his charhound hung around on duty; even Avar Kriss sometimes frowned. But Nib Assek had always been friendly with Ember, and as for the recent arrivals, Elzar

Mann grinned and Orla Jareni even whistled, which made Ember cock her head as she came up to Burryaga's side. (Burry had rapidly become a favorite of the charhound's, and vice versa. Maybe it was a fur-solidarity kind of thing.)

I think people who like pets are more in touch with the Force, Bell thought. Then he wondered whether that was a small-minded way to look at things—and a very convenient one, for the guardian of a charhound. Still, wasn't there something to it? A friendship with an entirely different sort of life-form, one with which there could be no direct communication—wasn't that a sign that your spirit was welcoming to the Force in whatever form it took?

In the far distance of a side corridor, Bell glimpsed a small work crew in dark coveralls: a Pau'an, an Ithorian, and a human, all bustling from one job to the next. No surprise they were busy.

Orla let the Force guide her through the corridors; she encountered droids as she went, but no living beings. There was a definite destination—perhaps the main cargo bay, she thought—but the closer she came to it, the more uncertain she was of her own conclusions. The Force usually guided her steps more surely.

Footfalls along another corridor made her tense, and she whirled around to see another Jedi emerging from the side. He was a few years younger than her, quite tall, with messy brown hair and a friendly smile. Orla liked him on sight.

"You feel it too, huh?" the Jedi said, instead of hello.

"Definitely. Or I did. The closer I get, the farther away I feel." Orla shook her head as if to clear it. "By the way, I'm Orla Jareni."

This won her a grin. "The Wayseeker! I've heard a lot about you. My name's Regald Coll."

"And what brings you here, Regald?" She said it with a smile, the better to defuse the tension that threatened to curl around her mind. "The same sense of—" She trailed off as the true weight of what she felt sank in. "This . . . insistent dread?"

Regald hesitated. "I'm actually trying to help one of my comrades by proving that there *isn't* some weird source of insistent dread on board Starlight, that we're all just tired and on edge . . . but you asking that question kind of blows a hole in my theory."

They had by this time reached the cargo bay. Its doors slid open to reveal—nothing but cargo ships sitting or hovering in their berths, everything precisely as it should be. Orla no longer felt as certain that this was the correct destination, but surely it had some meaning. She turned to a nearby astromech droid. "Can you bring up a complete manifest?"

With a whistle, the little astromech projected the full, lengthy screen. Orla ran her fingers along it, the tips dipping into the light, as she searched them.

"Seeing any trouble?" Regald asked.

"No. I mean, not unless you count the fact that we have not one but two ships here fool enough to haul rathtars." Orla shrugged. "They're the worst. But rathtars aren't responsible for what we're feeling."

Regald tried to make light of it. "Oh, come on, they might be bad, but the worst? More awful than a sarlacc? Badder than a rancor?"

"A small pastime of mine is learning the literary collective names of things," Orla said. "You know, like a grove of Wookiees or a tinker of droids?"

"Or a bulge of Hutts." Regald nodded. "I admit, I've always liked an illumination of Jedi."

"Well, the collective name for these guys is a remorse of rathtars." She gave him a look. "They weren't given that moniker lightly."

Maybe the issue is the rathtars, Orla thought. *Maybe they're not being properly contained. If rathtars got loose aboard Starlight, that would create a whole new level of chaos. We should check and see. But—that makes no sense, rathtars don't influence the Force more or less than any other living creature—*

Orla's personal comlink chirped, jerking her back into the present. "Jareni here."

"Welcome to Starlight, Orla." Stellan's voice sounded warmer than she would've expected. Why was it so difficult, sometimes, to remember that they truly liked and respected each other?

Well. There were reasons. But Orla smiled as she said, "Much appreciated, Stellan. A fine station you have here."

"I'd appreciate the chance to talk with you about Elzar's progress—without betraying any confidences, of course—"

"He's your friend. You worry. I get it." Orla adjusted her pale robes, already preparing for the meeting. "I can tell you a little bit."

"I'll be waiting," Stellan replied, signing out. That meant he wanted to see her now.

And there was no reason not to go. Orla's trip to this cargo bay had resulted in nothing but some vague, unfounded worries about rathtar storage. Regald Coll, too, seemed nonplussed by their very ordinary surroundings. He shrugged, falling into step beside her as she left the bay.

I'll investigate more later, Orla decided. *Maybe my head will be clearer.* At present, her connection to the Force was too confused for her to be sure of her thinking. Why was that happening? What would have the ability to do that to a *Jedi*?

Sooner or later—hopefully sooner—Orla intended to find out.

Chapter 9

Beyond the crowded docking bay, Starlight Beacon felt almost normal. Still active, still bustling with personnel and droids. Thank goodness he'd ultimately turned down the position as head of the outpost temple on Valo; not only had Elzar recognized he was in no fit place to lead, but he also would've denied himself the pleasure of returning to Starlight. Tension he hadn't realized he felt uncoiled within his chest, and despite all the uncertainty that surrounded them, Elzar began to smile. He could be in this familiar place without reverting to the thought patterns that had led him down such troubling paths.

I still carry what I learned on Ledalau, he thought. *No—I don't carry it. It's a part of me now. Not something to be lost at the first challenge.*

Yes, he remained somewhat more closed off to the Force than a Jedi should be, but Orla had said that could be healthy. Elzar had come to trust her judgment.

Finally, Elzar reached Ops. A smile dawned on his face as he strode confidently into this familiar room—alight with the finest technology the Republic had to offer, filled with some of the greatest Jedi of the age. It felt like stepping into the sun again after too long in the shade. "Oh, Master Gios of the Jedi Council," he called with mock gravity. "Did you miss me?"

Stellan Gios was, at that moment, bent over a control panel, leaning away from the door. When he stood up, Elzar expected to see his friend's hands outstretched in greeting.

Instead he saw an uncertain man, one with dark circles under his eyes—as though he had not slept for many days, still propping half his weight on the panel. Elzar felt the smile slip from his face.

"Elzar," Stellan said. His voice was raspy. Had he been ill? "Welcome back."

"I—ah—do you have a moment?" Obviously something was going on, but he knew his friend well enough to understand that Stellan wouldn't appreciate being questioned about it in public. Elzar gestured toward the marshal's office. "If so, I'd appreciate a chance to get caught up."

It took Stellan a moment to nod. Every movement, every reaction, seemed somewhat slowed, as though the man were underwater. "Of course. Come. We'll talk."

Most other Jedi would, in a similar situation, have found a tactful way to indicate that they'd noticed Stellan's distress. Elzar Mann waited not half a second after the closing of the office door to say, "What's wrong with you? Should I call a pill droid? I know we've got a handful of refugees in need, but—"

"Do I look that bad?" Stellan laughed raggedly. "I suppose I must. It's nothing, really. Wretched insomnia, no more. Besides—" He became focused again, more like his usual self. "—We have more important matters to attend to."

Elzar nodded mechanically as Stellan updated him on the Nihil activity, the growing number of people stranded by the same, the stalled work on Eiram—all things Elzar already knew, more or less. Instead his attention remained focused on the evident distress Stellan felt, even if he wouldn't admit it. Yes, sleeplessness could be terrible, particularly over an extended period of time. But a night or two wouldn't bring down a Jedi as vital as Stellan Gios.

Within a few minutes, Elzar had reached a conclusion, one he didn't like: Stellan was not attempting to hide physical pain. Instead he was doing a very poor job of concealing emotional distress.

When Stellan finished, Elzar didn't even bother pretending he'd been paying close attention. "Will you tell me now what's troubling you?"

He expected more denials. Instead Stellan's face fell. "Would you believe—it is no more than a dream?"

"A dream? This can't be because of a mere nightmare."

"This dream lingers on and on—intruding on every waking moment." Stellan leaned heavily against the desk, shoulders slumped. "It nags at me. It demands attention. And yet the details seem so insignificant. For some reason I can't fully comprehend, this nightmare . . . this nightmare has darkened my connection to the Force."

That phrase shivered along Elzar's skin. Was Stellan Gios struggling with the dark side now, just as Elzar had been struggling months before? It seemed unfathomable, not least because that meant Elzar would have to take on the mantle of being the steadfast one. Not his specialty.

But maybe there was a ready explanation. His journey on the *Vessel* reminded him of the reports Orla Jareni and Master Cohmac had filed after their time on the Amaxine station. "Do you suspect the presence of the Drengir? They're said to be strong with the dark side. Those Jedi on the Amaxine station reported feelings of lingering dread."

Stellan shook his head. "I doubt it. Avar defeated them, the ones we put on ice are still very much frozen, and I can't imagine who would have brought them here. At any rate, they haven't made their presence known, and the Drengir aren't known for subtlety."

"Fair enough," Elzar admitted.

"Besides—what I'm experiencing isn't the presence of the dark side. It's—it's indescribable."

"Do you even have an image? A word?"

"If I could come up with anything like that," Stellan said, "this would be half over."

None of this made sense to Elzar, but it didn't have to. When he'd needed help, Stellan had provided it—

—*not personally, as he promised,* whispered the less worthy voice within Elzar's head—

And if Stellan now needed help, Elzar intended to give it in return. "Then tell me some task I can take up for you, to ease your burdens until Avar returns."

The mention of Avar prompted an odd look from Stellan, but he said only, "There's not much you can do for me. Everything is centered here, and—oh, seven hells of the Sith. The *prisoners.*"

"What prisoners?" Elzar frowned.

At that moment, the doors to the marshal's office slid open again, and Orla Jareni entered. She stopped short when she caught sight of Stellan. Elzar had believed he was being direct, an illusion shattered when Orla flatly said, "You look like death itself."

"Nice to see you again, too, Orla." Stellan shook his head, though the shadow of a smile appeared on his face. "Tactful as ever."

"I find tact only slows conversations down." Orla stepped closer, and Elzar sensed real concern there. "Any chance you'll talk about it?"

"There's honestly not much to share," Stellan insisted, "and the best help either of you can give is by picking up some of the things I've let slide. Namely, the prisoners I'd like Elzar to question next."

Elzar focused on the task ahead. "Did we capture some of these Nihil stragglers?"

"Maybe. Two people were captured on one of Avar's raids. Known Nihil collaborator Chancey Yarrow and a girl of apprentice age, known only as Nan. Nan is confirmed to have been affiliated with the Nihil as recently as a few months prior. They claim to be employed by someone else these days, but there's a good chance they have at least some useful intel." Stellan rubbed his temples. "That is, if we do something besides leaving them to rot in a cell, which is what I've inadvertently done."

"I'll look into it," Elzar promised. "Besides, it won't do them any harm to cool their hyperdrives for a while."

Nan sat on her flat metal bunk in the cell, staring up at the light that came from the grid above. "Why haven't they come for us?"

"Other things to do," Chancey replied. She was idly tracing invisible designs on the wall of the cell next to her bunk, on which she stretched as if she had not a care in the worlds. A few of her long braids dangled off the edge of the bunk. "Besides, it's a classic interrogation technique. Let 'em sweat. If we get nervous, think they've forgotten us, we wear ourselves down before they even start asking questions. So don't do the Jedi's work for them, all right?"

"All right." It was an easy thing to promise. Not an easy thing to deliver. But Nan intended to try.

She kept her other concerns to herself, because she knew Chancey Yarrow wouldn't be sympathetic. The fact was, their arrest had made Nan doubt many of her choices—especially, above all, her decision to temporarily leave the Nihil.

Nan had had dreams of becoming an information broker, a power player, a spy with the kind of knowledge and connections that would make her valuable to anyone, underworld or legitimate. The Grafs were only the beginning. But even at the height of her dreaming, she had always intended to return to the Nihil someday—hopefully, more useful to the Eye than ever before.

She had rarely been farther from her dreams than she was at this moment, trapped in a Jedi holding cell, apparently forgotten.

Why did I ever leave? Nan asked herself as she hugged her knees to her chest. The galaxy could be brutal; it was better not to be on your own. Better by far to be a part of something bigger, something powerful, something like the Nihil. Her individual desires had blinded her to that for a while, but she saw it only too clearly now.

Still—Nan *had* left. She was facing the consequences, and the Nihil weren't coming to save her. If she ever hoped to rejoin them, she'd have to get out of this mess on her own.

Leox Gyasi was not a man to hold grudges. Unfortunately, he had learned that it only took one person to hold a grudge—and if someone chose to hold one against him, he might have little choice but to respond in kind.

Koley Linn was not only the kind of guy who held grudges, he was the kind of guy who *enjoyed* them. If there was ever a time and place when trouble was likely to be fomented, Leox figured it was Starlight Beacon on that very day.

A dozen years ago, when Leox was still working his way up to pilot status in the Byne Guild, he and Koley Linn had been assigned as techs to the same ship. Koley had gotten there first and made a big show of teaching Leox the ship's ins and outs—all of which were pretty ordinary quirks, nothing anybody with any experience couldn't figure out on his own. It was Koley's attempt to show dominance, to make Leox look small. Might've shaken some guys up.

But status came very low on the list of things Leox Gyasi cared about, somewhere between "fashion" and "owning good toenail clippers." So he just kept rolling.

As it turned out, Koley wasn't only trying to put Leox in his place with those explanations; he was attempting to mislead him. He'd claimed this ship's power cells lost energy a little too quickly because they were older and needed updating. However, Leox soon realized that the cells were low on power because someone—namely, Koley Linn—was siphoning them off into portable cells, which he promptly sold on the black market during shore leaves.

Leox decided not to report Koley. He wasn't a snitch. However, instead of performing his maintenance checks the way Koley had suggested, Leox instead did them properly. This pointed out the discrepancy almost immediately, which promptly got Koley transferred to another position on another ship, where he could do less damage.

It wasn't like Leox set Koley back so far. The Byne Guild cut too many corners to care much when its members showed a little entrepreneurial initiative. Koley wound up having to leave the guild to get a ship of his own—but he *had* gotten the *Ace of Staves,* and had even partnered with guild pilots from time to time. Given these circumstances, Leox would've figured Koley Linn's annoyance level with him to be pretty mild. The sort of thing you might razz a guy about over a couple mugs of Port in a Storm.

Instead Koley Linn hated Leox Gyasi the way you'd hate someone who'd plunged a Mandalorian *kal* into your heart. By this point, Leox knew nothing would ever change that.

So, as a rule, he steered clear of Koley Linn, and intended to obey that rule aboard Starlight Beacon.

Leox's first plan was simply to draw a mental diagram that halved the main Starlight docking bay, with one part for the *Vessel* and the other for Koley's ship, the *Ace of Staves.* This plan's flaw was that it required Koley Linn to stick to his half, which it appeared the man had no intention of doing. Leox discovered this when he walked down the ramp to find Koley standing there, waiting for him.

"Looks like you're stuck." Koley's arms were folded across his chest, his expression smug.

"Don't know if you've noticed, but we're *all* stuck." Leox gestured around the crowded bay.

"*I'm* only stuck because these Jedi tyrants won't allow me to fly free. *You're* stuck because your *poodoo* ship's broken down. Again."

Leox thought about mentioning their rescue mission, decided against it. That wasn't anything Koley Linn would respect. "Are you here to offer assistance? Because, forgive my mentioning it, that doesn't sound like you."

"I can help out," Koley said, surprising Leox until he added, "For a price. If you're not low on funds, that is."

Times were hard now that they operated independently, without the Byne Guild, but they'd have to get a damn sight harder before Leox would do business with the likes of Koley Linn. "We're fine, thanks."

"Whatever, Gyasi. Stay mired here as long as you like. Tell that rock hello, unless you've replaced him with some mud and dirt."

"Geode is an individual with a rich and vibrant personality," Leox said, "though those of limited perception often fail to see it."

Which was a lesson for Koley Linn, if he'd have cared to learn one, but instead he was walking away, studying the other stranded ships, perhaps looking for someone desperate enough to strike a bad deal.

Orla could've respected Stellan's privacy, excused herself when Elzar left, and minded her own business.

But where was the fun in that?

"You'll wind up telling me eventually, you know." She sat opposite Stellan's desk, giving him the full intensity of her gaze. "No point in putting it off."

"There isn't much to tell," Stellan insisted. "I've had insomnia. I've had nightmares. I'm not rested, and there's too much to do on Starlight, and—isn't that enough to tire any man?"

"Most men, sure. Stellan Gios? Hardly. You're one of the bravest and most resourceful Jedi Knights I've ever known—even if I did have to totally save your hindquarters back on Pamarthe."

Stellan groaned, sounding a bit like himself again. "Are you ever going to let me live that down?"

"Surely you realize by now the answer is no."

"I do, I do." When Stellan smiled at her, Orla felt like some of his protective shell was beginning to crack at last. And then he had to go and add, "You're wasted as a Wayseeker. You ought to be an investigator working alongside Caphtor."

And there it was: the disdain for her choices that Orla knew Stellan felt, deep down, even if he had only intended to make a joke. "You've always had an issue with Wayseekers. I have a theory as to why, but—you tell me."

For a moment Stellan looked wearier than ever, and Orla regretted bringing it up. But he responded with surprising resolve. "The Jedi are meant to find meaning in the Order. In one another. In doing our duty. If it's difficult to stay that course sometimes—that's a sign we need to work harder, not to step back. It's also a sign that our own self-ish desires might be turning into attachments, and that those desires need to be sacrificed. Forgive me, Orla, but—you've never found it easy to walk a line."

"No, I haven't." Which didn't have a damn thing to do with selfish-ness or an unwillingness to sacrifice. Orla felt no need to defend herself, but decided it might be time for Stellan to hear a few of her thoughts in return. "You've found it all too easy, though, haven't you? Stellan Gios, the brightest of the bright, bravest of the brave, symbol of all that is good in the Jedi Order, youngest member of the Council in quite a while, and front and center of every publicity effort the Republic makes on our be-half. Don't misunderstand me—you look good in the spotlight, Stellan. But I know you well enough to realize how uneasy you are there. You've always had to be the golden child of the Order. You've never felt free to search, or to fail. You've never had the luxury to chart your own path. Is that why you're threatened by the Wayseekers who do?"

Stellan's face had seemingly turned to stone. "I'm not threatened. And we're meant to follow the path the Order and the Force show us."

Orla shook her head. "That's where we differ. You still think the Jedi Order and the Force are the same thing." She rose to her feet and put one hand on his. "I wouldn't say any of this if I didn't think the world of you, Stellan. As opposite as we are—I respect you and every-thing you've done, more than you can know. But I think you're in danger of disappearing into that spotlight. Someday, when this present crisis has ended—maybe take a little time for yourself."

"No, we don't see things the same way." Stellan managed to smile back at her, but stiffly. "I hope you know that I respect you, too."

"Of course you do," Orla said airily as she sauntered out of the room. "How could you not?"

Several of the maintenance shafts within Starlight Beacon housed info panels from which various systems could be checked—or, if you knew what you were doing, manipulated. Leyel knew what she was doing.

She also figured she might as well collect a little extra intel on what was going on inside Starlight. Cale always liked to stick to the letter of the plan, but what if conditions had changed in a way that thwarted the will of the Eye? They had been entrusted with his most important mission—with what deserved to be his single greatest triumph. Leyel would not see it endangered.

As various data sets scrolled past her, one intriguing item caught her attention. "Look at this," she said to Cale and Werrera, who paused in their work on the station's stabilizer connections. "'Suspected Nihil' prisoners, here, aboard the station."

Cale leaned in to examine the panel, too. "I don't know this Chancey Yarrow. But Nan—didn't she used to travel with Hague? He was a fine man, a capable warrior. He fell victim to the Jedi."

Werrera hissed with anger and contempt, emotions Leyel shared. She'd known Hague, too. The Nihil had no fiercer fighters than Hague had been.

"We shouldn't leave them trapped in their cell," Leyel argued. "We shouldn't give the Jedi the satisfaction."

Although Cale seemed wary, he finally nodded. "After we've completed the most critical preliminaries, when it won't matter as much if an alarm is raised. Who knows? Maybe they can help us."

Leyel tried to imagine going from being a helpless prisoner, at the Jedi's mercy, to instantly being given the power to destroy them all. What a gift. She almost envied those two women their captivity. Their release would be that sweet.

And then they, too, could serve the Eye's great plan.

Chapter 10

Starlight Beacon was not the only place in the galaxy where the Jedi offered refuge to those recently attacked by the Nihil. Some temples in and near the frontier lands opened their doors as well. No instructions went out from the Council on Coruscant dictating this; the decision was spontaneous, echoed by one Jedi Master after another, across vast stretches of space. Those who needed help—those who sought protection and assistance in dangerous times—would find it among the Jedi.

One such temple stood on the thickly forested world of Chespea, just within the border of the space newly sworn to the Republic. It was a temple of considerable age, one that had housed a small contingent of the Jedi for many generations. In some ways, the practices and customs of Jedi Knights here differed—they were independent, and private, and preferred it so—but not in their willingness to provide help to those who needed it.

So on that day the golden-roofed Chespea Temple, normally surrounded by nothing but kilometers of woodland and birdsong, instead was circled by tents and makeshift shelters, through which milled nearly one hundred people of various species and civilizations. In the few nearby clearings were parked carbon-scored, battered ships, the craft that had struggled so hard to reach a place of refuge. Yet the scene was peaceful in its way.

The calm before the Storm.

High in orbit, a Nihil Cloud leader nodded as the schematics zoomed in, tighter and tighter, until the temple's golden roof shone bright as a bull's-eye. "Don't bother with the ships," he said.

An underling who had not yet learned her place ventured, "But—if the goal is to cause damage and confusion—to leave them unclear of our intentions—"

"That was only for the first wave of our efforts," the Cloud leader snapped. "This wave is about sending a message to the Jedi. From now on they'll know—this is *about them.*"

So Marchion Ro had commanded. So would it be.

Those on the surface of Chespea at first believed that the swirling shapes far overhead must be a flock of birds. But that comforting illusion vanished within seconds. Moans of dismay turned into shrieks of panic as people jumped up, ran for their ships, or simply dashed into the woods in search of someplace, anyplace to hide. Otherwise they would surely be mowed down by the Nihil's merciless assault.

But none of these travelers were in any danger.

The head of the temple, Master Imgree, looked up and, for the first time in her life, said the words, "Call Coruscant."

Her Padawan nodded. "And tell them we're under attack?"

Imgree shook her head. The Force had already told her what was near. "Tell them we are gone."

The Padawan hesitated only momentarily before bravely doing what he was told. He had not been finished for more than one breath before Nihil fire blasted through the golden roof, incinerating everyone and everything inside, until the Chespea Temple was no more.

———

"Their target was indeed a Jedi temple," said aide Norel Quo, bringing up holo after holo to float above Chancellor Lina Soh's desk—portraits of devastation. "An isolated one, but still, a temple of the Order just the same. It was completely obliterated. So far as we know, no Jedi there survived."

Chancellor Soh shook her head, dismayed and disbelieving in equal measures. "We'd come to believe the Nihil no longer presented much of a threat. Even if these are only remnants and stragglers, lashing out—the threat they pose may have been reduced, but clearly it remains quite real."

Quo asked, "Should we inform Starlight Beacon?"

"Surely the Jedi Order has already told them." Being chancellor of the Republic often meant delivering bad news; Soh never shrank from this task, but she also saw no point in undertaking it when unnecessary.

Quo looked downcast. "It's hard to hear of this and think that we can do nothing."

"We'll send patrols along the hyperspace lanes, at least," Soh said. Like her aide, she felt better taking some kind of action, even if unnecessary. "If the Nihil send a fleet toward Starlight, we'll know about it—and we'll meet them with all the power we can muster. Contact Jedi Masters Adampo and Rosason, send our official sympathies . . . and unofficially let them know that the next time the Nihil try something, those guys are in for a nasty surprise."

"Does anyone have a T-7 anx I can buy or borrow?"

"We're looking for power converters, compatible with a Corellian model YG-2500."

"Hull plating? Metal that could become hull plating? Hull patches? Anything?"

Affie Hollow stood in the midst of the group at the center of the Starlight docking bay, trying to listen for both the things the *Vessel* needed and the ones they might be able to provide. Although the Jedi and the Republic were providing what tools, parts, and assistance they had to those stranded on the station, there wasn't quite enough to go around. So a kind of grassroots bartering place had formed, with everyone offering what they could do or spare in the hope of receiving what they needed in return.

Great in concept, Affie thought, *but kinda loud in action.*

She'd begun to step back from the huddle when she heard a voice call out, "Anybody here know how to fuse a new coupling?"

"I do!" Affie lifted one hand and looked around. "My shipmates and I can handle that."

"That's a relief." The speaker turned out to be a man of perhaps forty years, with a square but pleasant face. Holding on to his arm was a woman with riotously curly hair. "This is Pikka Adren, and I'm Joss, and are we glad to meet you. Not many people can fuse their own couplings any longer—"

"We *can,*" Pikka interjected, "but only the couplings that we can build with a polarity torch, and who carries around a polarity torch anymore?"

"Not us," Joss admitted. "Which will change in future, but that gets us nowhere today."

"Well, we can help you. I'm Affie Hollow. My pilot, Leox Gyasi, likes to do a lot of things the old-fashioned way, which means he's been making his own couplings for forever. I'm pretty good at it, too. Of course, we'll need micrax—"

"We've got micrax," said Joss, with a grin. "Let me guess. You don't, and are hoping we'll share?"

Affie smiled back. She'd have teamed up with anybody who had the materials the *Vessel* required . . . but it felt better to join forces with individuals who seemed honorable. She was starting to trust her instincts about people.

The news about the attack on the Jedi temple at Chespea would have been a terrible blow coming at any time. Coming at *this* time—with

Starlight both overcrowded and seemingly haunted by some strange disturbance in the Force—it felt like every burden had become heavier to bear.

You've dealt with worse than this, Stellan reminded himself sternly as he and the other senior Jedi on board took their places around the wide table. *You're only overwhelmed because something's interfering with your connection to the Force.*

Though he would never have admitted it, he was also reckoning with Orla Jareni's words earlier. She wondered if he knew who he was without the Order. That made Stellan wonder if he knew who he was without the Force at his beck and call, as it seemed to be no longer . . .

No. You remain bound to the Force. The connection is simply . . . disquieted for a while.

Stellan understood this on a purely logical level—*nothing* could destroy a Jedi's connection to the energy that linked all living beings. However, the instability in that connection at present was leading to a certain shakiness of his moods and thinking. Looking around the room at a group of powerful Jedi experiencing their own levels of distress, Stellan knew he wasn't the only one.

But he'd keep it together. He had to, for the good of this station, and perhaps the whole galaxy.

"Why should the Nihil attack such a small temple?" Indeera Stokes asked. "How are they a threat?"

"It's not about threats, it's about sending a message." Orla Jareni stood apart from the others, as usual, distinct in her snowy robes. "The question is why now?"

Nib Assek said, "Do we think the Nihil have something to do with this—strangeness aboard Starlight Beacon?"

With a shrug, Regald Coll said, "How would that even work? In other words, no."

"Then—with all respect to the fallen—" Elzar took a deep breath. "We need to set aside the question of Chespea for now. The Republic is taking action to police the hyperspace lanes, and the Council is already spreading the word, ensuring that other temples will be able to defend themselves. That means our most immediate concern remains taking care of the people who've taken refuge here."

Bell Zettifar leaned forward, clearly hesitant to speak but compelled to do so. "With all due respect, I disagree. Our first priority should be investigating this disturbance in the Force on the station."

He was right. Stellan felt a twinge of annoyance, because that was precisely what he ought to have said himself. The constant static at the edges of his consciousness—the prickling absence of his full communication with the Force—kept Stellan from ordering his thoughts as he should. He even had that strange nursery rhyme running through his head over and over, the one that began *Shrii ka rai ka rai—*

Focus, he told himself. "Is there a locus to the disturbance?" Stellan asked the group at large. He swiftly brought up a holoschematic of the station. "A place where we have each sensed this most strongly?"

From the corner, the logistics droid suddenly piped up, "I would be more than happy to compile all reports and map them on schematics of Starlight Beacon! This data could prove informative."

Stellan nearly said yes, just to give JJ-5145 something to do. Before he could, however, Indeera Stokes said, "That won't be necessary." She rose and walked toward the holo, raising her hand to brush very near the dividing locks that connected the top and bottom parts of the station. "Here," she murmured. "Somewhere around here."

Stellan had not known that was the place until she said it, but through what strength in the Force remained to him, the rightness of her words reverberated within his mind. Beyond that—it wasn't very far from the quartermaster's office, where he'd been sleeping when the nightmare overwhelmed him. "Yes. Yes, that's it."

"Okay, what do we have around there?" Elzar gestured to zoom in on the holo. "Engineering—raw material stores—the main cargo bay—"

"Both Orla and I were drawn to the main cargo bay earlier," Regald interjected. "We didn't discover anything out of the ordinary there, and we were soon called away, but I'd say that's more evidence that we need to center our efforts on that area."

"Yes. So we search," said Nib. "We find whatever this is. We learn what it is. And then we form a plan."

Every bone in Stellan's body told him *not* to search, not to get any closer. But that couldn't be the Force warning him. The Force had been pushed too far away. It was fear whispering to him now, and he refused to give way to fear. Stellan would stand for it no longer. "I realize we all have other responsibilities at the moment, but insofar as our duties allow—yes, we search. Whatever this is, we'll get to the bottom of it."

Maybe, if he was lucky, the cause of their trouble would be something he could jettison into the closest star.

Just as Koley Linn had suspected—yes, there stood Leox Gyasi like a chump, waiting with all the other fools in the line for rations. Why didn't he send the girl to do it? Koley traveled alone, but if he *did* have an assistant, damned if he'd be doing any grunt work.

(He knew that, supposedly, Leox worked for Affie Hollow. Koley didn't buy that. That stupid kid had ruined the Byne Guild and everybody who worked for it; even Gyasi couldn't be fool enough to listen to her ever again. No, probably they pretended she was the boss because it gave them an excuse when things went wrong.)

Still, Leox's stupidity gave Koley an opportunity—because he was pretty sure he'd seen Affie hanging around with some other pilots, working on some odd job or other. That meant the *Vessel* was ripe for exploration.

Koley strolled toward the ship, studying it as he went. As much as he ragged Leox about the antiquity of this ship, Koley knew it was also fast, maneuverable, and capable of handling a wide array of work. He also knew that, until recently, the *Vessel* had benefited from the well-funded maintenance budget of the late Byne Guild. That might yet turn out to be Koley's good fortune. Yeah, the *Vessel* had taken some damage, but there were probably some systems in good order—with new, top-quality parts just ripe for the scavenging—

Koley stooped down to check the ship's undercarriage, then heard a low hum and a thunk. He stood upright with a jolt and saw that the ramp was down, and he was being watched.

Geode stood there, expressionless, never turning away from Koley Linn.

"You," Koley muttered. "I heard a rumor you'd taken on other work. Though I'm not sure why I thought there would be more than one ship in the galaxy willing to hire a rock."

His jibe had no effect on Geode's hard, cold stare.

"Whatever." Koley shrugged as he turned to go. Not that he was scared of Geode or anyone else, but if he got reported to Starlight command, who knew how long the *Ace of Staves*'s departure would be delayed?

Still, it stung to turn back empty-handed. The *Vessel* was far from unguarded—at least, for the moment. But he'd keep his eyes open for other chances.

Koley pulled out his comm receiver, hoping to eavesdrop on official communications and get some better idea when he could get the hell out of here. As he clicked it on, though, static popped through it at strange, irregular, yet somehow ordered intervals. It lasted only a moment, but that was long enough for Koley to know that it was definitely weird.

Something is not right on this station, he thought.

Aboard the *Gaze Electric,* Thaya Ferr reviewed the scans and smiled. "Our first shipment of cargo is arriving now, my lord."

"Let us go to receive it." Marchion Ro normally left such tasks to the lowest members of his crew; they were beneath his dignity. But this was no regular receipt of cargo, and besides . . .

. . . the *Gaze Electric* now stood all but empty. The only living beings present were Thaya Ferr and Ro himself.

They reached the docking bay in time to see the first crate hovering in, guided solely by cargo droids. (Ro noted that Thaya had wisely arranged for droid-only delivery; there would be no wagging tongues spreading word about this.) He watched as the crate settled into the ship's hold with a heavy, satisfying thud.

The cargo droids flitted away to grab the next crate. If Ro waited, they would unpack all the crates for him, leaving nothing else for him to do. But he wanted to see the items he'd bought. They meant safety. Security. Dominance. They meant never having to waste time wiping out another insubordinate crewmember ever again.

Ro nodded toward Thaya, who quickly punched in the receiving code. The crate hinged open to reveal its contents: row after row of enforcer droids. Their flat, mirrored faces stared back, reflecting Ro's mask back at him a dozen times over.

Enforcer droids had been made illegal many decades before. This made them difficult to find, particularly in such quantities. Thaya Ferr had found them, however, and at a price he had been able to take from the Nihil coffers without attracting any notice.

If any of my Tempest Runners were as competent as my lackey, Ro thought, *only imagine what I could do.*

Chapter 11

At first the Nihil saboteur team had been careful to move quietly and stay out of sight. However, as the third day of their work dawned, it became increasingly obvious that this caution was no longer necessary. The stranded travelers marooned aboard Starlight Beacon made up a motley bunch, and they wandered throughout the station. It was easy enough for Werrera, Leyel, and Cale to blend in with the groups and travel where they would.

This way, they even got lunch.

"Ithorian," said a young Jedi with dark skin, who inexplicably kept a charhound dozing by his ankles while he worked at the rations table. "I think that's Nutrition Bracket Zeta Two?"

Werrera nodded, and the Jedi handed over a foil-sealed packet before turning his attention to the others. Within five minutes, they had taken seats on benches at the far end of the docking bay and were practically having a picnic. What fools these Jedi were.

But they had made the mistake of assuming everyone on board the station to be equally foolish.

"Hello there," said a trader, a human man with tightly coiled red hair. "Enjoying yourselves?"

Cale made a noncommittal sound, which seemed to be as much response as expected.

But the trader instead leaned against the wall and grinned at them unpleasantly. "I've noticed you guys around. In side corridors, back areas, those sorts of places. The kinds of places we're not supposed to be."

Werrera's eyes met Leyel's. Both were armed, of course, but they could scarcely shoot someone in the crowded docking bay. All the chaos and clamor wouldn't be enough to keep *that* from drawing attention.

Cale, however, remained steady. "You shouldn't admit going to forbidden places."

"I don't intend to admit it to the Jedi," said the trader. "Just like I'm not going to tell the Jedi what you're up to, either. Think of it as a favor."

"Favors are often done in expectation of reward," Cale replied. "What is it you want from us?"

"Just a slice of the action." The man had an unpleasant grin. "I'm Koley Linn—that's my ship over there, the *Ace of Staves*. Whatever you collect from this station, send a little of it my way. You can keep doing what you're doing, we both leave here the richer, and neither the Republic nor the Jedi has to know a thing."

He thought they were no more than thieves. Insulting, but convenient. "Whatever we collect here," Cale pledged, "you shall receive an ample share."

Koley nodded as he took it in. "I'll be checking in on you guys, so make sure you follow through."

Cale smiled back, bloodless and calm. "Have no doubt. We will."

One part of that promise could not be kept. Werrera, Leyel, and Cale had come to this station for the greater glory of the Nihil, and of

Marchion Ro the Eye; for that, they would ever be honored. Such honor could not be shared with the likes of Linn.

But they would find something else here, something they had all accepted as the price of that glory, what had to be paid in order for the will of the Eye to be done.

That, Koley Linn would share in full.

Even through the ongoing weirdness of the Force—

—and Regald Coll was calling it "weirdness" until they had something more definite to name it by—

—warnings could definitely be felt, and Regald was feeling one at that moment. Freshly done with distributing rations, he scanned the docking bay with his eyes narrowed, in search of the source of this particular stab of unease.

His gaze fell upon a small group at the far edge of the bay: three maintenance workers eating their food, and a red-haired pilot who seemed to have interrupted them. From where Regald stood, it was impossible to overhear them. It was also unnecessary. While the workers remained impassive, the pilot's satisfaction in the exchange was all too clear from his smirk and the way he swaggered off afterward.

Regald swiftly checked the manifest: LINN, KOLEY/*ACE OF STAVES*. Well, he'd keep an eye on that one.

The Force had provided a warning. A troublemaker had been identified. Regald was poised to take whatever action was necessary. And yet, still, he remained uneasy.

His attention drifted toward one of the doors to the docking bay— the one that led, roughly, in the direction of engineering and the cargo bays. The source, it appeared, of the greater problem affecting every Jedi aboard.

So far, Regald wasn't as badly impacted as the others seemed to be. He still thought that exhaustion and the ongoing tension about the Nihil was probably playing a role in everyone's disquiet. But with every single Force-sensitive person on board sensing the same thing, they all concurred: The problem was real.

As soon as they had no other duties, they were to investigate—and as Regald saw it, his duties were more or less fulfilled for the moment. He'd handed out so many rations he never wanted to look at food again.

He found himself thinking of his days minding the crèche at the Coruscant Temple. It wasn't the task he needed to be doing forever—Regald had always understood that—but as frantic and difficult as it had sometimes been, it had provided such a source of deep, abiding joy. The way the younglings' little faces lit up every time he announced a new game, the way their unguarded, unformed minds fluttered delicate and beautiful at the edges of Regald's consciousness, even the soft sounds they made as they napped on their mats at midday: He suddenly missed it all so sharply that it felt almost like a physical ache in his side.

Maybe, after my time on the frontier, I'll go back to the crèche for a while, Regald decided. *It's important for me to challenge myself, but there's also something to be said for knowing your strengths, right?*

Until then, though, he'd have to deal with more immediate, less concrete problems than toddlers with burgeoning Force abilities. Like, whatever the hell it was lurking on this station and pushing them all off balance.

Regald packed up the makeshift table he'd used for distribution and set off, determined not to return until he'd explored the station thoroughly enough to discover the true source of their problems.

"I just feel like I ought to be one of the ones to investigate," Bell said as he returned his rations distribution gear to its rightful place. "I don't mean to speak out of turn, Master—"

"You aren't," Master Indeera reassured him. "Obviously, we must soon make a search of the station to discover the source of the—the problem."

Bell noted that even his stoic, stalwart Master didn't want to speak directly of the issue they were all experiencing with the Force. Maybe it should've made him feel better about his own unease. Instead it gave him a strange quiver deep in his belly: *The Masters are worried about this. More, even, than they've let on. Maybe more than they've admitted to themselves.*

Master Indeera continued, "Our first duty, however, is not to protect ourselves. It is to protect those who have sought help and refuge aboard this station."

"Of course, Master." Bell couldn't resist adding, "But if we don't take care of ourselves—then who will take care of them?" Inwardly he winced, waiting for a reprimand.

It never came. Instead Master Indeera's expression softened. "You are wise, my Padawan learner. Yes, we must always strike a balance. So it will reassure you to hear that, once full ration distribution has finished, I intend to join the investigation of the levels around engineering and the cargo bay."

That was both the best news Bell had heard in a while and deeply scary. "You shouldn't go alone."

"Others will be searching as well."

"I meant—I should go with you," Bell explained.

"No," she said. "You have other tasks to perform, because we have yet to fully review all the refugee vessels' cargo manifests."

More make-work—but that was an apprentice's lot. Bell nodded, yet he remained uneasy. "But there will always be someone with you?"

Master Indeera cocked her head. "You're worried about me."

"It's not that I doubt your abilities, Master. I would never do that, it's just that—"

"—that you lost your previous Master, and you do not wish to lose this one." Master Indeera's hand closed gently around Bell's shoulder. "First of all, there is no particular reason for you to fear. This disturbance in the Force has not harmed anyone so far, and there is no reason to assume that it will."

Nightmares, panic attacks, and insomnia sounded like "harm" to Bell, but he knew what Master Indeera meant. "Right. Of course."

"Beyond that," she continued, "no Jedi can run away from risk. Not the risks to herself, nor the risks to others. Our great gifts demand even greater courage. We face danger because we are capable of facing it when others are not." Her vivid-blue eyes met Bell's evenly—and, he felt, for the first time she was looking on him more as a Jedi and an equal, rather than a mere apprentice. "To put it simply, Bell, you must always be willing to lose me, if it is necessary to do what we ought. I must be willing to lose you. We must be willing to sacrifice ourselves, and each other, for the greater good."

"Yes, Master."

Then, to his astonishment, she winked. "Just don't sacrifice me before it's strictly necessary, okay?"

Bell smiled back at her. "I promise."

"All right, then. Turn to those manifests. I'll report back soon." Master Indeera paused, then stooped to scratch Ember behind her ear for one moment before rising to leave.

The Jedi aboard Starlight Beacon had a lot of administrative work to do.

What luck, then, that one of the many small tediums Wayseekers didn't have to deal with was administration.

Orla Jareni drew her white cloak more closely around her as she took the lift downward toward the station's cargo bay. When she'd been down here before with Regald Coll, she'd sensed something was afoot— though, at the time, she'd been distracted by trivialities such as rath-tars and the idiots who transported them. On this trip, she would remain more focused on the real crisis at hand.

The lift doors slid open before the correct level, and Indeera Stokes stepped on. She and Orla exchanged brief nods, no more. Then, on the very next level—still too high—the doors opened again to admit Regald Coll, who gave a little half wave of welcome.

As they resumed their descent, Orla said, "I'm glad we're doing this together. More people means we can cover more ground."

"And I am definitely less likely to get into trouble for this if I'm not the only one down here on my own recognizance." Regald paused as he ran one hand through his shaggy brown hair. "Should I have admitted that out loud?"

Indeera shrugged. "Probably not."

"Stellan already gave us the go-ahead," Orla reminded them—but she realized, even as she spoke, that their doubts were reflections of the uncertainty this disturbance was causing them all. Their brains might be interpreting it as worry about correctly obeying orders; really, the tension was far more amorphous, far less malleable to logic. "Let's just keep going."

The lift doors opened, and the three of them walked out onto the level above engineering. Below this point, she understood, Estala Maru and his astromech would handle matters. (Apparently he, too, was noticing the eerie, soporific silence of the Force at work.) Orla said, "How about we keep it simple? I'll head left, Indeera, you can head right—"

"—And I'll go straight ahead." With a nod, Regald began walking, though he held up his comlink. "Let's stay in touch, all right?"

"Good plan," Orla said. Already she was projecting her attention ahead. Probably it was for the best that she was moving away from the cargo bay. The farther she stayed from rathtars, the better.

Indeera Stokes moved forward through relatively empty, quiet corridors. This level was largely used for storage, and she felt a moment's dismay that they hadn't been able to set up some temporary quarters down here for the refugees aboard. So much room, and the docking bay was becoming so crowded—

—but those people had their ships, which for the most part they wished to remain near. And while some of these compartments were empty, others were stocked with valuable components that couldn't simply be left available to all and sundry.

You're distracting yourself, she realized. *You're musing and mulling instead of opening yourself to the Force. That's not going to help.*

Do your work.

Indeera took a deep breath and reached out with her feelings. What she found was—

—was *nothing.*

The Force was not speaking to her here. There was the faintest . . . call it a whisper . . . proof that she hadn't lost her mind, that the Force continued ever on, as it must. But for the first time since she was a youngling, Indeera had trouble connecting herself to the Force.

The sheer wrongness of it made her stumble. Indeera stopped and put one hand to her head. She had to concentrate. Why couldn't she think? She should've eaten, earlier—it was hard to shake the thought that she was hungry—

Her comlink buzzed. Indeera took it up. "Stokes here—"

"*Help me.*" The sheer terror in Regald Coll's voice sent chills along Indeera's skin. "*Please—please—help me!*"

Indeera pivoted on her heel and ran back the way she'd come, intent on tracking Regald down. What was happening to him? She was suddenly, sharply afraid for him, more afraid than she'd ever been even for her own life. Her boots pounded against the floor as she turned this way, then that, seeking the path she'd seen Regald take earlier. This seemed to be the right direction . . .

Her steps slowed. Indeera swayed as she went, until finally she stumbled and had to catch herself against the nearest wall. She couldn't see Regald, though she knew he could only be a few meters ahead of her. Why was it so dark here?

The lights were on, but it was as though—as though she couldn't take in the light—

Indeera's eyes opened wider as the floor began to melt. As the walls shifted color and shape. She knew she was hallucinating, but knowing did no good; reality was nowhere to be found. This phantasmagoria surrounded her, entrapped her, took away everything that was true and good.

The floor slapped her across her cheek, kicked her shoulder, shoved her hip. Indeera pawed feebly at her side for her lightsaber, but she couldn't close her hand around it, and what good would it do besides? There was no enemy to fight. There was no place to stand.

There was no Force to guide her. It was gone, gone, gone forever, and she had not known it was possible to feel so frightened, so alone.

Tears welled in Indeera's eyes, blurring everything around her until she could see no more.

On a hunch, Orla had shimmied into a maintenance shaft where, she sensed, something had recently been done—though what, and by whom, remained a mystery—when Regald's call for help came over her comlink. So it took her precious seconds to clamber out again. She swore to herself as she struggled back to the corridor, then took off running the first second she was able. Her hand closed around the hilt of her double-bladed lightsaber, ready to unfold it the instant she glimpsed whatever was menacing Regald Coll.

Orla reached out with the Force, and though her perceptions remained frustratingly muffled, she had a sense of something moving away—retreating, perhaps? Maybe Regald had managed to handle this on his own. Still, she didn't slow down.

What she sensed didn't feel exactly like retreat. It felt more like . . . satiation.

She skidded around a bend in the corridor Regald had taken, then only just managed to catch her balance before she tripped over Indeera Stokes, who lay unconscious on the floor. "Indeera?" Orla knelt by the Tholothian woman's side and put two fingers to her throat. Yes, merely unconscious, not dead—but Indeera's breaths were shallow and irregular, and her skin was shockingly cold and clammy to the touch.

What had happened to her? Time to figure that out later. If the same thing that had done this to Indeera was menacing Regald, then Orla needed to keep moving.

Dashing onward, Orla pushed herself to run even faster until she reached a larger cargo area, a sudden wide, dark chasm deep within the station. The space appeared to be entirely empty. But as she blinked, her vision adjusting to the dimness, she saw a form lying on the floor a few meters away.

"Regald!" Orla called, hurrying to his side. Was he in the same state as Indeera?

No, she realized. The situation was far worse. Regald wasn't moving—wasn't even breathing.

Maybe there was some chance of resuscitation. Orla ran the last few steps, then halted as she reached him. Her eyes widened as she took in what lay before her.

Regald Coll was dead. But instead of his body, on the floor in front of Orla lay something that mimicked and mocked the outlines of his form—a horrifying, desiccated husk.

Chapter 12

"What do you mean?" Stellan Gios demanded, staring at his comlink as though he could see Orla Jareni looking back at him. "Regald Coll is *dead*?"

"*Worse than dead,*" came Orla's response. "*His body has been—changed, somehow. Into this dry, almost powdery version of itself. I haven't touched him because I'm scared he'll fall apart.*"

Stellan looked across the Hub at Nib Assek and Elzar Mann, whose dismay mirrored his own. "Another husk," Stellan said. "And this time, on Starlight itself."

Whatever horror had finally stolen the life of Loden Greatstorm had made its way aboard the station. Starlight—supposedly a place of refuge—had become another source of danger.

Orla said, "*What do you mean, another one? This is a thing that's been happening?*"

"Being cut off from the business of the Order is one of the prices of being a Wayseeker," Stellan pointed out. "We'll brief you in full when you return to the Hub."

"First you need to send a med team, or at least some droids and a hovergurney. Indeera Stokes was searching the level with us, several meters away—but still too close—"

"Not Indeera, too!" Nib blurted out. Stellan put one hand on her shoulder, briefly, helping her restore calm. They needed to remain centered now more than ever.

"Indeera's alive, at least for now," Orla said. *"But whatever killed Regald hurt her badly. She's unconscious, her breathing is weak and uneven, and—and she doesn't look good. She needs medical help right away."*

"Dispatching a med droid to your location immediately," Stellan said. "Once you've seen her to safety, report back to Ops." With that he clicked off the comm.

Elzar said, "At least when Indeera wakes up, she might be able to give us some idea what we're dealing with."

"Perhaps." Stellan envied Elzar his confidence that Indeera would, indeed, wake up. More than that, Stellan envied that level of concentration. With his attention no longer focused by the call, his exhaustion was catching up to him. The intense dread that had been suffusing him for almost two days, ever since the nightmare, deepened with the knowledge that the danger he'd sensed was very real—and had already cost one of Stellan's people his life.

"Stellan." Elzar had come to his side without Stellan even observing it. "You're not yourself. If you need to rest, go. I can watch things here."

"And *I* can watch *him*," Nib added, with the faintest hint of her usual humor. "If he won't take it easy of his own free will, I'll call my Padawan. See if I don't."

"No Wookiee enforcement will be necessary," Stellan insisted. "I'll—sit. Rest a little. But more than anything I want to talk to Orla, and hopefully Indeera, so we can get some answers about just what happened here."

———

They were being watched.

"This changes nothing," Cale warned the other members of the Nihil as they left the docking bay. "The human man with orange hair is a fool."

"Fools talk," Leyel pointed out, shouldering her tool bag. "That's one of the things they're best known for."

Cale remained undaunted. "But nobody is listening. How can they? The Eye's plan has thrown this station into bedlam. That gives us an opportunity."

The opportunity in question was their one deviation from Marchion Ro's plan. Breaking out the other Nihil in captivity—it carried risks. Now, however, that they had seen the state of Starlight Beacon for themselves, all three team members felt that the risks could be managed.

There even seemed to be a good chance the Jedi wouldn't realize their captives were gone, at least not in the brief amount of time they would have before being extremely distracted.

Starlight's brig had been built for short-term containment, not extended incarceration. Therefore it lacked the reinforcements standard on prison stations and ships: double-thick walls, metal-sealed ceilings and floors, force fields in nearby maintenance tubes and ducts. Of course it would be well guarded—even the Republic couldn't be so arrogant as to leave their prisoners without supervision—but probably such oversight was limited to the floor the cells were actually on, and was more likely to consist of droid sentries rather than sentient guards.

So the Nihil team had assumed, and within minutes of arriving on the next floor up, they had reason to believe they were correct. This floor, which seemed to be given over to conference rooms for policy summits and treaty discussions, was deserted except for a maintenance droid that kept sullenly to its task of vacuuming the air vents.

Werrera held up one of their devices preloaded with the station specs and blueprints that had been sent to the Nihil by Ghirra Starros.

This map showed them the way. At the point directly above the brig, Leyel withdrew a scrambler; it was a crude device, capable of disorienting droids only in its very immediate vicinity, and for no more than a few minutes—but that was all they required.

"In and out within six minutes." Cale smiled broadly as he took up the tools they'd need to peel away the floor. "Let's begin."

"The pacing is getting old," Chancey said as she stared at the blank cell wall before her.

"It is for me, too," Nan admitted, "but I can't sit still any longer. I need to *move.*"

"I remember feeling like that when I was younger." Chancey stretched out on her bunk, closing her eyes. "These days, I don't turn down too many chances to get some sleep."

Nan said nothing, but privately thought that if she were ever so decrepit as that, they could toss her on the funeral pyres and she'd light the first match herself. And Chancey couldn't be older than forty-five or so!

"Wonder if they've told Sylvestri that I've been arrested," Chancey said. Her eyes remained closed, and the tone of her voice was difficult to read. "She wouldn't be sorry, I imagine."

Sylvestri Yarrow was Chancey's daughter, a girl roughly Nan's own age, one who had turned down the chance to join her mother in working for the Grafs. Every single day since, Nan had been keenly aware that, however encouraging Chancey was, she'd rather it had been Sylvestri next to her. It turned out to be no fun, coming in as only second-best.

(Sylvestri Yarrow had been in the company of Padawan Reath Silas when Nan last saw her. Was there a connection between the two of them? Nan didn't want to be curious about this, about Reath, but couldn't deny that she was.)

In the end, all that mattered was this truth: Chancey Yarrow missed her daughter. That meant that, no matter how sleek and confident and badass Chancey acted (which was very), there was an emptiness within her.

That emptiness might be fulfilled by taking care of another young woman. Taking the fall for her, even, if Nan played her cards right . . .

For a moment she was jarred by her own thoughts. How could it be so easy to turn on someone who, only days before, had been her mentor?

Because we were only ever using each other, Nan realized. *Chancey's not like Hague.*

Her childhood guardian's wrinkled Zabrak face appeared in her mind, tightened her throat. Nan scarcely remembered her parents; it was Hague who had truly raised her, taught her nearly everything she knew. She hadn't realized that she wanted Chancey to fill that absence until now.

In the main docking bay, Affie Hollow looked over the Adrens' ship with approval. "Nice little skiff," she said. "We can have her back in top shape in no time."

"Good," Joss replied absently. "Good." He was staring into the distance, and his tone of voice had shifted from easygoing humor to something darker. Affie's ears pricked up. What had gone wrong? Only minutes had passed since both Adrens had inspected the *Vessel* with her, met Leox and Geode, and offered up plenty of ways to help. At that very moment, Leox was probably going through his audio files, because it turned out he and the Adrens were fans of the same simjo band.

So everybody was friendly. Getting along. Exchanging files, even. How could that already have changed for Joss Adren? "Um," she began. "What's the problem?"

Joss let out a long sigh. "Listen. I know there's nothing for me to worry about. Not really. But that doesn't mean I appreciate people flirting with my wife in front of my very eyes."

"Oh, Leox isn't flirting," Affie said. "He winds up hugging everybody sooner or later."

"Leox Gyasi isn't the problem," Joss huffed. "It's that damn rock."

Affie angled her body around the side of the Adrens' ship to see the *Vessel*. Its hatch was open, Geode at the top of the ramp . . . upon which sat Pikka Adren, her curly hair bouncing as she laughed.

Affie hurriedly said, "Geode's a Vintian. It's not like there's anything he could do with a human, even if he wanted to, which he doesn't. He dates in-species only. Which for most people I think is kind of narrow-minded? But you have to admit, for Vintians, it's kind of unavoidable."

Joss looked over her shoulder and sighed. "I guess you're right."

Affie smiled at him, relieved to have restored his mood, while inwardly thinking, *Oh, great, Geode's on the prowl again.*

Elzar went down to the cargo bay level, determined to see for himself what had become of Regald Coll. Really, Stellan should've gone—but Stellan was near the end of his endurance, whether he recognized it or not. Elzar had no interest in pushing the man even harder.

Besides, Elzar simply wasn't as affected by this strangeness aboard the station as all the other Jedi appeared to be. Was it because he was still closing himself off to the Force somewhat? That seemed wrong to Elzar—the Force strengthened a Jedi, never weakening him except through its absence.

The causes didn't matter, in the end. At the moment, Stellan couldn't handle this. So he took the responsibility on himself.

He arrived just after the medical team, in time to see them hurrying away with a hovergurney carrying the unconscious Indeera Stokes. She twitched where she lay—less like someone regaining awareness, more like someone potentially on the verge of a seizure. Elzar's brief glimpse of her face was enough to shock him: She looked ten years older than she had just hours prior. *It's like something literally sucked the life out of her,* he thought.

From the shadows farther down the corridor appeared a figure in white. "Come," Orla said. "You should see this. Someone besides me should, anyway. I'm not sure I believe my eyes."

Elzar went to her side. There, before them, lay what remained of Regald Coll: mere dust in the shape of a man. Though the husk had some kind of fibrous quality as well—

In Elzar's mind, a memory flashed: Regald laughing over breakfast that very morning, making light of the tasks ahead of them, refusing to give way to the darkness shadowing them all.

Only hours later, the darkness had swallowed Regald whole.

"What power can do something like this?" Orla whispered. "It's as if—as if life itself were torn from him."

That's impossible, Elzar wanted to say. But he didn't know if he believed in its impossibility any longer.

The bridge of the *Gaze Electric* was almost completely silent. Thaya checked the activation sequences on the second shipment of droids from her station, far off in the corner, while Marchion Ro remained in his chair, staring into a middle distance. The dim lights of the consoles reflected on the impassive visage of his mask. Few ever saw him off guard like this, she realized: What thoughts might be running through his mind?

Thaya had little time to consider this question before an approach signal began chiming, requesting permission for boarding. She sat up in alarm, but Ro made a lazy gesture with one hand. "Our guest is expected."

Better to have told me, so I could make arrangements, Thaya thought but didn't say. It wasn't Marchion Ro's responsibility to make her job easier; it was Thaya's responsibility to adapt to whatever his needs might be.

Ro flicked on the comm himself. "This is *Gaze Electric,*" he said. "What took you so long?" His tone was warm, almost teasing . . . and, to Thaya's ears, rather false.

The holo flickered to life, grainy and shadowed, revealing a woman in her early forties, wide-eyed and breathless as a girl. After an instant, Thaya recognized her: Senator Ghirra Starros, Republic official and Nihil spy. Thaya had often wondered how Ro managed to subvert and turn a Republic senator to their side. Now she knew: He'd used the oldest, most obvious trick there was. And Starros had fallen for it.

Was there nothing Marchion Ro couldn't do?

"Marchion," Starros said. "You received all my transmissions?"

Ro nodded. "Every word." Again that knowing, mischievous tone— one he would never use with a true intimate, assuming he had any. "Come and claim your reward."

The emphasis he put on the last word made it clear what that reward would be. Thaya felt a moment's gratitude for the relative darkness of the bridge, which hid her blush. She said nothing, simply transmitted the docking codes to Starros's tiny ship.

"I'll be there within moments," Starros promised. "I can't wait to see you."

The holo blinked out, leaving the bridge dark and quiet once more. Ro said, "I'll greet our guest personally."

"I'll get quarters ready for her." Thaya smiled brightly. "Alfkenda's old rooms?" Now reassigned to another ship, Alfkenda had been a highly valued engineer. As such, her former quarters were some of the nicest on the ship, save for Ro's own.

They were also located half the length of the ship away from Ro's suite. Ro would be able to visit Senator Starros whenever he wished . . . but wouldn't have to deal with any intrusions on his privacy.

"Those will be ideal," Ro said. "You've comprehended my needs exactly."

Thaya bowed her head. For her there could be no greater praise.

Getting out of here is going to be a lot of work, Leox thought as he sat in the *Vessel* cockpit, looking out at the docking bay. Starlight's crew had done superb work layering so many ships in so little space—but it would be difficult for more than one or two to take off and exit at a time. Given that everybody would be anxious to be on their way as soon as it was safe, it was a good bet that not everyone would want to wait their turn for departure.

Especially not beekmonkeys like Koley Linn.

They'd be looking at a three-dimensional traffic jam even if the Jedi weren't in a hurry. And if they were—

"Leox?" Affie's voice rang through the ship as he heard her footsteps on the ramp. "Where's Geode?"

"Sleeping, I think." Vintians kept odd hours.

Affie appeared in the cockpit door, eyes wide. "He's in his bunk . . . *alone,* right?"

"Of course. You know he only flirts around."

"Yeah, but this time he's flirting with one of the mechanics who can get us out of here." Affie plopped down in the seat beside Leox, shaking her head. "Who happens to be married to the *other* mechanic who can get us out of here."

"Hey, the guy can't help it," Leox said with a shrug. "The ladies go for those strong, silent types."

This won him a scowl from Affie. "He can help it more than he does, and this time, he'd better."

"All right, all right, all right. I'll talk to him when he gets up." Leox couldn't help thinking about more predatory types aboard. "Koley Linn hasn't given you any trouble, has he?"

"No, except by existing." Affie helped herself to one of Leox's mint sticks. She still thought their biggest problem was Geode not knowing when to turn off the charm.

Leox hoped she was right.

A thump overhead made Chancey look up. Nan flinched on her bunk, whispering, "What's that?"

"Something going on upstairs," Chancey replied. She glanced at the sentry droids, just visible from their cell; they stood in place, vibrating slightly, not reacting.

That's a scrambler at work, she thought. Something serious was about to go down, and it looked like they were standing at the center of it.

Another thump brought both women to their feet. Sparks sprayed around one of the ceiling panels, and then it lifted free to reveal three beings staring down at her.

"All glory to the Eye," said the Pau'an male.

The Nihil? What the *hell*? This made no sense to Chancey whatsoever.

But Nan had already jumped to her feet, relief washing over her face. "All glory to the Eye," she returned. "How have you—did someone send you—"

"We knew Hague," said the human female. "For his sake, we've come to help you."

The Pau'an added, "In return, you will help us." It wasn't a question.

Chancey wanted to know a lot more about what they were helping with, and why—but she also knew this was no time to be stubborn. "I've made worse bargains," she said, scooting one of the bunks beneath the open ceiling panel, the better for them to reach. "Let's move."

Chapter 13

In the medical tower, the situation was—well, not serene, but as close as any part of Starlight Beacon could come to it at present. When Bell Zettifar had first begun assisting the tower personnel in preparing for an influx of patients, he'd thought they'd be scrambling to keep up for some time to come.

But he'd underestimated the medical staff, the patients, the droids, the Force, even himself. They'd had to pull a few extra beds, but the wards remained orderly. All patients were being cared for, and they had (just barely) enough medical droids and supplies to go around.

"Can you believe it?" Bell asked Burryaga. "We actually pulled this off."

Burryaga pointed out that the reward for restoring order in the medical tower would probably be getting assigned to restore order in the main docking bay.

"Then we'll manage that, too." For the first time in days, Bell felt almost like himself. The eerie distortion of the Force barely touched him, and he dared to hope that perhaps it was ending, fading away as mysteriously as it had begun.

A med droid in the corridor whined in dismay at the sound of foot-steps hurrying toward their ward. Bell and Burryaga exchanged glances—another patient? They each knew that no more ships were supposed to be docking at Starlight Beacon anytime soon—before heading out to help. He just hoped there hadn't been another Nihil attack; already, the number was beginning to make him nervous that this wasn't just a few last remnants striking out, but perhaps a sign that the Nihil had more life in them than the Republic and the Jedi had hoped.

Upon stepping into the corridor, Bell saw that Orla Jareni was walk-ing alongside a hovergurney, on which lay a Tholothian—

No, Bell thought in that first horrified moment. *It can't be, I would have felt it, how could I not have felt it?*

His Master, Indeera Stokes, lay on the stretcher as gray as death.

Another of Bell's Masters had been cut down, and the Force had told him nothing.

The Republic had to be made up of foolishly trusting people, Nan de-cided, because the station's regulation-issue work coveralls turned out to be stored at an easily accessible location, inside a locker that opened without code or key.

"We don't exactly match the rest of you," Chancey Yarrow said as she cuffed her coverall's sleeves, "but it's close enough that I suspect no one will notice the difference."

The Pau'an team leader nodded. "None of them have noticed that what we're wearing is any different from what they usually see."

Nan couldn't resist a small smile as she thought of the high-and-mighty Jedi being brought down by something as simple as this: the revelation that they didn't look very carefully at those who did menial tasks for them.

"Still no alarms going off," Chancey noted. "No announcements about escaped prisoners. Maybe the Jedi *have* forgotten about us."

"I'm just glad we're out of there," Nan said. "And that we finally have something to do. Sitting around and waiting—I hate it."

"Our work for the Eye is vital," the Pau'an said, "and you will be glad to know that it is very nearly complete."

"Very glad," Nan replied. It felt so good to have *purpose* again. "Now how can we help you?"

"If you're planning on making some trouble aboard Starlight, I'm not a bad engineer," Chancey said, with what Nan knew to be false modesty. "Give me a look at some schematics, and I can probably put a few kinks in their system." She was still being careful of the Nihil team, holding something back.

Should Nan do that, too?

The Nihil team members exchanged glances. "We already have a comprehensive plan, one that is very near completion," said the human woman on the team—Leyel, or something like that. Nan hadn't bothered listening closely to their names. "But the final stage will be easier, with your assistance."

The Pau'an interjected, "You must follow our instructions *precisely.* We cannot be too cautious. Too much depends on the mission the Eye has entrusted to us."

Nan felt a stab of jealousy: These people were special to Marchion Ro already. That wasn't supposed to matter to her any longer—but it did.

"No problem with that," Chancey said. She might feel no loyalty to the Nihil, but Nan thought the woman seemed genuinely willing to assist them. Gratitude carried more weight with her than the Nihil did. "Nan, you know your way around a tool kit, right?"

"Of course," Nan said. As though anybody who'd been spacefaring since infancy wouldn't.

"What about you?" Leyel narrowed her eyes as she stared at Chancey. "Are you capable with tools? Do you understand station technology?"

Chancey's mouth quirked, a stifled smile. "I think I can manage."

Nan wanted to tell the Nihil who they were really dealing with—an elite scientist who had just developed an entirely new type of gravitic weapon—but that would mean openly betraying Chancey, something she wasn't ready to do. Besides, the Nihil already had a plan, didn't they? Chancey's expertise didn't come into it. Yet.

The Pau'an simply nodded. "It is nearly time to take the final steps. Follow us."

Meanwhile, within the Hub, Stellan Gios was attempting to regain some measure of balance. A hard thing to do, without the steady guidance of the Force—but the Force had not yet entirely abandoned them here. It remained, perceptible but faint, making its influence known in swift moments. Those moments were buoys in the stormy sea of Stellan's mind.

He clung to the memory of them especially strongly at the moment, because it would not do to have the head of Starlight Beacon show weakness to a planetary leader.

"We've heard the latest reports that people and ships have taken refuge aboard Starlight," said Queen Thandeka of Eiram, shimmering in the hologram before him. "Is it not a burden to your operations?"

"It is," Stellan admitted, "but one we are capable of handling. You need not worry—we don't expect any overflow on Eiram."

The queen tilted her head, studying him. "You misunderstand the purpose of my call, Master Gios. The people of Eiram do not fear the arrival of refugees. We wish to welcome them if it will be of assistance."

"Your planet is in no shape for that," Stellan insisted, realizing only as he spoke that it was highly presumptuous to explain to a queen the condition of her own world. Still, the facts were undeniable. "You have barely enough water for your citizens, and many of your greater structures have taken considerable damage."

Thandeka lifted her chin. "We have medical personnel capable of traveling to Starlight to assist in treating the injured. Although we are a small world with no real fleet to speak of, we do have a medical cruiser that can be dispatched. And though we are still working on repairs from the groundquake, we are not without shelter for those in need. What we have, we can share."

Other protests bubbled up in Stellan's mind, but he had the sense not to speak them. "Queen Thandeka," he began, "the generosity of Eiram cannot be doubted. But Starlight Beacon is meant to offer help to those in need, not to receive it."

The queen shook her head. "'We are all the Republic.' Are those mere words, or do you mean them?"

"—Of course we mean them, but—"

"If Eiram is no less a part of the Republic than any other world, then we are no less bound to offer whatever help is in our capacity to give." Humor glinted in her dark eyes. "Or are the Jedi too proud to ask for help?"

Stellan knew when he'd been bested. He held up his hands, a brief gesture of concession. "We are not as proud as that, Your Majesty. I promise you, if and when we require Eiram's assistance, we will call upon your people. But for the time being, the situation here is stable. Our medical tower is more than capable of handling the injured we have, and at this point it would be more burdensome for us to try to move them again than it is to take care of them where they are. Our medical supplies and rations are sufficient and will remain so for some days to come."

Her posture relaxed somewhat, and her smile became easier. "You've handled your problems very well, Master Gios. I congratulate you."

"Save your congratulations for the end of this crisis."

The queen laughed. "Superstitious?"

"Only prudent. Thank you again, Queen Thandeka."

She nodded as her hologram shimmered to black.

Once he could no longer be seen by anyone outside the Hub, Stellan slumped back into the nearest chair.

What would the galaxy at large say, if they could see him now? Stellan Gios, scion of the Jedi, Council member, and leader of Starlight

Beacon, no longer the confident guardian of peace and justice—just a tired, confused man who feels older than his years—

He imagined Orla Jareni raising an eyebrow. Indeed, he knew exactly what she'd say if she were here: *Why are you comparing yourself with a fiction constructed by the media of the Republic? You're doing the best you can at this time. No one can ask more.*

So loosen up already.

If she'd actually been present to speak the words, he might even have been able to believe her.

Stellan had the sudden, irrational thought, *I am being punished for my pride. For thinking I knew better than Avar Kriss, that I alone knew the right course of action to take against the Nihil, for Starlight—*

But was it his pride that had created this falseness? Or had the Republic and the Jedi fashioned it, then draped the mantle over his shoulders?

It didn't matter, Stellan realized. The point was recognizing it for what it was. Not comparing himself with something he'd never been and could never be.

But without that—who was he?

The Nihil team—newly five beings strong—had made its way to the base of the station, to the very wall of the structure's foundation.

"What's kept here?" said the younger human they had rescued, the girl called Nan. "Or is it solid?"

"This," Leyel said, giving the metal wall a satisfied pat, "houses the reactor core that powers the entire station."

The older human woman, Chancey, nodded. "Take this offline, and they'll be begging for help within hours. Plus our rescue ship can fly up safe as you please to get us out of here."

Werrera, Cale, and Leyel all exchanged quick glances. This was not the plan—but there was no need to tell the newcomers that just yet. It also seemed that Chancey knew a bit more about engineering than she'd let on, but they could ensure she did not disrupt the Eye's plan.

Cale said only, "We've disabled the alarms that would sense activity along the core wall. So they should detect nothing." Already Leyel and Werrera were unpacking their plasma torches.

Chancey bent down to open a nearby maintenance shaft—sure enough, they had more plasma torches here just waiting for orderly repairs when necessary. These torches weren't as strong as those the Nihil had brought, but they would help get the job done. Once both of the women they'd freed had the torches in hand, Cale turned to stare at the wall they were about to rip apart. "Begin."

It was very nearly "evening" aboard the station. Bell Zettifar was overdue to collect his dinner ration, but he refused to leave his Master's side. Even Ember had taken a place beneath the medical bed and curled into a ball to sleep.

Master Indeera remained unconscious. Her frightening twitching had ceased, but Bell didn't know whether that was a good sign or a terrible one. The med droids had reported that all of her vital functions had slowed tremendously—as they might in someone of very great age—but that they continued to flow. While there was life, there was hope. Yet Bell felt farther away from that hope than he had been in a long time.

A soft growl made him look up. Burryaga stood there, holding not one but two packets of dinner rations.

For the first time since Master Indeera had been brought in, Bell was able to smile, sort of. "Thanks. I appreciate it."

Burryaga handed him the smaller of the two packets (Wookiee rations were, understandably, more ample), and together they wordlessly took places at a small table nearby. The food had so little flavor that Bell thought he might as well have been munching leaves.

No, scratch that, he realized. *Some leaves taste great. Emergency rations don't.*

It was Burryaga who broke the silence, asking kindly after Master Indeera, though surely her condition was obvious.

"Nothing's changed," Bell said. "I wish I could reach her through the Force, but I can't."

Burryaga growled a suggestion—what if they worked together? If they both reached out, perhaps they would prove stronger than whoever or whatever was muffling the Force aboard Starlight.

Bell wasn't certain. The Force didn't operate according to mathematical principles. Two Jedi working in combination might have a greater effect, or might not.

Still, it wouldn't hurt to try.

After finishing their rations, they returned to Master Indeera's bedside. Bell stood facing Burryaga, and something about that moment made him realize that their friendship had deepened, these past few days—and he'd needed a friend more than he'd realized. "Thanks for being here," he said quietly.

Burryaga simply inclined his head, then closed his eyes, silently summoning Bell to begin.

Bell closed his eyes, too. He took a deep breath—then another—then began reaching out with his feelings. A memory from the crèche drifted through his mind: Master Yoda teaching the younglings how to do this for the first time, whispering to them, *Let go.* To this day, it helped Bell to imagine how Yoda had sounded when he said it.

At least, it usually did.

Today was different.

Bell reached out and did not find the Force. He could still sense it, but at a great distance, and it did not flow through him. It was . . . distorted. Twisted. *Wrong.*

He couldn't connect with Master Indeera, even subconsciously. Bell could only barely detect Burryaga's presence, and that was with Burry not even a meter away and actively reaching out to him as well.

Bell's eyes opened to see Burryaga looking equally stricken. He whispered, "It's all wrong for you, too?"

Burryaga nodded.

"It can't go on like this," Bell blurted out. "Whatever's happening on this station—it can't last forever. The Force is eternal. Nothing can permanently damage it. Nothing ever could."

With a growl, Burryaga agreed that this situation couldn't last forever. Sooner or later, everything would change.

The question was how.

Chapter 14

As an apprentice, Orla Jareni had once traveled on a mission to a world that had been known for its beautifully realistic sculpture. Its artists crafted forms so lifelike from their famously iridescent gray native stone that they seemed to have softness, texture, even spirit.

She thought of those statues as she stared at the husk that had been Regald Coll.

His features had been preserved so finely that he could have been one of those statues—gray as stone, delicate as any artwork. But the illusion of vitality those sculptors had created was totally absent. Only hours ago, Regald had been joking, laughing, utterly alive. At this moment, looking at the husk left behind, it seemed impossible to imagine anything more lifeless.

Stellan's overeager logistics droid had taken undue pleasure in activating one chamber's hazmat pod protocol. The air had the flat scent of sterility; the faint hiss of atmospheric filters came from every direction. Sophisticated analysis droids whirred around the table where Regald's husk lay, taking readings, but Orla felt certain that the mystery of what had happened here would not be solved by mere data.

The doors slid open, and Elzar Mann walked in, graver than she had ever seen him.

"This isn't the first time, you know," he said as he came to her side. "Loden Greatstorm was found like this, though his—husk, whatever you want to call it—fell to ash at the first touch."

"This has more substance to it," Orla said. It had been transported to the hazmat pod without difficulty. "But you feel sure it's the same thing?"

Elzar nodded. "The question remains, what the hell is it? What has the power to do something like this?"

Orla had been asking herself that. Although she had come up with no definite answers, she had reached the next question, one even more ominous: "The disturbance in the Force—do you believe it's the cause of Regald's death?"

"You'd know more than I," Elzar said. "So far . . . well, it hasn't affected me much."

"Of course." Orla couldn't believe she hadn't realized this for herself; then again, neither she nor the other Jedi were exactly themselves, at present. "You're not calling upon the Force in the same way you once were. That's shielded you, to a degree—protected you. Elzar Mann, you may be our only hope."

Elzar gave her a look, which seemed to say, *Anything but that.* He didn't fully trust himself again yet, then. No matter. Orla was confident that Elzar would rise to whatever challenges confronted them.

If only she could feel so sure of herself.

Orla had strong mastery over her fear; it had not greatly troubled her since her earliest days as a Padawan, regardless of the danger she'd found herself in through the years. Yet a wave of it swept through her as she thought, *We need to get off this station. We need to get out of here* now. *Open the docking bay doors and board the ships along with their pilots. The Nihil may still be out there, but we're better off facing the Nihil than we are against . . . whatever this is. At least with the Nihil, we know how to fight—*

She took a deep breath, regained her control. Her expression had never wavered for an instant. "We need to search again."

Elzar didn't look enthused. "The last search wound up with Regald dead."

"If we don't find what's doing this and stop it," Orla replied, "he won't be the last to die."

When Nan had been very small, when her parents were still alive, they had shared one of the bonding rituals of most spacefaring families. Among her few memories of them was of sitting on her father's lap while he showed her how to rewire a basic conduit, and the way her mother had hovered nearby the first time Nan took a T-7 anx into her hands. Learning how to repair and modify their ship—their home— was a rite of passage for any child who spent most of her life among the stars.

Who could've guessed, Nan thought as she worked with the plasma torch, sparks flying around her, *that I'd wind up using my skills for this?*

"Almost there," Leyel said. "Step back and let me finish."

Nan, Chancey, and the other Nihil team members did as Leyel asked, allowing the older woman to complete the last bit of cutting. Then Werrera, the Ithorian, applied a magnetic clamp and pulled out the large slab of metal they'd cut from the core casing. Internal panels and workings hummed and glowed with signals meant for only maintenance workers to see. From where she stood, Nan couldn't glimpse any more than that, but she knew that if they peered upward into that hollow darkness, they'd have a view all the way through the station.

Cale, the Pau'an, nodded with satisfaction. "Almost exactly on time. We have less than an hour to wait."

"If only the Eye could know how well this has gone," Leyel said.

"It will be obvious from the results." Pride emanated from Cale— from the entire Nihil team, really.

But Chancey shot Nan a look, one she understood instantly. It meant, *Why wouldn't the Eye know about this? Aren't they going to tell him how it went? It's his big plan, after all.*

Nan could think of only one reason the team wouldn't tell Marchion Ro about this: They would never get the chance.

Werrera took off the backpack he'd been wearing all along and let it drop to the ground with a heavy thud. When it was unsealed, Nan saw what was inside. Her gut clenched, and her body went cold as she realized: *Those are explosives.*

The image of Regald Coll's remains lingered in Elzar Mann's mind, almost blinding him to his surroundings. After the third time he nearly walked straight into a droid, he stopped himself and remembered his teachings. *The past is gone. The future is only a dream. The present is all.*

That was what Yoda would say, were he here. But Yoda's teachings could guide Elzar to serenity even in his absence.

And just then, as though the Force were taunting his ambitions for balance and harmony, station comms buzzed with an announcement: "*Republic ship* Ataraxia *requesting permission to board.*"

The *Ataraxia.* The ship carrying Avar Kriss.

At least this filled his mind with new images, even if those images were distinctly unhelpful: Avar's golden hair draped across his pillow, her eyes as bright as the jewel she wore in her headband, her fingers entwined with his—

"Stay in the present," Elzar muttered, willing himself to follow through.

During their time on Ledalau, Orla had told Elzar that guarding against darkness was about more than simply avoiding an excess of fear or anger. Negative emotions might be overwhelming at times, but it was easy to name them for what they were. *The real danger,* she had said, *lies in those emotions that seem positive at first, but take too great a hold over our minds and hearts. Give way to those feelings, embrace them, and before you know it, they've been twisted into something else far more damaging.*

Elzar could not make himself reject his feelings about Avar. But he couldn't let those feelings turn poisonous. That would be the ultimate betrayal—of Avar's goodness, of his emotions, of every memory they'd made together.

"Steady on," he told himself, and it seemed that he had regained his balance.

But he'd make himself scarce for a little while. No point in tempting fate.

After JJ-5145 had finished setting up the hazmat pod, Stellan found further stalling impossible. "You will greatly appreciate the efficiency and cleanliness of the new marshal's office," the droid insisted. "In addition, I have arranged all equipment and furnishings in a fashionably minimalist style."

If there was anything in the galaxy Stellan cared less about than having a stylish office, he wasn't sure what it could be. Still, inspecting the droid's efforts was a task he felt up to, and so he accompanied JJ-5145 down to the level of the station that housed the docking bays and what had been, until recently, the quartermaster's office.

"What do you think?" JJ-5145 swiveled on his base, clearly eager for approval. "Will it not suit your every need?"

"I . . . believe that it will." Against his expectations, Stellan was impressed. Though the quartermaster's office was only a fraction as large as the Hub, JJ-5145 had managed to set up arrays with readouts that provided constant updates on all major station systems. His chair seemed almost like the pilot's seat in a small, hyperefficient ship, with everything he could possibly need within arm's reach. And a decorative mobile hung in one corner. "You've done amazing work here, Forfive. Thank you."

"It has been my great pleasure!" JJ-5145 chirped. "What other tasks may I perform for you? If there are no major station matters to attend to, I can help with your personal needs. Does your clothing require organization?"

Stellan did not intend to have a droid rooting around in his sock drawer and would've said so had the announcement over the comm not interrupted him.

"The *Ataraxia*?" he said, in unwelcome amazement. As though they didn't have enough to worry about, Avar had decided to abandon her obsessive quest to capture the Nihil Eye just long enough to drop by for a visit?

Perhaps other members of the Council had informed her that she was no longer marshal of Starlight Beacon, and she was here to protest. Or maybe she didn't yet know. If that were the case, she was in for a rude awakening. Stellan wouldn't hesitate to provide one.

Pride, this is your pride talking to you and it is unworthy, repudiate it.

This unknown power aboard the station is draining me of the ability to feel almost anything.

Pride is the last emotion I have left.

And if he fell apart during this crisis, he wouldn't even have that.

Stellan pulled himself together insofar as possible and nodded to the communications tech. "Patch them through."

"Starlight, this is the *Ataraxia*. Come in, please."

The hologram shimmered to life before him, revealing Avar Kriss, her golden hair surrounding her face as though she glowed. "This is Starlight," Stellan replied.

Her first reaction was to frown. "Stellan—I . . . is everything okay? Where's Maru?"

I must look even worse than I feel, he thought. "Attending to his duties in the Hub. I've just begun operating from the quartermaster's office."

Avar's frown deepened. "Operating in what capacity?"

"As the marshal of Starlight Beacon."

Saying it was every bit as fulfilling as it shouldn't have been. Her eyes widened. Avar would've been less shocked if he'd walked up and slapped her.

(Which he wouldn't do, which he would never do, why was he having these thoughts, where was the Force to guide him?)

She collected herself quickly, however. "You mean, until I returned."

"I mean, permanently. We warned you, Avar. I warned you, and yet you abandoned your post—"

"Abandoned?" Avar said, cutting him off. "Stellan, you can't mean that."

It felt too good, defying her. "You abandoned your post, defying the Council, and for what? A wild mynock chase."

"Stellan, you need to listen to me." Avar remained undaunted. "The 'wild mynock chase' was a success. We have—"

A loud BOOM shook the walls, floors, Stellan himself, everything. The lights flickered; Avar's hologram vanished. The reverberations continued, on and on, as though they were planetside in a tremendous thunderstorm.

Something's gone wrong, Stellan realized. *Something's exploded.*

In the medical tower, the jolt sent Bell sprawling; he was barely able to catch himself against the side of Master Indeera's bed.

"What was that?" cried one of the patients, echoed by Burryaga's alarmed whine. Ember crept to his side, tail between her legs.

"They'll tell us," Bell said, as reassuringly as he could manage. "Probably there'll be an announcement really soon. Within a few seconds."

No sooner had he spoken than the lights flickered, dimming the ward into almost total darkness.

Koley Linn slammed sideways into his ship so hard, it was as though it had struck him. He managed to stay on his feet, however, which was more than could be said for most of the people in the docking bay. Cries of dismay and alarm rose from all over.

I need to get out of here as fast as possible, he thought, *and I'm trapped on this damn thing.*

Elzar Mann's ears rang from the blast as he braced himself against the corridor wall. His first thought was that something had happened to the *Ataraxia*—but that made no sense. The vibration beneath his feet told him the explosion had been a great deal closer, and that Starlight had taken considerable damage.

His personal comlink wasn't picking up anything at the moment. The wall next to him held a comm panel within easy reach—maybe it still had a good connection? Elzar staggered to it. "Stellan? What's happened?"

No response from the quartermaster's office.

Stellan wouldn't have all the information yet anyway, Elzar decided as he called the Hub instead. "Maru? It's Elzar Mann. What's going on?"

No response.

Comms were down, which meant that, for the moment, every person on this station was on their own.

Affie Hollow picked herself up from the floor of the *Vessel* with the assistance of Leox's helping hand. The sabacc cards from their game had scattered across the floor. Her first instinct was to call to Geode, to tell him there was a problem, but she realized, *Not even Geode could sleep through that.* He'd be there shortly.

"Did one of the ships in the docking bay blow up?" Affie wondered if they'd be able to see it from the cockpit.

"Don't think so," Leox said. His expression was unusually grim. "We'd have heard debris against the hull, and fire suppression systems would be going off like crazy."

"What else aboard this station could explode like that?"

Her gut dropped when Leox replied, "It's gotta be the station itself."

It had taken all Orla Jareni's considerable talent in the Force to remain upright when the explosion rippled through the station and the lights in her quarters flickered down almost to black. She waited for the tightness in her ears that would signal decompression, which would of course be followed by her swift and painful demise, along with the deaths of everyone else aboard Starlight.

Fifteen seconds passed. The tightness never came. *Not dead yet,* Orla thought, *which means we've got work to do.*

Nan coughed, crawling along the floor away from the thick smoke. Chancey was by her side, and it sounded like the rest of the Nihil team was right behind her. They'd all survived, then. But Nan wasn't sure how much good that did them.

The core of the station had been massively, permanently compromised. Nan could *feel* the instability, the subtle shifting that rendered the floor unsteady beneath their feet. She'd ridden on too many patched-together ships not to know when a structure was on the verge of falling apart. Starlight Beacon was in danger of that now.

The web of gravity reinforcement that bound the station together and oriented everyone aboard with a sense of "up" and "down" was faltering. Nan realized true "down" was slipping by a few degrees. The taut invisible framework holding the station together had begun to go slack.

Once they'd made their way to a less smoky corridor, they all got to their feet. As Nan wiped soot from her face and hands, she expected to hear the Nihil team's fear and regret. They'd used too many explosives, surely. Or detonated at the wrong spot.

But no. They were smiling. They were *glad.*

Chancey didn't look one bit surprised. "Tell me you've got a way off this station."

Cale shook his head. "If we could escape, so could others. That would defeat the Eye's plan."

"We need nothing else," Leyel added. "We've completed his work. The galaxy will see this and finally understand the might of the Nihil."

Nan had wondered before, but finally she knew: This was a suicide mission.

The station was going to be destroyed, and Nan would die with it— as would every other being aboard Starlight Beacon.

Chapter 15

Aboard the *Gaze Electric,* the news came as a simple comm chime, one that might've meant no more than a distant Cloud making contact. But this was the time Marchion Ro had dictated—and, it appeared, his team had met his expectations.

He rose from the captain's chair, which meant dislodging Ghirra Starros from his lap. Laughing, she said, "Isn't there anyone at *all* aboard your ship? You need someone around to take care of things like this for you. I thought that was what that Ferr woman was for."

Marchion didn't address the question of who else was aboard his ship. Starros would learn that in time, and he'd deal with her reaction— or not—later. Hearing this communication was far more pressing.

Just as he reached the console, Thaya Ferr hurried in. Starros made a small huff of irritation. Ro paid neither of them any mind.

He hit the switch himself. All screens on board lit up with the simple, automated text communication: *An explosion has damaged the Starlight Beacon station core. All systems responding as predicted.*

"We've done it, then." Starros, with great and obvious effort, sounded cheerful. "You've pulled it off. While Lourna Dee and all the other

Tempest Runners are off pursuing their own selfish concerns, running after glory, you've struck at the heart of their enemy."

"And drawn blood," Ro said, before turning to Thaya Ferr. "Keep monitoring that channel."

Ghirra Starros interrupted. "There will be...more?" Her face seemed pale.

"So much more," Ro said. Did she not fully comprehend what she had done? Only a fool wouldn't. But Starros was undoubtedly like most beings—capable of considerable denial when it came to the harm she could do. He had never had any need for such self-deceit. Let her face the truth of what she'd wrought. "You see, we could have detonated the kind of device that would've destroyed Starlight instantly. Smuggling it on board would've been more difficult...but, with our intel, not impossible. Yet that would've defeated the purpose. The entire galaxy must see this. They must watch it happen. They must know the true power of the Nihil."

Stellan Gios did not know if the disturbance in the Force aboard Starlight had been destroyed in the explosion, or if he'd finally pushed past the effects of insomnia, or whether the immediate demands of a crisis had helped him throw off the stupor that disturbance had created. Regardless, he could focus again, and just as the station needed him the most.

Elzar reached him within minutes of the blast, with Nib Assek trailing along behind. She looked rumpled, no worse, but he had a small scrape along one cheekbone that hadn't been there earlier in the day. "What's happening?"

"No solid information yet," Stellan said, tossing on his robe as he hurried out from the quartermaster's office toward the nearest lifts. Elzar fell into step beside him. "Internal comms are down. The droids aren't able to pull up system-wide information. Hell, we don't even know whether this was an internal systems failure or a bomb."

"My money's on the bomb," Elzar replied.

That was Stellan's guess, too, which meant they had the additional problem of saboteurs on board. But he said, "Speculation won't help us as much as getting the actual facts as to what's gone wrong. Once we've reached the Hub, we ought to be able to get a better picture of the overall situation."

However, the first lifts they tried weren't working. Neither were the next lifts. To judge from the murmurs of dismay Stellan heard from every clustered group along the way—more and more as they went on—every lift on Starlight had been rendered inoperable, as a precaution against faltering internal integrity systems. The obvious next step was taking one of the maintenance shafts; that would be a long climb, time Stellan wished they didn't have to waste, but at least it could be done.

Or so he thought, until the three of them looked up into the maintenance tunnel and saw the shimmering ray shield well above—one that was holding back glowing waves of radiation. A glance downward revealed that another such ray shield had been automatically generated several levels below them, too.

"Do those shields run all the way through the station?" Nib asked.

Elzar sighed. "If so, we're stuck here."

Stellan felt almost ablaze with the need to reach the Hub—the new setup in the quartermaster's office seemed comprehensive, and yet he would've preferred to take no chances. But he summoned all his patience. "Let's talk to the Hub, then. Some of the comm panels are damaged, but surely they aren't all offline. If I know Maru, he's probably already analyzed every bit of damage and come up with pro and con lists for each possible solution." That won him a flinty smile from Elzar, a real smile from Nib.

But those smiles faded as they tried one comm after another, to no avail.

"This is impossible!" Stellan said. "There are independent power and signal banks for comms throughout the station. No explosion should be able to take them all out while the station remains intact."

Nib looked grave. "What if they're not broken? What if they're being blocked?"

As soon as Nib had spoken, Stellan knew she'd hit upon the truth. "Saboteurs, then. They not only hit us with an explosive device, they've kept us from calling for help, even from talking to one another. What else might they have done?"

With a grimace, Elzar said, "I have a feeling we're going to find out."

JJ-5145, who'd been quietly running analysis, piped up. "At minimum, they have sabotaged the escape pods."

"What?" Elzar said sharply. "How?"

"Power to the escape pods has been cut, apparently permanently," said JJ-5145. "Each individual pod would require its own power cell, of sufficient strength to fully and independently launch. We do not keep a supply of such strong cells aboard Starlight."

"All right, then," Stellan said, projecting more confidence than he felt. "No escape pods. We have to find a way to open the docking bay doors to let everyone out. So let's get started on that."

When the others were gone, and could not see him falter, Stellan leaned against the nearest wall to gather his wits. *At least the disturbance in the Force is gone now,* he reminded himself. *Whatever the cause was, the saboteurs must have destroyed it completely.*

The cause had not been destroyed. In fact, it was now on the move.

Damage from the blast had been greater within the cargo bay than in many other areas, due both to its proximity to the explosion itself, and to the percussive resonance that spread across so many unbattened cargo containers and vessels. While some ships remained intact and in good order, others had been upended or sent crashing into one another.

One ship—the one brought to Starlight by Cale, Leyel, and Werrera—looked as if it had been somehow cracked open by the force of the explosion. Instead the lock on its cargo hold had released, as it was programmed to do, after detecting extreme seismic shock.

It didn't take long for their cargo to realize they were finally free.

"This is Bell Zettifar calling to the Hub—to anybody who might be checking our communications—anyone?" Bell had been repeating variations on this for a few minutes, but finally gave up. Comms were down for the moment, and his time would be better spent helping out in the medical tower.

The shock waves in this location had been intense. Patients had been tipped out of their beds onto the floor; pill droids had crashed into walls. Burryaga had assigned himself the task of putting the heavier items to rights, which left Bell to console and check on people as much as possible.

He took an extra moment by his Master's bedside. Indeera's condition remained stable. Despite still having no idea what exactly had happened to her, Bell was increasingly convinced that she could survive—but only if they were able to keep her stable long enough for her to heal. That was a hard thing to feel confident about while working with only emergency lights for guidance. Still, even without speaking to the rest of the station, he knew that many Jedi and Republic officials were working hard to set right whatever had gone wrong.

Bell then knelt on the floor. Beneath Master Indeera's bed, Ember lay curled in a ball, tail tucked between her legs. Charhounds didn't like big scary noises. Bell didn't blame them.

"It's okay, girl," he murmured, stroking her warm fur. "I think the worst is over."

Next he went to Burryaga's side to see if he needed help. Burryaga good-naturedly pointed out that Bell had waited to do this until after all the heaviest stuff had already been moved.

Bell made a face, then got back to business. "Listen, comms are still down. Should we send a droid to the Hub to get info? Or should I run it myself? Looks like sending somebody is the only way we're going to find out what's happened. It's like the old frontier messenger days again."

Burryaga shook his head, growling as he explained that he'd tried going for help himself immediately after the blast—and had run directly into an air lock that wouldn't unseal. Anyone who had ever traveled in space knew: It was highly unwise to blow a sticky air lock, because there was a good chance that air lock was stuck for a good reason, namely, keeping out the bone-chilling vacuum of space.

The reality sank in, heavy on Bell's shoulders. "In other words," he said, "we're trapped."

At that moment—though virtually nobody else on Starlight knew it— Avar Kriss and a handful of the others who'd arrived on the *Ataraxia* were boarding the station. Even this had taken considerable ingenuity, as they'd been unable to signal for any of the docking bay doors to open. The Jedi were instead reduced to carving through the station's outer hull with their lightsabers, thanks to the powerful seal within the *Ataraxia*'s cofferdam.

"The midsection juncture is flooded with radiation!" Frozian Jedi Nooranbakarakana warned as Avar strode through the corridors, intent upon reaching the Hub. "The top and bottom halves of the station are almost entirely cut off from each other. The conductive elements designed to transmit energy throughout the station are now serving as conduits for radiation, with limiters and dampening fields meant to prevent such a cascade overwhelmed. If this was an accident, it was a profoundly unfortunate one."

Nooranbakarakana didn't think it was an accident. Avar could tell. She didn't think it was accidental, either.

She paused, considered, decided. "For the moment, we devote our energies to helping here in the top half of the station. Once we've done that, maybe we can find a way to connect the two."

(Certain beings were traversing the divide at that very moment—

beings incapable of understanding what havoc radiation would work on their bodies within a few days. They understood nothing beyond their terrible hunger, and the desperation to feed.)

As Avar continued resolutely on her way toward the Hub, she found herself compelled to reach Stellan Gios if at all possible. He'd taken her position as marshal—stolen it out from under her, while she was trying to save the galaxy from the threat of the Nihil by capturing their leader. And what was the result? *This.* Stellan hadn't even had charge of Starlight for a month before disaster struck.

Despite that compulsion, she couldn't help thinking of Elzar Mann, too. He'd be on her side. Maybe he could even make Stellan understand. His loyalty—that was something Avar never had to question.

Her steps quickened. Would she find him above, or was he within the bottom half of the station, trapped on the other side of the barrier between them?

Wherever he was, whoever was with him, Avar felt sure that Elzar would be fighting as hard as she was to save them all.

Is Avar all right? Was the Ataraxia *affected by the blast?*

After that one sudden, piercing moment of concern for Avar, Elzar forced himself to put such worries aside. He could not concentrate on his fear for one life and still do his best to protect all the many lives presently at risk on Starlight Beacon.

As he worked on the comm panel nearest the quartermaster's office, hoping to restore some fragment of signal, a figure in white appeared through the emergency-light gloom: Orla Jareni, concerned but calm. She said, "I'm assuming you're as cut off as everyone else?"

"So it would seem," Elzar replied, looking her up and down. "Are you ever going to explain how you keep those robes pristine white even through explosions?"

"No. Now stop wisecracking and fill me in."

Elzar told her what little he could, leading to the latest and worst news: "The astromechs' ability to obtain data is severely limited, but based on what readings we do have, it looks as though the top and bottom halves of the station are almost inaccessible to each other—and the joining between the halves has been structurally compromised. It may not hold. Right now we can really only reach the medical tower. Everything else above is off limits."

Orla nodded as she took that in. "As long as both halves remain airtight, it's still something that can be fixed."

How did you put two halves of a space station back together? No doubt there were Republic engineers who could manage it, given time and material, but Elzar hoped they wouldn't have to find out.

Stellan emerged from his office, haggard but focused. "Any luck?" Elzar shook his head. "Then I guess we need to assume the worst-case scenario and act accordingly."

Orla said, "Which means one of our first priorities should be getting the refugee ships off this station."

"Exactly," Stellan said. "Elzar, Orla, I'm putting you on point for this. Not every ship is spaceworthy yet, but the ones that are need to prepare for takeoff within the hour."

It'll be chaos, Elzar thought, but he had a feeling that even the most uncooperative pilots would follow the plan if it meant they could get off Starlight faster.

"We're not in great shape, but we can fly out of here, make our way down to Eiram," said Leox Gyasi as he and Affie began going through the preflight checks. Geode already sat at navigation, steady despite the chaos. "It may be a lump of a planet in the middle of nowhere, but it's got breathable air. Starlight Beacon may not be able to say the same before long."

Affie looked stricken. "Air circulation—of course, that's powered, too. How long do you think they can hold on?"

"Depends on the damage—a couple days, maybe?" Leox knew the thought of leaving behind people in distress would upset Affie even more, so he added, "The best thing we can do for them is leave. The more people who get out of here, the more breathable air is left over for the ones still on the station."

From the cockpit he saw an astromech roll up; seconds later their takeoff slot and coordinates appeared on the controls. Affie breathed out in relief. "We're in the first wave."

"See? The station's luck might've run out, but ours is still holding." Leox started the engines; the *Vessel* hummed to life. On the console the countdown to their takeoff window began.

His hands were tense on the controls, ready to take them into flight the instant the docking bay doors slid open. Those doors, there to keep them safe in case of hostilities or disaster, were now just the bars on their cage. Leox wouldn't be sad to see the last of them. He counted the last moments down silently in his head: *three, two, one.*

The doors didn't open.

Maybe the droids weren't in perfect sync—hardly surprising given the chaotic situation. But as the seconds went on, Leox's gut began to tighten, and the bay doors remained shut.

"They should open," Affie said. "The problems with the power source shouldn't matter. Starlight Beacon's bay doors have their own independent emergency power sources—Orla told me that. They should work no matter what!"

"They should," Leox agreed. "But apparently they don't."

Geode had gone very still. Affie whispered, "You mean we're stuck here?"

Leox wished he could pretty this up for her, but he didn't like to lie. "We're trapped."

Networking together a group of astromechs was a poor substitute for a proper command center—but at least they had this much, and Stellan was grateful for it. Combined with JJ-5145's earlier efforts, they were producing a level of analysis that the Hub itself would find difficult to match. As data finally began rolling in, he, Elzar, Nib, and Orla gathered together to study it.

"They're able to get our position via Eiram's satellites?" Nib murmured.

Stellan nodded. "More or less."

"Let me guess," Orla said. "We're not where we're supposed to be."

"Doesn't look like it." Elzar's voice sounded strange. Probably that was because he had just looked at the data stream Stellan was studying—the one that was tracking Starlight's position in real time. That position was changing moment by moment. "And it looks like we're getting even farther off track."

By this point Elzar must have realized the truth. Maybe he simply didn't want to say it out loud. Or maybe Stellan really was the only one who'd seen it yet.

But it couldn't be concealed for very long.

"The change in our position is slowly accelerating," Stellan said. "That wouldn't happen if our movement was purely a result of the explosion."

Nib's eyes widened. Orla put one hand to her chest as she said, "You mean—we've drifted into the planet's gravitational pull."

"And without control of our positional thrusters, we have no way to free ourselves from it," Elzar added. His eyes met Stellan's in mutual, terrible understanding.

Stellan forced himself to say it: "This station is going to crash."

Chapter 16

They're literally sitting down and waiting to die, Nan thought.

The Nihil team considered its work done. Their *lives* done. Although they'd accompanied Nan and Chancey as they fled the uncomfortably smoky area near the explosion, once the group had reached a clear corridor, any sense of urgency vanished. Werrera and Leyel took seats on the floor, while Cale leaned against a wall with all the contentment of an artisan who'd just finished a momentous creation.

Chancey wiped soot from her face. "I suggest you find another place to relax. They'll have a team up here within minutes."

"Doubtful," Cale replied. "Our preparations lasted for days—and I assure you, we've taken care of everything. One way or another, we have compromised every system on this station save for the most obscure— entertainment systems, retrofit backup systems, and the like. We've taken over communications. We've powered down independent energy cells. We've even closed off the lifts. Travel through the station will be difficult, if not impossible, and the Jedi and the Republic will be too busy keeping themselves alive to worry about the cause of the explosion."

"Not forever," Nan snapped. "Sooner or later, they're going to come after us."

Leyel laughed out loud. Cale shook his head, sly and satisfied, as he said, "Sooner? They have bigger problems. Later? There is no later."

Nan and Chancey exchanged glances. That swift look was enough to tell Nan that yes, Chancey believed the Nihil team. They might not have actually dealt Starlight Beacon a fatal blow, but they certainly believed that they had.

Which meant it was time to get the hell out of here.

"Thanks for the jailbreak," Chancey said. "If you don't mind, I think it's time we parted company—both with you, and with this station."

Cale bowed. "Thank you for your assistance. We couldn't have—well, no. We could've done it without you. But you helped us do it faster."

I sped up a disaster that might kill us, Nan thought. *Go, me.*

She and Chancey hurried down the hallway, putting distance between themselves and the Nihil as quickly as they could. But she still heard Leyel calling after them, "You won't be parting company with this station anytime soon—and neither will anyone else."

The quartermaster's office—briefly the calm, ordered, "fashionably minimalist" center of Stellan Gios's authority on Starlight Beacon—now looked like a droidsmith's workshop.

More and more astromechs had wheeled in to join the group that had been networked together to make up for the loss of the Hub. But this was nothing like the hastily cobbled-together droid lifeline that proved so essential in stemming the Great Hyperspace Disaster fallout; thanks to JJ-5145's advance efforts, they formed an efficient, well-ordered array. They had nothing like the same level of computational power, as the Hub and their inputs were limited to the few damaged connections that could be established from the quartermaster's office. Still, it was better than the alternative . . . which was to say, nothing.

Stellan pored over the data from the linked astromechs, analyzing what they'd been able to collect over the past several hours of station operations. Although this information was scattershot so far, he had finally detected the pattern: shutdowns of various warning systems, followed by disruptions in the areas those systems were meant to protect. Some of these disruptions were so minor that Stellan could hardly believe anybody would take the trouble. But overall, the sabotage efforts added up to a badly injured station that had been robbed of its ability to fully catalog its own damage, much less compensate for it.

One deviation in particular caught his attention. "The holding cell—all systems in that area were switched off some hours ago." He put one hand to his forehead, as though he could push back the headache that was brewing. "I'd tell you to check on the prisoners, Elzar, but I'm fairly sure they're not incarcerated any longer."

Elzar considered that. "Nan, at least, had been connected with the Nihil. She was a former member, and one who'd left their ranks pretty recently. Doesn't that suggest this is Nihil sabotage we're dealing with?"

"Probably," Stellan agreed. It was possible that their saboteur might simply have sprung the prisoners to add to the overall chaos on the station—but who else had such hatred for the Republic? Who else had shown such a pattern of hostility and aggression toward the Jedi?

No, this was Nihil work, and Stellan hadn't seen it until it was too late. Why hadn't the Force warned him? Why hadn't every Jedi aboard Starlight been on alert?

Because of the strange distortion in the Force they'd all sensed. Somehow their ability to foresee danger had been removed just as that danger became most acute. Were the Nihil responsible for that? If so— *how*?

Orla Jareni chose this moment to interject, "Who did this doesn't matter as much at the moment as what we're going to do about it."

Elzar gestured toward the astromechs doggedly churning out data. "That's what we're trying to figure out. There's not much else we can do yet besides help the injured—"

"But we can give the people on board the truth," Orla said. "They deserve to know their lives are in danger."

Stellan fixed her in a hard stare. "If we tell them that before we've figured out how to help them escape, all we'll do is start a panic." Koley Linn flashed through his mind, argumentative and angry. "If I knew more of these pilots—if I could predict their reactions, know that they would remain reasonable and calm—yes, I'd agree, we should tell them. But I don't know them all, and some of those I've met have already proved to be difficult at best. It only takes one short fuse in the group to make the whole situation blow up, and I guarantee you, we have at least one on board."

Orla didn't seem convinced. "If those short fuses figure out the danger on their own, the panic will be ten times worse."

"If it took us all this to get the data," Stellan pointed out, meaning the dozen astromechs blinking and beeping all around them, "nobody out there has a chance of figuring it out."

Leox Gyasi stood at one of the docking bay's few windows, a small rectangular space just at his eye level. He gazed through the viewer of the wood-and-metal device he held in his hands, carefully adjusting the small mirrors on its frame.

"What is that thing?" Affie asked. She stood by his shoulder, mostly for lack of anything else to do.

"It's an astrometrical sextant."

"It looks like something out of a museum."

"You'd be more likely to find one in a museum than in most spacecraft these days," Leox agreed. "Me, I prefer to do things the old-fashioned way sometimes. Mostly to connect with the ancestors—to understand how they found their way in a vast and chaotic galaxy—

but on the rare occasions all of our present-day technological marvels fail, as indeed they have today, old tools can be damn useful."

He hoped this might distract Affie for a little while, get her started on some of her teasing about his "antiques." Instead she said, "But what exactly is it you're doing the old-fashioned way?"

Shoulda known Little Bit wouldn't let me off that easily, Leox thought. "I'm measuring the relative distances between the stars and Eiram's horizon."

"The only reason to do that would be if you think our location is changing. Shifting relative to Eiram."

"You got it in one."

"But what does it matter?" Affie asked. "The explosion could only have thrown Starlight off by so much, and we couldn't be moving very fast from the force of that alone."

Leox double-checked his fourth reading of the past ten minutes, accepted the truth, and lowered the sextant so he could look her in the eyes. "Other forces are coming into play, namely, Eiram's gravity."

It was horrible to see the realization setting in, the dread on her young face. "You mean, the station's falling."

"We've got a long way to go yet," Leox said quickly. "And I'm sure they're getting Starlight back under control as we speak."

"Of course they are. Of course." Affie ran a hand through her dark-brown hair, which was one way she calmed herself. "But—have you figured out how long we do have?"

"Not yet." Which was the truth, though he already realized they were looking at hours, not days . . . and not that many hours, either. "Look. The Republic's got the best people, the best equipment. No doubt they're already calling for help halfway across the galaxy. Any minute now, some Longbeams are going to show up and pull us out of harm's way. Hell, we might get to see a hyperspace tow for ourselves."

Affie half smiled. "That'd be cool."

Leox patted her shoulder, but he was looking past her at the rest of the docking bay. People were, for the most part, working on their ships (the better to launch once the bay doors could finally be pried open) or huddled in groups, talking, killing time. Leox wasn't the only one who expected the Republic to take care of the situation pretty soon.

He just hoped the situation got taken care of before more people figured out the danger, because the one thing that could make this situation worse would be panic.

In the medical tower, Bell felt like order had been restored—more or less.

More, in that people had calmed down, everything and everyone had been put back in place, and no other explosions or disturbances seemed to be forthcoming. Less, in that they still had only emergency light to go by, communications remained down, and they continued to be cut off from the rest of the station, both top and bottom.

"We've done everything we can do," Bell said to Burryaga as they walked slowly through the ward. Ember trotted beside him, wagging her tail; as far as she was concerned, all was well. Bell wished he could be as easily reassured. "Is it crazy, to wish we still had more to do? Because at least then we'd be busy?"

Burryaga said it wasn't, because it was difficult to face a problem when there was no way to *fix* that problem. But, he added with a soft growl, the galaxy contained many problems that could not be easily fixed, and sometimes those had to be faced. So they would be wise to learn how to handle such moments.

"I know," Bell said. "I just wish we didn't have to learn it *today.*"

It wasn't much of a joke, but they were both tired, and nothing felt quite as good as letting the tension break. Burryaga chuckled; Bell snickered; Burryaga guffawed; and then they were both covering their mouths, trying not to disturb the patients by bursting out in laughter.

Bell's eyes were teary by the time they'd pulled themselves together. "So. How are we for supplies?"

Medical supplies were thin but would hold for another day or more, assuming no further injuries, Burryaga reported. Food rations, unfortunately, would only cover about one more meal for everyone in the tower.

"We shouldn't need more than that." Although the fact that they'd received no communication so far was worrisome, Bell felt certain Masters Stellan, Maru, and the rest would get on top of the situation soon. And hadn't the *Ataraxia* just arrived? That meant Avar Kriss was on it, too. Bell leaned down to scratch Ember behind her ears. "Don't worry, girl. I'll split my ration with you."

Burryaga said he'd counted Ember all along, and Bell smiled.

Orla Jareni wished violently that she'd brought the *Lightseeker* with her on this journey. Even though the docking bay doors would have remained as stubbornly closed to her ship as they did to everyone else's, she'd have liked to know that it was there waiting for her once this crisis had passed.

Not that she had any intention of abandoning any persons aboard Starlight Beacon. No, Orla's desire to leave had less to do with the current emergency than it did with the crisis before that—the one that both Stellan and Elzar seemed to have put out of their minds in the wake of the Nihil blast.

The ghostly husk left behind by Regald Coll wasn't something she could as easily forget.

Nor would the others be able to ignore it much longer, Orla suspected. As the immediate aftermath of the explosion settled, she was becoming more and more aware that the disturbance in the Force had not vanished. It remained present—more diffuse, somehow?—but she sensed that the source might be even closer than before.

What can that source be? Orla paced along the corridor outside Stellan Gios's office; motion sometimes helped her think. *What could have the power to disturb a Jedi's connection to the Force? And what could do* that *to poor Regald?* Although she had heard of the fates that had nearly befallen the Jedi twins Terec and Ceret, and the grotesque end of Loden

Greatstorm, she hadn't seen the results—and what had happened to Regald had been even more horrific than that.

She was no closer to those answers than she had ever been, but a new realization struck her then, one that stopped her in her tracks: Whatever the source of the disturbance was, it must have been brought to Starlight from the Nihil.

And if the Nihil had found a way to attack the Jedi by attacking the Force itself, they were a far more dangerous enemy than anybody from the Republic had ever guessed.

Chancey and Nan had found a small operational array that remained functional—sort of. It wasn't good for much beyond telling them how screwed they were.

"We can tap into their communications," Nan suggested. "Hear whether they've got rescue vessels coming that the Nihil could attack. Or piggyback a signal within one of their own, get word to the *Gaze Electric* that we need help."

"For one, neither Marchion Ro nor anyone else on his ship gives a damn that we need help." Chancey frowned at the latest scans coming up on the array's tiny screen. "For two, those zealots may be crazy, but they knew what they were doing when they went after Starlight's comms."

Nan felt a queasy flutter in her gut. "Are *all* the communications systems down?"

"None of them are down. However, all of them are currently broad-casting blank signal." At Nan's confused expression, Chancey elaborated, "Blank signal is made up of copied loops of data that give the illusion everything's fine, nothing's changed. So not only can Starlight not call the Republic for help, but if the Republic happens to check on them for any reason, the comms will also make it look like there's no problem here whatsoever. Granted, that won't stand up to any direct attempts at contact—but delaying communication by even a few hours

makes it a lot less likely that help from the Republic can reach this station in time."

As much as Nan hated counting on the Republic to do something,
she hated the knowledge that they weren't coming even more. "The
blockers on individual power sources mean none of the bay doors will
open, so even if we could steal a ship, we couldn't fly it out of here."
That left only one option. "Can you pull up the location of the station's
escape pods?"

Chancey nodded, but she hesitated. "The Nihil team sounded confident they'd trapped everybody on board. They wouldn't say that if
they hadn't dealt with the escape pods, too."

"They can't have had time to interfere with everything on this station, no matter what they say," Nan insisted.

"Hope not," Chancey said as she began searching for the escape
pods. "Because that's looking like our last chance—and everybody else
on this station is about to figure out the exact same thing."

Chapter 17

Those in the lower half of Starlight Beacon had begun congregating in and near the main docking bay. Republic officials, maintenance workers, even droids milled around in the corridors just outside the bay, sharing the few scraps of information they had. The overall mood remained calm. They had faith in the Republic; they expected help to arrive soon; this was a considerable mishap, and the station would require repair, but none of them suspected the situation could be worse than that.

Orla Jareni didn't know whether to pity them or envy them. What she wanted was to enlighten them. But Stellan still wouldn't hear of it.

"People have a right to know," Orla insisted. "In their place, I'd want the truth."

"I don't intend to deny them the truth forever," Stellan said. "Not even for very much longer. But the situation—and some of the individuals within it—it's volatile. Once we've been able to establish contact with the Republic, once we *have a plan*, then we can make the announcement. Koley Linn and those like him won't have a chance to make problems if we come to them with a solution already in hand."

Orla could see the wisdom in this. But she could see the flaws, too. "All this is predicated on the belief that we actually *can* contact the Republic in the near future. Right now we have absolutely no proof of that."

"It has to be possible," Stellan insisted. His eyes had taken on that shine they sometimes had—that absolute, utter faith—that made Orla understand exactly why the Council had chosen him as the public exemplar of all Jedi. "The Nihil are strong, and they're vicious. But they're not necessarily smart. They win by brute force and deceit. Any technological sabotage they've pulled? We'll be able to unravel it. We just have to find the right string to pull."

The Nihil have been smart enough to outwit us time and time again! Orla nearly snapped—but she held on to her temper. Barely. "I hope you're right, Stellan," she said. "The stakes are too high if you're wrong."

As she stalked off, the angry words she hadn't spoken boiled inside her. *You always need the Council's approval, don't you, Stellan? You don't know who you are without it.* It took all her self-control not to turn back, confront Stellan, lash out at him in order to argue the point further, more hotly, until . . .

I'm not myself, she realized.

Her temper had long been her most difficult companion, but she possessed more self-control than this—or at least she did when she was in communion with the Force.

But her connection to the Force was again disturbed. As was Stellan's, she'd wager. Whatever had gone wrong before hadn't conveniently departed when this crisis began. Instead it lay in wait, chipping away at every Jedi on board.

We have to do something, Orla thought. *No. I have to do something.*

Bell's first spark of hope came when a droid piped up: "Eiram medical cruiser approaching Starlight."

"They are?" Bell scrambled to his feet from his place on the floor at Master Indeera's bedside, waking Ember. Already Burryaga was lumbering closer. "You've been able to get through on comms?"

"Negative," the droid said. "But look." It pointed its metallic arm at the nearest viewport. Sure enough, the Eiram ship was out there, hovering close, apparently unsure what to do next.

Burryaga growled that if they weren't docking, that probably meant they *couldn't* dock.

"I hate to say it, but I agree," Bell said. "The docking bays must have been screwed up by the blast, too." Which he'd more or less guessed before this, but the confirmation was daunting.

Still, the medical cruiser was a potential source of help—the first they'd had—and they needed to make the most of the opportunity.

Bell turned to the droid. "Okay, so, station-wide communication is still a no-go—"

"Affirmative."

"—But is there some other way for us to send a signal at a shorter range. Say, just to the Eiram vessel?" Bell looked back and forth between the droid and Burryaga, hoping one of them would have the answer that was eluding him.

Burryaga thoughtfully growled that some droids had strong enough arrays—like, for instance, this LT-16 here.

"Why didn't you say so?" Bell asked the droid.

The LT cheerfully replied, "I'm afraid I'm designed to work in tandem with larger systems for communications. I lack the transmitter strength to send any signal that could cover a distance over one hundred meters."

"The Eiram ship's close, but there's no way it's going to get *that* close without docking—which, apparently, it can't do." Bell ran one hand through his hair, thinking fast. "But if we can boost the transmitter strength . . ."

Burryaga went to the nearest wall and peeled off a panel with a metallic clang that startled the patients, exposing circuits and wires. Bell smiled as he spotted a small power cell relay wedged in the works.

"Burry," he said, "you're brilliant."

Modestly Burryaga admitted this was true, but currently beside the point. With great care, he detached the power cell from its relay cable; a couple of the emergency lights dimmed, but it didn't get too much darker—which was a relief, because Bell very much needed to be able to see what he was doing.

"Could you open your maintenance panel?" he asked the LT droid.

"Affirmative." LT-16 seemed somewhat reluctant, as well he might be, since he was about to get hit with the droid equivalent of triple adrenaline. But he opened the maintenance panel and allowed Bell to attach the power cell. Once he was done, he opened the energy flow—and the droid's visor panel glowed brighter and brighter. Its metal body began to vibrate. "Oh my," it said.

"Can you transmit my voice?" Bell asked.

"Text only." LT-16 whirred louder. "Oh my oh my oh my."

"Then tell the Eiram cruiser that there's been an explosion, that we're contacting them from this tower, and we still need medical help, all right?" Bell said. Ember whimpered slightly at his side, and he stroked her neck as the droid continued buzzing and whirring.

His eyes met Burryaga's. If this didn't work—

"They read," the droid said. "They read and are conducting scans. Will report."

"We've made contact." Bell grinned up at Burryaga. This was only the first of many, many steps to bring everyone aboard the medical tower to safety—but at least they'd finally begun.

From the corner of his eye, Elzar Mann saw a flutter of white. He immediately left his post, where he was hotwiring yet more astromechs in the hope of gaining greater computational power, and hurried after. "Orla? Where are you going?"

She stopped at the sound of her name. "Am I in trouble for defying the edicts of Stellan Gios?"

Elzar gave her a look. "I'd be just about the last person in the galaxy to give you a problem for bending the rules. But we shouldn't be wandering off. The radiation levels from the base of the station are spiking—there's going to be even more instability soon."

"I realize that," Orla said, even as she shook her head no. "But that disturbance in the Force—it's still out there, Elzar. If anything, it's growing stronger. Do you truly not sense it at all?"

He had to admit, "If anything, I've held myself back from the Force even more than before. Which I know is the exact opposite of what a Jedi should do—"

"Not here," Orla said. "Not today. Trust your instincts, Elzar. They're steering you in the right direction."

For once, Elzar thought, but he remained quiet.

Orla continued, "I'm not myself. Stellan is—better, at least, than he was, but still not operating at top capacity, don't you agree? Probably every other Jedi aboard Starlight is suffering from the malign influence of . . . of whatever that is." Orla sighed heavily. "We must stop it. In order to stop it, we must identify it. In order to identify it, we first have to find the damn thing. Which is what I'm about to do."

Elzar gripped her arm, unwilling to let her go. "But—what happened to Regald, and even to Indeera—we'd all agreed, nobody else should pursue this until we have more support, and the crisis is over—"

"I recognize the risks," Orla said. "We're going to need all our strength to get through this crisis, and whatever this is has sapped away that strength. We can't save the station without taking it on." With the shadow of a smile, she added, "Don't worry. I can be surprisingly careful, when I want to be."

He wanted to stop her, but she was right. "If you're not back within the hour, I'm coming after you."

"I'd expect no less." With that, Orla gave him a surprisingly easy grin. "Watch your temper until I return to watch it for you." Then Elzar could only watch her go.

———

One of the few non-Jedi aboard Starlight who knew the depth of the danger they were in was, at that moment, passionately wishing she had no idea.

If I didn't know, then this would just be mildly irritating, Affie thought, walking numbly through the crowded docking bay back toward the *Vessel. I'd kill time playing sabacc with Geode and Leox. We'd be having fun, right up until a few minutes before—*

A shudder went through her as she imagined what it might be like for the station to descend into Eiram's atmosphere, gravity seizing them ever tighter into its grip until they were plummeting at maximum velocity straight down to—

"Hi there!" Pikka Adren seemed to appear from midair directly in Affie's path, though Affie was fairly sure that was only because she hadn't been paying attention. "Listen, thanks for your help with the . . . the couplings . . . Affie, are you okay?"

"Not particularly." Affie tried to smile. She must not have done a very good job, because Pikka's face fell. "It's just rough, you know? Being stuck here."

"Well, it's no fun." Pikka leaned in closer and whispered, "Is that Koley Linn guy giving you trouble? We've seen him following you around, watching your ship. Looks like he's up to no good."

Affie hadn't even noticed Koley Linn following her. *Great.* "We've had run-ins with him before. Usually he's more of a nuisance than a danger, but—he can be dangerous, so give him a wide berth if you can."

Pikka's eyes widened with outrage. "He *is* pestering you. Listen, if he ever approaches you and your crewmates aren't around, come and find us, or just give a shout. Joss and I will be there as fast as we can."

"You're good people," Affie said. The thought of the Adrens being trapped on this station struck her with new force. It was one thing to be frightened for yourself, another to be frightened for others. It was beginning to fully sink in that every single being on Starlight was in mortal danger. "Seriously. Thank you. I appreciate it. But—"

"But that's not what's bothering you." Pikka put one hand on her shoulder, an almost motherly gesture. Affie hadn't had any mothering in a long time. "Do you want to talk about it?"

As badly as Affie wished she didn't know the truth, she also didn't want to lie to anybody else. *Besides,* she told herself, *the more people who know, the more people who'll be working on a solution.*

"We should talk," she said to Pikka. "But first, you need to sit down."

"Oh my," the LT-16 droid chirped, still almost vibrating with borrowed power. "Oh my, oh my, scans incoming."

"Finally!" Bell connected the droid to the nearest screen; Burryaga bent over his shoulder to look, too. The surge of excitement they each felt dimmed, however, as the scans began to unfurl.

What they were seeing was barely recognizable as Starlight Beacon. The middle of the station had been rendered no more than a glowing blur. Normally scans would have shown Starlight lit up with power in every wall, on every level, but instead large sections of the station had gone all but completely dark. The medical tower wasn't the only area working solely under emergency lights. Worst of all, to Bell's eyes, was the darkness around the docking bays. Without those, it would be impossible to evacuate the patients, much less leave themselves.

"Trajectory readings coming in," LT-16 said. "Oh my."

I need to unhitch that thing from the extra power soon, Bell thought. The LT-16 was, for now, their one connection to anything outside of this tower; he didn't want to fry its circuits. "What do you mean, trajectory?"

The droid replied by bringing up a schematic on the screen, which showed Starlight Beacon, Eiram, and some extremely discouraging arrows. It was nothing the station's positional thrusters couldn't fix, but on the earlier scans, those thrusters had been dark and powerless. When the schematic's full meaning sank in, Bell looked up at Burryaga to see, on his face, just as much dismay as Bell felt himself.

According to the schematic, Starlight would enter the planet's atmosphere within three hours.

Bell willed himself to remain calm. "Tell the medical cruiser that we're looking at the new data and will get back to them shortly."

"Message delivered," LT-16 said, still trembling.

Slowly and deliberately, Bell unplugged the droid from the amplified power. It went still with a long whistle that could only be interpreted as relief. "What now?" Bell said to Burryaga. "What can we do that's even remotely constructive?"

Burryaga brought the schematic back on-screen. Was he going to show Bell something, or was he searching for any kind of answer? It didn't matter, because when Bell studied it this time, he spotted an opportunity.

Quickly he pointed to the outline of a nearby maintenance shaft. "This would normally be shut off in case of emergency, but it's open. Which means—"

Burryaga growled in triumph. They finally had a way to reach the rest of the station—and if that wasn't a solution, it was at least a place to begin.

Elzar Mann would have been greatly surprised to learn that his warnings to Orla had—in part—been heeded.

As much as Orla liked to think of herself as an exception to most rules, there was no reason to believe that she would be more aware of the danger, or able to defend against it, than Regald Coll and Indeera Stokes had been. Yes, something had to be done, but that didn't necessarily involve confrontation.

Instead she had decided to simply seal the area off.

We ought to have done that at the beginning, Orla thought. It seemed so obvious to her now, but it should have been obvious to all of them, immediately. This was yet more proof that whatever was aboard this station was affecting their judgment; fear clouded the thoughts as effectively as any Jedi mind trick, if not more.

And sealing off the area would probably contain whatever was causing the problem . . . but it wouldn't end those effects. The disturbance
in the Force would remain.

Still. Taking this action might not fix everything, but inaction
would fix nothing. Once the area was sealed, the source of this disrup-
tion in the Force couldn't get any closer; at least that represented some
kind of limit.

And once it's trapped, Orla thought—still not knowing what *it* might
be—*our options for dealing with it increase.*

As she approached the spot where Regald had fallen, very near the
cargo bay, the air took on a chill. Climate controls on this level appeared to be failing. Soon Orla could see her breath, visible as faint
gray puffs. As mundane as this sight was, it always made her smile; it
reminded her of a long-ago day when Yoda had taken her group of
younglings to the roof of the temple to play in one of the planet's rare
snowfalls.

Orla had toddled close to the side, and he had caught her with his
walking stick . . .

That was what had happened. She remembered it well. But in her
mind, the images had changed. Her memory was no longer her own.

*Toddling to the side, tripping over the side, crying out as she fell, then tumbling
forever and ever down through the gilded maze of Coruscant's buildings, inexora-
bly toward her death—*

Stop it, Orla told herself. There was no point in imagining how that
day might have gone if Yoda hadn't been careful.

As ever, when she was troubled by the stray morbid thought, Orla
called upon the Force to bolster and guide her. That still worked . . .
more or less.

Her steps took her into a long corridor marked only by a few random storage bins—some short, some tall. Orla peered into the distance at a taller stack of bins many meters ahead.

Above the stack were grayish-white puffs of breath—far too large to
represent the breath of anything humanoid. This was something else.

Doesn't mean it's the cause of the trouble, she told herself. *It could just be a lost Trandoshan, something like that.*

Still, terror spiked through her, threatening to hold her fast.

Orla forced herself to begin walking forward, but each step became more difficult than the last—as though she were trying to walk through frigid water that came up to her calves, then her thighs, then her chest. Instead of the weightlessness that came with being in water, though, she felt infinitely heavier.

Like the waves she'd commanded Elzar to face on Ledalau—but worse, darker, higher, stronger, threatening to toss her aside and crush her on the nearest rocks—

It knows I'm coming, she thought.

And then—without knowing where the knowledge came from—*It's hungry.*

Not for her flesh, Orla knew. For something much worse.

She tried to reach out with her feelings, but it was impossible. She couldn't remember how, couldn't regain her focus, couldn't think at all. Her eyes remained fixed on the far end of the corridor, and she saw motion—but without shape.

Or, rather, with a thousand shapes all at once, writhing and vanishing and reappearing and roiling ever closer, and she couldn't even run.

It's melting, she thought as the shapes poured downward all around her, falling and falling and falling without end. *The station is melting. Or the galaxy. Or—or—*

Nothing made sense to her any longer. She sensed that rather than knew it; Orla had slipped past the point when anything in her brain could still be considered thought. Instead she was at the mercy of the hallucinogenic twisting and turning that had swallowed her whole.

Orla's mind was no longer her own. The Force had gone silent, but it still existed. It *had* to exist.

Didn't it?

The Force would find her, it would find her, she wouldn't just vanish into the void, she wouldn't just become nothing—or no one—

Cold seized Orla, piercing her flesh, seemingly freezing her very bones. She wanted to hug herself against the brutal chill, but her arms no longer obeyed her commands. Her legs wouldn't move. Nor her head and neck—she wanted to look down and see what had gripped her, but she couldn't any longer.

Her face became even whiter. Then gray as ash. She fell onto the floor, unable to move, ever again.

The Force was silent, and nothing was left of Orla but fear.

Chapter 18

The mood in the docking bay was shifting, from "tense" to something much stranger and more ominous. Leox could think of plenty of reasons for that: Nobody liked being trapped, the Jedi weren't doing a great job of keeping everyone briefed, and the sensors aboard individual ships were no doubt being used to establish just how messed up Starlight Beacon really was.

But that was nothing compared with how things were going to change once more people figured out this station was going down.

Leox, Affie, and Geode all sat in the cockpit of the *Vessel,* in what he reckoned were varying degrees of numbness. Geode had shut down completely, saying nothing; Affie wasn't much better. Leox, who prided himself on taking a philosophical approach to life, was somewhat disappointed to discover that he couldn't face his own likely death with a greater sense of calm.

Wish I could at least say goodbye to my sister, he thought.

Then he said, "Communications."

Affie turned to him. "What?"

"Communications." Leox thought fast. "We're in a top-level emergency, which means emergency protocols are supposed to snap into place. Which would block communications by independent ships docked aboard Starlight."

"Which *do* block communications," Affie said, pointing at the red indicator light that told the tale.

"Maybe not." Leox turned to Geode. "Hey, run a scan on those frequencies. Show me what we've got."

Another screen began fluctuating with data, and a slow smile began to spread across Leox's face. "Sometimes the beneficence of the galaxy astounds me."

"They're *not* sending the emergency signal on all frequencies?" Affie was having trouble wrapping her mind around it. "Why not? If this isn't an emergency, what is? And if they aren't sending the emergency signal, then why do our sensors say our communications on the *Vessel* are blocked?"

"Whoever sabotaged this station went all-out." Leox said. "There's tricks within tricks, lies within lies."

Geode gave him the flat look that generally meant Leox needed to get to the point already.

"Okay, start with the basics," he explained. "Starlight Beacon's emergency signal is just like the one on a whole lot of space stations: It's made up of two almost entirely separate systems. There's one system that actually broadcasts for help on every available frequency, and another, separate system that handles more localized tasks—including, and most pertinent to our current situation, telling ships docked on the station that communications are blocked. If somebody wanted to sabotage this station—as somebody obviously very much did—an obvious first step would be blocking Starlight's ability to call for help. Which appears to be exactly what happened."

Affie's face lit up. "And an obvious second step would be separating those two emergency systems, so every ship on board would think their communications were blocked by Starlight. So those ships wouldn't call for help themselves, thinking they couldn't—but they actually could. I mean, we can!"

"That is precisely what I'm telling you." Leox took a moment to consider, then decided the last station they'd been docked at, the one orbiting Parlatal, was their best bet. "This is the *Vessel* calling, reporting an emergency at Starlight Beacon. Repeat, we have an emergency on Starlight Beacon, station crashing, multiple trapped ships aboard, possibility of catastrophic impact. Please confirm signal."

It took a few seconds for a reply, which came in a bored drawl. "*Vessel, this joke isn't funny.*"

"Nor is it a joke," Leox said. "This is for real."

"*Okay, sure,*" said Parlatal station control in much the same tone of voice. "*And you're telling us this instead of Starlight personnel—why, exactly?*"

There were plenty of reasons why, but little point in elaborating on them when a better solution was at hand. Leox turned to Affie. "Go find somebody in charge and get them over here pronto. Or to any other ship. We've gotta call for help while the help might still have a chance of getting here in time."

Stellan was equally relieved and chagrined. Relieved that he at last had a way of alerting the Republic of the danger Starlight was in; chagrined that he had simply accepted the signals instead of double-checking the communication frequencies for himself. How could he have had such an inexplicable blind spot?

"Doesn't seem so inexplicable to me," said Leox Gyasi as he led Stellan inside the *Vessel*. "You're Republic. You're *Jedi*. Where you guys come from, if you're told something doesn't work? Yeah, it probably doesn't work. Out here on the margins, we don't trust anything we haven't personally verified. We ask more questions. And when you ask more questions, you get more answers."

"That makes sense." Which it did, on one level. But Stellan couldn't absolve himself so easily. His blindness had cost the station valuable time—and could make the difference between salvation and destruction for all aboard.

Was it the disturbance in the Force that had muddled his thinking? Possibly so. However, another suspicion haunted Stellan far more. Orla Jareni had said he was too used to following the path the Jedi had set out for him; this was an accusation that it did not occur to him to deny. He trusted the Order as he trusted in the Force. He might disagree or argue with the Order sometimes, but he never questioned it.

Ask fewer questions, he thought, *get fewer answers.*

Perhaps he should meditate deeply on this question, even talk to Orla about that, when all this was over. But Stellan laid the matter aside for later, when they had the leisure to do so. His first priority was contacting the Council and the Republic, and thanks to the *Vessel*'s comm system, he was able to do so right away.

"We read you, Master Gios," came the voice of Master Rosason from the Coruscant Temple. "Rest assured that we are in full communication with the chancellor and other Republic officials." He could hear that for himself; the bustle of activity around Rosason had audibly increased during the few minutes of their conversation. "Help should be on its way to you within three hours."

"Three hours?" There *had* to be a hyperspace shortcut faster than that. "We may not have three hours!"

Master Rosason said, "Ships are coming as quickly as they can. But resources are spread thin—some Jedi went to help the worlds and stations affected by the scattered Nihil attacks. Republic vessels were routed to those worlds for protection and recovery efforts. We can't get through to the Jedi outpost on Banchii, but we've sent people to Chespea, to investigate the destruction of the temple there . . ."

Her voice trailed off, no doubt because she was having the same realization Stellan had just reached: "The Nihil attacks weren't scattered," he said, sitting up straighter. "They weren't random. Chespea and Banchii were targeted because it takes several hyperspace jumps to get from here to either planet. This wasn't a few stragglers lashing out in any direction—it was a *coordinated attack*."

Leox Gyasi, standing nearby, drew himself upright, registering the terrible news, too. His expression matched Rosason's tone as she answered, "They didn't detonate the device aboard Starlight until they knew both the Jedi and the Republic had scattered their forces."

"So much for Lourna Dee being the Eye of the Nihil." Had Stellan learned this a few days earlier, it would've felt like a point scored against Avar Kriss. The power play between them seemed so petty now, so small. Why had he let their disagreement become personal, on any level? It mattered so little compared with the real danger that had descended upon them both. "The Nihil's true leader is still out there, somewhere."

"So it would seem," Master Rosason said. "That must inform our efforts going forward, but at the moment it must remain a secondary concern. We can and must find a way to assist Starlight Beacon. Have hope, Stellan."

He still had hope. What he didn't have was a plan. But now that communication had been restored, there was a reason to believe they could prevent the Nihil plan from reaching its full, fatal conclusion.

Bell and Burryaga crept forward through the maintenance shaft. It was slow going, as they had next to no light, and the dimensions of the shaft had not been built with Wookiees in mind. The cramped space had been rendered even narrower, and more hazardous, thanks to various ruptured joists, bent plating, and other obstacles that bowed more and jutted farther in than the station's architects ever intended. Despite a few tight squeezes, however, the two apprentices managed to travel around some of the blocked areas and were currently approaching the main docking bay.

At least, Bell *hoped* they were. If they'd gotten mixed up and turned a wrong corner somewhere, they might be headed straight toward an irradiated zone.

A long whine echoed through the tube. "I know," Bell said, carefully stepping over a high joining. "This isn't the most fun I've had today, either."

Burryaga pointed out that he never thought he'd miss the medical tower but had become almost homesick for the place.

Bell recalled the moment they'd left it, gear strapped to their belts, unsure of where to go. "Stay with Master Indeera," he'd commanded Ember, and she had gone straight to Indeera's bed and sat down, keeping the vigil Bell had been forced to abandon. Leaving them behind had been hard—but at least he was finally on the verge of getting some real help.

Or dying. One or the other.

They came to a door and shared a quick glance before Burryaga pushed it open. Bell grinned as he saw the corridor that led to the quartermaster's office and, beyond that, to the docking bay. "We made it!"

Burryaga guffawed in triumph. Almost immediately, a familiar face appeared—Elzar Mann, sooty and disheveled but otherwise well. "Thank goodness you're both all right," he said, coming toward them. "We were guessing you were in the medical tower—it's undamaged?"

"Relatively speaking," Bell said. "But getting in and out is a challenge."

"Are you able to access the rest of the top half of the station from there?"

Bell's spirits sank. "No. Which means—what, Starlight's been split in two?"

"We're holding together so far, but I don't know for how much longer. The rest of the station is becoming more unstable by the minute, and is on a trajectory to strike Eiram in about three hours' time, perhaps slightly less," Elzar said. Though Bell had grasped as much, hearing the information still felt like a punch to the solar plexus. "Still, we've finally been able to make contact with the Republic. Help is on the way. We just have to hope it reaches us in time."

"Of course." Bell hadn't doubted for a second that help was already near. It turned out he'd been too optimistic. But he swallowed hard and kept going. "We're trying to find a way for the Eiram medical cruiser to dock with the station somehow, maybe even just through a standard air lock in the medical tower. Got any ideas?"

"Not one," Elzar said flatly. "As for our Force disturbance, Orla's looking into it—we can't face this challenge if we're not at our best."

Bell was about to ask where Orla was when a more cheerful voice called, "There you are!" Nib Assek came up to them, her arms wide, and Burryaga welcomed his Master's embrace, practically burying her tiny frame in his shaggy fur. "Goodness. I knew you were all right, wherever you were, but I didn't know when I'd ever see you again."

With a gruffle, Burryaga made it clear that his Master wouldn't be able to get rid of him that easily. Seeing Master and apprentice so joyfully reunited made Bell's heart ache, in the best way. Maybe it would be like that for him and Master Indeera when she woke—*if* she woke—

—but that would never happen with Loden Greatstorm, and deep inside, Bell was still hoping helplessly, endlessly, for a reunion that could never come—

Elzar brought Bell back to the here and now. "Tell you what—I'll think about that Eiram medical cruiser while you two help us get the situation under control here, all right?"

Burryaga nodded, and Bell fell into step behind them as they went, thinking, *They'll come up with answers. Or I will. We have three hours.*

A lot can happen in three hours.

What Elzar meant by "getting the situation under control" was calming down the many people trapped in the docking bay because the mood was darkening by the minute.

Koley Linn, true to form, wasn't helping.

"We're definitely crashing," he said to a terrified pair of Arcona huddled near their ship. "I overheard that girl from the *Vessel* telling the woman with the curly hair—that one." He pointed toward Pikka

Adren, who was at the moment helping her husband work on their ship. "They didn't think the rest of us deserved to know."

He'd given variations of this information to nearly everyone in the docking bay by this point. Koley's goals were twofold: First, to get people to trust him, because trust might come in very handy in the next short while.

Second, to get people to distrust the crew of the *Vessel,* for the exact same reason. Koley badly wanted to escape from Starlight Beacon, but getting out of here would be even sweeter if he could ensure that Leox Gyasi and his friends got left behind. Leox was a traitor and a snitch. He deserved whatever came to him.

If Koley Linn had known that his own behavior had motivated the decision not to inform the pilots aboard of the station's peril—he would only have shrugged. His mistakes were no one else's to criticize; other people's mistakes were opportunities upon which to capitalize, if possible.

The more Koley talked, the more the news spread.

The more the news spread, the more afraid people became.

Affie had already learned that being in a group intensified emotion. Many individually brave people could unify into an incredibly courageous whole. However, many frightened people could easily degenerate into a panicked mob.

She was pretty sure that she was seeing the mob forming before her eyes.

As she walked toward the Adrens' ship—they were all keeping on with repairs because that was the only constructive thing to do—Affie saw people staring at her. No, *glaring* at her. In the distance, others seemed to be accosting every single Republic crewmember or Jedi they could find, pointing fingers and raising voices that she could hear even over the low, troubled murmur of the crowd.

When Affie reached the Adrens, they were both tense and pale. "It's getting ugly in here," Pikka confided. "More people realize the danger we're in, and they seem to blame *us*."

"That doesn't make any sense," Affie said, though she knew "panic" and "sense" didn't have a lot to do with each other.

"It maybe does? Kind of? A little bit?" Pikka winced. "The docking bay doors—the ones currently trapping us inside—well, Joss and I helped install those after the Great Hyperspace Disaster. They were meant to be a safeguard against the Nihil. Instead the Nihil found a way to use them against us."

"That doesn't make this your fault," Affie insisted. "Let's just keep our heads down."

But it didn't look like they were going to get the chance. Nearby, a Neimoidian had become angry enough to accost a Republic crewer. "You're keeping us here against our will! You could open the doors, but you won't!"

The crewer tried to protest, but the Neimoidian's angry shout had sparked a flame. People began crowding around, shouting in various degrees of fear and fury:

"Just open the doors! Do whatever you have to!"

"Maybe the Nihil have taken control of the whole station. Maybe you're working with them!"

"We're sick and tired of this! Let us go or *face the consequences*!"

That last came from Koley Linn. Affie thought the situation couldn't get any worse until Koley pulled his blaster.

A nearby Wookie Jedi put out his broad arms, shielding the nearest people, but Koley aimed his weapon at the tall ceiling of the docking bay. He shouted, "We've had *enough*!"—and fired.

Which was how every visitor to the station discovered that the main docking bay on Starlight was magnetically sealed.

Affie dived for the floor as the blaster bolt ricocheted around at tremendous speed, bouncing off walls and floors until they might as well have been caught in a firefight. The Wookiee bellowed in protest, and the curse words of three dozen worlds were shouted and screamed. Beneath the Adrens' ship, Affie and Pikka shared a look; they both knew that bolt wasn't going to stop until it hit something besides a wall, which meant either a ship was going to get damaged or somebody was about to get killed.

The bolt zapped by them and—*szzzzzzzz.*

At the instant of that strange sizzling sound, the bolt stopped. Like everyone else, Affie looked up to see Geode standing there, burn mark in his midsection still smoking, completely undaunted. He'd thrown himself in front of the blasterfire and taken the hit. As she watched, he sloughed off the scorched dust and gravel and let it crumble to the floor.

"No time for pain," Joss Adren said, admiringly. "I had the wrong idea about you, man."

Geode modestly said nothing, even as others began to applaud. Pikka still seemed concerned, but she got to her feet. "Isn't he hurt?"

"He's fine." Affie grinned at her friend. "Vintians can choose to be magnetically sealed or not. For them it's as easy as holding their breath." She patted Geode on the back.

Koley Linn could've taken this opportunity to apologize for firing his blaster as a stunt, if he had been a completely different sort of person. Instead he said, "We're still trapped here, and the Jedi aren't helping."

"They're doing everything they can!" Affie put her hands on her hips. "Stellan Gios is in the *Vessel* right now, calling for assistance, which happens to be on the way. Until then, if we need help, we have to help ourselves—and each other. So why don't we try that for a change?"

The crowd was sufficiently sobered by the blasterfire incident to listen, at least for the moment. People began talking to one another in earnest. The Wookiee Jedi gave Geode a quick hug before hurrying away. Affie returned her attention to the Adrens and their ship, which was nearly fully spaceworthy again.

Koley Linn watched her go with narrowed eyes, determined to score a point against the crew of the *Vessel* before this was all through. They'd wrecked the Byne Guild; he didn't intend to let them wreck any more of his plans, ever again.

Besides, he always wanted someone else to blame.

Chapter 19

Starlight only has manual opening controls on the exterior of the station, Elzar Mann noted as he studied the schematics on display in Stellan's office. *The situation's too unstable to send anyone out in a vac suit yet. Maybe we can hook up independent power cells to the doors?*

Despite the best efforts of JJ-5145, the sheer number of astromechs currently networked together in the office crowded the space, and they'd been bleeping and screeching in various states of warning from the moment they'd been tied together. So it took Elzar a few moments to realize that the pitch of their alarm had risen. He looked up from the schematics to check their readouts.

Radiation levels were rising. The remaining links between the top and bottom halves of the station—already damaged and frayed, all but useless—were beginning to sever completely. Worst of all, the internal stability levels of the innermost structure of Starlight were plummeting.

Elzar had known from very shortly after the explosion that there was a risk this station could break in two. But Starlight Beacon had been created as the ultimate symbol of the Republic, designed by its greatest scientists, built by the fabled craftworkers of Riosa. He'd been so sure that it would withstand this damage, at least long enough for help to arrive. Never had he seriously contemplated it falling apart—

—until this moment.

The floor jolted out from under Bell Zettifar—or so it seemed to him as he stumbled sideways, catching himself against the wall. "What was that?" he asked, looking over at Burryaga.

His Wookiee friend had joined him near the entrance to the docking bay, where they were theoretically ensuring that nobody else pulled a blaster and created further problems. Burryaga, who'd had to grab a service ladder to remain upright, looked no more confident than Bell felt himself. With a whine, Burryaga admitted that he had no idea what had caused that jolt, but it couldn't be good.

"None of this is good," Bell said, "but I didn't think it could get *worse.*"

Burryaga replied that as long as you were alive to worry about it, the situation could always get worse. It was a good point, but not one Bell particularly wanted to dwell on at the moment.

He went to the nearest control panel, which had been more or less functional only a few minutes before. No readouts, no power. The emergency lights flickered.

Worst of all, however, was a deep shuddering vibration that passed through the station, rumbling beneath their feet.

Bell looked over at Burryaga. "We should probably report this to Master Stellan, right?"

Burryaga thought that Stellan probably already knew about the increasing instability in the station—but the situation was changing fast. It would be wise to get as much information as possible, while they still could.

Would it? Bell wasn't as sure. This struck him as the kind of situation where more information might prove paralyzing rather than helpful.

But if the worst-case scenario was coming to pass—Starlight fully falling apart, exposing them all to the quick bleak death of being spaced—Bell would want to be by Master Indeera's side when it happened. He would want to have Ember in his arms. That was worth facing whatever terrors the truth might hold.

He rested one hand against the wall, taking a breath as he steadied his emotion—then yanked his hand back. "Ow. That's warm. *Too* warm."

Burryaga reached toward the same section of wall, stopping just millimeters before coming into direct contact. He whined that something was overheating.

Mentally Bell reviewed the schematics of Starlight Beacon as best he knew them. While he was no engineer, he'd studied the details enough to feel reasonably sure of his conclusion. "Burry, I think the station's auxiliary power system—something's seriously wrong."

Stellan felt something like himself again, and not one moment too soon. Elzar, Bell, Burryaga, Nib, and JJ-5145 all ringed his desk, surrounded by astromechs, awaiting his orders—and, at last, Stellan was sure of the orders to give.

"Our first priority has to be stabilizing auxiliary power," he told them. "Without that, we don't have life support. We don't even have light. If we lose those things, any other repair or rescue efforts will become impossible. Our analyses suggest we can still shore it up to run another two to four hours."

"But the structural instability!" Elzar didn't seem to understand that there was nothing else to be done. "You're talking about hours from now, but Stellan—I'm not positive the station's going to last even that long."

"What should we do, then?" Stellan demanded. "Do you have a crew of engineers from a radiation-resistant species, ready to go in with thousands of tons of durasteel and build a new skeleton for this station?"

"—of course not, and yet—"

"We can only put our energies toward our absolute top priority." Stellan looked intently into Elzar's eyes, willing him to understand. "Nothing can be higher priority than keeping air in our lungs and light to work by." A handful of Republic techs and Jedi aboard were of species that did not rely on sight as their primary sense, but they were neither numerous nor specialized enough to perform the level of work necessary on their own—and even they needed to breathe. "There are dangers at work that we are powerless to prevent. If we allow them to distract us from the few tools we have to increase our chances of survival, then we waste those chances. Besides—honestly, if the station's breaking in two, I don't know that there's much we can do about it."

Finally the truth seemed to have sunk in. Elzar's face had paled. "You should know—the astromechs think we'll hit the breaking point within the half hour. Maybe within the next fifteen minutes."

"I imagine we'll recognize it when it comes," Stellan said drily.

"But the people up there—" Nib protested. "—and the *Ataraxia*'s docked on the top half of the station, so what happens to them?"

"That weight lies heavily on us all," Stellan said. "But we can do literally nothing for them. We have to trust that Maru and Avar and all the others are doing their best for everyone there. They're in good hands. So for now, we keep working. If we lose half of this station, we keep working. Unless and until the instant the walls come apart and we lose air, *we keep working.* Think about reinforcing the auxiliary life support. Don't think about anything else."

"Understood," Nib said, squaring her tiny shoulders.

Where's Orla? Stellan thought. She should have been back before now. Probably she'd run into one of the countless mini crises on board and was trying to handle it on her own, the way she generally did.

His line of thought was interrupted when Bell asked, "Our assignments?"

Making decisions had gotten a great deal easier for Stellan at exactly the right moment. "Nib, I'd like you to break down the auxiliary systems into smaller arrays—they're compartmentalized, so you should be able to do it. Then we can localize the problems and fix them. After that, see if you can locate Orla Jareni; we need her on this, too. Elzar, you need to retrieve as many individual power cells as you can to help fuel some of the smaller arrays; we can expect more localized power failures as the station grows more unstable. Burryaga, Bell, you'll lead the main repair team."

Elzar nodded, as did Burryaga. Bell looked concerned—the young man's lack of confidence since the death of one Master and injuring of another was holding him back, but that, too, was a matter to be dealt with another day. It was Nib who said, wearily, "I'd hoped it wouldn't come to this."

Stellan sighed. In this moment—focused on the problem at hand, thinking only of others—he felt something like himself again, for the first time in days. "This is what hope *is*. It isn't pretending that nothing will go wrong if only we try hard enough. It's looking squarely at all the obstacles in the way—knowing the limits of our own power, and the possibility of failure—and moving ahead anyway. That is how we must proceed. With hope."

Others were absorbing this information with sentiments very far removed from hope.

"This place is royally *kriffed,*" Chancey Yarrow said, crawling through a maintenance shaft on her belly, "and we are getting kriffed right along with it."

"Kriffing up Starlight is what Marchion Ro sent the team to do," Nan pointed out. She was a meter or so ahead of Chancey, periodically pausing to shine a glow rod and see if they were still headed in the right direction.

Chancey made a huffing sound that wasn't quite a laugh. "They did a great job."

"Never thought I'd wish for anyone of the Nihil to make some mistakes," Nan answered, "but here we are."

On one level, she was almost ashamed of that feeling. This was a great triumph for the Nihil—perhaps their greatest ever—and proof beyond any doubt of Marchion Ro's brilliance and power.

Yet the Nihil encouraged ruthlessness in the pursuit of one's goals, and what goal could be more vital than staying alive? Nan wasn't betraying her former self—the part of her that still, within, remained Nihil—by looking out for her own skin.

By this point she and Chancey had reached one of the lower levels, closer to the main docking bay. The goal was to get to the outer rim of the station before descending further, mostly because this level was almost certainly the most crowded, and therefore the one where they were most likely to get caught.

But the next jolt was so strong that it seemed to jar Nan's very bones. She accidentally bit down on her tongue hard enough to taste blood. An eerie rattle began to echo the length of the maintenance shaft.

Chancey said, "I don't think these tubes have the same atmospheric controls as the station at large. And I suspect air quality is about to become a *lot* bigger issue than it already is."

"What do you mean?"

"Notice how it's gotten a lot warmer as we crawl farther along? Something's overheating, and my guess is it's auxiliary life support. If that fails—it's lights out, first literally, then figuratively. That's our second-biggest problem."

Nan didn't like asking this: "Then what's our actual biggest problem?"

"Pretty sure the station's top and bottom halves are about to kiss each other goodbye. So how about we find some escape pods already?"

She thinks Starlight's going to fall apart, Nan thought. *Ro has literally torn the station in two.* For a second, despite the danger she herself was in, Nan felt a flash of pure pride in the might of the Nihil. They'd taken the symbol of the Republic and the Jedi and snapped it in half as easily as a twig.

Self-preservation kicked in again swiftly. "So first we need to get out of these shafts, even if we're still on a crowded level."

"As soon as possible," Chancey confirmed. "Who knows? The Jedi may not even notice us. They're about to have bigger problems to deal with."

Elzar saw the wisdom in Stellan's advice. Life support absolutely had to be their first priority. But as he hurried through the docking bay and saw the stranded people—most of them working together, finally, in small clusters around the most damaged ships—he couldn't help thinking about the danger they were in.

No, he wasn't about to stand up and shout, *The station is falling apart!* That would only incite riotous panic. To do so when he had no solution to offer would be unspeakably cruel.

But his impatience nagged at him, sparking against his temper, which was the last thing Elzar or anybody around him needed.

Still, there was one thing he could do that might help. Elzar dashed to the docking bay's speaker, which was still functional for projecting sound throughout the bay. He hit the controls to address them all: "This is Jedi Knight Elzar Mann. All persons are to return *immediately* to their vessels if those vessels are currently spaceworthy. If your neighbor's vessel is not spaceworthy, please allow aboard as many individuals as you can safely carry. All vessels are required to take on station personnel, whether Republic, Jedi, or civilian, in the quantity that they can safely transport. Repeat, *do this immediately.* Mann out."

Instantly people began to scatter for their ships, summoning their crewmates, gesturing for station workers to join them. Elzar felt one brief moment's relief. At least if the station disintegrated entirely, those within airtight spacecraft had some slim chance of survival.

Otherwise they had none.

This announcement came as Bell and Burryaga led a repair team toward an auxiliary system juncture, and it stopped them all in their tracks.

They exchanged glances, understanding the implications immediately. "The split's really happening," Bell said. "Are we going to be able to get the life support stabilized in time?"

Burryaga said he wasn't sure, but they had a chance: The auxiliary system could break down into component units, so the work they did here could sustain the lower part of the station, even if the upper part were to break away.

"Right. Let's get on it." Bell sounded more confident than he felt as he led Burryaga and the group of Republic techs onward.

A deep metallic groan sounded throughout the depths of the station, like the moan of an enormous dying animal. Bell's hair stood on end; so did Burryaga's, which was a fearsome sight to behold.

Burryaga shook his head no. After hearing that sound, Bell knew he was right. The moment of truth was coming, within mere minutes. As desperate as the life support situation might be, it would have to wait to see if any of them lived through the impending split.

He closed his eyes tightly and imagined Ember sitting next to Master Indeera. At least they were together. At least he hadn't left either of them alone.

"Should we grab breath masks?" Bell said. "Since the passengers are going to be aboard their own ships?"

Burryaga couldn't think of anything else useful to do, so they might as well, and he began leading the repair team toward the nearest storage crate that might have masks inside.

It was almost futile—a loss of atmospheric pressure would almost certainly lead to their being sucked out into the frigid vacuum of space. But staying alive meant returning to save his Master, and his charhound, so Bell was going to do it or die trying.

Leox hit the switches to pull up the *Vessel*'s ramp. Geode had already returned to his navigator's station, and Affie clambered back into her seat. "Harness up," Leox said. "We may be about to take a bumpy ride."

"It's not falling apart, is it?" Affie said, even though she was more than smart enough to put this together for herself. She knew. She just didn't want to believe it. "Starlight wouldn't just . . . disintegrate?"

Geode's silence spoke volumes. Affie slumped back in her seat, crushed by the realization.

"Look at the bright side," Leox said as he tightened his own harness. "We wanted those docking bay doors open, right?"

"That's *not funny*." Affie glared at him before turning to her own harness.

"Not meant to be. We might survive the debris cluster and reach open space. If not, well—at least we don't die alone."

Affie's face gentled. She swiveled her seat around so that she could touch Geode with one hand, Leox's arm with the other. Leox gave her the best smile he could. Thinking of Affie and Geode dying was harder than facing his own likely demise. That was love for you.

But he'd rather die with them than survive alone, so let fate bring what it may.

A storage area a few levels below the cargo bay—just beneath engineering—held a trove of independent power cells. Reaching them meant getting even closer to a heavily irradiated zone, which also happened to be the area where the station was most in danger of breaking apart. In other words, not the place most people would want to be at that particular time.

But if Starlight survived the impending breakup, the power cells could keep life support running, and therefore would make the difference between life and death. That made it Elzar Mann's job to collect as many as he possibly could.

Wearing a breath mask, he clambered up the ladder and exited on the correct level. Starlight Beacon had felt shaky down near the docking bay, but that had been nothing compared with this. Even the emergency lights were down to half power, if not less, so everything was rendered in shadow and gray. The floor, the walls, the stranded bits of debris that had been knocked loose—everything trembled, so strongly that Elzar had difficulty keeping his balance. For the first time in this crisis, he called upon the Force to help him; it answered, but only as a shadow of itself. A shiver traveled along his spine. Whatever was disturbing the Jedi's connections to the Force was stronger here . . .

He shut down. No more Force, no more Jedi powers. They could only harm him now, and the station had no time. He didn't require the Force to get his work done and get the hell out.

Steadying himself against one wall, Elzar made his way toward the storage area. The identi-lock, thank goodness, remained operational; when he pressed his hand against it, the door slid open instantly. Even better, a repulsor pallet had wisely been kept in one corner. Elzar powered it up and began loading power cells, as many as it would safely hold and a few more besides. Having something constructive to do gave him a greater sense of calm than he'd been able to muster since the initial blast. If they could just ride this part out, maybe they'd be okay.

Done. Moving as fast as he could, which wasn't that fast given the difficulty in keeping his balance, Elzar hauled the power cells to the murky maintenance shaft. Adjusting the repulsor pallet for horizontal took a second, but then he was able to lower it into the tube; it would power itself the rest of the way. Elzar climbed in after it, hustling down the ladder as fast as he could—

—and the ladder twisted, buckling directly beneath Elzar so that his feet slipped free. He clung tight with his hands until he could find his footing again. By this point the moaning of the tormented metal within the station core had become constant, higher-pitched, almost a howl. The vibrations grew stronger and stronger, until Elzar wasn't certain he'd even be able to hold on to the ladder any longer.

He let go. For one instant, he was in free fall—but then the anti-gravity of the repulsor pallet caught him, more or less, allowing him to settle upon it. Breathless, Elzar stared upward. The shaking was intensifying here, but even more the farther up it went.

Despite the disturbance, the Force remained with him enough that he knew the second he had to act. Elzar pushed the repulsor pallet down faster until they reached one of the rare control panels within the maintenance shaft. His palms were sweaty as he fiddled with the controls in the near dark, thinking, *go go go go go—*

A containment field shimmered into existence half a meter above him. Three seconds later, the station gave way.

The shrieking of metal pierced Elzar's eardrums. He covered the sides of his head with his hands as he stared upward in horror, watching the metal twist, tear, and disintegrate. Showers of sparks from ripped wiring lit up the maintenance shaft like flashes of lightning. Elzar could only watch as the hole grew wider and wider, then exploded outward, revealing the black starfield of space beyond.

By the Force, Elzar thought. He could see the shape of the upper half of the station, still fizzling with thousands upon thousands of sparking wires, shrinking in size as the two halves went separate ways, each toward its own fate. *Damn the Nihil. Damn them to every hell in every mythology of the galaxy!*

At least both individual halves' structures seemed to have held. The emergency lights remained on. There was still some chance for survival, embodied in the power cells Elzar needed to transport immediately.

Still, before he did so, Elzar took one last moment to look at the small vanishing image of the top half of the station, as it had been and never would be again. Starlight Beacon was no more.

Chapter 20

For Stellan, the split came in a terrible shuddering of the floors and walls of the quartermaster's office, the screeching alarms of networked astromechs, and a flickering of the lights. He braced himself against his desk, closing his eyes against the wave of fear and pain he felt reverberating from almost every living thing aboard the station—

—followed by something even worse: the knowledge that half of those lives were already growing more distant as the two parts of the station fell apart.

JJ-5145 had wobbled on his spherical base but was already righted. "It appears that the station has divided into halves," he said with totally incongruous cheer.

This undeniable truth was written in every graph, scan, and line of data that surrounded them, but it was an almost impossibly difficult thing to accept. Stellan forced himself to say the words: "Yes. Starlight has broken in two."

A small, shaky holo shone from one of the astromechs: their half of Starlight, as indicated by their scans. The bottom half of the station,

Stellan's half, had taken the medical tower with it in the divide. Otherwise, the top of Starlight Beacon was entirely blank. What was happening to Maru? To Avar? No way to know, at this point. Stellan had to let it go.

He stood in the quartermaster's office amid the nest of networked astromechs who had now fallen all but silent. The droids had less to report. Everything felt still and steady again—for the moment. Stellan wondered if the many people huddled in the docking bay thought something good had happened. Maybe they believed the worst was over. If so, he envied them.

"Recalculating organizational needs based on new station parameters," JJ-5145 said. "We have lost some critical ship functions, but other systems may operate more efficiently for a time, as they now only need to service half of the station. Of course, those systems will soon cease to operate entirely, but that would be hours from this point, or upon our crashing onto the planet's surface."

"That's not much of a bright side, Forfive." But the mention of the crash sparked another idea for Stellan: *Could breaking apart have altered either half's trajectory, preventing the crash? Maybe even* both *halves?*

It was a slim hope, and a short-lived one. Stellan tapped the screen that told the tale: two arcs, rather than just one, each headed toward Eiram's surface. The top section would actually hit the atmosphere first, and far too soon. This bottom section of the station would follow it shortly thereafter.

JJ-5145's idea about some station systems being able to work more efficiently appeared to have been borne out. Auxiliary life support, though still under great strain, had rebounded slightly. At least that bought them some repair time. But none of the other vaguely, temporarily improved functions helped them.

Except—

"The positional thrusters," Stellan said, new energy in his voice. "They couldn't be restored to full power, and anything less wouldn't have helped us. But now that the thrusters only have to lift half the station, rather than the whole, we could probably stay aloft indefinitely!"

If JJ-5145 felt smug about having been correct, the droid gave no sign. "I will begin the necessary repair calculations immediately!"

Stellan felt a moment of despair for those aboard the top half of the station—without thrusters, without any way of altering their course or their fate—but he pushed it aside. Fearing for them would change nothing; mourning for them, if and when it came, would be done in its due time. From this point on he had to concentrate only on those lives he could still save.

Nan and Chancey Yarrow remained crouched in a storage area at the far rim of Starlight's docking bay level. The terrible sound of ripping metal had ceased, as had the vibrations that had rattled Nan to the point of nausea. Still, it was hard to trust that this stage of the danger had passed.

Finally, however, Chancey got to her feet. "Okay. Sounds like Starlight Beacon lost a level, or split apart, or whatever it did, and we're still alive."

"They actually destroyed it." Nan felt something almost like reverence. Who could doubt Marchion Ro now?

Chancey, on the other hand, didn't seem interested in the big picture. "Right now things feel stable, but we can't assume that they are. My guess is this station, or what remains of it, only has so long left before it falls apart completely. Our best bet is to grab an escape pod, make our way to Eiram, and take it from there."

"We'll want weapons," Nan said. "Because we won't be the only ones trying for an escape pod."

"The big question is whether any pods are left. They might already have launched." Chancey considered for a second. "Maybe nobody else can reach the pods. We'll have to hope so, anyway. Otherwise, we're even more kriffed than I thought."

Nan felt a quiver of fear in her belly but suppressed it. She would bear witness to Marchion Ro's greatest triumph *and* live to tell the tale.

Although only scant minutes had passed since the station's breakup, people from the stranded ships in the main docking bay had already ventured out to ask what had happened and demand answers. Bell wished he had more to give them.

"Are we no longer headed for the planet's surface?" Joss Adren asked. "Did that maybe shift our trajectory?"

"How long can we remain airtight?" This was from a small Twi'lek with green skin and eyes enormous with fright. "How do we know it hasn't been compromised?"

Koley Linn demanded, "Why aren't you getting us out of here?"

Burryaga growled for everyone to stay calm. Either he expressed himself well, or people were naturally intimidated by enormous growling Wookiees, because the crowd settled somewhat.

However, Koley Linn was less subdued than most. "My question stands. All right, the escape pods aren't working. The docking bay doors aren't working. But you're *the Jedi.* You're supposed to be capable of working miracles, moving things with just your minds. So why don't you use the Force or whatever you call it to open the docking bay doors?"

It was a good question, one that unfortunately had a depressing answer. "Because it's not just a matter of opening the doors," Bell said. "Smaller containment fields are working, but we haven't been able to activate larger ones—like, docking-bay-sized ones. So we'd have to use the Force to hold in all the breathable air to keep from destabilizing the station, maybe even killing everyone else on board. Doing either of those things would be difficult, even for us. Doing both of them at the same time is impossible."

Maybe it wouldn't be, Bell thought, *if we had a chance to meditate. If we could get more than a handful of overworked Jedi Knights together at once. And if the disturbance in the Force on this station finally vanished. But that's not happening.*

"Some miracle workers you are," Koley said before stalking off. The others, however, seemed to hear him, and the crowd quieted—at least, for the moment.

As soon as Bell and Burryaga had been left alone for a second, they hurried together toward one of the still-functioning (mostly) terminals. Bell knew they shared the same concern. No doubt Stellan Gios would fill them in shortly, but they had to know what had become of the medical tower. Had it been ripped away in the breakup, too?

I can't lose another Master, Bell thought. *And Ember—Ember has to be so scared—*

Then the screen lit up with an image of what remained of Starlight Beacon. To virtually anyone else, this would have been a portrait of pure destruction. But Bell laughed out loud as Burryaga cheered.

"They're still with us!" Bell said. "We can still get to them."

Before long, he'd be reunited with his charhound—he'd help care for the helpless injured—and he *would* save Indeera Stokes.

Being a Jedi involved performing many tasks that were generally considered "heroic"—but Elzar had rarely felt like more of a hero than he did the moment he reentered the docking bay hauling a repulsor pallet of power cells. It wasn't just the stranded passengers who began whooping and cheering; Nib Assek looked like she might kiss him. "You made it," Nib said breathlessly. "We can stabilize auxiliary life support!"

"Maybe," Elzar said. He couldn't share in the good cheer—the Force alone knew what was happening to the top half of that station and everyone aboard it, including Avar Kriss—but he had something productive to do and needed to focus on that, rather than on the anger he felt about what the Nihil had done to Starlight. "What's our full status?"

This came in a briefing not five minutes later, in which Stellan, Elzar, and Nib gathered in the quartermaster's office to go over what data JJ-5145 and the astromechs had been able to collect. Elzar felt as though he were standing in a nest of wires as the small, crude holo-gram appeared in the center of the room.

"It appears that this is what remains of Starlight," Stellan said. The ragged lower half of the station, outlined in bluish light, rotated in midair before them all. "Our trajectory, although altered, still takes us within the pull of Eiram's gravity and onto their surface in just under two and a half hours. But we have a better chance of activating the positional thrusters now—not at full capacity, which has been ren-dered impossible, but at enough strength to keep this station from crashing for days or even weeks."

"Somebody will reach us by then," Nib said with total confidence. Elzar knew she had every reason for her faith, but the saboteur-imposed silence and isolation rattled him.

"You two, join in Bell and Burryaga's efforts with auxiliary life sup-port. Forfive and I will work on activating the positional thrusters, if we can." The droid swiveled about, apparently in pride at his important assignment. "Once those two things have been accomplished, I believe we can hold out until help arrives from the Republic."

"We have hope again," Elzar said, acknowledging Stellan with a nod. "But wait—where's Orla?"

"Putting out other fires. Figuratively, maybe literally." Nib was head-ing toward the door before Elzar was done speaking. "I'll bring her back as soon as possible."

Elzar didn't feel as confident about anyone's safety at this point. Could Orla have been lost in the station's breakup? Elzar felt a ragged jab of worry for his mentor.

But Stellan was correct. They had to optimize their best chances. For the moment, that meant stabilizing life support, and having faith. Besides, if anyone could take care of herself, it was Orla Jareni.

The chatter traveling through the docking bay (where gossip was rap-idly approaching hyperspace speeds) was that the situation was look-ing up thanks to more power cells. Affie didn't know how these people were getting "good news" from the fact that they were on a space station that had just *split in two.*

Thanks to her earlier experiences with the Jedi, in particular her friendship with Orla Jareni, Affie trusted them more than some did in this region of space. But as Leox had taught her, the best results came when you both trusted with an open heart and watched your own damn back.

So, while the others milled around discussing the new possibilities and the Jedi attended some super special meeting, Affie set out in search of escape pods.

The escape pods weren't working, the Jedi said. But the Jedi had also believed communications weren't working when they were. Was it such a stretch to wonder whether the escape pods might be in better shape than the computers claimed?

A spacefarer since her infancy, Affie knew how a variety of escape pods worked. There might be ways to rig even a sabotaged pod. She'd do whatever it took to make sure Leox got to safety.

But Geode wouldn't fit into an escape pod . . .

The doors on the pods are too small for anyone who can't bend or crouch, but maybe he could go out an air lock, Affie thought as she made her way through a darkened, debris-scattered corridor on the far outer rim of the docking bay level. *He'd be okay for a good long while. We'd just have to make sure somebody could pick him up.*

(Vintians rarely embraced space travel, preferring to remain settled on Vint. However, the few who took it up, like Geode, were in demand largely because of their extreme sturdiness, which fell on the outer edge of what biological life-forms were capable of. An hour or two in the void of space would do a Vintian no harm. What could harm them, however, was gravity. If Geode fell into Eiram's atmosphere and then to its surface, he would die as surely as any human who plummeted from such a height.)

As she considered the possibilities, Affie was almost completely lost in thought—but snapped back to the present when she heard voices coming from up ahead. *Hushed* voices, the words of those who didn't wish to be overheard.

She crouched close to the wall and crept forward, triply careful of the clutter strewn at her feet. Thanks to the curve in the corridor, it took a few minutes for her to get close enough to see the speakers: two human women, or a woman and a girl, who were shining a glow rod ahead of them but—luckily—not looking back.

The woman said, "If I remember the schematics right, there ought to be a few pods up ahead."

So, Affie wasn't the only one who wanted advance info about the escape pods. Well, fair was fair. She opened her mouth to call out to them—best to work as a team—when she heard the younger woman say, "I just hope they haven't been launched already."

I know that voice, Affie realized as her gut clenched. *That's Nan! That's one of the Nihil!*

It had been months since the *Vessel* had been stranded on the Amaxine station, but Affie would never forget the sense of shock and betrayal she'd felt upon learning that two of the others stranded there had been Nihil. Nan had been one of them: small as a child, apparently sweetly curious about the Republic, so eager to be friendly to all of them but especially to the Jedi. In other words, Nan had played them all expertly, which was reason enough not to forgive her.

But since Nan had apparently been one of the ones who helped blow up Starlight Beacon—

Affie paused, stooped to the floor, and carefully picked up a long metal pole that had fallen there. She didn't intend to let Nan walk away from this, and that meant she needed to be ready to fight.

In days to come, Stellan suspected, he'd be uncomfortable with the way he'd taken over the *Vessel* as a makeshift communications hub. For the moment, however, he remained focused on the call that had just come in.

"Master Gios, we grieve with you in this terrible time. We wish to be of what assistance we can." Queen Thandeka of Eiram, in holographic form, floated in the ship's cockpit. "However, Queen Dima and I must think of our planet and our people. Our strategists' analyses suggest that the top half of the station—having no positional thrusters—is likely to come in so fast that it will burn up on its descent through our atmosphere."

Maru, Stellan thought. *Avar.* The reality of it pierced him anew.

Queen Thandeka continued, "If you're able to reactivate the thrusters in time, your half of the station may survive. But if you cannot, it seems likely to strike one of our planet's largest cities, located on the coast of our northernmost continent. It looks as if . . . as if the only way to save that city's inhabitants is by shooting the station down."

"By blasting us to atoms, you mean." Stellan couldn't blame the woman. Any good leader would have to consider this option.

She looked stricken. "Please know that this is our last-ditch option. We would never—not if any other possibilities—"

"You need not apologize," he replied. "If it comes down to sacrificing the hundreds of lives on this half of the station to save many thousands on the planet's surface, then that is what you must do. But it won't come to that."

"Are you certain?" Queen Thandeka's hands were clasped in front of her, fidgety with worry.

Stellan shrugged. "Absolutely certain? No. But I know the Jedi aboard this station. I know what they're capable of. What *we're* capable of. We will not let Starlight fall. You have already trusted in us, Queen Thandeka. I must ask you to do so again. Trust us to save this station."

She hesitated—but only for a moment. Lifting her chin, she said, "Then we are proud to again put our faith in the Jedi."

Stellan only hoped the Jedi deserved her faith.

Chapter 21

Chancey Yarrow wondered which would fall to pieces first—the remainder of Starlight Beacon, or this girl Nan.

She still wants to believe in Marchion Ro so fiercely, Chancey thought as the two of them continued the search for escape pods. *She may have even convinced herself that she* does *believe.*

But a doubter could also see the doubt in others, even when they couldn't see it for themselves. Chancey had used the Nihil for her own purposes, the same way she was using the Grafs, but she hadn't needed to believe in some charismatic leader or any higher, greater purpose in a very long time. It was a much more efficient way to live, and a lot less disappointing.

Nan, on the other hand, still searched for validation in someone or something outside of herself. Chancey had hoped that setting out on her own would spark some independence within Nan, but that adulation she had for the Nihil still glowed brightly within the girl's heart.

Will we actually have to catch fire and burn up with this thing before she realizes Ro doesn't give a damn about anyone in his path? Chancey wondered. *If we don't find some escape pods soon, I guess I'll find out.*

Weirdly, Chancey found herself reminded of her daughter, Sylves-tri. In some ways, Nan and Sylvestri were very much alike—more, she suspected, than either one would ever care to admit. But they each had an idealistic streak that wouldn't serve them well in the long run. Prob-ably the reason she'd taken Nan on was so she could teach some young woman the things her own daughter had refused to learn. So Chancey could then figure out how to get through to Sylvestri, and they might be together again—the way she'd always intended, even if Sylvestri couldn't see that yet—

Well, the years would probably take care of Sylvestri's idealism. Nan's hero worship, too, assuming she had years left.

Chancey's glow rod beam swept back and forth across the curving corridor they followed, until finally light landed upon something in-teresting. "There." Chancey nudged Nan with an elbow.

"A pod!" Nan lit up. "All we have to do now is detonate the explosive launchers, and we're out of here!"

Chancey wasn't as sure. "Let's take a look."

Most escape pods worked exactly as Nan had suggested, outfitted with chemical explosives that would launch them clear of the mother ship or station, so that they could be used even when no power was available. They should have been able to get these going no matter what.

But they couldn't.

"Republic arrogance," Nan said, her face darkening into a scowl. "They thought nothing could go wrong on their station, so they didn't worry about having escape pods that work—"

"Or, just maybe, the same team that sabotaged the rest of this sta-tion took out the pods, too," Chancey pointed out. "Which of these possibilities seems more likely to you? At any rate, we'd better hope these things were sabotaged, since then maybe we can slice them."

Nan began rolling up the sleeves of her coverall. "I can slice any-thing."

Chancey, a scientist almost without peer, scarcely needed help with a little slicing, but there was no need to say so. Besides, who knew?

Maybe Nan's time with the Nihil had taught her exactly what she'd need to undo Nihil sabotage. There were two pods—one for each of them to work on—so as long as either of them could get the job done, they'd both survive . . .

There it was again. A faint shuffling sound behind them. Chancey hadn't been imagining it.

Her eyes met Nan's. They both realized they were no longer alone.

Auxiliary life support turned out to actually be easier to fix with the top of the station almost entirely gone—strange, but true. Bell had been able to "tie off" different areas of the bottom half of the station, separating the backup life support into separate, independent pods, each of which was stable enough to last for a while.

At least until we crash into the ground, he thought, dark humor he didn't speak aloud.

He kept at his task, setting duplicate and triplicate reinforcements on each system, even restoring a few intership communications systems, until Burryaga whined inquisitively.

"What's that?" Bell poked his head out of the lower compartment he was working in; Burryaga, naturally enough, had taken over with some junctures located higher up.

Burryaga pointed out that Master Nib had been gone for a while now.

"She's looking for Orla Jareni, right?" Once they'd completed the primary work on the auxiliary life support, Nib had undertaken her secondary task. "It could take a while, given the state of Starlight."

Although Burryaga realized this was reasonable, he also couldn't help remembering that they had lost Regald Coll, and nearly lost Indeera Stokes, to the strange disturbance in the Force—and while that disturbance had waxed and waned, particularly since the explosion, it had not vanished.

Bell pushed a heavy industrial toggle into place, then scooted back to look up at Burryaga's worried face. "We've done as much here as we're going to be able to do. Should we task some droids to look for Master Nib?"

They could, Burryaga gruffly conceded, but he wished to search for his Master himself.

That feeling was one Bell understood all too well. "Okay, we have a few minutes. Let's go."

Nib would have started her search in the last place Orla was known to be headed: in the area of the cargo bay, the same area that appeared to be the center of the disturbances in the Force. This was also the last place on Starlight that Bell wanted to visit. But Burryaga wouldn't rest until he'd found his Master safe and sound, and Bell wouldn't deny any other Padawan the kind of joyful reunion he had been denied with Loden Greatstorm.

When they approached the cargo bay, the corridors branched off in a dozen different directions. Burryaga suggested they split up to cover more ground.

"Oh no, we're not," Bell said. "Haven't you ever watched a fright holo? Splitting up is the worst thing we could do."

Burryaga pointed out that he'd been watching fright holos since long before Bell was born, and not one of them had ever borne much resemblance to real life.

It was a valid point. Within minutes, Bell was making his way along the left corridor alone. He walked as quickly as he could while still being careful to look for any hint of Orla's presence. In truth, he mostly wanted to return to the medical tower as soon as possible. Master Indeera needed him. Ember needed him.

And he needed them, too.

Bell stopped as his glow rod swept across an unfamiliar gray shape on the floor. The texture of it was peculiar—*cobwebby? Not many arachnids on a space station.* He took another few steps forward, trying to make out the details.

Are those . . . feet?

And then it hit him that this was the shape of a human body lying on its side in the fetal position. Its back was to him, but Bell had no doubt that he'd just found what remained of Orla Jareni.

Affie winced the moment her foot scraped against a fallen ceiling tile—it only made the smallest sound, but both of the women she was stalking heard it. They tensed and looked at each other, which was Affie's cue to take the initiative.

"Back it up," she said, striding forward with the metal rod in her hands, projecting the kind of confidence she imagined from official station security. "Step away from those pods."

They each stood, apparently obeying—but then recognition flickered in Nan's eyes. "I know you. You're no Jedi. You're that girl from the *Vessel*, Addie."

Affie nearly corrected her but caught herself. No point in giving saboteurs any more information than they already had. "And you're Nan, one of the Nihil."

"You can't sneer at the Nihil any longer," Nan retorted as she stepped forward. "Not after this."

"You were stupid enough to blow up a space station while you're *still on it*," Affie said. "So I'm not impressed."

The other woman acted as though none of this were any big deal. "Listen, Addie," she said, "I'm called Chancey, and I know only three things about you: your name, that you don't have any actual authority on this station, and that you're in as much danger as we are. Or did the Jedi give you special permission to take an escape pod?"

Make that two things, Affie thought. "I just came here to check the pods out, not to steal one."

"But you want one pretty badly, don't you?" Chancey's smile seemed almost natural. "Listen, you two were on opposite sides at one point. Don't let it blind you to the fact that you're on the same side now.

There's enough escape pods here for all of us, plus a couple friends of yours. Help us get these things ready to launch, call your buddies, and let's all get the hell off this thing."

For one second, it made so much sense. Affie sympathized with the Jedi and with everyone else on board, but getting the chance to save her friends . . .

If Geode would've fit into an escape pod, she might've gone for it.

Instead she said, "I'll never be on the same side as Nihil intruders." Affie raised her pole the instant Nan rushed her.

"We're not *intruders!*" Nan shouted, She'd nabbed some random bit of pipe from the floor and kept hacking at Affie, striking the pole so hard it jarred every bone in her arms. "We were brought here as prisoners!"

"I'm not sure—*unh*—" Affie shoved Nan backward as forcefully as she could, but it barely budged her. The girl knew how to fight. "Not sure that helps your case."

Nan's eyes blazed with a near-feverish light. "If the Jedi couldn't contain us—if they underestimated the Nihil—that's their problem."

Chancey cut in, shouting, "Nan!" Her voice was loud enough that Nan actually stopped for a second, long enough at least for Affie to catch her breath. Chancey continued, "This is a distraction, and a dangerous one. Let it go and *come with me.*"

Nan stared back at Affie for a long second. They'd barely known each other on the Amaxine station—Nan had spent more time cozying up to Reath Silas, in order to pump him for more information about the Jedi—but from this she'd managed to kindle a blaze of hatred.

We weren't enemies before, Affie thought, *but we always will be from here on.*

When Nan turned to run away with Chancey, there was no point in wasting time trying to chase them. Two on one equaled bad odds.

Better to get to the docking bay and let the Jedi know just who they were dealing with.

———

"Bell Zettifar to Master Stellan—"

"Good timing," Master Stellan said before Bell could get out another word. "Both on restoring a few comms—saw that on scans, good work—and on your call itself. One of the civilian pilots encountered two prisoners, potentially the Nihil saboteurs, approximately seventy meters from the cargo bay. We need a team to investigate the surrounding area. Forfive says you were working not far from there, right?"

"Yes, sir, I am, but . . . I've just found Orla Jareni. I mean, what's left of her."

A long pause followed, during which Burryaga appeared at the end of the corridor; he had heard Bell's shout moments before. Burryaga must have realized that Orla hadn't been located alive and well, but he whined in dismay at the sight of her lying at Bell's feet.

Finally Master Stellan said, his voice rough, "Is she in the—they're calling it the husked state?"

As hollow and dead as "husked" sounded, Bell thought the term didn't come close to the horror of the truth. The gray, papery, fragile shell before him was almost a mockery of the vibrant woman whose body this had once been. Worse, for Bell, it was a terrible reminder of the tragic end of Loden Greatstorm. "Yes," he said. "She's husked."

"By the Force. And we can't save her remains for study, even provide a pyre. Orla deserved a pyre." But Master Stellan, shaken as he apparently was, quickly refocused on the task at hand. "Put up some kind of protective field around Orla's—around Orla. I'm on my way to join you for the search. If the Nihil are behind what happened to Orla and Regald, too, it's more important than ever that we find the saboteurs and get some answers."

"Understood, sir." But Master Stellan had already cut the connection. Bell looked up at Burryaga as he began fumbling in his equipment belt for a portable containment field. "What has the power to do something like this?"

Burryaga said he didn't know, but they had a more immediate problem.

"I know, I know, the station's crashing—"

More immediate even than that, Burryaga pointed out: They still hadn't found his Master, Nib Assek.

"And this is the part of the station where she was headed." Realization sank within Bell like a stone. "Oh no."

Stellan Gios had never managed to get the last word with Orla Jareni, and now he never would.

Maybe you were right about me, Stellan thought. *I wish I'd had a chance to say that to you.* It felt so wrong that he'd never again be honored by her unflinching honesty. She had gone forth bravely, trying to solve one of the few problems on this station that had any chance of a permanent solution, and the cost had been her life.

Whatever's causing this disturbance in the Force, he decided as he strode toward the cargo bay, *must simply be avoided.* Investigation, so important before, was all but futile; they'd already lost two fine Jedi to the search, with no further answers. Whatever or whoever was interfering with the Jedi's connection to the Force was likely to perish along with this space station. *If I can save Starlight,* then *it will be time to get to the heart of that mystery.*

He thought again of Orla Jareni—first as the laughing young girl he'd met on Pamarthe all those years ago, then as she'd told him that he let himself be defined by the Order. How long ago had it been? A day? Three? More?

It seemed as though he should know that. But Stellan couldn't find the answer anywhere within his thoughts. The memory of Orla wavered, shimmered, like a heat mirage. Was sorrow for his lost comrade undermining his ability to think straight?

No. It was the disturbance in the Force that had again clouded his thoughts. Stellan remembered it so clearly, that terrible piercing coldness that seeped through every pore of his skin . . .

He shivered.

No. No, I'm not even close yet—not that close—and yet—

He was not remembering his nightmare. It was happening to him all over again.

Stellan grabbed his lightsaber and ignited it. Even though it seemed this foe was one that could not be fought, he intended to go down fighting. Whatever had killed Regald and Orla had found Stellan Gios at last.

Chapter 22

Color died first.

One moment Stellan could see, despite the dim emergency lighting, any number of colors: the red flare of warning lights on every electronic interface, the white-and-gold of his robes, the blue blade and quillons of his lightsaber. Then, as the chill took him, every shade and hue drained from existence, leaving him in a reality that seemed to be made of nothing but shadows.

It's coming, he thought, though he could not have said what, nor how he knew.

Fear came next, pure biological fear, the reflexes of the animal self that least obeyed Jedi teaching. His heart rate sped; his blood pressure intensified until his temples throbbed; sweat went clammy on his skin. If Stellan had actually been afraid of something specific—anything—he could have talked himself down from it.

But this was a different category of fear, settling around him like a cold wet cloak, heavy and sodden. It was tangible, even palpable. He could no more have exorcised it from his thoughts than he could have wished a sun from its sky.

It's coming, Stellan thought again. His vision had blurred; the corridor in which he stood went wavy and liquid, then darker, then lighter again. He *thought* he could see something moving toward him, but he wasn't certain. There was no being certain of anything any longer.

Could he get away? Stellan tried to run but couldn't. He could barely even walk. The floor pitched and swayed beneath his feet as though he were on the deck of a sailing ship during a storm. Nausea gripped him, and he had to gasp for breath. Almost flailing, he reached out for the wall to brace himself.

His hand made contact with a box. The box was called . . . something . . . something Stellan ought to remember . . .

It's coming it's coming it's coming

Stellan hit the switch on the box. Immediately, a full air lock blast shield slammed down, cutting off the corridor less than a meter from where he stood. The thickness of the metal seemed to provide some small comfort—enough for him to stagger away—but he knew this was not an escape.

It was only a delay.

Whatever was behind that wall would come for him again, and soon.

"Thanks for running off," Nan snapped as she and Chancey made their way down another level. The search for escape pods obviously had to be relocated, because the level they'd just left would be crawling with Jedi within seconds, assuming it wasn't already. "Nice to know you've got my back."

"Spare me," Chancey said, almost congenially. "You seem more interested in defending the Nihil than helping me, so who's the traitor here? If the fake outrage makes you feel better, have fun with that, but I've got bigger tip-yip to fry."

Nan would've liked to argue this point, but Chancey was right. They had become partners, but never allies. Chancey was her companion as a matter of expedience, no more. This, too, made the Nihil seem brighter in contrast—there, people shared a creed. They shared a leader. They made sacrifices together. It could be cutthroat, yes, but there was always something greater to consider, bigger plans at work.

They emerged onto the new level to find it deserted. Anyone this close to the docking bay, she reasoned, would have gone there already if they could. But they were still close enough to the bay that finding escape pods seemed likely.

She said as much to Chancey, who didn't seem impressed. "Fact is," she said, "any Nihil sabotage that affected the power cells we've found so far probably affects them all. I say we don't worry about the pods until we've found some individual power cells. Maybe one of those would juice up a pod enough to manually break free of Starlight."

"Makes sense." Nan still felt unsettled, even angry. Chancey was right that she wasn't the cause of her disquiet. It would be easy to say that she was scared—that the devastation she saw around her, with loose wiring hanging from walls and ceiling, with detritus scattered on the floor, with everything gone yellowish in dim emergency lighting, had her frightened for her life—but Nan refused to admit that. The Nihil had taught her bravery before almost anything else.

It's that girl Addie, she finally decided. *She gets to fly around the galaxy having fun and acting self-righteous, and she never stops to think about how hard the rest of us are working. She never dreams about having to suffer, or sacrifice. She doesn't know how good she has it.*

If Nan ever got the chance, she decided, she'd teach Addie Hollow a lesson or two.

On Eiram's surface, it had until recently been possible to be completely unaware that Starlight Beacon was even above the planet, much less having trouble. If you ignored news broadcasts and weren't monitoring the skies for any particular reason, Starlight had appeared as no more than one bright spot among thousands in the firmament.

However, by this point, the only thing you had to do to realize there was trouble was to live on the southeastern continent and to look up.

It was late at night there, but those few who were awake had begun to rouse others. They pointed up at a sky thick with stars—two of which were growing larger and brighter by the moment. One of them had begun to glow a terrible shade of red.

It's burning, said some.

It can't, said others. It's the symbol of the Republic. It's the best technology the whole galaxy has to offer. It can't have been taken down so easily.

But they said it less often as the sky brightened with the approaching dawn, and they could better see the blaze that was beginning to streak across the sky.

Queen Thandeka's announcement came just as the sun first crested the horizon: "*—advise all residents of the coastal cities to move inland as soon as possible. Do not panic. This move is a precaution only.*"

The people of Eiram were a steady lot. They did not panic. They did, however, get moving in a hurry. Before full light, speeders and slides of every variety had begun clogging the streets, packed with both individuals and possessions. One tiny two-person landspeeder wobbled along carrying four humans, a Bith, and three tooka-cats—only to be caught, along with all the other traffic, on the congested roads that led to safety but had begun moving nowhere.

The mood in the docking bay had not yet become panicked again, but the calm that had been established early was only temporary, and its time was running out.

So it seemed to Leox Gyasi, who was finishing soldering some damaged clamps within a Cerean pilot's air lock. He lifted up his goggles, ready to announce the job was done, but first took a moment to fully assess the situation surrounding him.

Those whose ships were repaired, or nearly so, were by and large acting productively: double-checking systems, assisting neighbors, prepping for the moment when they'd get a chance to take off. However, those whose ships were more severely damaged had gone ominously quiet. Some of them weren't even moving. They stared at the more fortunate around them with large eyes, sometimes filled with fear, but other times—more dangerously—with envy, or even anger.

Worst of all, near the back, a small huddled group of Sullustans was deep in conversation with none other than that ultimate waste of carbon, Koley Linn. Leox was much too far away to hear anything specifically being said, but he could tell from the body language of the Sullustans that they were getting more fearful and angry by the second. He could also tell from the smirk on Koley's face that he enjoyed winding them up.

Some individuals feed on conflict the way plants feed on light, Leox reminded himself. *It's as natural to them as photosynthesis to a leaf.*

However, Drengir aside, plants didn't often make a situation worse. Koley Linn almost always did. And this current situation was one that needed to improve, not devolve.

If the time came when Koley Linn needed to be shut up—Leox would take that duty on with a smile.

The low, deep groaning of metal within Starlight reminded Bell of the depths of an oceangoing ship, and of a long-ago mission with Loden Greatstorm. It felt good to remember his Master as he'd truly been—his face damp with sea spray, his lekku unfurled in the strong winds—not as the desiccated husk he had become.

Not the way Bell had just left Orla Jareni.

Burryaga howled for his Master, an eerie sound that echoed up and down the long corridor they traveled. No response from Nib Assek or from anyone else.

"Maybe she just can't hear us," Bell said.

This suggestion got all the response it deserved, which was none. Burryaga remained intent on the search.

In this section of the station, the vibrations from the explosion or separation must have been especially violent. Entire beams had fallen, as had enormous metal panels from walls and ceilings. Burryaga could scale the obstacles easily enough, but Bell had to work to keep up. He very nearly stumbled over one beam, and on the next plank of paneling he skidded backward and caught himself just before falling.

As he straightened, he caught a glimpse of something lying beneath the paneling—something pale, sort of dusty—

Bell went very still. Burryaga didn't notice at first, but after several more steps turned around and whined questioningly.

"I'm not sure what it is," Bell said, which was true no matter how strong his suspicions were. "But—I think we need to clear this area and see."

It can't be. It can't have happened again. Burryaga won't be able to bear it—

His tone of voice must have told Burryaga much, because the Wookiee had returned to his side in a mere instant. Burryaga lifted the panel and tossed it aside.

This revealed the next husk.

Nib Assek's outline was clearer than any of the others Bell had yet seen. She might have been carved of stone, so fine were the details of her face, her robe, even her long hair fallen free from its usual bun. But even the faint stirring of air within the corridor whisked away particles from her surface, and when Burryaga reached out—at the first touch, she disintegrated into dust and nothingness, gone forever.

Elzar Mann was never, ever buying a droid as a practical joke ever again.

"Perhaps you should try rerouting the polarity reflectors," JJ-5145 suggested as Elzar continued his work in the quartermaster's office, trying hard to get the positional thrusters back online. "This is often effective."

"You realize I tried that already," Elzar said. "Right?"

"Yes, but as you have attempted multiple methods without success, there are few further possibilities to suggest. Therefore you may wish to begin repeating methods you have tried before."

Elzar glanced up at the endlessly chipper droid. "Why would they work now when they didn't before?"

"They would not. But you would be less frustrated if you had more tasks to perform. It is well known that most sentients function less efficiently when frustrated."

"Let me get this straight, Forfive. You're suggesting that doing things I know *won't* work will refresh my mind so that I'm able to think of something that *will* work?"

The droid swiveled happily on his spherical base. "That is correct, Master Elzar."

This was absolutely ludicrous, of course, and Elzar intended to discuss other potential workarounds with Stellan as soon as he returned. Until, then, however—might as well try it JJ-5145's way. Elzar would make himself go through the motions of every single option one more time, just in case one of them—

"Wait." He stared down at the screen before him, where several red lights had just turned green, or at least a promising orange. "Wait. Did that just work? Have we got positional thrusters?"

The astromechs in the quartermaster's office all beeped and burbled cheerfully as a smile lit up his face. That bypass had worked . . . more or less. Elzar hadn't regained full control over the thrusters, but he'd ignited them at one-third power.

"Also, sometimes repeating a method provides a different result," JJ-5145 said, with a certain smugness he honestly deserved. "Within reason, of course."

"I doubt the power we've got is enough to keep the station from crashing into Eiram forever," Elzar said, "but that should work to keep us from burning up in the atmosphere, right?"

"Yes, we are no longer in imminent danger of death by incineration," JJ-5145 said happily. "It is now ninety-eight point one percent likely that we will instead die on impact with the planet's surface. This is excellent progress!"

Heady with hope, Elzar laughed out loud. At least he'd bought them valuable time. And if the positional thrusters could be activated to that level, then there was every reason to believe he might be able to bring them fully online.

At the moment, however, the only ways he could think of to do that involved interacting manually with the thruster mechanisms, which involved sending someone through unsurvivable radiation, stuff that would scramble even a droid . . .

Footsteps in the corridor just outside the quartermaster's office made Elzar turn away from his work with a grin. "Get ready," he said, "whoever you are, because I think you're about to—Stellan?"

Stellan Gios shuffled toward him, one hand on the wall as though to remind him where it was, or which way was up. His face was white with shock, his eyes dead and unseeing. Elzar clutched one of Stellan's arms to provide support; it seemed possible the man would collapse at any second.

"Elzar," Stellan said. His voice cracked with the effort of speaking. "It came after me."

". . . *what* came after you?"

"Whatever it is. It's hungry. It's *so hungry.* And it's not done with us—not even close—"

"The Drengir?" Which made no sense—if the Drengir had returned, they'd know—but the species' rampant appetite for sentient flesh couldn't help but come to mind.

"No. Worse. So—so much worse." Tears welled in Stellan's eyes.

"And I keep hearing it—*shrii ka rai, ka rai*—over and over—"

The station was on the brink of apocalypse and Stellan's mind was clouded with nursery rhymes? What had happened to him? What could've done this to a Jedi as strong and proud as Stellan Gios?

Swiftly, Elzar ushered him into the quartermaster's office, both to rest and to avoid his being seen by any of the stranded pilots. If they saw the head of Starlight Beacon at the point of collapse, the result would surely be panic.

The people out there thought their biggest problem was the impending crash of the station. Even moments before, Elzar would have agreed with them.

Now, however, he suspected the crash wasn't nearly as dangerous as whatever else stalked the corridors of this station.

Chapter 23

Bell didn't need any special empathy through the Force to understand the anguish Burryaga felt. He'd been there himself when Loden Greatstorm was lost.

Burryaga remained bent over the ashes that were the sole remains of Master Nib. His yowls of grief had quieted but not ended; he showed no signs of wanting to get up again.

Regald Coll. Orla Jareni. Now Nib Assek. Three Jedi, each one more powerful than a couple of apprentices. If this thing finds us, how long can we possibly hope to hold out against it?

At least Master Indeera had survived. If she recovered, she might be able to tell them what they were up against. But that wasn't the only reason Bell wanted to return to the medical tower. At this time more than ever before, he felt the need to protect her. He wanted the comfort of Ember's presence. He wanted to be back in a place with other people, where the problems he faced were known and tangible.

The corridor in which they stood remained forbiddingly murky. It seemed to Bell that in the distance—amid a patch of dust shaken loose from collapsing metalwork—there was some sort of a track, the footprint of something very large. Was that the attacker? Or was it just a member of some larger sentient species aboard?

All Bell knew was that investigating this thing got people killed. Yes, they needed the truth, but at this point, the priority had to be staying alive, saving others—and letting Masters Stellan and Elzar know what had happened here.

First he had to take care of his friend.

"Burryaga?" Bell's voice was soft. "We need to go report this."

Burryaga's plaintive sounds of grief stilled, but he didn't move. He stared down at the ashes that lay before them as if the intensity of his attention could somehow resurrect Nib Assek.

There was no describing the grief that came from losing a Master. Bell had carried it ever since Loden Greatstorm's initial abduction by the Nihil; then the pain had redoubled upon learning how he had failed his late Master, not searching for him, allowing him to be tortured grotesquely by the Nihil. His next Master, Indeera Stokes, at that moment lay in the medical tower, insensate, suspended between life and death. So he knew by heart the terrible shock and loss that no doubt nearly paralyzed Burryaga.

Yet for Burryaga's sake, Bell could glimpse the greater perspective that had so often eluded him with his own losses.

Bell knelt beside the Wookiee. "She'd want us to warn the others. She'd urge us not to grieve. She'd tell us to do our duty." *Just as Master Loden would. Just like Master Stokes will, if she wakes from this.*

Burryaga didn't react at first. Bell wondered if he'd been heard. But then Burryaga rose to his feet, ready at last to walk away from his Master.

No pill droids could be spared from the medical tower, plus traveling to and from it was difficult enough—and besides, Elzar figured that the kind of help Stellan needed wasn't the sort a pill droid could dispense.

The quartermaster's office had already been transformed into a makeshift Hub; next it had become another medbay, one dedicated to Force-related injuries. Elzar had found enough emergency blankets to fashion a bed for Stellan to rest upon, in the corner, almost entirely walled off by the still-bleeping astromechs.

Stellan had remained nearly inert throughout Elzar's preparations; the lone move he made to help himself was to walk to the bed rather than having to be carried. His eyes remained fixed on something that could no longer be seen.

He needs a temple healer, Elzar thought as he stood there, looking down at where Stellan lay. *Or even someone more empathetic—Avar would know what to do—*

At that moment he was startled by the sound of the doors sliding open. Elzar was relieved to see Burryaga and Bell Zettifar, but only for the second it took him to read the expressions on their faces. "Oh no," he said. "Not Orla, too?"

"And Nib Assek as well." Bell lowered his head.

Both of them, gone? "Did you see what happened?"

Burryaga shook his head. Bell added, "We'd split up, which I think was a mistake we shouldn't repeat."

Elzar felt queasy. Orla had been, for the past two months, the buoy he clung to in a turbulent ocean. That support had been forever lost. Stellan had so badly wanted control of this station, but at its moment of greatest crisis, he had been rendered incapable of taking on that responsibility.

It's up to me, Elzar thought.

It didn't matter if he'd failed recently. It didn't matter if he felt shaky, or uncertain, or alone. Duty called upon him to rise to this moment, and Elzar would be damned if he'd falter again.

If he had to step up to fill Stellan's shoes—if he had to reach out through the Force in ways he remained unsure of—then that was what Elzar intended to do.

"All right," he said, projecting a confidence he didn't feel. "Something's apparently attacking Force-users, or the Force itself. The two conclusions we can take from that? One, non-Force-users appear to be safe. None of them have reported feeling any problems at all. Two, we need to seal off the area the disturbance is originating from."

Burryaga whined inquisitively. Bell said, "How?"

"Blast shields. Air locks. We collapse tunnels if we have to. This is hardly the time to worry about causing more damage." Elzar ran one hand through his black hair. "And we put non-Force-users on it. They're not endangered in the same way."

"You mean we're telling them everything now?" Bell said.

"Do you disagree?" Elzar hadn't been a fan of Stellan's decision, but that didn't mean he didn't understand the reasons at work—or that Bell might not have something to say that would change his mind.

But Bell shook his head. "I think we should've done it long ago."

Elzar gave him an encouraging smile. "Good. Then you'll enjoy talking it through with the passengers. Besides, if they're working on sealing off that section of the station, we can dedicate our energies to getting the positional thrusters fully online."

"They're working again?" Bell brightened. It felt like forever since Elzar had been able to give someone good news. "The station's safe?"

"Not yet," Elzar said, "but our chances just got a whole lot better. Let's not waste them."

Having been brought up on a peaceable world, Leox Gyasi was only vaguely familiar with the idea of a draft—but he was pretty sure he was seeing one now.

"The threat to the Jedi aboard this station is a threat to the survival of this station," declared Elzar Mann. He stood on a small platform overlooking the docking bay, where the assembled crews had all gathered. "You need us to keep this station intact and in the air. That means we need you to seal off a large section of the station. Burryaga and Bell Zettifar will show you how."

Two Jedi apprentices nodded in acknowledgment. Leox felt a pang of loss—they'd been told of Orla Jareni's death, little though it meant to anyone else aboard beyond the crew of the *Vessel. Surely these two kids shouldn't be sent back into danger. Orla was tough. Anything that could take her out had to be formidable.*

But it seemed it didn't come after regular folks. Only Force-users. That meant Leox was probably safe. (Well, safe as it was possible to be on a malfunctioning chunk of a space station currently hurtling toward the ground.) And that made it his responsibility to do what he could.

"In Orla's name," he murmured under his breath, before stepping forward to be one of the first volunteers.

Even Koley Linn hadn't been able to believe Leox Gyasi stupid enough to sign up for some suicide mission just on the Jedi's say-so, but there he was, doing it. Unbelievable.

Then again, he'd been stupid enough to log hours correctly on that damn freighter, ruining it for anybody sane who wanted to profit for himself. So there was no telling what idiocy Gyasi would be up to next.

One man's foolishness could always be another man's opportunity, if he played his cards right. Koley prided himself on making the most out of every hand.

"You coming?"

He was startled back to the moment by the sight of a pretty woman with hair nearly as curly as his own, staring at him with her hands on her hips. Pikka Adren, he remembered. Too friendly with Gyasi for Koley's liking. "What's it to you?"

"Just thought, since you like talking about people so much, you might like to *do* something for a change," she retorted before heading off with the others. Obviously she had no idea that Koley Linn was making plans to do a good deal.

That damn rock will stay behind to watch the ship, he thought, staring sideways at the *Vessel. But it looks like most people in this bay are joining the team that's going to collapse something or cut something off or basically waste time doing anything that isn't getting the hell out of here.*

Would that meddlesome girl Leox traveled with go on the mission, too? Koley would have to wait and see. His strategy would depend on whether he'd need to deal with her.

Regardless, as long as even a few individuals remained behind, he'd have his chance to suggest a new plan.

Nearly forty people wound up volunteering for the team, which was more than Bell had dared hope for. Certainly it was a sufficient number to get a lot of work done, and quickly. He hoped it would be quick enough.

"All right," he called to the group, which was trooping along with him through the darkened corridors, their boots crunching against some of the smaller pieces of debris scattered there. Every being was bathed in dim yellowish emergency light, which gave them a look of unity they might not have had otherwise. "Every space station is designed to deal with potential hull breaches. In other words, there are dozens of air locks deep within the station—redundant until we activate them in case of emergency."

Pikka Adren muttered to the rangy blond pilot she stood next to— obviously not realizing she was loud enough to be overheard—"Does the poor kid think this is our first day in space?"

Bell felt grateful that the heat flushing his cheeks didn't show. *These people have been spacefaring longer than you've been alive! Do them the courtesy of remembering that.* "Obviously you're all familiar with that concept. What you might not know is how to activate an internal air lock without sensors reporting a hull breach."

"Let me guess," said the rangy pilot, whose name was something like Leox. "We trick the sensors."

"Normally that's how we'd do it," Bell agreed, "but our sensors are currently going haywire. We don't want to confuse them any more than we already have. There's a simple, manual release for the air locks. I'll demonstrate on one, let you all practice on a few more, and then I'm going to leave you to it. Sound good?"

The group seemed not only willing but also eager to get started.

This surprised Bell until he realized that almost all pilots were gearheads—there was nothing they loved more than learning a new trick with machinery.

Good, he thought. *If they're having fun with it, maybe they'll work even faster.* As far as he was concerned, they couldn't seal away this section quickly enough.

Burryaga boosted Bell onto his shoulders, which was *really* high up. It allowed Bell to reach a small octagonal dial at the ceiling, just by the nearly invisible grooves in the wall that hid internal air lock doors. He shined a light on it so the company could see. "If you turn this in a pattern—it's quick, once you've gotten the hang of it—the manual air lock kicks in. Everyone, come stand on this side of the doors and I'll demonstrate."

He did so. The doors slid shut with a reassuring clang, followed by the faint hiss of pressurization. Everyone nodded, and at the next lock, a Sullustan performed it successfully, albeit by using one of the service ladders instead of climbing atop Burryaga. After that, it was simple to divide everyone into teams and let them go their own ways.

"Okay, that leaves you two to take on the area nearest the cargo bay," Bell said, issuing the final set of orders. Then he stopped and thought about it. "Wait. Wait just a second."

Burryaga whined inquisitively—the first sign of curiosity, or any other positive emotion, he'd shown since Master Nib's death.

Bell said, "I'm not sure, but I think I've got a plan."

Ghirra Starros didn't second-guess her choices, as a rule. She liked to say, *The past is the only thing beyond your control. So don't look back. Look ahead.*

Forging an alliance with Marchion Ro—using her status as a senator to assist the Nihil, particularly in their strike against Starlight Beacon—that had been a tactical move, a way to put herself on both sides of the conflict in this new part of the Republic. Whoever won, Ghirra intended to stand with them on top. The relationship with Marchion wasn't her primary motivator, just a pleasurable side benefit.

Very, very pleasurable. But it didn't muddy her thought; Ghirra knew what their alliance was and wasn't. If anyone was likely to get carried away with emotion, no doubt it would be Marchion, not her.

Or so she believed, until they were together again on his ship.

Their reunion on the *Gaze Electric* had been every bit as passionate as Ghirra had fantasized it would be. Of course, nothing was perfect: Marchion's attention was unavoidably divided between her and the events on Starlight; she hadn't yet solidified her alibi for this period of time (she might not need one, but best to be careful); and his ship was oddly deserted, save for that omnipresent assistant of his, Thaya Ferr.

Did Thaya envy her? Ghirra wondered. (She liked it when people envied her.) It was easy to imagine this mousy, forgettable creature longing for the attention of such a powerful, dynamic leader. To envision her realizing, with despair, that she could never be the equal partner Marchion deserved, that her humdrum life, her utterly ordinary self, could never outshine a senator of the Republic who was skillfully playing both sides and enjoying it richly. These fantasies went so far as picturing Thaya looking down at her plain coverall in despair after seeing Ghirra's elegant traveling robe of sea-green Nubian silk.

But Thaya Ferr showed no hint of envy. Her respect for Marchion was evident, but she seemed entirely without any romantic longing for him. She swiftly attended to any of Ghirra's needs, when asked, then efficiently went back to completing Marchion's trivial busywork.

So there was no rivalry to be had there, and Ghirra had enough self-awareness to know that if she wanted one—if she needed someone to oppose her and be defeated—it was a hint that maybe she wasn't as sure about her path as she wanted to be. It is easier to believe in things when we are fighting for them.

Still, no changing the past. So Ghirra noted her internal disquiet and moved on.

After her arrival on board, and Marchion's enthusiastic greeting, Ghirra had badly needed to rest; it felt as though she hadn't slept in days. When she woke on the *Gaze Electric*, Ghirra's first thought was that it was still "night"—even though she'd rested for some hours. Most space stations and ships approximated a diurnal cycle through gradual brightening and dimming of the lights, but Marchion, it seemed, kept his ship in a perpetual night. It was cold, too—not frigid but on the cusp of human discomfort. Perhaps that was the temperature his species preferred.

Surely it was the only reason for the chill that trembled along her skin.

Ghirra strode through the corridors, head held high. Let everybody who passed her witness the pride she felt in aiding Marchion with his greatest task of all. Let them realize who stood alone as his greatest ally.

But nobody passed her.

Her boots sounded unnaturally loud against the metal floors as Ghirra made her way to the ship's bridge. The farther she walked, the more uneasy she became. Where was the crew?

Ghirra turned a corner, stopped short, and gasped.

Standing in front of her were two droids—but droids of no type she recognized. Their forms were humanoid, even more so than the average protocol droid, but their casings were peculiarly smooth, devoid of the usual ports and widgets. This was strange enough, but what unsettled Ghirra was the droids' heads: They were oval, shiny, brushed so fine that they seemed to reflect her own face back at her.

Normally a droid in a corridor was busy doing something, even if just moving from task to task. But these droids stood stock-still, like sentries, in front of the doors to the bridge.

Those doors slid open, and Ghirra startled. The bridge was filled with these uncanny, unsettling droids, all of them at the stations that had formerly been occupied by Nihil warriors. Yet sitting in his captain's chair, seemingly at ease, was Marchion Ro.

"Ah," he said. "Ghirra. You're awake at last." He held out a hand for her to join him, one Ghirra hurried to take.

"Marchion, these droids . . . what *are* they?"

"They," he said, "are the new crew of the *Gaze Electric.*"

Ghirra slowly looked around the bridge; the only other living being present was Thaya Ferr, tapping away at her console as though this were completely ordinary. It was anything but, as anyone else in the galaxy would've agreed.

Droids didn't pilot alone. There were functions that would never, ever be entirely turned over to them, no matter how much more efficient a droid might be, or how much more quickly they could perform calculations or maneuvers. Ghirra knew she felt this more strongly than some sentients did, but she also knew most would agree with the basic point. It was as though sentients had learned, at some point in their technological development, that droids had to be kept in their place or the consequences would be dire.

Droid pilots and crew were usually only used by criminals. By smugglers. By the very lowest of the low.

How could Marchion Ro stoop to this?

"How do you like my new crew?" he said. At times it was as though he could read her thoughts.

Ghirra knew better than to answer. "I've never seen droids like these before. Where—where did you get them?"

"There are certain merchants who deal in forbidden cargo, as I'm sure you're aware."

"Your crew—why did you—"

"No more backstabbing," Marchion said. "No more plots and intrigues in the back corridors. No more ambitious Tempest Runners bribing and coaxing my underlings for information, leading them into sedition. From this day, the *Gaze Electric* is wholly, completely, unalterably under my control alone."

Ghirra swallowed hard. "I see the wisdom of it," she said, which on one level was true. But the revulsion she felt as she witnessed droids in total control of a ship this large and powerful—it would take time for that to subside. She wasn't certain she wanted it to.

From the shadows in the back of the bridge came some movement, a shape unlike that of the eerie mirrored droids around them. The tension in Ghirra's chest eased slightly—at least one other sentient was aboard—but then the shape moved into the light, and her horror returned tenfold.

The droid that hovered toward her was massive, nearly two meters high, broad at the midsection, narrowing down to the repulsor base. Its surface was as unusual as its make; whatever it was didn't appear to be metal, but something almost crystalline, a pale ghostly blue that reminded Ghirra of the lips of the dying. Instead of the mock-face many human-sized droids had, or the reflective nothingness on the crew droids around her, this droid had two horizontal slits, both bright red, like gashes cut into flesh . . . or strikes of lightning scalding a stormy sky. Faint illumination shone from each slit. It was as though it could look at her, and snarl at her, even without motion and sound.

"It seems Carnine wishes to introduce himself." Marchion motioned the KA-R9 even closer. "I need more than crewmembers, you see. I need enforcers as well. And Carnine is excellent at his work."

Ghirra put one hand on Marchion's shoulder, hoping it would steady her. It did not. "I don't doubt it."

The positional thrusters remained at only one-third power. Elzar had been sure he'd find another workaround that would add to this, but he'd now exhausted every trick he knew without having any further effect. The Nihil saboteurs had known exactly what they were doing.

I wish Estala Maru had been in the lower half of the station when it broke, Elzar thought. *He'd know just how to get the thrusters going.*

It was remembering Maru that did it. Elzar felt a prickle of awareness at the edges of his consciousness—sensitive and wrong, like the split second between touching something hot and feeling the pain.

Then the pain hit, and it was unspeakably terrible. Anguish almost beyond imagining—

"The top half of the station," he gasped. "Do you feel it?"

Stellan barely seemed to know that Elzar had spoken; he showed no reaction, just lay there blank and numb.

Swiftly Elzar dashed into the docking bay—quieter, but not deserted—and toward the nearest ship he knew, which happened to be the *Vessel.* He jogged up the ramp, calling, "Can you get a visual on the top half of the station?"

His response came when he made his way into the cockpit to find Geode sitting there solemnly, a holo already picked up from satellites and projected into midair. Elzar sank into a seat, staring at the nightmare vision before him.

Starlight Beacon was burning.

The top half of the station arced through Eiram's atmosphere like a meteor, leaving behind a long trail of glowing, incinerating debris. By this point the structure was shaking so violently it could be seen even from this great distance, and there was no way it could hold together much longer.

Already parts of it were ablaze. Elzar could feel those people's pain almost as though it were his own—and those who were Jedi were even more vivid to him than the rest, stabbing into his awareness like red-hot knives.

The temple spire. The Hub. The beacon itself. They were all immolating.

Avar, please, please don't be there, he thought. They'd already had readings suggesting the *Ataraxia* had made its escape, but Elzar couldn't help worrying. It was wrong to wish for one person's survival more than any other's—a sign of "attachment"—but at the moment Elzar didn't give a damn.

Somewhere in the heart of all that pain, he sensed an incredible power of will—someone exerting the kind of effort through the Force that could very nearly drain one's own life. Elzar didn't know who it was, but he knew that this act of heroism was saving lives every second it could be sustained.

And then it snapped.

Starlight Beacon's upper half fell apart entirely in a burst of flame. The spire twisted violently as it turned into a plume of sparks and ash.

Then Elzar spotted the glowing egglike shape that had to have been the Hub—people in there were still alive as the fire consumed them. Amid it all, Starlight's beacon pulsed one last time, the light nearly lost in Eiram's dazzling sky—then fell dark forever.

The pain within the station intensified, fractured, died out. Tears of pain and even rage welled in Elzar's eyes as the last of it faded away.

No one had survived.

The *Vessel* was not the only ship that had been able to patch into Eiram's satellites. A small, select group of pilots watched aboard the *Ace of Staves.*

That was, most of them watched. Koley Linn stared at those he had invited, gauging their reactions. He'd have picked a different crew, if there had been more choice; those not working on shutting down the rest of the station tended to be very young, rather elderly, or in some way vulnerable, like the heavily pregnant Shistavanan who watched with her hand clasped over her muzzle.

Still, they could all fly a ship, and they could all shoot. That meant they could serve Koley's purpose.

Once the top half of the station had gone black and broken up and ceased to be interesting, he said, "The Jedi couldn't save that half. What makes them think this half will be any different?"

Nobody seemed able to reply. People got so shaken up about things, even when they happened to other people—Koley had never understood that.

He continued, "We can't sit here waiting for the Jedi to fix this. We can't sacrifice our lives in a futile effort to save people who are already doomed. All of us have spaceworthy ships. All we need is an open door—or a hole big enough to fly through." Koley grinned. "What say we open one up?"

Chapter 24

There was little enough good news at the moment, and Elzar Mann was grateful for any. This, however, would have given him some measure of joy at any time.

"Confirmed," said JJ-5145 as he wheeled through the web of cables that networked the astromechs in the quartermaster's office. "The *Ataraxia* launched clear of the destruction of the other half of the station. Presumably many individuals aboard the top half of the station evacuated with the ship."

Avar lives. Elzar had not sensed her death, which surely he would have. Still, the confirmation lit one spark of light in his dark mood.

JJ-5145 jerked his head side-to-side in apparent confusion. "These trajectories for the top half of the station do not compute. It ought to have fallen even faster than it did."

"No doubt the Jedi aboard used the Force to hold the station together as long as they could." Elzar had felt the titanic effort of it—the utterly heroic attempt—but had taken heed from its failure. He'd already considered trying something like that with this half of Starlight (all that remained of Starlight, now); it would mean fully reconnecting to the Force again in a way he hadn't since Ledalau, in a way he did not yet fully trust again, but if that was what it took, Elzar would do it. However, between the loss of so many Jedi and the eerie disturbance in the Force aboard, he suspected they'd have no better luck than those on the top half of the station.

The Force couldn't solve everything. Sometimes even the most powerful Jedi had to deal with the material world as they found it. This was one of those times.

Get the positional thrusters online, Elzar told himself, *and worry about the limitations of the Force later.*

But his next task promised to be harder than either.

Stellan Gios drifted in and out of—consciousness? Sleep? He couldn't tell the difference and no longer cared. His body demanded rest; his weary mind was all too ready to give it.

Then a hand shook his shoulder, forcing him to acknowledge the world beyond his skin. "Yes," he rasped. "Yes, I'm awake. I'm here."

"Stellan, it's Elzar." Elzar's tone was gentled, the way it might have been if he were speaking to a frightened child. "Do you understand me?"

"I understand." Stellan managed to push himself into a seated position so he could look Elzar in the eye. The dismay he saw there made Stellan wonder if he looked as bad as Indeera Stokes had; he felt only vaguely more conscious. "Are we—is the station—"

"Still falling, but the positional thrusters are back online at one-third power. If we can boost them even to two-thirds, we can remain aloft a long time, probably enough for help. And if we can boost them all the way, we can hang on indefinitely."

Stellan's mood brightened—not much, but more than he would've thought possible. "Excellent. How is the top half of the station faring?"

Elzar took a deep breath. "They tried using the Force to hold the station together, to slow its descent. But it didn't work."

"Then they need our assistance—"

"No," Elzar said. "Not that we have any assistance to give. But they're past that now. I'm sorry, Stellan—the top half of Starlight Beacon has been destroyed, along with all aboard."

Estala Maru. Every Republic staffer. Every civilian aboard. So many other Jedi—every single one of them, gone, and the Republic humbled—no, *humiliated* by the Nihil. It was a failure so complete, so appalling, that Stellan could scarcely comprehend it.

The symbol of the Jedi. Their public pride and joy. Under my watch, Starlight was destroyed.

Elzar cocked his head. "Stellan? Can you hear me?"

Of course Stellan could, but he couldn't react to it. Couldn't act at all. Whatever evil lurked aboard this station had stolen more than the Force. It had stolen his pride, his will, his tongue. If only it could steal his pain.

In the cockpit of the *Vessel,* Affie and Geode were thinking hard. Ever since their ship had become the makeshift communications center for the remainder of Starlight Beacon, Affie had felt a greater sense of responsibility for the station's welfare. It was easier to work saving others' lives than to sit and be frightened for her own.

"So, we've figured out how to reach Eiram's communications networks, and we can talk to the planet and any ships in our immediate vicinity," she mused out loud. "They're connecting our messages to Coruscant via relay, but we can't contact anyone else who might be farther away."

Geode, still deep in thought, said nothing. He knew when to let Affie talk through a problem.

"The biggest issue with that is, we can't issue a wider distress call. All those Republic ships diverted to deal with the earlier Nihil raids can only get here so quickly. But there must be other ships, civilian ships, that could and would arrive to help us, if they only knew we needed help."

A screen on the *Vessel*'s console shifted to a view of Eiram's full satellite network. It looked like any other small planet's: crisscrossing orbits, small silvery satellites bouncing signals around that world. It looked . . . vulnerable.

"Great thinking, Geode," Affie said. "It's an easy target, isn't it? If you have slice codes, which we do. And if we, let's say, 'commandeer' the planet's satellite network, we can send distress calls all over!"

Penalties for interfering with planetary comms systems were extremely severe. Most people, upon hearing Affie's suggestion, would immediately have said something about getting into trouble with Eiram for taking those steps, or about being censured or punished by the Jedi for overstepping their (nonexistent) authority. Geode didn't bother. He wasn't the kind of guy who wasted time asking for permission, not when lives were on the line.

Within moments, the satellite network began to glow various shades of orange as signals from the *Vessel* started giving them new instructions.

The distress call that went out was generic in form, one that spoke in computer-generated tones. (Affie had no problem taking the initiative to seize a whole planet's communications network, but she drew the line at literally speaking for the Republic.) It stated the situation in the driest, briefest possible terms. And yet it stunned all who heard it:

Starlight Beacon has fallen under Nihil attack. Hundreds are trapped aboard. The top half of the station is already destroyed; the bottom half requires immediate help. All ships capable of providing any assistance are asked to travel to the Eiram system immediately.

Many who heard this signal believed it to be a prank. Others thought it a propaganda move by the Nihil, one that exaggerated the actual damage.

However, those worlds and ships that had already witnessed what the Nihil could do—they believed. Within mere minutes, spacecraft had started preparing for the leap into hyperspace. Some planetary leaders and ruling councils went so far as to begin larger-scale relief efforts, readying flotillas and caravans of ships well equipped with medical supplies.

Word of the message did reach Coruscant itself, and it was swiftly passed on to Chancellor Lina Soh. She sat between Voru and Matari, reading the message transcript in increasing horror. Even through the last hours of suspense, she had always believed that the brilliant minds aboard Starlight Beacon would find answers. The Jedi always did. They would protect the station and those aboard it from the worst.

Instead—half of Starlight gone? The greatest of all the Great Works, ripped apart, burning up?

I should've called for a civilian effort before, Soh realized. She hadn't done so in part because it had seemed so impossible that Starlight Beacon could truly be falling. But she would amplify this call and add her own. That, at least, she could do. May the Force allow her to be in time!

Then she remembered the Jedi she had met—the ones who had helped save her boy at the ill-fated Republic fair—the ones who had celebrated with her, via holo, only days before. So many of them were already dead.

And Lina Soh, chancellor of the greatest Republic the galaxy had ever known, had been powerless to prevent it.

Among the first to hear the message were those who already knew the horror, even more fully than anyone on Starlight's bottom half. They were those few who had escaped from the top half before the fiery end.

Avar Kriss stood on Eiram's surface, soot and grit marring her clothes, blinking against the bright sunlight. The dark streaks that marked the incineration of the last fragments of the station—of Maru, and of so many others—were already dissipating into the atmosphere. As gruesome as they were to witness, Avar could hardly bear the fact that they were vanishing. Soon there would be no trace left of those people, that station, the hopes of the entire Republic.

Her mind went to Elzar, then to Stellan, both of whom she knew must be struggling valiantly to save the bottom half. She closed her eyes and willed them strength. *The Force will guide them. We will not lose the station entire.*

The message also reached those who weren't shocked by the information at all.

"Half of it already burning!" Marchion Ro stood at the center of the *Gaze Electric*'s bridge, his arms outstretched. Even here, he wore his helmet; his smiles were not for the likes of others to see. "Half of it doomed! The Republic, the mighty Jedi, forced to go begging for help from the galaxy at large! They are *nothing* compared with the might of the Nihil!"

"They are nothing compared with the Eye of the Nihil," said Ghirra breathily. Another plus of wearing the mask: Ghirra couldn't see him rolling his eyes.

"Ships are responding to Starlight's distress call," said Thaya Ferr from her station off to the side

"Small civilian craft, mostly. Nothing with the power to change the course of events."

Ro shrugged. "Let them try their best. They'll beg for help, they'll turn to Corellia, they'll look high and low for solutions. But we've blocked them at every turn. They won't be able to prevent the full, complete destruction of Starlight Beacon. After that, none will be able to deny that the Nihil are the true masters of the Outer Rim."

Ghirra Starros looked pale. Surely she had understood the implications of her actions? Was she fretting about that child of hers? If so, she should've thought about her offspring's fate before. Ro had little patience for those with such myopic perception, or such weak stomachs. KA-R9 hovered close by, as though the droid could cut the station to shreds himself. (Which, given the devastating vibroscalpels he was equipped with, was probably true.)

Meanwhile, Thaya Ferr gave Ro a cheerful nod, no more, before turning back to her tasks. Her smile, though bright, lacked the near-intoxicated zeal of most of his Nihil followers. She didn't believe in the dream he sold the rank and file . . . but she did Ro's bidding gladly anyway, and he'd begun to believe she always would. At any rate, she would never try to stab him in the back, which was more than he could say for anyone else among the Nihil elite.

Time, he decided, to bring Ferr more closely into his operations. A loyal assistant was worth ten cargo holds' worth of coaxium.

Ferr said, "What now, my lord?"

"When their desperate attempts at salvation have degenerated into chaos . . . when no one will know or care who has crowded into the system where Starlight will die . . . the *Gaze Electric* will join the throng." Ghirra's intel had confirmed, for Ro, that his ship remained utterly unknown to the Republic. They would be one spacecraft among many, no more. "And together, we will watch Starlight Beacon burn."

Every astromech aboard Starlight had been networked by this point; Elzar only hoped that what they lost in increased glitchiness would be made up for by greater computing power. He'd exhausted every option for activating the positional thrusters that didn't require him to go into the mechanical workings themselves—assuming they could even get through the surrounding areas to reach those workings, which were currently on fire. Hopefully the droids would come up with a third path, and soon.

In the meantime, Elzar had somebody to save.

He sat with Stellan in a quiet cargo hold in the back of the *Vessel.* (The quartermaster's office, chock-full of bleeping and blinking droids, no longer counted as "peaceful.") Stellan had taken Elzar's suggestion with troubling willingness, and his stare remained unfocused— a shadow of what his sharp gaze had so recently been.

"Without the Force," Stellan said, still gazing into a vague distance. "This is where you've been. Where I am now."

"You're not fully cut off from the Force." Elzar didn't know exactly what was plaguing the Jedi on Starlight Beacon, but he refused to believe they could be severed from the Force entirely. The Force was too vast for that; its power was eternal and universal, and would always be. "It's just more difficult for you to call upon right now."

"And this is what you chose for yourself, in order to turn away from darkness." Stellan's face creased in a small, sad smile. "I wouldn't have had the courage."

Elzar couldn't have heard that correctly. "What?"

"I've never asked myself who I would be without my control of the Force. Without the Jedi Order to structure and define my life."

"Because you're a great Jedi, one of the greatest of us all," Elzar said. "Stellan, surely you don't doubt that?"

Stellan shrugged, his gaze still looked far past Elzar, past this room. "Greatness can mean a lot of different things. I've always believed it meant—duty, honor, selflessness. But how can you be selfless if you've never defined yourself? Because I never have, Elzar. I've lived as the Jedi exemplar—poured myself into a mold shaped by others. Take away my ability to use the Force, and I find myself left as . . . as a man I hardly know."

Elzar put his hands on his friend's shoulders. "Stellan. You're hurting. This isn't the time to question your entire existence—"

"It's exactly the time." Stellan shook his head and, at last, met Elzar's eyes; the openness Elzar saw there, the vulnerability, was something the two of them had not shared since they were Padawans. Stellan had shielded himself so slowly, so gradually, that Elzar hadn't even noticed it.

My friend has returned to me, Elzar thought, *the one I didn't even realize was gone.*

Stellan continued, "You've had the strength to walk your own path. Even if that path was crooked at times, it was yours and yours alone. You and Avar, you've always known who you were. You've never let the Order do your thinking for you. You always shone . . . that little bit brighter."

"You're hardly a pushover," Elzar protested. "You've stood up to the Council before."

"But it's different, and you know it, don't you?" Stellan glanced down for a moment before continuing, "You've always known I was wary of the—the intimacy between you and Avar."

This was the last topic Elzar had dreamed would come up, and very nearly the last he wanted to mention at the moment. "I—uhm—"

"You thought it was because I obeyed the rules, but that wasn't the whole truth. Really, I was jealous, that the two of you had a connection I didn't share." Stellan cocked his head, studying Elzar as though they hadn't seen each other in a long while. "A constellation of three stars, but two were much closer together."

Elzar felt his throat tighten. "But you were our polestar. Our guide. Don't you know that?"

Stellan took a deep breath. "I'm glad you think so."

They needed to get to work; as important as this conversation was, and as much as they needed to return to it, this was not the day. "I don't know what injury the Force has suffered," Elzar began, "or whether it's our ability to connect to the Force that's devastating us so. Regardless, you've taken the brunt of it. Orla taught me a meditation technique—a kind of self-healing. It might help. Will you try this with me?"

Stellan nodded. It seemed that he trusted Elzar completely.

Now Elzar had to trust himself.

"Close your eyes," Elzar said as he did the same. In his mind's eye, he pictured Orla Jareni standing on the Ledalau beach. Behind her rolled the eternal tides.

You see the Force as an ocean, Orla had said on their first day of the meditation retreat. *But you've fallen into the habit of believing that the ocean is something you can control. That's the first step toward thinking of the Force merely as a tool to be wielded however you wish. No ocean obeys any living creature—high time you remembered that.*

Elzar couldn't re-create that experience for Stellan, nor did he think it was what was needed. Stellan knew too much about powerlessness, at the moment. What he could do was find that serenity within his own mind, and share it as fully as possible.

He would not call upon the Force from any external source—only from what he found inside himself.

It took courage for Stellan to brace himself outside of the Force's guidance. It also took courage for Elzar to fully return to the Force, to believe in his ability to wield it fully once again.

Before long, he imagined he could hear the ocean. Elzar thought perhaps Stellan heard it, too.

Leox Gyasi had had more fun in his life than he was having on this particular day, but if he couldn't enjoy riding on a Wookiee's shoulders just a little bit . . . why, then, he might as well be dead. So he let himself grin as he prepped one more air lock, then shouted, "Get clear!"

His small team got clear, Leox triggered the mechanism, and SHOOMP—the air lock shut.

"That's got us about seventy-five percent of the way," he said, remaining on Burryaga's shoulders. "You about ready to try this cockamamie scheme of yours?"

Young Bell Zettifar managed to smile. "It's not cocka—whatever you said. But yeah. It's almost time. We just have to make sure the routes in and out are clear, that they'll work like they're supposed to."

Leox sure as hell hoped they would—because then at least a few people had a chance to survive.

Once Stellan was resting again, Elzar studied his sleeping countenance for a few moments. Although Stellan's energy remained low, he seemed to be a little more like himself. Maybe, when he woke, he'd be back to himself enough to help Elzar with some of the countless decisions that had to be made.

No. Elzar could make those decisions on his own; what he truly wanted was some basic sense of calm. To find something pure and good that would cast out the anger within. To know that someone else was with him in this struggle.

Only one person in the galaxy ever made Elzar feel that way.

Avar, he thought, closing his eyes again as he called her telepathically. *Avar, please, be with me. Be with me here for just one moment.*

It wasn't as though she could hear the words inside his head, much less reply. But there were other forms of communication through the Force, other ways of understanding and being understood.

Elzar filled his mind with memories of her: the sound of her voice, the way she dueled in the lightsaber ring, even the scent of her skin. The more real she became in his mind, the more chance he had of—

And then he heard it.

Just for a moment. Just a brief sense of melody. But still.

It was the song of the Force as Avar Kriss heard it—and for this instant, she had gifted it to him.

The shock and delight of it broke his concentration. Elzar was back in the present, as far away from Avar Kriss as ever. Yet he was stronger for that moment of communion.

He hoped that Avar, whatever she was doing, whatever troubles she faced, had shared a moment when she heard the waves on the sea.

Both far away and very near, Avar levitated with her arms outstretched, calling upon the song of the Force to sustain them all and give them strength as every Jedi in or near Starlight Beacon fought to save the station and all those aboard. Every individual was a note in the greatest, most meaningful chord she had ever known.

Between those notes lay another sound, so subtle she barely recognized it: the sound of the waves, the roaring of the sea.

Chapter 25

Bell Zettifar led the group into the station bay reserved for cargo only. As a general rule, cargo ships were left unattended, save by droids; pilots spent almost all of their time on the rest of the station. Some of these pilots were part of the band to seal off this section; others, who had been enjoying the hospitality offered on the top half of Starlight Beacon, had already been killed.

"This is my thought," Bell said, ostensibly to Burryaga but really to everyone within earshot. "We open up *these* bay doors and let all the cargo ships escape, along with as many passengers as they can carry. That doesn't save everyone, and it means a lot of people lose the spacecraft left behind in the main docking bay—but we still save a lot of lives."

The pilot named Leox looked skeptical. "How come you can open up these doors but not the other ones, in the main docking bay?"

"Because, in the main docking bay, it's more complex—we'd have to hold in the atmosphere, handle pressurization, keep the ships that can't go into space right now in place, close the doors again in time—basically, it's so complicated as to be impossible, even for experienced

Force-users." It made Bell's head hurt just thinking about it. "Here, though—all of these ships remain spaceworthy. We've already sealed off this area from most of the rest of the station. Meaning, all we have to do here is get the doors open. It'll be explosive depressurization. People will have to be braced for it. But then they can leave."

Burryaga gruffled encouragingly. Leox raised an eyebrow that seemed to say, *Good thinking, kid.* The others huddled nearby began eagerly discussing how it might work, what different ships might be able to carry, and so on. It was Pikka Adren who asked, "But how do we decide who stays and who goes?"

If handled badly, Bell could see that this could turn into a flashpoint for conflict, but he thought he knew how it ought to be done. "Obviously, the pilots and crews of these ships get to be aboard them. Each ship will then be filled to capacity with people, that capacity to be determined by droids. Once we know how many people there are spots for, we distribute slots at random."

An Ardennian near the back, one of the cargo pilots, appeared wary, folding all four of her arms across her chest. "Does that mean we have to dump cargo?"

"Almost certainly," Bell said. "This is an extreme emergency. Surely you—and your employers—will see that." The Ardennian nodded, already resigned to the loss.

Pikka spoke up again, asking a question Bell hadn't anticipated: "What if we don't want to abandon our ships? For some of us, our ships are our lives." Several people murmured in agreement.

This seemed suicidal to Bell, but these people knew the facts, and could make their own decisions. "Nobody would be forced to go."

Burryaga growled inquisitively; he'd taken up a datapad and was reviewing a cargo manifest of everything in the bay. Two ships were carrying living creatures—would they have to be spaced like other cargo? Or should they be saved?

"What living creatures?" Bell first thought of charhounds like Ember; the idea of spacing even one of them made his heart ache.

But then Burryaga explained that, improbably, both ships were carrying rathtars.

"*Rathtars?*" Bell wouldn't have expected anybody to be fool enough to haul those things around, much less two different pilots within the same week. To judge by the laughter and disbelieving stares of the group at large, he wasn't the only one.

Pikka shook her head. "Yeah, we can just space those."

Burryaga, however, had become unexpectedly grave. He said that the last time he'd seen Orla Jareni, she had mentioned the rathtars. She found the label suspicious, probably false—designed to keep anybody from looking inside those cargo holds to see what was really inside.

They had to hurry—Bell felt that urgency in his every cell—but what if this had been the Nihil tactic used to sabotage the station? What if another act of sabotage still lay ahead?

"Okay," he said. "We check those cargo holds. Then we finish prep. Within half an hour we need to blow this thing."

"What did they do to these things?" Nan struck the entry ring for the latest set of escape pods so hard the metal bit into her hand. The pain hardly mattered. "I've gone through every type of slice I've ever heard of, and invented a few new ones. And the pods still won't launch!"

"That Nihil group knew what they were doing," pointed out Chancey Yarrow, "and since we joined forces with them and helped manufacture this particular crisis, we've only got ourselves to blame."

Nan felt like there was more than enough blame to go around, but discussing this with Chancey only made her angrier, so she dropped it.

They'd traveled down far enough to put themselves in radiation danger; this was the lowest deck, their last attempt. But none of the escape pods were wired any differently. This would have mattered less if Nan and Chancey had been able to find any power cells to manually activate a pod or two. No such luck.

"We're going to have to go back to the docking bay level," Chancey said.

"We go up there, we get caught." Nan could just imagine what glee Addie had taken in reporting them to the Jedi. She'd been expecting a capture team to pounce on them at any second.

Chancey shook her head. "I'm not so sure. Yeah, any other time, they'd be scouring the station high and low for any sign of us. But they've got bigger problems right now."

This made some sense, Nan supposed. Still, going up to the docking bay level and assuming nobody knew to look out for them . . . they were pushing their luck.

Then again, if they were captured, and the Jedi found some way to escape Starlight Beacon, the Republic would probably save its prisoners, too. They were just idiotic enough for that.

Nan preferred to leave on her own terms, but Chancey was right. "Okay. Let's give it a try."

The first rathtar transport—so-called—that Leox and the rest came upon sat there with its cargo hold door wide open, and the hold itself completely empty.

"A break-in," guessed Bell Zettifar.

Leox shook his head; he'd led the kind of life that taught you what robberies looked like or didn't. "The doors haven't been forced. Whatever was in this hold, it's been taken out—or let out—by the people who brought the ship here in the first place."

"Explosives." Pikka Adren, at least, was catching on. "Is this how the Nihil got them on board?"

"My guess is security systems would've picked up any large devices on scans," Leox said. "Besides, you don't need anything big to do damage. Pick the right material, and you could rip the guts out of this station with a device no bigger than your palm."

"Well, they didn't release a bunch of rathtars onto the station," Bell said. "Explosion or no, we would've noticed *that*."

Burryaga had walked into the cargo hold to nose around for himself. Literally: He growled that he'd encountered rathtars before, and while he smelled some kind of animal that had been in the hold, it had to be a different species, one Burryaga had never come across before.

"Animals?" Leox couldn't wrap his head around this one. "Why would anybody haul a bunch of animals up here as part of a terrorist attack? Especially since the animals haven't caused anybody a lick of trouble the whole time."

Then Burryaga suggested that the animals might have been not the attacking element but a ruse, included so that their strong scent would throw off detection of the *real* threat. While Leox didn't think most Jedi were as odor-sensitive as Wookiees, it was a theory worth considering.

Bell pointed to another cargo ship docked less than fifty meters away. "That's the other ship that said it was hauling rathtars, and it looks like it's still holding its cargo."

Burryaga and Bell headed toward that ship, and several people— Leox and Pikka included—went along with them. Whatever this was, Leox wanted to see it. He had half an idea that they'd be innocent creatures, more lives to save.

But maybe the Jedi already knew. He asked, "What's the Force telling you about this?"

"Not much," Bell admitted. "Something's been clouding the Force on Starlight for days. Otherwise, the Nihil could never have taken out this station."

That was quite the revelation. Leox welcomed the frankness— seemed to him like the time for tact had run out about point four seconds after that Nihil bomb went off. Granted, it also made him a bit uneasy, because he'd rather have had the Jedi at their best during a disaster. But you always had to play whatever sabacc hand you were dealt.

"Okay," Bell said. "Get ready. We're opening this on the count of three. One—"

Leox looked back at the open, empty cargo hold they'd just left behind. Wild animals had been let loose and were running free around Starlight—the Force was blocked—was there a chance those two things were related?

"—Two—"

It seemed unlikely. Still, Leox was about to ask when Bell said, "—Three."

On that mark, Burryaga sprang the doors on the new ship and let them slide open. For one split second, nobody—and nothing—moved.

Then Bell said, "Okay, so these *are* rathtars."

Which was when the rathtars woke up, and all hell broke loose.

Elzar caught a sense of alarm—new alarm, sharper than the rest—but lost it almost instantly. He breathed out in frustration. Now that he had stopped shielding himself and once again sought the full guidance of the Force, he understood more how compromised his comrades had been. The dampening, and damaging, of the Force on this station . . . it was like having to work with one arm strapped to his side. While this was happening, he couldn't be his whole, best self, and that was what he needed to be to save Starlight Beacon.

As it was, he was fighting with all he had left—and it still looked like it wouldn't be enough.

So he was talking it out, mostly to himself, but also with JJ-5145.

"There's no way to safely get through the irradiated levels to the positional thruster mechanisms." Elzar kept staring at the holo cross section of Starlight, which he'd maneuvered not to show the top half anymore. Being reminded of that pain could only distract him. "Where are the radiation suits?"

JJ-5145 obligingly reported: "Radiation suits were stored in two main areas aboard Starlight Beacon, on both one of the most topmost levels and one of the bottommost."

"We've lost the upper level suits, obviously, but—"

"The lower storage area for the radiation suits is currently inaccessible due to radiation," the droid reported with no sense of irony whatsoever. Elzar managed not to groan out loud. "Some species are more resistant to radiation. Are any of those on board, Forfive?"

"One of the maintenance supervisors, Ar Prace, is a Fian," said JJ-5145, which gave Elzar hope for the brief moment before the droid continued, "but it appears she was on the top half of the station when Starlight split in two."

One more person gone Elzar hadn't yet reckoned with. "How long will it take for the radiation to die down?"

"Approximately ten thousand years."

"That's slightly more time than we have to spare." Elzar ran his hands along the side of his face, the scratch of stubble against his palms. "Ships can fly through that level of radiation, if they're shielded, but we can't get any ships out of the docking bay . . ."

No, that's a lunatic idea.

It's also the only one I've got.

"Maybe," Elzar said. "If we can't fly the ships out of the station, maybe we can fly *through* it."

Bell's lightsaber was in his hand within a microsecond, ignited and ready—

—but the rathtars were ready, too.

They rolled out with terrifying speed, tentacles whipping in every direction, hundreds of creepy soulless eyes and one enormous mouth. Everyone scattered, except for the Jedi, who somehow had to deal with this.

Bell swung up savagely toward one of the rathtars, ready to bisect it cleanly, only to find his stroke blocked by Burryaga's lightsaber. "What are you doing?" Bell yelped, diving out of the enraged rathtar's immediate path, though another of its brethren was rolling right after it. "I had him, Burry!"

With a long and mighty roar, Burryaga explained that rathtars reproduce by fission, and he didn't know if cutting one in half made two rathtars or not, but this was no time to find out.

"Don't cut them in half," Bell said, leaping through the air to the top of one of the other docked ships. "Good strategy. Thanks for passing that along."

He needed to defend the civilians if he could, but they were already instinctively employing the best strategy, which was scattering widely throughout the bay. The six freed rathtars couldn't chase everyone at once.

As it turned out, they could climb the sides of ships, as Bell discovered when one of them rolled atop the one he'd taken shelter upon. Tentacles flailing, it lurched toward Bell.

Don't slice, he told himself. *Stab.*

He had to slash through the tentacles, spinning his lightsaber right to left at tremendous speed; blood spattered everywhere, but the rathtar didn't slow down. Its horrid, many-toothed mouth opened wide to devour Bell whole.

Bell stabbed his lightsaber straight into the maw of the creature, his lunge taking the blade through almost its entire body. The rathtar howled one last cry before rolling, dead, to land heavily on the floor.

Where next? Burryaga had just dispatched another of the creatures, though he'd managed to stab it through the back. But that still left four rathtars loose, which were chasing after fleeing civilians.

Bell ran to the edge of the ship and leapt wide, about ten meters, to land between Pikka Adren and the nearest rathtar. He tried fighting it the same way as he had the last, but this one seemed determined to slaughter people with its tentacles and only then bring them to its mouth. Bell slashed through tentacles—slashed again—but there were always more, *how many tentacles do these things have—*

Blasterfire from behind Bell rang out, each bolt striking the rathtar dead center. It yowled and writhed for only a moment, then seemed to deflate. Bell looked behind him to Pikka standing with her blaster in hand. She gave him a grin, which he returned.

Nearby, however, Burryaga and another rathtar were locked in a messy fight—one angled so that Pikka couldn't fire without possibly hitting Burry. The other two rathtars were almost at the far edges of the bay at this point. Bell ran toward Burryaga and his opponent, thinking, *Usually teaming up helps, because most beings can't fight in two directions at once, but rathtars can fight in* every *direction at once.*

This one was considerably bigger than the others, too—so large that Bell wasn't sure even a strong lightsaber stab could penetrate to its heart.

If they couldn't defeat the thing, they'd have to escape it.

"Emergency flare!" Bell shouted as he leapt into the fray beside Burryaga. "Somebody find one and ignite it now!"

With that, Bell was back in battle mode, slashing and hacking his way through what seemed to be a forest of tentacles. Burryaga howled in fury as the rathtar kept coming, undaunted, always with more tentacles to spare.

"Heyyyyo!" Leox's voice rang out through the cargo hold. "Bet you'd like one of these!"

With that, he ignited an emergency flare. An almost blindingly white glow filled the hold like a miniature sun.

The nearly brainless rathtars only knew that something was very bright and so needed to be chased. With its eerie cry, the big one rolled away from Bell and Burryaga toward Leox and the flare; the other two followed. Once both Jedi were clear, Leox threw the flare with all his might. As it soared to the opposite end of the bay, every other being in the cargo bay ran like hell for the doors.

They made it out. But the flare didn't distract them for long. As they ran, Bell could hear the wet flolloping sound of tentacles slapping metal.

"Through the next air lock!" Bell shouted. "Burry, it's up to you!"

The next air lock was only a few meters ahead. The entire group made it through, with Burryaga bringing up the rear. As he reached it, Burryaga jumped up to grab the mechanism at the top of the air lock, then held himself there with one arm while hastily finishing the maneuver.

Bell looked back to see the rathtars rolling toward them, faster than ever, way too close—

—when Burryaga swung through the air lock, which then slammed shut with the rathtars on the other side.

Everyone exhaled at once; a few individuals swore. Bell leaned against the air lock doors, panting. "Well, that was fun."

This only won him dirty looks from the rest of the group—with one exception. "Wouldn't go that far," Leox said with a grin, "but what that incident lacked in serenity of mind will be more than made up for through the years in anecdotal value."

Weirdly, he was right.

Assuming they survived.

Chapter 26

"Please repeat that for me," Elzar Mann said evenly. This situation *couldn't* get worse. Obviously he had misheard.

But he hadn't. "There are three rathtars loose on the station," Bell Zettifar confirmed. "The other rathtar shipment turned out to be false, and I assumed this one was, too. There's no excuse for my error, and I—"

"Skip it." Elzar took a deep breath. "Every strength has a corresponding weakness. For us, our strength in the Force gives us confidence in our decisions . . . but then we grow too accustomed to leaning on it." Stellan had taught him that. "I might've opened the cargo hold, too."

Stellan Gios had woken not long before; although he remained a shadow of his usual self, he had regained comprehension and composure. "Look at it this way: Of all our current problems, the rathtars should be the easiest to solve."

The quartermaster's office, filled as it was with droids, scarcely functioned as a meeting space any longer. Elzar wished they hadn't moved the conversation here—but then, perhaps it was best that no civilian crew overheard them for a while. He said only, "Let's get back to the plan. You said we could evacuate some people through the cargo bay."

Bell still looked sheepish, but he nodded. "Yes, Master Elzar. I think there's a way."

As he explained the idea, Elzar took heart. Stellan, however, would require more convincing. "You're talking about a level of explosive decompression that smaller ships probably can't compensate for. The ships could crash into one another; the passengers could be killed before they even made it into space."

"It's risky," Bell said, "but these people know the danger."

Elzar nodded. "Besides, if the only other option we can offer is keeping them imprisoned on a station that's still crashing, we owe them a better shot. Even if it's not an ideal option—it's a chance, perhaps the only one they've got."

Stellan put one hand to his head; his skin was pale. Were they pushing him too hard? But he managed to say, "You're right. It's the only possibility we can give them now."

As badly as Elzar wanted to share his ideas about reaching the positional thruster mechanisms, he decided to wait a while longer. Stellan needed more time to process this, and Bell was already burdened enough—and was about to carry yet more weight.

"Bell, thank you for all that you've done here. But now we need you back at the medical tower. We won't be able to evacuate the badly injured through any conventional means, so we need you there to strategize." He put one hand on Bell's shoulder, a brief gesture he warmed with a smile. "Burryaga can stay here to help with the cargo bay evacuation."

Apparently he didn't need to console Bell about the assignment; not only did the apprentice not see it as a punishment, but he also lit up. That must have been where he truly wanted to be all the while. "Of course, sir. I'll head there right away."

Stellan nodded, as though he were still in a position to approve or disapprove. "Very good."

Bell headed out, but paused at the door. "About the cargo bay escape plan—now they also have to get past the rathtars."

Elzar sighed. "One problem at a time."

Bell didn't intend to hesitate on his way back to the medical tower; Starlight was running out of time, and that knowledge pressed down harder by the minute. But halfway there, Burryaga came across his path and growled a friendly greeting.

"Burry! I'm headed back to the medical tower." Bell clasped his friend's paw. "That sticks you with the rathtars, I'm afraid."

Burryaga informed Bell that this was a debt that would have to be repaid eventually, ideally with Bell buying him a Wookiee-sized dinner at the best restaurant on Coruscant.

That's it exactly, Bell thought. *We believe we're going to live. We have to believe it to make it possible at all.*

He grinned up at his friend. "Deal."

Nan had never considered herself a particularly unlucky person, but she was going to have to rethink that, because the minute she and Chancey returned to the docking bay level, so did a couple dozen other pilots, including Leox Gyasi of the *Vessel.* She ducked into a small alcove, but Leox seemed to have other priorities, hurrying back to his ship quickly enough not to notice her.

Chancey, who hadn't bothered hiding, gave her a sidelong look. "You realize you were more likely to draw his attention by jumping for cover like that?"

"We shouldn't have come," Nan muttered.

"We're probably safer if we get busted than if we don't," Chancey pointed out.

The idea of that stung Nan even worse than her fear of death. Her life was her own; she would not owe it to the Jedi. To be indebted to them would be a kind of living death, one Nan did not intend to endure. Better to perish in flame, gloriously free to the end.

Then it hit her—the reality of dying by fire, the agonizing pain of it—

"So." A red-haired man appeared in front of them; he must have been just around the corner. Which meant he'd overheard it all, as his smug grin confirmed. "You two don't want to be seen by the others. What exactly would you be busted for?"

"Smuggling," Chancey immediately replied. "Why exactly aren't you busting us?"

"I've got no desire to do the Jedi's work for them," he said. "Especially when it gives me the chance to make new friends instead. The name's Koley Linn, and I'm thinking we can strike a bargain."

Nan already knew this was going to be a bad bargain, one they'd have no choice but to accept.

Since not everyone spoke Shyriiwook, Leox Gyasi wound up translating the plan for everyone in the cargo bay. "At the moment, Elzar's working out which cargo pilots are still aboard. The other ships will be assigned by lottery to those who can fly them. Every ship in the cargo bay will be filled to capacity, though nobody has to go if they don't want. Yeah, that decompression's gonna be violent. So is colliding with Eiram's surface. So pick your poison."

Most people immediately headed toward Elzar, ready to sign up for what looked like the only possible escape. A few, however, remained. Joss and Pikka Adren were deep in conversation next to their ship—and the hands they rested gently on its hull suggested they wouldn't be quick to leave it behind. The Cerean pilot whose ship had a literal hole blown in the side stood there looking at it as though she could mend the hull through sheer force of will.

And then, of course, there were Affie and Geode. While Geode was putting up a good front, Affie's dark eyes were wide with heartbreak. She whispered, "We have to abandon the *Vessel*?"

"Nope." Leox took her hands in his. "The *Vessel* belongs to you and you alone. It's your decision to make."

Affie looked so frightened for a moment—before her resolve returned. Leox saw it in the squaring of her shoulders, the way she lifted her chin. "I'm staying with my ship. Maybe it's crazy to still believe the Jedi have a way out of this, but I do believe it. And as long as there's any chance at all, then I want to save the *Vessel.* But if you two want to go, please, get off this thing. I can handle the ship on my own, and you two still have jobs if—"

Leox spared her from having to finish that thought. "I'm with you, Little Bit." Next to him, Geode loyally remained by her side, stalwart to the last.

Affie hesitated before nodding. "Okay. All together then."

Koley Linn wished he'd had a cam droid over his shoulder to capture these ladies' faces when he'd explained the plan. The little one's jaw had dropped, and the older woman said, "Blow a hole *through* the bay doors? Do you have any idea how much firepower that takes?"

"A lot," Koley replied, "but get enough ships together, and we can do it. Which is why we could use a couple extra hands to operate weapons on ships whose crews are, shall we say, not cooperating."

"Then you all get sucked out into space through a jagged opening that's lava-hot," said the younger one, Nan. "You seriously think all the ships are going to make it through undamaged?"

"No, I think the ships that aren't prepped—the ones that haven't anchored themselves or set thrusters to reverse—are going to get sucked out first. They'll be torn to scrap. But they'll just widen the opening for the rest of us, who exit on our own power after."

"I'm not sure that works," said the older one, Chancey or something like it. "At any rate, it's a lot longer shot than you're making it out to be. Long enough that I suspect you're not sharing all the dangers with everyone. Long enough to make sure your own ship leaves last, when the path is clear."

Koley loved the moment when people realized just how badly he'd screwed them, and that they had no choice but to go along with it. "Put it this way. It's not as long a shot at survival as you'll have if you go it alone. And make no mistake—the Jedi aren't going to save us. If they had any answers, we'd have heard them by now. They can't even save their friends, so what do you think the chances are they'll help us?"

Chancey and Nan shared a look, one that told him he was ahead.

These two women, whatever they were—they were hard. They were tough. They were used to doing what it took to stay alive. Koley had seen that look in the mirror too many times not to recognize it in somebody else.

People like that could capture the non-cooperating ships with heavier weapons, and his escape plan could become a reality.

Stellan Gios felt like half of himself. His body was moving, his brain thinking, absent any communion with his soul. Maybe this was what it was like to be a droid.

Still, he could go through the motions. With Starlight in imminent danger, he had to give what he could.

"So, we need to open up the cargo bay," Elzar was saying to Burry-aga, "to as many ships as we possibly can. That means getting some of the smaller ships in the main docking bay to the cargo bay—literally flying them through the station."

Burryaga growled that opening up the station in this way would be hard to accomplish without explosives.

At that, Stellan had to speak. ". . . how can *setting off another bomb* possibly improve our situation?"

"We aren't," Elzar said. "We're activating the retrofitting subsystems."

This made no sense to Stellan. "Retrofitting—that's meant to facilitate restructuring of the station at a space dock. It's not going to magically create a flight path through Starlight."

"No, it won't. However, it *will* allow us to collapse certain walls and floors, opening up broader spaces, and those can work as flight paths—at least, for our current emergency purposes." Elzar tapped the

head of one of the many astromechs surrounding them, which obligingly began projecting a holographic cross section of the lower half of
Starlight Beacon. "The Nihil saboteur, whoever he, she, it, or they
might be, set blocks on virtually every main operating system throughout Starlight. One of the only functions left completely intact? The
retrofitting subsystem. They probably assumed it was too obscure to
worry about. But that subsystem lets us reconfigure almost the entire
internal workings of the station. When we reconfigure, smaller ships
will have room to maneuver through Starlight Beacon."

"How do we open that up without destroying everything else in
those areas?" Stellan asked.

Elzar gave him a look. "We don't. We should consider everything on
Starlight Beacon already lost, except for the lives aboard. Once we've
saved those, then we can worry about hardware. But not until."

Stellan finally saw the sense of it and nodded. Burryaga also agreed
with this plan—it might be drastic, but they were in a drastic situation.

"If it works," Elzar added, "we might be able to open up a downward
shaft nearer the middle of the station—and then I can take a repair
pod through the radiation levels, retrieve a suit, and get down to the
positional thrusters near Starlight's base. If I can do that, then maybe
I can get them one hundred percent online."

The plan had value. "You've made a brilliant leap, Elzar. Good
work." Elzar grinned back.

Inside, however, Stellan could only think that he would be no help
in opening the cargo bay doors. The Force was no longer his to command.

After a long, difficult journey back, Bell finally reached the medical
tower. He emerged to smiles from the few overworked sentient medical
staffers, but he couldn't smile in return until he reached Indeera Stokes
and Ember. When he entered the room where he'd left his Master, he

saw her still unconscious but alive, resting on her bed, with Ember loyally at her side.

And at some point, Master Indeera must have roused a little, because her hand lay atop Ember's head.

At least, it did until Ember realized Bell had returned. She leapt up, bounding toward him so joyfully that Bell couldn't help laughing out loud.

"Hey, girl," he murmured as he bent to give her a good scratch. "Good job taking care of Master Indeera." Ember wriggled in joy, her tail thumping against the floor.

That moment of happiness proved fleeting. Bell had spent the journey back to the medical tower wondering how he might be able to transport some or all of the patients to the cargo bay, so they had some chance of escaping the station. His few phantom plans evaporated as he looked around the makeshift medbay. These people couldn't be transported out of the tower in less than a few hours, and some were too badly injured to be safely moved at all.

Just outside one of the viewports he could see the Eiram medical cruiser, stocked with doctors and med droids and every possible supply, still floating helplessly near Starlight.

Air locks every few meters in countless passages through this station, Bell thought, *and not one they can use to dock.*

Unless . . . unless I can change that.

Chapter 27

Various beings reacted differently to the option of leaving their ships behind to escape via the cargo bay. Those who were merely travelers—who had been passengers aboard the vessels of others, or only thought of their small ships as means of getting from one place to another: They were already jostling for slots. Those who owned their ships as a necessary element of their trade: They were hesitating, but mostly choosing to head to the bay.

But those who—like Leox Gyasi—thought of their home not as a planet but as a spacecraft among the stars: They were remaining with their ships.

Still, Leox figured he had no less responsibility for clearing the path to the cargo bay just because he was staying put. Each individual was a small spark of the one great consciousness, the universe beholding itself; if you'd do something to save your own life, he figured, you ought to be willing to do it to save another's.

So he stood among the assembled group as preparation began for the run to the cargo bay.

"As everyone aboard now knows, we have three rathtars loose in the general area of the cargo bay," said Elzar Mann, who appeared to have taken charge. (Stellan Gios stood nearby, looking marginally better than Leox had last seen him, but saying nothing.) "This means taking people in on foot has become significantly riskier. While Burryaga, Stellan, and I can provide some cover with our lightsabers, rathtars are . . . challenging."

"Don't be polite! They're enormous tentacled *jerks*!" Pikka Adren called. It wasn't much of a joke, but most people chuckled. Almost anything leavened the increasingly tense mood aboard.

Elzar simply nodded. "I've been talking to those few people here in the main docking bay who arrived in small, single-pilot ships such as scout craft. Those pilots have courageously agreed to join in our efforts."

Leox raised an eyebrow. Was this going where he thought it was going?

Sure enough, Elzar continued, "We're going to essentially open several corridors between here and the last air lock currently separating that part of the station. This will allow those ships to fly through the station into the cargo bay—providing extra cover from the rathtars, and taking their own chance to escape when we open the cargo bay doors."

Leox mentally notched upward the likelihood of his dying in this effort, but he still had to say, "Wish we could sell tickets."

Elzar glanced sideways at Burryaga, who held his inactive lightsaber in his hands as if a rathtar might appear at any second. "You realize we're safe until we open up the corridors, right?"

Burryaga grunted agreement, but pointed out that they wouldn't be safe from rathtars very long after that. Best to be prepared.

"Good point." As Elzar took out his own blade, he had a fleeting remembrance of Orla Jareni's exquisite double-bladed lightsaber. She had encouraged his iconoclasm, always told him, *Doing things differently doesn't mean you're doing them wrong.*

He wished she'd survived to see this plan, because she would've loved it.

He nodded across the bay to Stellan, who would activate the countdown via the astromechs. A nearby anchor droid began to intone, "Ten—nine—eight—"

The four single-pilot scouts started their engines, sending a high whine through the docking bay.

"Six—five—four—"

All the scouts rose from the floor, hovering in midair. Those few people not coming along for the escape ducked back to the far edges of the room or retreated inside their ships.

"Two—one—*initiate*."

At that instant, the astromechs sent signals to joinings deep within the station's workings, joinings designed to facilitate its original construction and a theoretical reconstruction. They were only meant to give way in the case of a retrofit, but with the right codes they could be set loose at any time.

Down the corridor came a series of deep, vibrating thuds—the sound of metal separating and giving way. Elzar glanced at the assembled group and saw them ready to run. They would as soon as the pilots moved forward, which would happen as soon as . . .

The final corridor gave way, walls and ceiling folding away in front of them to reveal an enormous dark cavern that stretched out seemingly into infinity. Elzar yelled, "*Go!*"

Everyone began to run. The few mildly injured rode on mechnochairs, pushed by friends or new allies. Burryaga roared as he swiftly moved to the front, his glowing lightsaber leading the way, and some of the fleeing people cheered to boost their courage.

They shouldn't, the rathtars will hear it, Elzar fleetingly thought as he ran, *but no, the ship engines are louder, that will draw the beasts away—*

Still, he ignited his lightsaber, too, ready for the battle to come.

The rattle of entire levels of the station collapsing at once unsettled Nan even further. It wasn't the only impact she'd felt that day, definitely not the greatest, but there was a limit to how much she could take in a short period of time, and apparently she was about to hit it.

What kind of a weakling are you? Nan scolded herself. *You've fought in battles since you were a child. You can't take a little standing around and waiting?*

But that was exactly the problem. She was realizing that it was easier to fight—even to risk her life—than it was to wait in a situation beyond her control.

At least the waiting was nearly over.

Nan stood with Chancey Yarrow in a shadowy corner of the docking bay, where they weren't easy to see but weren't obviously hiding. Unfortunately, Addie Hollow and Geode had remained with the *Vessel,* which meant Nan could get busted at any moment. Soon, however, Koley Linn would give the signal and their small band would attempt the takeover of the docking bay, complete with blasting their way through the hull, into space, to safety.

Ideally, Nan would've been able to steal the *Vessel* for her escape. She'd liked the idea of flying away with it, leaving Addie and the rock in the dust. Still, the main thing was flying away at all.

"You look tense," Chancey said. "Try not to."

"Nobody's watching us," Nan insisted.

"Still, when you project a feeling on the outside, sometimes it sneaks into your gut. Becomes real." Chancey sounded . . . encouraging. "Act relaxed, and you might actually chill out long enough to pull this thing off."

Nan had to smile. Chancey rubbed one of her arms, a brief gesture before they were both back to business. For an instant, Nan even remembered why she'd left the Nihil and set out with Chancey Yarrow in the first place—what it felt like to want a life of one's own.

Koley Linn checked the charge on his blaster. Just his luck, he'd gotten stranded out here just as his favorite BlasTech B95 went on the fritz.

Still, 90 percent charge would take him a long way. He could wipe out a few dozen guys with that alone. Count the others who'd thrown in their lot with him, and they had more than enough firepower to overwhelm any resistance.

One Jedi had remained behind, the leader, Stellan Gios. But it seemed like the explosion had taken something out of Gios. The man standing there was a pale imitation of the one Koley had first spoken to. Could he even draw his lightsaber, the way he was now, much less fight with it?

Koley decided it didn't matter if Stellan Gios did manage to rouse himself. He glanced down at the parcel he'd just assembled and chuckled.

Jedi or no Jedi, his team was going to be the only ones on board with a bomb.

"I'm building a bomb," Bell said to Ember.

His charhound was the only one with both the time and consciousness to listen to Bell at the moment; all around him in the medical tower, patients dozed in varying states of awareness, and both personnel and pill droids hurried from being to being, dispensing what medicine and treatment remained. Okay, so Ember wasn't exactly going to point out flaws in the plan—but Bell was pretty sure there weren't any flaws. For the first time since Loden Greatstorm's disappearance, Bell felt utterly sure of his choices.

Ember cocked her head as Bell continued, "See, the Eiram medical cruiser could save us, even dock with us if we have an air lock available. At the moment we don't. The only air locks working are the internal ones."

A thump of Ember's tail would do for a response.

"The thing is, this tower isn't fully integrated into the main structure of Starlight Beacon, not since it split apart." Bell continued wiring his device. It was a simple enough explosive, the sort of thing any pilot of middling experience could construct in case of emergency. "A strong enough explosive placed in the exact right spot—well, it'll separate the tower from Starlight completely. But if we've already sealed off the bottom two air locks, not only will we still be fine in here, but the Eiram medical cruiser will be able to dock with us. From there they can evacuate patients, bring us medicine, and—best part—keep us from crashing."

Ember lay down next to the device, sniffing it with great interest. Her ears were slightly set back—could she sense the danger? Bell had learned that charhounds picked up on things many sentients wouldn't have suspected.

"The trick," Bell said, screwing one of the last connections in place, "is making a device strong enough to separate this tower from the rest of the station without overly damaging either. But I've done the calculations. They all work out."

Feeling so certain of himself had become such an unfamiliar state of mind that Bell had to pause. Was there a flaw in his plans he wasn't seeing?

No. It was time at last to trust himself again. Time to act.

Elzar ran through the hollowed-out shell of Starlight Beacon, keeping his attention focused on the path ahead. But his mind still had the space to wonder: *Whatever it is that's been damaging the Force—killing our people—have we just set it free again? If so, will we still have the strength to open the cargo bay doors?*

Only one way to find out.

The group reached the cargo bay with Burryaga still leading the charge. Once Elzar made it into the bay, he could see how profoundly the room had been changed: The ceiling and the former walls on each side had retracted, vastly widening the space and exposing the skeleton of the station, metal beams and dangling wiring. In the dark reaches above, Elzar could see the scout ships circling and swooping—and firing.

That, plus an eerie shriek that echoed through the rafters, told Elzar that at least one rathtar remained on the loose.

The scent of living flesh would draw the beasts quickly. Elzar shouted, "Everyone to your ships!"

People of two dozen species took off. The computers had retained the ship IDs with docking stations, so everyone knew where to find their assigned rides. Within minutes they'd all be on board and ready to go.

Let's just hope the rathtars give us that much time, Elzar thought. To Burryaga he called, "Atmospheric suits!"

But Burryaga was already hurrying toward the storage locker where each bay's atmospheric suits were kept. Luckily the suits were elastic enough to fit even a Wookiee, though Elzar didn't envy Burryaga the task of wrestling into one.

He was only steps behind when he heard a ghastly slithering sound overhead.

Elzar looked up to see a rathtar hurtling down the wall, tentacles flailing, heading directly for them both.

"It is a shame that the office has become so chaotic so soon after its initial organization," said JJ-5145, with the only sense of dismay the droid had expressed since the disaster began. "At our current trajectory and rate of descent it is unlikely that there will ever be an opportunity to reestablish order."

"In other words," Stellan said, "you think we're all going to die."

"*You* will die," JJ-5145 cheerfully specified. "I will merely become inactive."

Stellan couldn't resist a smile. "Find that silver lining, Forfive."

JJ-5145 swiveled with "Which lining? What do you want me to locate?"

". . . on second thought, it might be better if you monitored the astromech network for potential instability."

Once JJ-5145 was occupied, Stellan took a moment to center himself. The Force still felt muffled, twisted, far away—but the meditative trance, with Elzar steadying him, had helped. If Stellan could not yet function as a Jedi should, he could at least function as a leader should.

A comm chimed, startling Stellan at first; so many communications links were down at present. But thanks to some serious work by the astromechs, the medical tower had become one of the few exceptions, and Bell Zettifar's grainy holo appeared in the quartermaster's office. "Bell," Stellan said. "Everything's well where you are?"

"Yes, sir. And I think I know how to make it even better."

As Bell explained his plan to separate the medical tower from Starlight, profound relief washed over Stellan. At least some people would be saved. "When do you plan to detonate?"

"Soon, Master Stellan. If I wait too much longer, I'm not convinced the blast will take the medical tower far enough to escape Eiram's gravity."

He's not asking permission. He's not second-guessing himself. The doubt that has gripped Bell since Loden's initial disappearance has gone—and good riddance. "You've done well," Stellan said. "Indeera will be proud of you when she wakes. And Loden Greatstorm would have been proud, too."

Bell blinked fast, holding back emotion. "Thank you, sir."

Stellan held up one hand in farewell, wondering whether he would ever see Bell Zettifar again. At least, in this moment, he'd been granted a glimpse of the great Jedi Knight Bell would become. "May the Force be with you."

Bell began by closing the first air lock, the one within the station itself, only a few meters before the tangled tunnel of debris that led into the lower half of the station. This would protect the rest of Starlight Beacon from catastrophic decompression.

Next Bell placed his explosive device very carefully in the middle jointure, just where the structure should be the most fragile. Although this took mere seconds, it felt as though it lasted much longer; Bell remained very aware of the hiss of pressurized air, the faint singed smell of damaged wiring, the presence of Ember several steps behind.

"Wait for my signal," he said to the device as a kind of a joke. It didn't help much.

Bell sealed the next air lock to contain the blast. Then the one after that, hopefully for the Eiram medical ship to use for docking. Finally, the one after *that*—as a backup. Then he stood on the other side of a sealed air lock, breathing hard, with nothing else to do but act on faith.

"Come here," Bell said, bending to scoop Ember into his arms. He told himself he did this to keep her from being afraid when the blast occurred; she was warm against his chest.

Taking the detonator from his pocket, he reviewed every step in his head, making sure everything had been done, and done correctly. His thumb hovered on the button.

At last he whispered, "For light and for life," and pressed down.

BOOM!

The blast nearly threw Bell to the floor, but he managed to stay upright and hang on to Ember—barely. Cries of panic from the patients within disturbed him, but he kept his cool. Air still flowed. The power remained on. Bell dashed to the nearest viewport, peered outside, and shouted for joy. "We did it! Ember, we did it!"

Ember began wriggling happily in his arms, licking Bell's face. She knew only that he was happy, and he was *ecstatic,* because what he saw was the remainder of Starlight Beacon floating away, with the medical tower completely separate and free. Better yet, the force of the explosion had pushed the tower farther away from Eiram.

The LT-16 rolled up to him, squeaking, "Jedi Zettifar, the Eiram medical cruiser reports that they have us in their tractor beam. They'll move us out of the descent path and attempt boarding shortly."

"Great," Bell said, grinning widely. "Spread the news among the patients, okay?" He intended to follow shortly behind, in order to tell

Master Indeera himself; even if she couldn't hear him yet, it was important to him to be able to say the words, *You're safe.*

And perhaps she *could* hear him—Master Indeera's consciousness remained intact within her, even if stifled by her injury . . .

It hit Bell, then, just how much more he could perceive through the Force than he could've just minutes ago. As Starlight Beacon drifted farther and farther away, the terrible draining damage to his connection to the Force faded. His abilities were coming back in full; until this moment, Bell hadn't comprehended just how badly they had been diminished.

He thought of every Jedi still trapped aboard Starlight: Elzar Mann, Stellan Gios, and above all Burryaga. Bell knew now that they were all but separated from the Force. How could they ever overcome? Was there any hope for those still aboard Starlight Beacon?

Chapter 28

When Stellan saw the medical tower floating free, he felt a wave of gratitude. The plan—radical as it had been—had worked. He stared out the window of the quartermaster's office, watching as the Eiram medical cruiser brought the tower closer with its tractor beam, then proceeded to connect their air locks. Every person within that tower, most important the dozens who had come to the Jedi seeking assistance and shelter, had been saved.

Yes, the people of the galaxy would hear of the success of the Nihil attack—but now they would also hear of how so many had been saved through the ingenuity and courage of a Jedi.

Other ships had begun appearing in the darkness of space overhead: little craft, most of them, but they'd responded to the distress call. These people—not soldiers or planetary representatives, but private citizens—had braved the threat of the Nihil to travel hostile, dangerous hyperspace routes, in the hope of aiding Starlight Beacon.

We are all the Republic, Stellan thought. It had never been truer than it was in this moment.

He only wished there was some way they *could* help.

But there had to be something—a plan they hadn't yet envisioned, a trick still hiding up their sleeves. The same inspiration that had come to Bell would come to them as long as they didn't give up.

The good news: It wasn't a rathtar descending toward Elzar Mann and Burryaga.

The bad news: It was *two* rathtars.

Elzar leapt upward, slashing widely with his lightsaber, less with the aim of a fatal stroke, more in the hope of scaring the beasts into retreat. Unfortunately, these rathtars seemed to like shiny objects. Their tentacles flailed out toward Elzar, one of them lashing his wrist but failing to achieve a grip.

Elzar landed back on the deck in a combat-ready crouch, lightsaber still at the ready. Burryaga leapt up into the air, too, taking his turn slashing at the rathtar tentacles—but one thick tendril wrapped around the Wookiee's midsection, holding him in its powerful grip.

Elzar thought fast. Jumping up toward the rathtars might save time, but it also made for vulnerability midair. Instead he dashed to the service ladder on the side; normally hidden within a maintenance shaft, it had been exposed in the newly cavernous space of the cargo bay when they'd collapsed the walls. He climbed as quickly as he could, desperate to reach Burryaga before more harm was done.

Burryaga, however, wasn't done defending himself. He extended his claws to the fullest—a sight Elzar had never seen before, and a fearsome one—to slash at the rathtar that held him. It screeched in pain and let go.

For one instant, Elzar smiled. Burryaga would use the Force to catch himself, Elzar would jump down to him, and maybe the rathtars had learned their lesson.

They hadn't. The other rathtar bolted down the wall to grab Burryaga again. This time, its tentacle wrapped around his neck—tightly enough to suffocate anyone to death, even a Wookiee. Burryaga clawed at the tentacle again, but this rathtar was made of sterner stuff than the last. It only yowled in anticipation as it brought the Wookiee closer to its wide, hungry mouth.

The docking bay was all but empty. Almost everyone within it seemed distracted by the explosion that had just shuddered through the station, not to mention the detached tower that seemed to be floating around outside. Nan didn't bother going to look. She didn't care.

What mattered was that the few people currently focused on the present place and moment were all members of Koley Linn's small team.

Nearby, Chancey gave her a swift nod. An instant later, Koley's explosive went off in the docking bay.

Nan ducked, dodging debris and shrapnel; it wasn't much of a bomb, but it had decimated the ship it had been placed under, and now the bay was filling with smoke and screaming. She charged forward, heading straight toward the ship she'd been told to target. Her boots pounded against the deck, *go go go go—*

"Unhh!" Nan tripped over something and went sprawling onto the deck. A smoldering bit of metal on the floor either burned or cut a painful slash on her forearm. Worst of all, she looked over to see that she'd been tripped by none other than Addie Hollow, who was staring at her as if looks could kill.

Looks couldn't kill. Nan could. She lunged to her feet, ready to take Addie down—but halted when Koley Linn shouted, "Nobody move!"

Both she and Addie turned as one to see Koley standing near the center of the docking bay, his blaster aimed at a small child who lay sprawled on the floor, wailing pitifully. Everyone had frozen, Nan saw, both the members of their team and the others, who had begun fighting back faster than she would've thought possible. Even the stupefied Stellan Gios had emerged, lightsaber in hand, in battle stance at the far end of the bay.

It's a standoff, Nan realized.

Koley Linn called out, "Let me explain how this is going to work."

Though smoke continued to roll past, misty or opaque in turns, it looked as if everyone knew better than to take their chance with such momentary cover.

The small child on the floor wailed, and for one instant Koley vaguely felt a sensation he'd all but banished years ago: shame. There wasn't much pride to be found in a hostage so completely incapable of defending itself.

But he wasn't here for pride. Koley had the hostage; he had the element of surprise; he had the advantage. That was exactly how he liked it. The transient shame faded, never to return.

"There's a way off this station for those willing to take it," he said. "The rest of you can take your chances with the Jedi. But us? We're getting on the ships with the best weaponry and we're blowing through the hull of Starlight Beacon."

"You can't," said Stellan Gios, with more strength than Koley would've thought the guy could still muster. "The hangar's magnetized—"

"Yeah, that would be a problem, if we were shooting our way out with our blasters. But the blasters are for you guys"—Koley waggled the muzzle slightly, indicating some individuals he'd consider shooting first—"and don't worry. If I shoot at you, I won't miss. Shipboard weapons—that kind of firepower won't be held in by the magnetic seal you have in here, and don't think I don't know it." Typical Jedi, assuming they knew everything and nobody else had a clue.

Stellan remained undaunted. "Do you have any idea how long it would take to blast through the doors? Hours, probably—time we don't have."

From the back, Joss Adren piped up. "Plus you'd space the rest of us and our ships!"

Koley kept his eyes on Stellan, by far the biggest threat in the room. "Face it—your ships are lost already. Nobody here has to get spaced if they clear out." He didn't mind killing whoever he had to kill, but in this case cleaner was also faster, and time was precious. "As for the hull—you haven't done the calculations, Stell. I have. We can punch through it in about forty-five minutes. It's about an hour before we're fully in atmosphere and things get even uglier. So I'd like to get started right away."

The child on the floor near Koley suddenly stopped wailing. He half turned to see a thick patch of smoke clearing—and Geode, now standing, silent and resolute, between Koley and his former hostage.

How does that damn thing move? Koley thought, not for the first time. He gestured to his nearest co-conspirator, the girl called Nan, who swung her rifle around to target the child in his stead. Then Koley grinned. "You've gotten in my way for the last time, you idiot rock."

Geode didn't react. The guy put up a good front; Koley would give him that much.

"No idea how anybody ever took you seriously," he said, holding his blaster at the hip for the most accurate shot. Koley wasn't sure exactly how much fire it would take to turn a Vintian into rubble, but he was about to learn. "Now it's time to take you out."

Koley fired—

—in the instant his finger squeezed the trigger, he remembered something Affie Hollow had said before: *Vintians can decide whether to be magnetically sealed or not—*

—and the sound and flash of his first fire lanced through Koley's midsection.

He staggered backward. Geode stood in front of him, smoldering; the guy hadn't even moved.

But Geode had refracted Koley's own blasterfire directly back at him, which was why there was now a new hole in his gut.

Koley collapsed to the ground. The last thing he ever saw was Geode standing over his head, just like a tombstone.

Affie Hollow had understood Geode's plan immediately; she'd also been pretty sure Koley Linn was dumb enough to fall for it. So she'd focused on getting ready to stop Nan from making good on her implicit threat to the small child still sprawled on the deck nearby.

In the first instant after Koley fired—when he was still staggering backward—Affie launched herself at Nan. They both went down, falling at the same time Koley Linn dropped dead.

Prepared to fight, Affie scrambled to her feet again, but several of Linn's co-conspirators, not interested in a fight where they had no advantage, turned and ran. Nan was among these; she took off at impressive speed, vanishing into the darker shadows at the edge of the docking bay. Affie watched her go, inwardly seething, but determined to stay focused on what really mattered.

So she turned back to Geode. The child's mother already had her infant in her arms and was leaning against the Vintian in profound gratitude. Affie said, "Are you all right?" Obviously he was, but she'd feel better once she'd heard it from Geode himself.

But at that moment, Stellan called out, "Listen to me! Those of you who cast your lots with Koley Linn—I don't blame you for being afraid. I don't blame you for being desperate. You must now turn over your weapons, but if you do so, I give you my word as a Jedi that none of you will suffer any further consequence."

It took only a moment for people to begin complying. Affie could feel the anger in the room diminishing, replaced by—well, the best thing it could be called was "resignation," but it was a lot less volatile.

"We're looking for a way out," Stellan continued. "We will find a way out. We need you to help us find it. We need you to believe."

Elzar watched in horror as Burryaga—still choking in the rathtar's grip—slashed out wildly with his lightsaber. The other rathtar tried to grab the shiny thing with a tentacle and came close enough to knock the lightsaber out of Burryaga's hand. It tumbled downward, and Elzar reached out with the Force to grab it—

—but it was hard, *so hard,* as though even reaching for the Force caused pain, and it responded so feebly—

—and when Elzar finally caught it, he felt exhausted, as though he'd been trying to levitate for hours.

Is this what the other Jedi have been struggling through all this time?

Burryaga, still struggling within the rathtar's grip, had at least managed to get his neck free. He roared to Elzar not to worry about him; the people in the cargo bay needed to escape.

"Stop being noble!" Elzar had little patience with this kind of thing. "I need you to help me with the cargo bay doors!"

But Burryaga growled that Elzar could do it. He was strong enough. He was inventive enough. If any Jedi on this station could do it alone, it would be Elzar Mann.

He also wanted Elzar to tell Bell goodbye.

"Burryaga, no!" But Elzar could see that the two rathtars, now working together, were slithering farther and farther overhead, beyond Elzar's reach. If he exerted through the Force with everything he had left, maybe he could catch them . . .

. . . and afterward, Elzar would have no remaining strength to open the doors.

Elzar swore under his breath. Tears stung his eyes, but he refused to break down. He could only honor the Wookiee's sacrifice.

Their job was to save the people in this bay, and that meant letting Burryaga go.

Bell Zettifar lifted his head.

One of the Eiram medics looked at him curiously. "Are you all right?" she asked.

"I'm fine," he insisted. "It's Master Indeera who needs your help."

The Force told him that Burryaga was in trouble aboard Starlight Beacon. It was as though Bell could feel his friend's desperation, the wild need to lash out in every direction at once. What was happening?

No way to know. No way to go to Burry's aid.

Bell walked across the floor of the Eiram medical cruiser—newly laden with the wounded and injured from the medical tower—with Ember at his heels. Through the viewport he could see the bottom half of Starlight Beacon below them, on the very verge of entering Eiram's atmosphere. At that point, it was doomed.

"That *moron.*" Chancey Yarrow paced the length of the small, lower-level room where they'd taken refuge. "If he hadn't tried grandstanding, we might've had the jump on them! Instead he wanted to take a hostage? I can't believe we let *that* guy take the lead."

Nan sat in a corner of the room, exhausted and even sootier than before. It looked like their only hope of survival was the Jedi, which was worse, to her, than no hope at all.

The Jedi weren't even bothering to capture them. It was borderline insulting.

Chancey ran a hand through her hair, then refocused. "All right. Koley said we might regroup here, which didn't happen, but suggests there's something in this area worth having."

Nan didn't hold out much hope, but she began going through the nearest storage locker. It was crammed full of disparate stuff— suggesting that Koley Linn had been doing some low-level stealing during his time on Starlight Beacon. But what good was any of this junk to them now?

Then her hand closed around thick, silvery material. She pulled it up into the light and thought it didn't look like much, but her companion gasped.

"Radiation suits," Chancey breathed. "Thank every god in every religion on every planet there ever was."

"Our biggest problem isn't radiation." Nan figured the suits might keep them from burning for a while, which meant only that they'd die by being slammed into the ground at maximum velocity instead. Not exactly a win.

But Chancey said, "That's right. Our biggest problem is *gravity.* Our best defense against gravity is the station's positional thrusters, which are only partly online. We've heard them talking about repairing them, but they can't, because they don't have radiation suits. But we do!"

This at least sounded promising. Nan said, "Do you know how to repair the thrusters?"

"I invented a whole new type of gravitic weapon. I think I can handle the most basic antigrav mechanisms in existence." Chancey grinned. Already she was shrugging off her vest, ready to don the radiation suit. "If this station's positional thrusters can work at all—and apparently they can—then I can get them boosted to full power at least temporarily. That ought to be enough to get Starlight back into space and save our necks."

Nan considered this. "We'll also save everyone else on the station—including the Jedi."

Chancey shrugged. "No plan is perfect."

Chapter 29

Another of the scout ships fired at the rathtars overhead—the ones after Burryaga? Another? Elzar Mann couldn't tell—and the echoes of the blasts drowned out any sounds either rathtars or Burryaga could've made. The other ships had begun powering up their engines, the building sound making it impossible for Elzar to know whether Burryaga remained alive.

Yet Burryaga had been the first to say it didn't matter. Elzar's duty was to the people in these ships, who deserved a chance to live.

Now all he had to do was open these massive bay doors by himself . . .

More and more ships began arriving in the Eiram system. Some were larger spacecraft: transports, ore carriers, even one mid-space shipbuilder from Corellia. Most, however, were smaller—one- or two-person gigs, or standard payload haulers. They came from dozens of different planets, all in response to Starlight Beacon's desperate call, all willing to do whatever they could to help.

But they had no leader, no logistics. Nor could one emerge from

the thick swirl of overlapping communications that clogged every possible frequency. So it took precious time for them to coordinate efforts,
each ship so equipped bringing tractor beams to bear on the remaining
half of the station. However, as it happened, the timing didn't matter;
even their combined tractor beams lacked the strength to free Starlight
from the grip of Eiram's gravity.

Increasingly far-fetched plans were hatched, shared, debated. Could
they attach physical tow lines to the station, haul it up and away, just
like Starlight had been towed to Dalna and Eiram? But tow lines were
largely designed only for use with small to midsized ships, and even
when Starlight Beacon was structurally sound, such towing was risky
and had to be meticulously planned. Now it was beyond hope.

Yet they came. All the Republic shared in the dream that Starlight
Beacon represented. People and species from across the galaxy saw its
plight and were willing to do anything they could to help, even risking
reprisals from the Nihil.

And all of it did no good.

The system became ever more crowded with ships that could not
help—that could only stand and watch as Starlight fell.

All of this sounded ideal to Marchion Ro.

"Each of the Tempests has been made aware of your triumph, my
lord," said Thaya Ferr, bent over her console as she had been for hours,
scarcely budging. KA-R9 hovered behind her, a malevolent shadow
carved of ice, but she had not let it unnerve her. (This stood in sharp
contrast to Ghirra Starros, who remained on the far side of the bridge
from KA-R9 at all times.) "Two of the Runners have already asked to
bring Clouds and Strikes to the Eiram system, to raid the ships that
have come to assist—"

"It is forbidden," Ro said. "Any Nihil ship that enters this system
will be destroyed by the *Gaze Electric* itself. If they wish to see the devastation, they can do so on holonet—like billions of other beings
throughout the galaxy. Any other Nihil activity at this time will only

distract the witnesses from our ultimate victory." He rose from his chair and stared at the scene before them: the jagged remnant of Starlight descending into the outmost haze of Eiram's atmosphere. "*This* is what I want them to see. The *only* thing I want them to see."

Thaya Ferr bowed her head. "It shall be as you command, my lord."

There was another motivation for Ro's stance, one he preferred not to voice: Personally witnessing Starlight's demise from the Eiram system itself was a privilege that belonged to him and him alone.

The atmospheric suit helmet slipped easily over Elzar's head. When he hit the seal, a faint hiss around his neck became sharply audible as the sounds from all the ships and rathtars in the cargo bay were muffled to a fraction of their former volume. The respirator kicked in, pumping air from the pack on his back through the suit. Although the insulating shield remained silent, he could feel the energy humming along his skin, prepared to protect him against the frigid void of space.

But the same shielding that was so necessary for this moment was antithetical to the Jedi ideal of openness, awareness, connectedness. Wearing the suit caused a mental block only, but Elzar knew such blocks could be as impenetrable as any physical barrier.

It's not just the suit, Elzar thought. *It's believing that I deserve to fully connect to the Force again, after allowing myself to use its dark side.* He'd begun reopening himself to that power in order to help Stellan, but this would require more.

Orla Jareni's voice spoke in his head again: *Trust yourself, stupid.*

Elzar took a deep breath, strapped on his safety harness, and closed his eyes. In his mind, he once again stood on the surface of Ledalau, looking out at the broad expanse of the ocean. In his ears, he heard the tide.

You always imagined the Force as the ocean, Orla had said. *But the ocean isn't a power we get to control. It's a power we can partner with. First you have to decide: Are you going to keep fighting something too infinitely vast to be fought? Or are you going to study its currents and set sail?*

They had agreed that he wouldn't "tinker" with the Force again for a while, only until he'd reached a place of greater peace and strength. Elzar had thought that wise. But that, too, was fighting the current. The ocean had brought him here, to a place and a time where he could only save others by trusting himself.

Elzar lifted his hands and focused his attention—not ever outward, toward the totality of his surroundings, but forward. His spirit sought only those fellow beings aboard the waiting ships. Gradually, gently, he began to sense their fear and their panic, but also their hope. Their determination. Their faith.

The link strengthened. Elzar realized that he was drawing some of his power from these people, something a Jedi would normally never do. In this moment, however, he knew the rightness of it. Each one of these individuals would have given every shred of strength, would have fought with ultimate will, if it meant the chance between life and death. Their strength and their will flowed into Elzar, and—

—he felt the doors, but not their heaviness, they were mere objects, and their size mattered not—

—*Open,* he thought. *OPEN.*

A slash of light split the bay in two. Powerful suction clutched him, yanking him forward until the straps of Elzar's harness seemed as though they would cut through his chest. His feet left the floor. He barely noticed. More important were the ships in the bay, all of which were struggling against the suction's power at full engine strength.

Elzar's eyes widened as he saw the doors slowly, slowly sliding apart to reveal Eiram below. The planet was bathed in sunlight that streamed in, filling the bay. *Just a little more, just a little more—*

He glimpsed dark shapes overhead, being sucked through the gap at such speed they were unidentifiable. Were they smaller ships? Rathtars? The thought that one might be Burryaga pierced Elzar's heart, but he remained focused.

Finally, when the gap was wide enough, the first ships began to dart through. One by one by one, they took off, bursting into outer space and to safety.

I did this for you, Orla, he thought. *And for you, Burryaga, Nib, Regald. I did it* with *all of you.*

Grateful tears filled Elzar's eyes, catching the sunlight, until they seemed to swim with molten gold.

The networked droids had reported to Stellan that the cargo bay doors were opening—but he had not allowed himself to truly believe it until several minutes later, when Elzar returned, wearing an atmospheric suit and carrying a helmet under one arm.

"You've done it," Stellan said, a smile breaking across his weary face. "You got them all away?"

"Every ship," Elzar confirmed, but he wasn't smiling. That was when it hit Stellan that Elzar had come back alone.

"No. Not Burryaga—"

"The rathtars took him." Elzar swore under his breath, but after that continued with something that could almost pass for equanimity. "Burryaga called for me to complete the escape plan without him. That must have been his very last act."

I should have been the one to go with Elzar. It should have been me. Stellan said only, "His courage stands as an example to us all."

"Hey." Elzar stepped closer. "I've had a thought."

Stellan raised an eyebrow. "A useful one, I take it?"

"I was able to call powerfully upon the Force while I was in the cargo bay. Part of that was, well, ingenuity. But part of it may have been the absence or at least distance of the thing or things that have been causing such problems for every Force-user aboard the station." Elzar began removing the gloves of his atmospheric suit, preparing for greater action. "The varying locations, plus the fact that the Nihil transport was falsely marked as carrying wildlife, makes me think that it—no, *they*—are living creatures."

It was a rational deduction, one Stellan felt he'd probably have reached himself if he hadn't been so incapacitated. "How can we use that knowledge to our advantage?"

"At the present?" Elzar asked. "Only one way. We understand that any Jedi, anywhere aboard Starlight, is vulnerable to these . . . attacks, at any moment." His eyes met Stellan's, dark with foreboding. "Any of us—all of us—may fall."

The formerly crowded docking bay had become a lot quieter. While almost all the ships still remained, most of those had lost their crews. Affie Hollow, standing on the ramp of the *Vessel,* couldn't help wondering if she'd made a terrible mistake. Her ship was her world, but—her life was her life.

Leox emerged, chewing on a mint stick. "Lookin' kind of shaky, Little Bit."

"I'm not shaky," Affie insisted. "It's just hard. We don't have tons of time left, and I know the Jedi always think of something, but . . . I wish they'd go ahead and think of it already."

"No way out for them that I can think of," Leox said. "The only way out for us I can think involves cannibalizing the *Vessel.*"

Now that the possibility of abandoning her ship to destruction was real again, Affie remembered why she hadn't been able to bear the thought before. "What do you mean?"

"We get down in the guts of our ship, rip out her core power cells, use that to jump-start an escape pod." Leox offered her a mint stick. "But if we do that, it's the last flight the *Vessel* ever takes. It's a hell of a choice."

She went to take the mint, then gasped. "Leox, that's it!"

"You're really willing to let her go? I guess we're about there—"

"We can't dig the power core out of the *Vessel* without basically destroying the ship, even if the Jedi do save the station," she said. "But everybody who already left—they've *already abandoned* their ships. Those power cores are available. Which means—"

Leox finished it for her: "The escape pods are, too."

Chapter 30

Leox ran it by the Jedi first. Yeah, people needed to get the hell off this station, but Leox also needed not to have a "destruction of property" charge waiting for him at the next spaceport. To his relief, Stellan Gios did not allow his thinking to be blurred by the ethical quandaries of the situation. "At this point our priorities are saving lives, not preserving property. Get to it!"

So it was that Leox found himself working shoulder-to-shoulder with both Joss and Pikka Adren, removing power cores from the engines of abandoned ships and transporting them to the nearest ring of escape pods. There, Affie had her entire tool kit arrayed around her, working double-speed to attach pods to cores. These were two mechanical elements never meant to be linked, which meant the linkage was pretty clunky, but as Affie herself said, "It only has to work one time." Once he and the Adrens had removed every core that could be spared, they'd join her in the work, hopefully learning from whatever method she'd devised.

At one point Leox ducked into the *Vessel* to quickly grab his canteen—disemboweling engine parts was serious physical work—but hesitated at the door of the mess. Geode stood at the far end of the corridor, giving Leox a pointed look.

"Listen," Leox said, "I want to push Affie into an escape pod as badly as you do. I also know that if we do that, and are nonetheless fortunate enough to survive the current disaster, we will only die slower and more painfully later on, once she catches up with us."

Geode seemed unconvinced.

"Do *you* want to order her to get on an escape pod? Are you that sure you wouldn't be reduced to gravel? Because if so, go right on ahead." When Geode didn't move, Leox said, "Yeah, I thought not."

If it came right down to it, Leox knew he might wrestle Affie into an escape pod yet. But before he'd make that call for her, they'd have to be even closer to the wire than they already were.

The station rattled beneath his feet as he hurried toward the next ship they'd plunder. Eiram's atmosphere was beginning to show itself.

Elzar Mann was relieved that the pilots had come up with a means of powering the escape pods and had even undertaken the work themselves. That left him free to concentrate on finally reaching the positional thrusters.

"The radiation suits were stored in two primary compartments at the uppermost and lowermost levels of the station, both of which we've been cut off from in different ways," Elzar began, addressing Stellan and the handful of other personnel who remained. "In future I intend to suggest that all Republic space stations have much more decentralized radiation suit storage, but that's a point to raise with Chancellor Soh later. Without those suits, it had looked like we had no way to reach the Starlight's positional thrusters without exposing whoever went down there to fatal levels of radiation—so fatal they'd kill within minutes, so even heroic sacrifices weren't going to do us any good."

"There must be some more suits somewhere," protested Stellan. (To Elzar's great relief, his friend looked focused, active, vital—like himself once more.) "Never in galactic history has every single thing on a station been stored precisely, and only, where it's supposed to be."

Elzar pointed at him. "True. But none of our searching has turned up any so far, and we can't possibly go through every trunk or locker on the remainder of this station in the hope of a radiation suit turning up unexpectedly. We don't have the time. Which is why we need to do exactly what we did to get people into the cargo bay—we need to collapse more of Starlight's inner structure. We know now, from the cargo bay escape, that we can activate the retrofitting systems without causing larger-scale internal collapse. That means we can use them one more time to reach the positional thrusters."

Stellan nodded slowly. "All right, then. How do we do this?"

"I'm going to give them another twenty to thirty minutes to get as many escape pods away as possible," Elzar said. "Cutting it close, I know, but the lives aboard this station remain our first priority. Once they've managed that, the droids will initiate the partial retrofitting collapse downward, and I'll fly a maintenance pod down to the positional thrusters. There, maybe, finally, I can get them back online."

He didn't bother pointing out that collapsing the structure vertically was riskier than collapsing it horizontally, as they had before. Some of the lower sections were far more damaged and weakened than the levels they'd stuck to thus far. A partial collapse stood a greater chance of triggering an even more catastrophic one, which might kill everyone on board before the station's crash even happened.

But it wasn't *that* big a chance, Elzar reasoned, and besides—what did they have to lose?

By this point it was full morning in Barraza, Eiram's largest coastal city—or what had been its most populated city until a few hours prior. It had become several other things instead: a ghost town, a traffic jam, a far smaller city still populated by several thousand people unable to leave.

Flying craft had already departed if they could, though the frenzied escape had caused several crashes; smoldering aircraft parts lay on the rooftops where they'd fallen. Landspeeders and wheeled vehicles had attempted to follow, but the terrain surrounding Barraza was too rugged and uneven to go far off-road. This meant long, long lines of vehicles creeping forward at a pace too slow to ensure that those within were protected from the horror descending from above.

By now, the fiery death of the top half of Starlight Beacon had been shown on holonews stations across the planet; every screen on every device replayed the disaster, intercut with eyewitness statements and, sometimes, people holding up grisly, charred finds they had made from the zone below the inferno.

None of this was as fearsome to the people of the city as the slowly enlarging dark spot against the sky, directly overhead.

Nor were the people of Eiram the only ones watching in horror.

"This is a disaster." Chancellor Lina Soh leaned heavily against the targons on either side of her. Holos showing the broadcasts of—and reactions to—Starlight's descent on a dozen different worlds were projected around her. "The greatest disaster for the Republic in a century, perhaps more." *So far,* she thought, but was not morbid enough to add. "We can't get anyone there faster?"

"It won't be more than two hours now," said Norel Quo. But they all knew Starlight Beacon didn't have that long.

One of her newer aides decided this was a prime opportunity to get noticed. "I've taken the liberty, ma'am, of drafting several statements, each with slightly different nuance, for your review. What's most important at this point, of course, is demonstrating that the Republic remains strong and in control, and that your leadership can't be linked to this incident in any way—"

"Fool!" Soh shouted. She tried to be a temperate and generous leader, but this was a provocation beyond any restraint. "This is not a moment to worry about how to spin this for my reelection campaign.

This great tragedy deserves respect, of which you appear incapable. *Leave.*"

The aide clearly wanted to ask whether leave meant "now" or "forever." (It was the latter, as he'd eventually discover.) He managed wisdom enough to simply walk out without another word.

Tragedy can forge unity, thought Lina Soh. Her statement—which she alone would write—was beginning to take shape in her head. But this was not a matter of politics, not any attempt to salvage her own reputation. She looked at it the way a doctor might look at a wound, seeing whether there was any way to heal what could not be undone.

But for the sight of Starlight Beacon beneath, Bell might have been in excellent spirits.

The medical tower, fully docked with the Eiram medical cruiser, bustled with medics and pill droids. Every single injured person had treatment; every one of them was safe. Ember had curled into a contented ball at Bell's feet as he sat next to the bed of Indeera Stokes. Master Indeera had not yet regained full consciousness, but the medics assured him that her readings were slowly normalizing, and there was some indication that she was perceiving both sound and light. There was every reason to think that she not only would recover, but also might be able to explain exactly what horrific entity had taken Regald Coll and Orla Jareni's lives.

And Loden Greatstorm's.

We're going to get answers at last, Bell thought.

Still, at the edge of the medbay window, he could see the bottom half of Starlight—jagged and ugly at the top—getting smaller and smaller in the distance.

Bell took his comlink and tried once more. "Bell Zettifar to anyone aboard Starlight Beacon who can hear my—"

"*Padawan Zettifar.*" Stellan Gios's voice sounded thready and weak, yet better than Bell had last heard it. "*Good work with the medical tower.*"

"There's got to be something else I can do to help," Bell insisted. "There are a few medical shuttles on board. The staffers have offered me—"

"*Don't come back here,*" Stellan said. "*Enough lives are endangered without adding yours.*"

Although Bell could see the sense of this, it was difficult to accept that there might be no more he could do. Casting about for ideas, he said, "Listen, is there any way you could put Burryaga through? He and I are pretty good at putting our heads together. Maybe there are ways to separate other sections of the station, so they could be pulled to safety by tractor—"

"*I can't put him through. I'm afraid—I'm sorry, Bell. We have lost Burryaga.*"

Bell stared down at the comlink, as though that could somehow change the words he'd heard. "You mean . . . Burryaga's dead?"

"*Believed dead,*" Stellan replied. "*Apparently he gave his life protecting Elzar Mann from the rathtars, so that the ships from the cargo bay could escape in time.*"

Believed dead. That meant they didn't have a body.

After what had happened to Loden Greatstorm, Bell would never give up on anyone who was missing again.

Climbing down ladders wasn't much less tiring than climbing up them, and Nan had done a lot of both during this one impossibly long day. Her leg muscles seemed to have gone nearly gelatinous by the time she finally clambered onto the lower level of the station that housed the positional thrusters and closed the hatch that stood between them and deadly radiation.

Chancey Yarrow, though nearly as wobbly, righted herself first, pulling off her helmet with a sigh of relief. "After this is over—by which I mean, *all* of this—I'm going to find the nearest vacation planet with hot mineral springs and settle in for a long soak. I'm talking days. Droids are going to have to fly out and bring me my food. Plus at least two bottles of Toniray wine. After that, maybe—" Chancey's expression softened. "—Maybe I can catch up with my daughter, try to talk with her again. It'll go better, next time. Not that it could go much worse."

At this point, Nan's ambitions topped out at "not dying today." If she managed to achieve that, she certainly didn't intend to waste time on frivolous pursuits. But she was too exhausted to start that discussion. "What next?"

"Next we find the localized engineering array and boost the power to that thing."

"Do we need to find power cells, or—"

"There ought to be plenty hardwired in, for emergencies like this. Starlight just needs someone to flip the right switches, which is what we're here to do." Chancey grinned as she flipped open an equipment kit mounted on the nearest wall. "It's not too complicated. So perk up. The hard part is over."

"That's what you think," said a third voice—a familiar one.

Chancey and Nan turned as one to see the Nihil team standing there staring at them: Cale, Leyel, and Werrera, ragged and dirty, their radiation suits almost black with soot, but still very much alive. They were also very much armed, not with blasters but with lengths of pipe that could do plenty of damage.

Nan said, "What are you doing here?"

Cale's wintry Pau'an face had never looked more forbidding. "Our work didn't end with the blast. We ran analytics both following the blast and after the station split in two. It wasn't hard to see that the only way to save the station was by using the positional thrusters."

"So we put on some radiation suits we'd stashed, just to make sure we didn't wind up melting before we could finish our work," Leyel added. "Got down here and waited to make sure no one had the bright idea of undoing our hard work. But here you are. Unless you've come all this way to say goodbye?"

Chancey grabbed a tool from the equipment kit: a fusion laser, which could not only seal difficult-to-reach connections from a distance but also operate a lot like a blaster in a pinch. Nan had used them like that before herself. "I've come all this way to save my neck and fry anybody who gets in my way," Chancey said.

"You would snatch away the Nihil's greatest victory?" Cale's voice rose in pitch.

When he put it that way, Nan could see his point. But she also thought the Nihil victory was already undeniable. What did it matter if there were a handful of survivors? Did it really take away from what Marchion Ro had accomplished here?

Not much, she decided, as long as she was among those who lived.

More ships continued to arrive, spacecraft from all over. Nobody was cataloging them, not even droids.

Which was why one particular ship could dart into the system unheralded and unnoticed, but still get close enough for a wonderful view of Starlight's end.

The *Gaze Electric.*

All the rest would spread the tale among the Nihil until it was another of Ro's legends—the greatest yet.

But not the greatest ever, he thought. *That is yet to come.*

Ro spared a thought for the beings he had sacrificed aboard Starlight Beacon. He had sent seven—enough to be sure that they would have an effect, but also enough for him to feel their lack. They were not easily replaced.

Still, no one else had them at all. Ro alone held the advantage.

Chapter 31

Usually, in a firefight, the one who pulled their weapon first had the advantage.

It didn't work for Chancey Yarrow.

Chancey fired her fusion laser at the Nihil saboteurs, striking the Ithorian, Werrera, in the gut. But both Cale and Leyel dodged expertly, and even Werrera managed to hurl a heavy pipe at Nan's head before he fell. Nan hit the floor, letting the pipe clatter harmlessly behind her as she crawled back toward it. His weapon would soon become hers.

Leyel threw some kind of projectile as well—Nan didn't get a good look at it—but whatever it was struck Chancey in the temple. She staggered backward but didn't fall. Instead Chancey braced herself behind a metal column, catching her breath while waiting to see what the others might do next. Werrera lay on the floor, exposed and barely moving; anyone who had fought with the Nihil had seen enough death to know he wouldn't live much longer.

From her place on the floor, Nan looked up at Chancey. By this time Nan had curled her hand around the edge of the pipe; it was still warm from Werrera's hand. It felt good to be armed again.

But Chancey shook her head. "Don't throw anything yet," she muttered, barely audible over the heavy whir-hum of machinery surrounding them. "We do the wrong thing down here, we could wind up damaging the equipment so badly that getting the thrusters back online would be impossible. I can't even fire again unless I know I've got them dead in my sights."

So they just had to wait for Cale and Leyel to set the terms of the fight? Nan wanted to scream with frustration. Her hand tightened on the length of pipe as she reminded herself—she'd have an outlet for her anger soon enough.

A protocol droid aboard the Eiram medical cruiser, which must have been taken along because this mission was considered "diplomatic," didn't have that much to do—which meant he was focusing all his attention on Bell Zettifar, much to Bell's amusement.

"But, sir!" protested the silvery droid as it tottered along after Bell into the medical cruiser's launch bay. "You've only just escaped from Starlight Beacon!"

"They still need help," Bell said, scanning the bay for the shuttle he'd been granted access to. "That makes it my responsibility to get back there if I can."

The protocol droid would not be easily convinced. "But if nobody can yet exit Starlight, how can you possibly hope to enter it?"

"Remember, they've opened the cargo bay." It was the last place Burryaga had been seen—and the first place Bell intended to search for him. "From that point I can access the rest of the station."

"The station is unstable! On the verge of breaking up! Which is why no rescue vessels have been sent in—"

"It's risky," Bell agreed. "We couldn't ask anyone else to make the attempt. But the Force is with me, and I know this station, and—and these are *my people*. It's my job to help them if I can."

Probably the protocol droid had been programmed to keep diplomatic envoys out of harm's way if at all possible, because he waved his stiff metal arms about in dismay as Bell boarded the shuttle. "Sir, if you could only wait, perhaps more favorable conditions will arise. You must reconsider!"

Bell shook his head. "Starlight is almost out of time."

In the end, Elzar had insisted that his vehicle for the trip through the station would be a little one-person maintenance skimmer pod, the sort of thing intended only for minor hull repairs and other exterior odd jobs. Stellan had recommended something sturdier—the pods weren't intended for anything as hazardous as this, and a handful of single-pilot craft remained—but he said nothing as Elzar boarded.

He won't listen to me, Stellan thought. *The only person with a chance of getting through to him would be Avar.*

The third star in their constellation. The light in the night sky that Stellan had turned from, all because of a disagreement about tactics—one that now seemed shortsighted, even petty. How could they have let the Nihil, destroyers of so much, damage their friendship, too? That, Stellan now saw, was the greatest error either of them had ever made—and ironically, given that it had set them at odds, it was a mistake they had made equally, together.

He'd tell Avar that he hadn't appreciated her enough, should they ever meet again. Their constellation would shine in the firmament once more.

Seen from outside, what remained of Starlight Beacon looked even more broken and doomed than Bell would've expected—and he'd expected it to be bad. But his eyes widened as he took in the full horror: the bent, broken metal beams jabbing upward from the ugly break, the few standing walls from the break level that revealed where rooms— and people—had been, the forbidding darkness of a station largely illuminated only by emergency lights, so that it glowed sickly orange in the dark.

Worst of all, the curve of Eiram's surface had come to cover almost the entire horizon, and Bell could feel the subtle resistance of the first traces of planetary atmosphere. They had so little time.

He steered the shuttle around the curve of Starlight's hull, directing his full attention toward the cargo bay. Yes, he'd come here to help anyone and everyone he could, but his friend Burryaga remained foremost in his thoughts. Master Stellan had told him enough about Burryaga's disappearance for Bell to know that the odds weren't good. Still, his brain kept supplying possible ways his friend might have survived: *Burryaga could've managed to squeeze through an air lock on an upper level. Or, if he got free of the rathtars in time, he might've been able to put on his atmospheric suit and strap in, which means he wouldn't have been sucked into space when the bay doors opened.*

If Bell could think of those possibilities, then Burryaga could've, too.

He brought his shuttle in closer to the hull as he approached the cargo bay—within twenty meters. As he did so, Bell felt a tiny shiver of fear.

C'mon, he told himself. *You're a good enough pilot to handle this.* Which was true, and yet it did nothing to calm his concern.

Instead it heightened.

Something's wrong, he thought, the hair on his arms rising as his heartbeat quickened. *It's not supposed to be like this, not like this at all—*

The shuttle controls didn't make sense. What was he supposed to be doing? It felt as though the instrument panel changed every time he looked at it, while he was looking at it, and that only made everything scarier.

Then another voice inside his head, the one that spoke to him as Master Loden once had, said, *Get away from this place.*

Acting on instinct, Bell managed to push the controls enough to steer the shuttle away from Starlight Beacon. Within another hundred meters, the fear had begun to subside. He took deep breaths as he felt the terror growing more distant.

Somehow . . . fear itself had been placed aboard Starlight. And Bell had no doubt, it was this same fear that had killed Orla Jareni, Regald Coll, and Loden Greatstorm.

But what is it? How does it do this?

Those were questions that required investigation, and soon. At the moment, however, Bell was certain of only one thing: He must not return to Starlight. Whatever in there was poison to the Jedi, and if he went back in, he would only fall prey, too.

Instead he would have to find a way to help from out here.

"What was that?" Affie Hollow asked.

Pikka Adren—who was currently working side by side with Affie on the escape pods—leaned to look down the corridor, then shook her head. "I don't see anything."

"There was a shadow," Affie insisted, "and I thought I heard something heavy moving along."

"Maybe it's a Trodatome or something that got lost." Pikka was already at work. "Not that I've seen one on board, and lucky for them, since I'm not sure one would fit into an escape pod. They're kind of squidgy, though, so maybe one could smush in?"

Affie still felt uneasy, because she knew *something* was creeping around this station killing or hurting Jedi. Anything unknown could prove to be a threat.

Then again, the Jedi had described a sense of fear and confusion that surrounded them when the something approached, and Affie wasn't getting that at all. Even her understandable worries about getting off the station in time could be managed as long as she had a job to focus on, as she did at the moment. *I guess it was nothing,* she decided.

Pikka nodded and smacked the panel nearest the first escape pod they'd readied. "I think she's ready for her first launch."

Affie grinned. "Then let's do it."

Stellan Gios had chosen the first to board: a Caphex husband and wife who had wished to take part in the cargo bay escape but had been among those for whom there was no more room. With Affie's help, they both managed to climb inside the tiny pod; they fit, but barely.

"All right," Affie said, "Strap in, seal off, and we'll launch the minute we get the clear."

As the pod sealed, Affie and Pikka each looked at the control panel, which should've shown an all-clear to launch. Instead it blinked red. "What now?" Pikka wailed. "Is it just malfunctioning?"

"We can't launch them without knowing," Affie insisted. "We don't know what damage the exterior of the station took when it broke in two. There could be a dangling beam or something out there." Already Pikka was nodding; she saw it also. If they launched an escape pod only to have it almost instantly collide with metal, they would be costing lives instead of saving them.

A small knock came from within the pod. No doubt the Caphex were wondering when they would finally escape. Affie wished she had an answer.

At that moment, her comlink hissed, and then she heard a voice: *"This is Jedi apprentice Bell Zettifar, calling anyone who can hear me aboard Starlight Beacon. Do you read me?"*

"Reading you, Bell," said Affie. "I'm Affie Hollow—not a Jedi, but I'm working on the escape pods here. Do you want me to find Stellan Gios?"

"Maybe—but is there any way I can help you? I'm in a shuttle circling Starlight right now. Docking seems…" He hesitated a second before continuing, *"…inadvisable, but if there's anything I can—"*

"There is, and wow, do you have great timing." Maybe there was something to this Force thing after all, Affie reckoned.

Nan had never fought against other Nihil before. She'd wanted to, at times—but she'd kept her eyes on her goal. Murdering other Nihil was only advisable when it meant a move upward, when it got her closer to wealth, to power, to Marchion Ro. And it was foolish to work against any of Ro's plans.

Today was different.

She shouted from sheer exertion as she swung the metal pipe at Leyel, who blocked it with her own; the dull clang of metal on metal resonated with the answering pain in the bones of her arm. Nan kept swinging, kept hitting, driving Leyel farther back toward the wall.

If only Chancey Yarrow would kill them already! Yeah, yeah, a fusion laser wasn't nearly as accurate as a blaster, and misdirected fire could be fatal, but so would be crashing onto Eiram's surface. In Nan's opinion, it was time to take the risk already.

Instead Chancey and Cale were locked in a battle of attrition, hurling projectiles at each other, each trying to wrangle for position closer to the control panels for the station's thrusters.

(Neither Nan nor anyone else in the fight paid any further attention to the wounded Werrera, who now lay utterly still on the floor, dead or dying. Nobody would check to see which.)

Leyel swung lower than Nan was expecting, catching her in the gut and knocking the breath from her lungs. Nan went sprawling sideways, skidding across the floor as Leyel shouted, "Traitor! You're nothing but a *traitor*!"

I don't want to die for the Nihil, Nan decided. *Instead I will live for them.*

Already Leyel was running toward her, aiming a killing blow for Nan's brain. Nan rolled over and flung herself toward Chancey—specifically, toward her fusion laser. Her hand made contact with the grip, and even as Chancey tried to react, Nan shoved her sideways so she could yank the fusion laser up—even with Leyel's face—which was when she fired.

Leyel dropped. Before Cale could react, Nan wheeled around and fired at him, too. He staggered back two steps before falling not far from his comrade. They'd both been killed instantly. For a few moments, Nan and Chancey just stood there, breathing hard, staring at the carnage.

"I know what would've happened if I'd missed," Nan said. "But I *didn't miss*."

"We're going to have a conversation about this later." Chancey had begun rolling up her sleeves. "Right after I finish saving everyone's ass."

Chapter 32

"...although it has descended into our atmosphere, it's not too late to shoot Starlight out of the sky."

Eiram's defense minister, an Enso woman swaddled in a thick coat, nodded approvingly at her adviser before turning to the two queens of her planet. "Queen Dima, Queen Thandeka, you've heard the report. You can see it with your own eyes. How much longer can we continue to endanger our people?"

"We ask our people to accept a risk," Queen Dima replied. She was somewhat older than her consort, with thick gray hair twined in complicated braids upon her head. "To do otherwise means submitting all those on Starlight Beacon to certain slaughter."

The defense minister bowed her head. "With respect, Your Majesty—our first responsibility is to the people of Eiram."

Queen Dima glanced at her consort. Though Dima's rule was absolute, she listened carefully to her advisers—above all to her wife of thirty years. As the queen regnant had aged and become more frail, Thandeka as queen consort had taken on more responsibility, in particular when it came to dealing with dignitaries from other nations and, now, the Republic.

It was Queen Thandeka who had argued most strongly to give the Jedi time, and Dima had trusted her. At this point, however, doubts were creeping into Dima's mind—doubts Thandeka was beginning to share.

As much as Thandeka trusted the Republic, as greatly as she honored the Jedi, she knew their gifts had limits.

"How long until impact?" Thandeka asked.

The defense minister replied, "Approximately forty-five minutes—but we only have another ten to fifteen minutes to shoot them down. After that, we'll simply be scattering the debris over a wider field."

Queen Thandeka's shoulders slumped. She thought of the faces of the Jedi she had come to know over the past weeks. How many of them were lost already? How many were about to fall?

Then Queen Dima startled her by saying, "We cannot do this."

"But—" The defense minister's face fell. "Your Majesty, how can we not?"

"It is as I said before." Dima rose to her feet, looking each adviser in the eyes in turn. "We will not use the kind euphemism *preventive action* to justify killing. Did anyone on this planet not know of the Nihil before? Had anyone failed to learn that Starlight Beacon was one of their targets? Yet we invited Starlight here when we needed assistance—when it suited us. Our planet accepted those risks when we accepted the Republic's help . . . and we will not allow the Nihil to turn us into murderers."

Queen Dima looked at Thandeka last, and Thandeka didn't try to hide her tears. It was hard to see their people in danger, but it would have been far worse to lose the very soul of their world, all in the name of "safety."

The decision was made. After this, only the Jedi could determine what would happen next.

————

The path downward had been cleared, and so Elzar at last began his descent to the bottom of Starlight Beacon.

The tiny maintenance pod made its way slowly—only about a human's walking speed, if that—because Elzar couldn't be sure what jagged metal might be waiting below. It wouldn't take much of a bump to damage the hull; his pod was such a flimsy thing that it only barely protected him from the radiation he'd pass through. Once Elzar made it to the lowest level, he'd close up the floor above, which ought to shield him long enough to repair the station's positional thrusters.

But descending slowly meant having plenty of time to see everything he passed, and what he saw horrified him.

One level: fire-scarred, black on gray on black, with a few crumpled figures among the debris that had previously been the bodies of sentients.

The next level: what had been the beautiful arboretum, now dark and weighed down with soot so that the few standing furnishings and wall panels all sagged nearly to the point of collapse.

The level after that: almost empty, where before it had been bustling with energy and action. Somehow that was even worse—the simple absence of purpose where there had been so much before.

Seeing the damage to the station on every floor stoked Elzar's temper until it grew hotter and hotter, threatening to get the better of him. *The Nihil did this. They couldn't let one pure, good, noble thing stand. They couldn't endure a symbol of cooperation, friendship, and peace. So they made it ugly, and they cost people lives, and they always—*

Elzar caught himself. This wasn't the time. He had a job to focus on.

The pod went yet deeper, into sections where not even emergency lighting still ran. Only the faint glow from the pod controls illuminated Elzar's face. It was almost unnerving.

"C'mon," he muttered to himself, trying to ignore the chill he felt. "Aren't you a little old to be scared of the dark?"

But Elzar couldn't shake the deep sense that something was terribly wrong.

Were there more Nihil saboteurs lurking? Was some kind of internal collapse of the station imminent? Fear rose higher and higher within Elzar, like floodwaters up to his neck, quickening his breathing until he could scarcely focus.

The pod's controls didn't seem to make any sense anymore. Why was he in this pod? Where was everyone else, and—

—what was *that*?

A large shape, indistinct in the gloom of a poorly lit level, swam and morphed in Elzar's vision like a fever dream. He only knew that it was hideous, repellent, *wrong*. It was moving toward him—whatever it was—and everything in him recoiled. He slumped against the pod wall and lifted his arm to try to shield his eyes, but his arm was so heavy . . .

The pod descended another level; the shape disappeared. *What happened?* Elzar couldn't understand it. *Where am I? What's going on?*

Another level. His heartbeat still pounded against his rib cage so hard it seemed to hurt, and Elzar felt as though he'd like to claw his way out of this pod . . . but he remembered the pod, and his mission, and how to work the controls.

He also remembered what had just happened, and how strange it was. Elzar had been briefly—but totally—incapacitated by fear and confusion upon his nearness to something. The farther he got from it, the better he felt.

Although he racked his brain for any meaningful memory of it, he retained merely a few indistinct flickers of a large creature moving toward him. He knew only two things for certain:

1. This was the creature, or one of the creatures, that had been attacking the Jedi aboard Starlight Beacon— attacking them through the Force; and

2. If Elzar's pod had moved any slower, he'd probably already be dead.

————

Unbeknownst to Elzar, his encounter with the creature—his confusion, his fear, his mortal dread—had been sensed by another.

Stellan stood in the quartermaster's office, struggling to catch his breath. The link between Elzar and himself was exceptionally strong at present, no doubt due to the deep meditative bond Elzar had shared with Stellan to center him after his last encounter with these terrible, nameless creatures on board. He knew that Elzar had been at risk, but had escaped.

For the moment.

Too much depended on the next several minutes, Stellan realized. And he would not leave his friend to suffer as Stellan himself had suffered, alone.

"Forfive?" he said. "Prep a second maintenance pod."

The droid rolled toward him inquisitively. "Is there another area in need of imminent repair?"

"No. But Elzar needs backup." Stellan squared his shoulders. "I intend to be with him."

It had been a while since Bell had flown in-atmosphere, but it was coming back to him fast.

The sky over Starlight Beacon was no longer black but dark blue, a blue that brightened by the minute. So far the atmospheric drag on his shuttle was minimal, but it would only increase from here.

Luckily, Bell only had to get within a reasonable range of Starlight to do his job.

"Escape pod A is clear," he reported, hovering slightly above it. "Repeat, the pod is clear!"

Seconds later, the escape pod launched—the first one to get away from Starlight Beacon. Bell cheered, then winced; it didn't pay to be too loud while wearing a flight helmet.

But he couldn't help grinning. After so much grief and loss and fear, finally, *finally* things were going right.

Over the comm came the voice of Affie Hollow: "*Okay, pod B is loaded and ready for go. Can you confirm it is clear?*"

A small orange light around pod B was blinking; no debris stood in its way. Bell said, "Confirmed clear. Let's get them out of here!"

This pod, too, shot forward, launching in a long, graceful arc down toward Eiram's surface.

Burryaga could've gotten out of the bay, found a pod, found a way to juice it up, Bell thought. Anything was possible.

He set those hopes aside to focus on the present moment. Currently it was easy to confirm the pods clear, but after the next few, they'd get to an area of the station that showed more damage. Not all those pods could be safely sent away, and it would be Bell's job to let them know which they were.

No matter how many lives had already been lost, every one they saved would be a victory.

Affie had been hesitating about her choice to remain with the *Vessel* before—but never so much as she did the moment Pikka Adren put her hands on Affie's shoulders and said, "A ship is not a life."

"I know that," Affie managed to reply. "Still, it's mine—both my ship and my life."

"Of course it is. The decision is yours." Pikka shared a look with her husband, Joss, who was already lowering himself into the escape pod, before turning back to Affie. "I just want you to understand that it's always possible to start over. Believe it or not, before Joss and I were together, I worked on the crew of a small ship that I was so dedicated to I—I made sacrifices I shouldn't have made—" Pikka closed her eyes tightly, as if willing back the memories. "Long story. Slightly off topic. The point is, things are always replaceable. People aren't. That includes you."

"It also includes my crew," Affie said. Geode was no closer to fitting through the door of an escape pod than he'd ever been. "What kind of captain abandons her people?"

"Talk it over with your people, then. Ask them what they think."

Affie said nothing, because she already knew that if she asked Leox and Geode, they'd shove her into an escape pod so fast her head would still be spinning at landfall. She didn't want to leave them, and she didn't want to abandon the *Vessel,* and damnit, they still had upward of forty minutes! Escape pods could launch a lot later than that.

(Well. Not *a lot* later. But later.)

Either Pikka assumed Affie was going to take her suggestion, or she simply knew there was no time to argue further. She embraced Affie, who hugged her back, suddenly and sharply aware that she'd made a new friend, one she might not see again.

"Land safe," Affie whispered. "Meet you on the ground."

Elzar's pod finally came to rest on very nearly the bottom level of Starlight—the same level that housed the workings for the positional thrusters. Finally, a chance to undo some of the Nihil's damage, and to save every being still alive to be saved.

He worked with a methodical caution that would've startled Stellan. It might even have surprised Avar. Elzar was admittedly impressed with himself: going through checklists, sealing the three floors above to prevent any significant radiation leaks, double-inspecting his tools to make sure he had every single thing he might possibly need for the work to be done.

In moments such as this one—when Elzar could see himself as the Jedi he'd always truly hoped to be—it was easier to feel courage. To feel confident of a good result ahead.

My polestar, Elzar thought, *and my song. They're with me now, whether they know it or not.*

Elzar unsealed the pod door and stepped out. Although he felt reasonably certain that none of those . . . *things* he'd seen above were on this level, it was best to make absolutely sure. Their influence was too powerful; it appeared no Jedi could stop them. *Maybe,* he thought, *I should've sent a non-Force-user technician down here instead.*

He halted where he stood when he heard something. After only a second, he relaxed slightly—those were sentient voices, surely—but nobody had answered any of their previous attempts at communication, suggesting that either this level had been empty at the time of the explosion or everyone down here had died.

So who was here?

More important—what were they doing to the thruster controls?

Leox Gyasi liked the Jedi as much as the next guy, more if the next guy happened to be a Nihil, but the only beings in the galaxy he liked enough to trust with his life were Geode and Affie Hollow. This meant he was about done waiting for the Jedi to fix this situation. If they could've done it, they would've by now.

Time for a new plan—and that plan had to involve saving the *Vessel*.

Leox understood what the ship symbolized to Affie, maybe more than she did herself. The *Vessel* had become hers after she'd turned her cartel-running mother in for countless egregious violations of the laws protecting indentured pilots. That made the ship the one thing Affie had gained for all that she'd lost, the one bit of tangible proof that she hadn't torpedoed her whole life by doing the right thing.

In the end, he knew, to save their lives, Affie would give the *Vessel* up—but he was about as likely to let her do that as he was to let her cut off her own arm. Had to be another way.

Thinking fast, Leox headed to the cockpit to check a few readings. Geode stood there, utterly still, utterly blank. Leox stopped and gave him a withering look. "Come *on,* man, pull yourself together! I know it's scary as hell, but this is when we need our wits about us the most."

He grabbed some gear from a locker, shrugging a pack onto his back, strapping on goggles, and pulling out a device he'd had for quite some time. Had won it in a game of sabacc, actually, a long time before. At several points, Leox had considered selling it—the things weren't cheap—but he'd always wondered whether it might come in handy. Today it would.

Affie appeared in the cockpit doorway, slightly out of breath. "Okay, the first ring of the escape pods is away."

"Good work, Little Bit," Leox said. "We're about to be off ourselves. The only way left to open the launch bay doors is by using the manual controls."

"But—" Affie frowned. "Those are located on the exterior hull. Outside the station."

"Indeed they are." Leox stood upright, displaying the item from his locker to his crewmates for the very first time. Geode was again silent from shock, though of a very different sort than before. Affie's jaw literally dropped.

"Leox . . . is that—do you—" She stammered. "Are you holding a thermal detonator?"

He nodded. "Been saving it for a special occasion. Looks like that's today."

Chapter 33

Chancey Yarrow had forgotten that working on machinery could be *fun*. She'd spent so much damn time fighting and scraping and clawing for advantage, doing the best she could in a hard galaxy . . . and all the while, she could've been doing this instead: standing up to her elbows in space station mechanisms, analyzing their workings, forgetting anything and everything that lay beyond the reach of her hands. Even invention, with all the dazzling mental fireworks it provided, lacked something of the core satisfaction of simply fixing what needed repair.

I've been focusing on the wrong things lately, she mused as she checked the drivers powering the positional thrusters of Starlight Beacon. *I should get back to basics. There's something to be said for dealing with problems that can actually be resolved.*

"No pressure," said Nan, who stood next to her with folded arms, "but we only have a few minutes left."

Chancey understood that this didn't mean "a few minutes before Starlight collides with the planet's surface and kills us all." It meant "a few minutes before Starlight has fallen so low that the positional thrusters will no longer be able to avoid the collision." Still not good news—but the distinction helped keep her head clear.

Besides, she had finally glimpsed the solution. Just reroute a little power here, angle the thrusters like so—and within minutes, Starlight Beacon would be aloft again.

Would the Jedi ever admit that an escaped prisoner, one who'd worked with the Nihil, no less, had been the one to save the day?

Probably not. But they'd know the truth. Chancey wondered if they'd swallow their Republic pride to thank her. Maybe someday even Sylvestri would realize what her mother had accomplished this day, and that knowledge might be the first stone in a new bridge between them, one upon which they could finally find each other again.

Hope doesn't matter, Chancey reminded herself as she took the T-7 anx and got to work. *The only reward I need is survival.*

"Do you have any idea how many spaceport checklists ask about thermal detonators?" Affie demanded. "Lots of them. You know how many of those lists I lied on by saying no? Apparently *all* of them. How could you not tell me about this?"

Leox shrugged. The two of them stood on the *Vessel*'s ramp, where she'd stopped him sauntering out with a detonator like it was no big deal. He seemed to find all of this amusing, which just made Affie madder. His only reply: "The thermal detonator's been aboard the *Vessel* longer than you have. That sabacc game was a loooong time ago."

"But the *Vessel* is my ship! I had a right to know!"

The smirk finally faded from Leox's face. "I reckon you did. Back when I won it, though, the *Vessel* belonged to your mother, and I didn't think it would be wise to report it to her. No telling what she would've used it for."

As much as Affie hated to admit it, Leox was right. Her adoptive mother, Scover Byne, had had a ruthless streak. Many of her pilots had been pressured to take on unethical, dangerous, even doomed assignments. Scover Byne wasn't a person who could be trusted with a thermal detonator.

But still. "I've had the ship for a while now, Leox. You could've told me."

"Look at the bright side," he said, bringing his goggles down over his eyes. "After today, no more thermal detonator."

"What are you going to do with that thing?"

"This is the plan." Leox pointed toward the far corner of the docking bay. "I'm going to attach this detonator to that area of the station's hull, which as you can see used to be an air lock during station construction but is now just a little bit thinner. I'm going to blow the detonator, which ought to punch a hole straight through. We're in-atmosphere by this point, so decompression is no longer a catastrophic problem. Once we've got a hole through which I'm able to exit, I can use the manual controls exterior to the station to open the launching bay doors."

Affie shook her head. "Let's just get into an escape pod, Leox. I can get another ship."

"Yeah, but you're not the only one here who's unwilling to let go of a ship."

Indeed, not quite a dozen crews—some single pilots, others groups of two or three—remained, inseparable from their ships to the end. Affie knew that they were like her, people with no other work, no other home. Even the Cerean pilot whose ship had a huge hole cut in the hull had refused to leave it behind; it was the only possession she had.

She turned back to agree with Leox—it had to be tried—but he was already running toward his target, thermal detonator in hand.

Elzar crept forward, lightsaber in his hands, listening to the sounds— the voices—he heard from the thruster control room.

"Are you sure you've got it?"

"One more second, and then this ride is over."

He leaned forward at an angle and saw two figures that he recognized from footage Stellan had shown him: the prisoners who had been captured in the raids on the Nihil, the ones who had protested their innocence. Yet here they were, at the heart of the station's mechanisms, revealing themselves as the saboteurs.

They were still alive—while Regald Coll, Nib Assek, and Orla Jareni lay dead, husked into dusty remnants of themselves. Not only had the saboteurs brought aboard these mysterious creatures, not only had they detonated a device that killed many and doomed nearly all, but now they were also trying to destroy Elzar's last chance to save lives.

Was there no end to the evil they created? Were they completely without pity, mercy, common decency?

A thousand images flashed in Elzar's mind in an instant: the chaos created by the Hyperspace Disaster. Valo. The terrible fate of Loden Greatstorm. Stellan's pale, haggard face. The wounded ships drifting through space, dark and dead as the beings that had been within them. The lightning bolt. Their pride, their arrogance, their greed—

He could bear it no more.

He would bear it no more.

No more.

Elzar leapt into the room, igniting his lightsaber mid-flip, until he landed directly in front of the woman who stood deep in the workings of the positional thrusters. Her large eyes widened, and already she was going for a weapon, ready and willing to kill him if that was the only way she got to kill others—

Before she could reach it, Elzar swung his lightsaber, the blade splitting her in two. Instantly she fell, dead.

Sometimes, fate threw you a freebie.

Leox felt confident he'd have gone with this plan regardless—but it was kind of great that one of the ships parked nearest his target for the thermal detonator happened to be the *Ace of Staves.* Not only would no living owner be deprived of their ship due to damage from the impending explosion, but as a benefit, some of the last evidence of Koley Linn's existence was probably about to be sent into oblivion.

Holding grudges against the dead is unworthy, Leox chided himself. *Life is meant to be lived in the now, where the dead can no longer be.* He needed to transcend this pettiness—and he'd get right on that, as soon as he was sure they weren't all about to die.

One small twist clicked the thermal detonator into countdown mode. Leox stuffed the detonator into a small container in front of that bit of the hull and ran like hell. As long as he put the *Ace of Staves* between himself and the explosion, he ought to do okay . . .

The blast rocked the bay, nearly sending Leox toppling down. He heard a few shrieks in the instant before that section of the hull gave way—and then the bay was filled with howling wind and the sudden brilliance of sunlight. Leox's gut twisted at the absolute proof that this space station was in space no longer, and probably never would be again.

But he still had time to get out there and save the *Vessel.*

Leox activated the magnetic clamps on his gloves and ran for the hull opening. The next bit would be hard—but he could get the job done. He had to. Affie and Geode's lives depended on it.

The best of the show from space was already over. How quickly glory could pass.

Marchion Ro stood on the bridge of the *Gaze Electric,* looking down at the planet Eiram—a world so insignificant, so devoid of true riches, that his Nihil had never even bothered raiding it.

Thaya Ferr stood next to him, silently making notations on her datapad. On his other side stood Ghirra Starros, head held high, her hand wrapped around his arm. Was she foolish enough to think that these gestures would blind him to the wetness in her eyes?

There was no point in undertaking such an action if the consequences of that action were not fully understood and accepted from the start. This sort of behavior—regretting what one had done, when

STAR WARS: THE FALLEN STAR

one had fully succeeded—was the sort of thing Ro held in depthless contempt.

Ghirra had already served her most critical purpose. Ro briefly considered eliminating her on the spot; someone this weak would be more liability than ally in the days to come. He went so far as to look over toward KA-R9, hovering malevolently only steps away, and wonder how swiftly the droid could activate his laser scalpels.

But no. Ghirra remained Ro's best asset within the Galactic Senate. No point in getting rid of her until she'd done all she possibly could for him—or, of course, until he found someone better. For now, she'd do.

In a low voice he said, "In some ways, I wished I'd had the chance to send Starlight Beacon crashing down upon someplace far grander. On a planet the high-and-mighty Republic would pay more attention to."

"I think you've made your point," Ghirra said flatly.

Thaya Ferr, more quietly, asked, "This has a rightness to it as well, does it not?"

She understood much. "It does. The final resting place of the Republic's ultimate symbol—of the Jedi's pride—will be a backwater nowhere that didn't even appear on most star maps."

"Then it is perfection, my lord."

Ro nodded. Already Starlight was no more than an indistinct shape outlined against Eiram's clouds. Soon the station would pass through them and be invisible.

"Switch to planetary holonews," he commanded Ferr. "Let's watch this along with the rest of the galaxy."

Instantly the cloud-filled image on the main viewscreen was replaced by footage taken from Eiram's surface, where an enlarging dark mass was taking up more and more of their sky.

Even knowing how dangerous and powerful thermal detonators were, the blast that rocked the docking bay still caught Affie off guard. It knocked her out of her chair onto the cockpit floor of the *Vessel;* next to her, Geode wobbled precariously but managed not to fall. Metal debris clattered and clanged along her ship's hull—on every other ship remaining in the bay—and Affie suspected she wasn't the only one swearing.

But then an enormous shaft of light streamed through the bay, piercing through her anger and fear. "We're close," she said to Geode. "We're so close!"

Although the wind sweeping through the docking bay was fierce, only the slightest depressurization registered on her ship controls. The station had fallen well into atmosphere by this point. When the doors finally opened, they could fly out minus any problems.

Even the Cerean pilot can make it if she straps herself in, Affie thought, glancing over at the ship with a hole in its side. Sure enough, that pilot was already in her captain's chair, prepping for takeoff—as was pretty much everyone else remaining on the deck.

All Leox had to do was get the doors open, then get back.

He has magnetic clamp gloves, she reminded herself as she began working through her pre-launch checklist. The *Vessel* needed more work, but she'd fly to the surface smoothly enough. *He'll be locked onto the side of this station like a Shilian lamprey. No problems there.*

As if in reply, at that instant the docking bay doors finally, finally began to open.

They slid wider with what seemed like excruciating slowness—but Leox was working with manual controls, at what had to be the top possible speed. Affie could hardly imagine the effort it took; he had to be giving it his last measure of strength.

At last the doors opened wide enough for Affie to catch a glimpse of Leox: at an angle, his body just barely visible at the corner of the doors, his loose shirt and dark-blond curls whipping frantically in the wind. Even from here, she could tell how hard he was working.

"You've got it, you've got it." Affie wasn't even aware she was speaking out loud. "C'mon, Leox, get back in here and let's go!"

The first ship to speed out was the Cerean pilot, swooping past them to fly free into Eiram's sky. A couple of others followed, each one barely squeezing into the narrow opening between the bay doors, but making it through nonetheless. Affie's face lit up as she saw Leox begin working his way toward the opening—apparently he was coming in that way, not through the hole on the side—

—and then the wind caught him, yanked him backward, away from the station. For one moment it seemed as though Leox hung in the sky, before the gales tore him away, flinging him down toward the ground, and death.

Affie screamed. "No! No no no please no *please no*!" The words kept babbling out of her, like if she said them enough somehow what had just happened wouldn't have happened. But Leox was gone.

Geode managed to maintain his composure, locking in coordinates that would take them safely to the ground. Though tears welled in Affie's eyes, blurring the console, she knew the controls by heart. She punched the right toggles until the *Vessel* powered up, lifted off, and shot out of the doors.

The last thing Leox Gyasi had ever done was sacrifice his life for his friends, Affie thought. She wouldn't let his sacrifice go to waste.

Nan clung to the nearest metal strut, staring at the sight of Chancey Yarrow dead on the floor—both halves of her—and the murderous Jedi Knight who stood over the corpse. Surely Nan would be the next to fall, and she intended to give the Jedi some hell before she went.

But the Jedi just kept staring down at Chancey like an idiot. Like he hadn't meant to do what he had unquestionably just done.

"Why?" Nan said.

"You're Nihil," replied the dark-haired Jedi. His voice sounded hollow. Did he even believe his own words? "You did this to Starlight."

"Us? We'd left the Nihil months before you even captured us."

"Then how—how could—"

"The Nihil sent a saboteur team, three completely different people—who, by the way, *we* took out of commission." Nan gestured at Werrera's body lying on the floor. "We were prisoners here, remember? We didn't find out about this in advance any more than you did!"

This was all true, more or less. Nan hoped the Jedi wouldn't hear all the things she'd carefully left out. He couldn't stop staring at Chancey as he said, "You—*you* killed the Nihil who bombed this station? Why?"

"Because we were trying to save the station and our skins with it! Not to mention *yours*!"

The Jedi turned toward the controls that Chancey had been working on only moments before. "Right. The positional thrusters—it looks like she—like she'd already managed to repair the—"

A red light began flashing as a metallic, synthesized voice intoned, "Station below thruster operating level. Repeat, the station has descended below thruster operating level. Evacuate immediately."

The Jedi's face turned white as he realized what he'd done. Nan wondered if he'd stand there stupefied while the station crashed.

She took off running, though she couldn't resist shouting as she went: "You killed this station's last chance! You've *killed us all*!"

Chapter 34

Seconds before, Elzar Mann had been a Jedi, a hero, a man on a mission to save lives. Now he stood there a murderer. He looked down at the bisected corpse lying near his feet and thought he might be sick.

"*Evacuate immediately,*" the computer voice repeated, over and over. "*Warning. Collision imminent.*"

Elzar knew he had to move. The others needed his help. Still, even glancing away from the dead body of the woman he had just murdered felt like a desecration.

All the work he'd done with Orla Jareni on Ledalau. All his good intentions. All the progress he'd arrogantly believed he'd made. Every bit of it had vanished in one spark of rage. That was all it had taken to tear down Elzar Mann.

Then, as sharply as though she were still alive, Orla's voice sounded in his head: *What if you took a break from your self-pity and did something productive for a change?*

"Forgive me," Elzar said to the dead woman on the floor. Then he steeled himself to do everything he still could.

At that moment he heard a banging behind him—was the girl coming back? Elzar turned to see, to his shock, Stellan hurrying toward him. Behind him, at a distance, rolled JJ-5145, various tools and kits hung from his metallic frame. Elzar breathed, "Stellan? How—how did you—"

"There's more than one maintenance pod aboard." Stellan caught sight of the bodies lying strewn around the room. "What happened?"

"This woman was trying to save us." Elzar forced the words out. As horrible as it was to tell this truth, lying would have hurt even worse. At least he would claim the little integrity he had left. "But I didn't know that. I saw her bent over the thrusters, and I believed her to be Nihil, and I killed her. Stellan, I killed her in cold blood. So she never had her chance to save us, all because of me, and now it's too late—"

"As long as we're alive, it's not too late." Stellan paused for only a moment, as though thinking hard. Then he clapped one hand on Elzar's shoulder. "They need our help above. Take a pod upward, make sure that everyone else has escaped. We'll be right behind you."

Elzar couldn't argue. He didn't want to. Stellan was himself again—the polestar, the only light Elzar had to steer by.

Nan had only partially removed her radiation suit, so it didn't take her much time to re-protect herself for the journey upward. Still—it had been a long descent, would be a longer climb upward, and every muscle in her body quivered with exhaustion.

Can I make it? Nan briefly thought as she looked up the impossible stretch of the maintenance shaft that led to safety. But what a useless thing to wonder. She'd either make the climb or die. There were no other outcomes.

Nan moved upward as fast as she could while still pacing herself and maintaining a solid grip. To distract herself from the burning in her arms and legs, she started strategizing what might come next. Reaching an escape pod should be doable—and she knew that, by this point, the Republic had finally figured out how to recharge some of the pods. But would any of the charged pods remain?

Nothing to do but try, she told herself, and kept climbing.

Starlight Beacon shuddered around her. Its fall was near.

Once Elzar had made it above, he hurried through the docking bay level, calling out, "Is anybody still here? Anyone else? Make yourselves known!"

No response. Hopefully that meant everybody else had been taken to safety.

Some time back, Stellan had sent droids to search other accessible levels for people who somehow might not have found their way to the docking bay; apparently the droids had located no one else. At this point, the best Elzar could do was evacuate all remaining souls. Were he and Stellan the last ones remaining?

Footsteps pounding across the docking bay floor jolted Elzar from the morass of his sorrow. He wheeled around to see a girl—the Nihil prisoner, Nan, who seemed like someone he had encountered much longer ago—running through the bay, wild wind whipping her blue-streaked hair. She was heading straight for one of the few remaining abandoned ships. It had been damaged by the recent detonation and might not fly.

"Don't!" he called out. "It might not work! Come with us!"

Either Nan couldn't hear him over the roar of the wind, or she preferred to take her chances as a free woman than to live as a prisoner. Regardless, she ran into the ship without ever looking back.

If she had taken her chances, then she'd rolled lucky dice, because the ship's engines glowed to life almost instantly. Elzar simply stood at the entrance to the bay, hanging on tightly, to watch her go. At this point he saw her only as one more life saved. One more person he hadn't failed completely . . . unlike so many others.

A droid's beeping behind him made Elzar turn. His eyes widened as he saw that the droid had, in fact, found one more survivor: a badly dazed Sullustan who seemed to have suffered a head injury. Despite the blood oozing from her swollen temple, and a painful limp, the Sullustan was making her way toward him as best she could.

"There are a few more wired escape pods, right?" Elzar asked the droid, which whistled an affirmative. He glanced back toward the opening for the maintenance pods, wishing Stellan were back already. But Elzar's duty was clear. He slung the Sullustan's arm over his shoulder and began guiding her toward the escape pod. "Hang on. I'm getting you out of here."

One more life saved.

As the ship zipped out of the docking bay, Nan shouted in pure triumph. She sailed into pure blue sky, into light.

For a moment her smile faltered as she remembered Chancey Yarrow—briefly her partner, however uneasily, and now nothing but a grisly memory. But Nan didn't dwell on it long. She had to concentrate on finding the Nihil. If nothing else, she'd had the single best view of Starlight Beacon's fall; Marchion Ro would enjoy hearing the details. Yes, this would earn her a place at his side, at least for a few days. More than that . . . well, it would be up to her.

Nan realized then that she had also acquired a ship of her very own. A quick scroll through the computer ident systems revealed that it was called the *Ace of Staves*. *I like that name,* she decided. *I'll keep it.*

On the rocky ground beneath, jagged with cliffs and buttes, Nan spotted a few small ships that were circling for safe landing space, most of them familiar from the Starlight docking bay. One of them had to be the *Vessel*. Tempting, to figure out which one and test her new ship's weapons systems as a last goodbye . . .

That could wait. Marchion Ro came first.

Nan steered her ship upward, toward space, freedom, and the Nihil.

Powerful winds buffeted the *Vessel* as Affie skimmed across the planet's surface. Ostensibly she was searching for a place to land, but really she kept blinking back tears, trying to clear her vision. Leox had given his life for theirs. She refused to dishonor his sacrifice by immediately crashing her ship.

The scene before her was almost incomprehensible. From where the *Vessel* hovered, Affie and Geode had a broad view of rocky terrain that split into crevasses and cliffs; long roads in the distance stood out as brightly colored, jumbled lines of backed-up vehicles. In the very near distance stood a great coastal city, its spires swaying slightly in the ever-increasing wind. Several smaller craft and countless recorder droids littered the air, all of them aimed at the rapidly descending disaster above.

Looming over them all was Starlight Beacon, seemingly larger and larger by the second, its broadening shadow pooling over them all, darkening the city as it fell.

It's going to crush the city, Affie thought. *It's going to kill thousands— maybe millions—*

She sobbed once. Geode was too stricken to speak. They could only stand by helplessly and bear witness.

Although the computer voice continued to insist that it was too late to avoid crashing, that didn't mean it was too late to activate the station's positional thrusters. Stellan worked at the controls, bringing system after system back online. Finally every bar glowed green, indicating full power.

This was no longer enough to keep the station from crashing; it was enough, however, for Starlight to move.

According to the scans in front of Stellan and his droid, Eiram's coastal city Barraza sat almost directly beneath them. He activated the aft thrusters only, which roared to life so powerfully that the air around him hummed.

Even now, the station has so much strength—if I'd gotten down here myself, if I hadn't been so lost—

Stellan pushed the thoughts aside and focused. The arc of Starlight's fall shifted, edging closer and closer to the water. "Forfive?" he called over the humming of the machinery, which grew louder as the station approached the surface. "Run some simulations for me, will you? Tell me how much the course has changed!"

Almost immediately, JJ-5145 replied, "At this speed, at our new trajectory, the station will land in the ocean, not in Barraza."

"Effects of the crash?"

"It will create tremors and significant waves, even deadly ones. Yet the loss of sentient life has been vastly diminished, from tens of thousands to perhaps no more than a dozen."

"Twelve lives lost is still too many." Stellan leaned harder on the controls, putting his entire body weight into it.

He was fighting with his strength now, with his will. He was fighting without the Force—not as a Jedi, but as a man. And yet Stellan felt if he had done this before—if he had asked himself what that would mean, for him—it would've made a better Jedi of him.

This is the first time I have acted with no thought for the Order, he realized. *This is the first thing I have ever done only as myself, only because I knew it to be right.*

"Master Stellan?" JJ-5145 sounded uncharacteristically hesitant. "You must evacuate soon if you are to reach an escape pod in time."

"If I evacuate, and nobody's able to hang on to these controls, the station won't clear the city, will it?"

"No, Master Stellan." The droid swiveled about, clearly trying to determine whether it could hold the controls in Stellan's place—but his arms were slender, made for precision rather than strength. It would be impossible. Stellan had known that all along. "But you must evacuate, or you will die."

"I know what I'm doing, Forfive," Stellan said. He felt stronger than he had in days. Maybe stronger than he ever had in his life. He imagined Elzar Mann's face—then Avar's—then Orla Jareni's—and he smiled. "I know who I am."

Cries of astonishment and joy rose up from Barraza as the looming shadow overhead shifted toward the sea. Yet most others watching—even if they rejoiced in the many lives saved—could only feel crushing horror as Starlight Beacon finally fell.

It seemed to speed up as it reached the ground: an optical illusion, like the moon appearing larger near the horizon, but an unnerving one. Even many of those who knew themselves safe couldn't help recoiling or even screaming as the enormous, broken, bent machinery of the station plummeted toward the surface.

"The desalination plant," Queen Thandeka breathed. "It'll be crushed—"

"We rebuilt it once." Queen Dima put her arm around her wife's shoulders, steadfastly watching in her council chamber along with all her advisers. "We can do so again."

On Coruscant, the scene was being played on nearly every holoprojector in the city. Crowds had gathered at every square, platform, and walkway to watch in shared astonishment and sorrow. Chancellor Lina Soh watched not the holo itself—she had already seen more of Starlight's demise than she could bear—but the people observing it, the way they clung to one another and wept. They felt this loss as keenly as she did.

Truly, she thought, *we are all the Republic—and never more so than in this moment of shared tragedy.*

Sorrows could bind people even more closely together. The natural bloodlust for revenge that would follow: That could be shaped, tamed, turned into common purpose. That would be Chancellor Soh's task in the days to come. For the moment, however, she, the most influential being in the galaxy, remained utterly powerless.

The man at the heart of the crash could not see it. Stellan Gios braced himself with all his strength as Starlight shuddered around him, so violently he thought it might break apart before impact. It didn't much matter now. The station had cleared the shoreline. Lives had been saved. The last thing he'd ever do, he'd done right.

Stellan felt no fear. The firmament of the night sky shone no less brightly when one small star went dark. Another nebula would be born, glowing with its own new light.

By this point, Starlight itself was almost invisible to the Eiram medical cruiser. Although surely some comm units could pick up broadcasts, Bell Zettifar didn't seek one out. His place was with the living—with Master Indeera Stokes, who slept peacefully in her bed, and with Ember, who had curled into a warm ball in Bell's lap.

He could review footage of Starlight's fate in the hours or days to come. For now, Bell chose to remain with those in need, with the reminders of the small but real triumphs that had been wrested from the chaos of this disaster.

On the holos played publicly on every Nihil ship, Marchion Ro's people clapped and cheered louder and louder in the station's last moments. On the *Gaze Electric,* Ro felt an almost dizzying exhilaration as the viewer showed Starlight plummeting downward, thrusters firing uselessly, whipping up the waves—

—and finally, impact.

The crash sent enormous plumes of water spewing in every direction, all of them several stories high, scattering waterships and shore debris. Everyone aboard Nihil ships grew frenzied with celebration, more like the midnight fireworks at Canto Bight than anything generally engaged in by the Nihil.

His face safely hidden by his helmet, Ro allowed himself to smile broadly. "Glorious," he whispered.

Alone among all those watching, Ro felt a moment's pang—not for Starlight or those who'd been aboard it, nor for what it represented, but for the creatures he had sent there and had done his work so well. They weren't easy to replace.

But he knew where to get more.

From a cliffside overlooking the ocean, Affie Hollow stood near the edge, tears streaming down her cheeks as she watched Starlight Beacon fall. The displaced water looked like an explosion, and even though she was at least eight kilometers away, Affie thought they might be drenched by it—or even swept away. The coastal city was protected in part by energy shields, a luxury she and Geode didn't have. But the widest waves struck her cliff without reaching the top of it.

Geode remained next to her, for which Affie was grateful. It helped to have someone to lean on. She shook her head at the sight of the twisted, bent section of Starlight that briefly bobbed amid the churning waters before sinking beneath the surface forever.

From behind her came a voice: "That's a hell of a thing."

Affie spun around. "*Leox?*"

He was ambling toward them, goggles pushed up to his forehead, dragging an enormous length of . . . was it fabric? A sail? Affie didn't care because somehow Leox was alive.

She flung her arms around him. "You made it. You made it!"

"Until you began squeezing the breath outta me." But Leox was hugging her back. "Shame to die by strangulation just after surviving that fall."

"But how did you do it?"

He picked up a bit of the length of diaphanous fabric that trailed him; Affie now saw that it was attached to his backpack. "'Parachute.' Not many people use 'em anymore, now that they have hover-ejectors et cetera." Leox grinned. "But you know I'm an old-fashioned kinda guy."

Affie hugged him again; they might have fallen over in exhaustion and relief, had it not been for Geode supporting them firmly on the side. She knew that many lives had been lost today, that the Nihil had won a victory that might change the balance of power in the galaxy.

But she'd worry about that later. For now, their little family was reunited and safe. It was enough.

Chapter 35

The escape pod had carved a rut into the rocky ground that ran almost half a kilometer, kicking up dust that turned the air hazy. Elzar Mann had emerged from it, coughing and unsteady, but knowing that he had to see what he could of Starlight's last moments.

I need to find other Jedi, he thought. *And to keep a lookout for Stellan's escape pod.* For the moment, however, he could only stand and watch.

Starlight passed directly overhead—crashing in slow motion, thanks to the thrusters that had been activated too late, but crashing all the same. Its shadow briefly blotted out the sun, a momentary eclipse. In another instant it was past them, arcing relentlessly downward toward the distant sea.

The station passed out of his sight, and seconds later an enormous shock wave hit. Elzar hung on to the side of the escape pod as the ground rattled beneath his feet and enormous plumes of water shot up toward the sky.

Worse than any of that was the psychic blow—the sudden awareness that at least a few others had been alive and trapped elsewhere on the station, because their deaths ripped through Elzar's consciousness, a terrible call of anguish that could never be answered, could never be healed.

And worst of all was the inner silence that followed.

He began trudging away from the pod, toward other small groups huddled in the near and far distance: evacuees from the nearby coastal city, crews from smaller ships that had landed. Elzar paid them no particular mind until someone broke from one of the most distant groups and began running toward him—and then he recognized the Jedi robe, and the long blond hair streaming behind her.

"Avar," he breathed, then shouted her name with all his might, "*Avar!*" Let the others hear him. Let the world see.

Elzar ran toward her until they met in the middle and clutched each other in their arms. He buried his face in the curve of her neck, willing away anything in the worlds farther away than this.

"You made it," she said, her voice hoarse with unshed tears. "I was so afraid you hadn't."

"I knew you were alive." Elzar stroked her hair. "You had to be."

While the city of Barraza had narrowly avoided obliteration, it had not escaped the station's crash unscathed. Despite the city's energy shielding, the massive waves unleashed by Starlight's fall had battered and flooded countless buildings on the shoreline, leaving the streets muddy and sand-logged, littered with debris and broken glass. Fishing boats had been tossed aside, crumpled, and left in strange places, like a careless child's toys. While almost all had evacuated the dangerous areas in time, not everybody had been able to leave, or had even chosen to do so; already Eiram's medical crews were searching through the most damaged areas for the bodies that undoubtedly lay there.

Droid probes had been immediately dispatched to check the wreckage, just in case . . . but it was clear to all that the crash had been unsurvivable for anyone who might still have been on board. In-depth retrieval searches would of course begin soon, with more droids sent in to contain and remove radioactive materials and other hazards. But they were on gravediggers' errands, and everyone knew it.

"We exchanged one disaster for another," said Queen Thandeka, who was one of the first wave of volunteers, making her way through sodden heaps of sand in what had been a busy thoroughfare. "First the quakes, now this."

Queen Dima, working next to her, nodded. "And now we're back to where we were before the Jedi ever arrived." She gestured toward the desalination plant—so near completion, so brief a time ago, and now lodged off-kilter, crooked, and unable to deliver fresh water to anyone. The next crisis would be water deprivation . . . and it would be upon them before the day was out.

"Where's Stellan?" Avar asked as she and Elzar led the other Jedi toward the coastline, where Eiram's queens were establishing disaster relief efforts.

"He would've taken a later pod." Elzar scanned around, still seeing no sign of it. "Hope he didn't make another water landing."

They shared a smile, remembering a long-ago ship-evacuation drill when they were young Padawans, one in which Stellan had wound up dunking himself thoroughly. But the reminiscence didn't last long; they had too much to do.

The journey to the shoreline wasn't a long one, even on foot, and more and more Jedi joined Elzar and Avar as they went. Groups of Eiram's citizens were flocking toward the coast, too; this was a planet with a strong sense of unity, a commitment to helping one another even at the height of crisis.

Elzar knew eventually he'd have to tell Avar what he'd done, how he'd given in to anger, killed a woman trying to rescue them, and doomed the last chance Starlight had left. But to do so at this time would be to assert that his personal despair was more important than this planet's crisis. The truth would keep.

He brightened as he saw a familiar droid rolling up to them. "For-five!" Elzar called. "About time. Where's Stellan?"

JJ-5145, for once, sounded solemn. "Master Stellan remained at the thruster controls to ensure that the station did not hit the coastal city of Barraza."

Elzar's mind went numb. It was Avar who said, "No. Please, no."

"He ordered me to take the final escape pod from Starlight," JJ-5145 reported. "He said that I was his gift to you, Master Elzar. And he wished for me to bring you this."

A panel on JJ-5145's chest slid open, revealing Stellan's lightsaber.

"He knew," Elzar whispered as he took the lightsaber in hand, holding it reverently. "Stellan would never have given up his lightsaber if he hadn't known—"

"He's gone," Avar said, with the searching look that told Elzar she'd been searching the song of the Force for Stellan's note, and that she hadn't found it. She never would again. "Stellan Gios is dead."

Although the traffic jam of would-be rescuers and blatant gawkers would hover within Eiram airspace for days to come, a few ships left almost immediately—which meant that Marchion Ro could do the same without attracting any attention. This freed the *Gaze Electric* to return to the Nihil, and to the greatest celebration that group had ever known.

He had prepared for victory, had anticipated the feast and frenzy that had to follow. Thaya Ferr had already made arrangements for a vast celebration in a small star system beyond the Republic's control, one where they could carouse wildly with no chance of restraint; automated signals had gone out, inviting the entirety of the Nihil to join them, and indeed, all did. (Except Lourna Dee, who went uninvited for several reasons, and whose whereabouts were unknown regardless.) Ro understood his people needed to literally taste the victory over the Jedi—and what better way to mark this win forever with *his* name, *his* will, *his* intent?

Thousands upon thousands of Nihil had gathered together on the chosen planet's surface before Thaya Ferr signaled the droids that it was time to begin distributing the massive stores of food and intoxicants laid aside in preparation for this day. Wines and ales flowed like fountains; tip-yip and gornt were brought out steaming on long platters. It was opulent. It was decadent. It was the greatest victory celebration the Nihil had ever known.

Only one gathering would ever be grander: the one Marchion Ro intended to hold as soon as the Jedi had been crushed forever.

He smiled to himself, beneath his mask, secure in the knowledge he wouldn't have to wait very long.

Elzar winced as they walked past the desalination plant, which had been so close to complete. *We should have finished the work before we celebrated,* he thought dully. *We tempted fate by toasting a project not yet done.*

No, worse. We tempted the Nihil.

The cost had been Eiram's safety, Starlight Beacon's existence, and Stellan's life.

Remorse threatened to swallow any resolve or concentration Elzar had when Avar stopped and made a gesture, one that drew all the other Jedi close.

"The desalination plant's connection is only slightly off," Avar said. Sunlight caught the jewel on her forehead, making it sparkle above her tear-reddened eyes. "We can put it back into place, if we all work together."

The others' smiles were fragile and uncertain—the kind of smiles that can surface in the face of tragedy. Elzar couldn't manage one at all.

But the only way they could make up for their hubris, for all the lost lives, was to get back to work saving this planet.

The Jedi stood together at a promontory near the coastline, looking out over the water plant and the most heavily damaged area of the waterfront. Elzar felt sharply aware that they were being observed by dozens, even hundreds of citizens gathering near, but the other Jedi paid that no attention, so he attempted to do the same.

The desalination plant seemed more distant than it had only moments before. As one, the Jedi each held out an arm, pointing their hand toward the object of their plan. This wasn't necessary—but many Jedi found that it helped to focus their efforts. Elzar reached out, too, and called upon the power within him, the one he distrusted but had to use for good, to prove that was still possible.

He found that power—but more important, he found the others.

It suffused every cell of Elzar's body—the power of it—as he sensed the enormous effort coming from Avar, Bell, and all the rest, the purity of their goodwill, the tremendous energy they had found and shaped and wielded—

The surrounding crowds gasped with surprise and relief as the desalination plant's connection slowly, slowly, shifted back into alignment, then settled in with an audible thunk. As one, the Jedi all exhaled . . . even Elzar.

You would be proud of this, he thought, imagining Stellan's face. *Even without Starlight, the Jedi have much to give the galaxy.*

I will learn how to give the best of myself, how to constrain the worst part of myself.

My actions deprived the galaxy of one of its greatest Jedi. For the rest of my life, I will be trying to create some small fraction of the goodness he still had to give.

Moving the desalination plant had helped center Bell anew. Learning of Master Stellan's death had shaken him. As had the temple attacks. And there was a battle on Corellia. Plus dozens and dozens of Jedi were still unaccounted for. But duty was stronger than grief. Stellan Gios would've been the first to say so . . . unless Master Loden had beaten him to it.

As Bell headed back toward his shuttle, he was stopped by Elzar

Mann. "Hey," Elzar said. He looked pale, haggard; Bell remembered then that Mann and Gios had been good friends from childhood. But it was not of his own loss that Elzar spoke. "I wanted to say . . . I'm sorry about Burryaga. You two were friends, weren't you?"

"We still are." When Elzar gave him a questioning look, Bell continued, "I assumed—we *all* assumed that Master Loden was lost when really he was being held captive by the Nihil. If I'd kept the faith—if I'd insisted on looking for him—we'd have spared him a great deal of suffering, and we'd probably have saved his life. So I'm not giving up on anyone else like that, ever again. That starts with Burryaga."

Elzar didn't seem convinced. He spoke gently, like a man attempting to break bad news. "What happened to Burryaga was very different. He couldn't have been captured. I don't see how he could have survived the rathtar, the opening of the cargo bay, *and* the crash."

"If there was any way, Burryaga would've found it." New as their close friendship was, Bell already felt certain of that much. "Even if there wasn't a way—even if he's gone—I'm going to search until I know for sure, and nobody's going to stop me."

"I wouldn't dream of trying." Elzar held up his hands in mock-surrender.

Bell resumed the walk back to his shuttle. "Check on Master Indeera in the medical cruiser for me, will you? And make sure Ember has her dinner."

"I promise," Elzar said, and Bell believed him.

Now to find his friend.

"Your ship's seen better days," said Joss Adren to Affie Hollow, "but she'll see plenty more once we're done with her."

Affie patted the side of the hull fondly. "We'll have her shining like new. Well, not today. But soon."

In the past few hours, everyone who'd escaped via pods had regathered near the coast, so it hadn't been hard to find Joss and Pikka Adren again. Affie had made them a deal: transport to wherever they needed to go in the galaxy, as long as they helped with the *Vessel*'s last necessary repairs. It was a good deal, and the Adrens knew it, which was why they'd been working alongside Affie, Leox, and Geode for a while now.

"Thank goodness we took out a policy on our ship," Pikka said as she double-checked some wiring by the ramp. Leox, who sat between Pikka and Geode as a kind of buffer, nodded sagely. "We'll be able to get another craft, though I don't know where we'll find one we like so well."

"If it's the right ship," Leox said, "you'll know it. Soon you won't be able to imagine your lives without it."

Affie wondered if she could've replaced the *Vessel* so easily. Thank goodness she didn't have to find out today, or hopefully for a long, long time to come.

As evening fell on Barraza, the Jedi continued assisting in the planet's relief efforts. Now that water readily flowed, cleanup was simplified and the populace was at least partly reassured. More and more citizens of the city who'd fled were returning, not to their homes but to the places that needed the most work. Long lines of people sweeping, bailing, bandaging, cooking, comforting . . . doing whatever could be done to console and restore those damaged by Starlight's fall.

Elzar Mann couldn't help but look out at the water, which by this point appeared almost tranquil. Starlight Beacon was the one part of this that could never be put right again. Its loss remained an open wound within him—within them all, surely—one that would not heal for a long time to come.

And it's partly my fault, he thought.

Already Elzar burned to confess to someone that he'd murdered a Nihil woman who had actually been trying to save all their lives. Avar Kriss would be the person he'd find it hardest to talk to, which meant she was *exactly* the person he must talk to.

He glanced across the long first-aid line in which he currently worked; at the far end stood Avar, bent over a young patient, a tender expression on her face. Elzar hoped she'd show him a little of that mercy.

When a brief pause came in their labors, Elzar made his way to Avar's side. She gazed upward at the darkening sky, and as he reached her, she stretched out one hand. He took it and looked up with her. Amid the emerging stars were tiny specks that he knew to be some of the ships that had swarmed here, hoping to help, but powerless in the face of destruction.

It still matters that they came, he reminded himself. *It will always matter. That unity, that compassion, that courage . . . this is what the Nihil lack. We will not win by stooping to their level, but by rising so far above it that even the Nihil cannot reach.*

Avar murmured, "Stellan always saw the Force as the firmament. As brilliant and expansive as all the stars in the galaxy."

"He told me that he saw the three of us as a constellation." Elzar's vision blurred with tears he fiercely blinked away. "An incomplete one now."

"No. He's still with us, as surely as the Force is with us. Stellan has become one with the Force, after all." Avar leaned her head against Elzar's shoulder. "And when we think of him—we can always find him, as long as we look to the sky."

Elzar held her close. "Our polestar still shines."

Epilogue

Marchion Ro's victory would be complete very, very soon.

He had cultivated the art of patience—an art fools like Lourna Dee could never grasp—but at this moment, as Starlight's last cinders faded into the approaching dusk, the need to speak nearly overcame him. *What is taking that lackey of mine so long—*

"Slicing into the communication buoys complete," said Thaya Ferr, never looking up from her console. "The message will be sent on the same frequency Starlight Beacon once used."

It was an excellent touch, if Ro said so himself. An extra twist of the knife currently buried in the hearts of the Jedi and the Republic. "Put me through."

In the last second before the holocam light came on, Ro heard Ghirra Starros scurrying even farther out of frame. Such pathetic cowardice. True courage came from putting one's own name to one's deeds—which was what Marchion Ro intended to do at last.

The light blinked brightly, and Ro began.

"Our entire galaxy has watched Starlight Beacon splinter, crash, and burn. By now most understand that the Nihil are responsible. Until this hour, however, very few have understood who is responsible for the Nihil. In other words—it's high time I introduced myself. I am Marchion Ro. I am the Eye of the Storm. I am the Eye of the Nihil."

He paused. Those watching in groups might well be exclaiming, talking among themselves, awestruck and horrified. Ro did not intend for their dismay to drown out his words.

"Much was made of the idea that Starlight Beacon was a symbol of hope," he continued. "But there is no hope in this part of the galaxy. There is only despair. There is only the Nihil. It was the Nihil who created the Great Hyperspace Disaster—and we can do so again. It was the Nihil who attacked the Republic Fair at Valo and left your high and mighty chancellor bleeding at our feet. And today it is the Nihil who have burned Starlight from the sky. The Republic can't protect you. The Jedi can't protect you. We have proved they can't even protect themselves. We go where we want. We strike where we want. Our will is the only authority in this part of the galaxy, and the only one there ever will be."

Ghirra Starros made a small sound; to judge from her tone of dismay, she either was horrified at his words—in which case, she was even more ridiculous than Ro had believed—or had bumped into KA-R9. Would the sound have come through on his broadcast? The idea irritated Ro for the brief moment it took him to realize how much fun it would be if it had: watching the sound clip being analyzed over and over again, Ghirra's inevitable identification, and the spectacular fallout that would follow. Better if he could have spoken uninterrupted, but the true philosopher found opportunities for satisfaction everywhere.

Ro refocused his attention entirely on that one small light. In that spark cowered the entire galaxy. His words were the true law; now they all knew it.

"I do not wish to rule the galaxy," he said. "If I did, you would be under my boot even now. But I will take what I wish, when I wish it, and no one will stand in my way—Republic, Jedi, or anyone else. They *cannot* stand in my way. The Nihil have proven our power, and we will use that power however we choose. This galaxy—"

He knew he should say *is ours*. He should reference all the Nihil in his statement, unify them in this ultimate statement of purpose.

Instead, Ro said what he truly believed: "This galaxy is mine."

ORLAND P̶ ̶ ̶ ̶ ̶C LIBRARY

Acknowledgments

My first and greatest thanks go to my fellow writers in the High Republic: Justina Ireland, Daniel Jose Older, Cavan Scott, and Charles Soule, as well as to Mike Siglain, who helps keep us all inspired, informed, and on track. Their professionalism, creativity, humor, and kindness shone a bright light on a very difficult couple of years. Thanks also to Jen Heddle, Pablo Hidalgo, Matt Martin, and the rest of the Lucasfilm and DelRey crews who work so hard to help us tell the story of the High Republic.

Massive thank-yous go out to my assistant, Sarah Simpson Weiss, who keeps me organized—no small task. Her endless good cheer has brightened many a tough workday.

Personally, I'd like to thank several fellow writers who know when to lend a sympathetic ear and when to tell me to get back to work on edits already: Marti Dumas, Stephanie Knapp, Brittany Williams Older, and Sarah Tolcser. Other friends who happily let me burrow down to meet deadlines and welcome me back with open arms when it's all done: Rodney Crouther, Stephanie Davis, Ruth Morrison, Madeline Nelson, and Amy and Gary Reggio.

My family has always been supportive of my writing, ever since the local newspaper printed my very bad poetry when I was a kid, the clippings of which they still have. This is either a sign of great love or blackmail material, possibly both. Thanks, Mom, Dad, Matthew, Melissa, Eli, Ari, and all the uncles, aunts, and cousins out there.

Finally, for my husband, Paul: All my gratitude, all my love.

About the Author

CLAUDIA GRAY is the *New York Times* bestselling author of the *Star Wars* books *The High Republic: Into the Dark; Bloodline; Leia, Princess of Alderaan;* and *Lost Stars.* Her other books include the Constellation, Evernight, Spellcaster, and Firebird series. She makes her home in New Orleans with her husband, Paul, and assorted small dogs.

claudiagray.com
Facebook.com/authorclaudiagray
Twitter: @claudiagray
Instagram: @claudia_gray

About the Type

This book was set in Hermann, a typeface created in 2019 by Chilean designers Diego Aravena and Salvador Rodriguez for W Type Foundry. Hermann was developed as a modern tribute to classic novels, taking its name from the author Hermann Hesse. It combines key legibility features from the typefaces Sabon and Garamond with more dynamic and bolder visual components.